The 7:30 Boat

Art Cappabianca

PAGE PUBLISHING, INC.
New York, NY

First originally published by Page Publishing, Inc. 2019

ISBN 978-1-64462-610-8 (Paperback)
ISBN 978-1-64462-611-5 (Digital)

Printed in the United States of America

CHAPTER 1

Carlos Reyes elbowed his way uncomfortably through the crowd that packed John O'Connor's loft in Brooklyn's Red Hook neighborhood. Located in the fetid backwaters of Brooklyn's Erie Basin, the pungent odors of the water wafted heavily with the breeze.

The building itself was a remarkable throwback to the nineteenth century, constructed of red brick and cement with heavy cast-iron riveted doors and shutters. It was a substantial building with thick, worn-out timbered floors, giving the impression of being an armory more than a pier warehouse. Semioccupied since the early 1960s, the warehouse was a sturdy structure even though the pointing on the waterside brick walls was showing the effects of prolonged exposure to salt air and water.

Currently, John and his girlfriend, Thea Bennett, were occupying the second-floor rooms at the far end of the building. John, known as Jack to his friends and associates, was an artist whose primary focus was documenting maritime New York. A graduate of Philadelphia's Art Institute, Jack pursued a bohemian way of life. He was a lanky twenty-eight-year-old with a mop of graying hair that prematurely aged his outward appearance.

Jack grew up on the water, his rough hands reflecting the years of hard labor. But his most distinctive feature was the piercing gray eyes he had inherited from his father. He reveled in the exploration of the debris and decay of the shoreline; the abandoned islands, vessels, and buildings that littered the harbor were always a source of wonder and amazement.

As Thea approached Carlos, making contact with his deep-set dark eyes, she found herself experiencing an inexplicable sense of uneasiness. She shook off that feeling as silliness on her part and made small conversation. "Hey, man, how's it going? Can I get you anything, a beer, some smoke, some blow, anything?"

Carlos smiled, answering, "Yeah, a bottle of cold water or a soda would be great." He couldn't help but think there was a special place for him waiting in paradise for taking on this job.

Jack O'Connor lived off the largesse of others, and as an artist of some repute in his community, he was continuously awarded grants, that being the reason for Carlos's appearance. Carlos represented Manuel Pabon, the owner of the Pabon Group. Manuel had made his legitimate capital in real estate, and after accumulating some wealth, he became a supporter of the arts. He was currently financing Jack's next show to the tune of $75,000. Manuel often entertained the ambitions of young artists in order to facilitate his own goals, which had nothing to do with the arts. Carlos was there for one reason: to dangle a substantial cash carrot in front of Jack and establish a parasitic relationship.

Manuel was a Cuban Marxist and intentional 1980 Marielito who had associates in unfriendly Latin and South American governments. A provocateur of covert ops, he was a link in a sinuous chain that led all the way back to Venezuela.

As he circulated, just marking time, someone caught Carlos's eye and diverted his attention. Elrod Rodgers shoved his way through the crowd, making his way toward him. Carlos knew he was about to be cornered in an awkward encounter. "Hey, Felix, how you doin', man?"

Rodgers was a midlevel drug dealer from New Jersey and the very last man Carlos wanted to run into, especially here and now. He raged to himself internally, *Shit! Damn it, I don't need this now!*

"I'm sorry, friend, you must have me confused with someone else. My name is Carlos, Carlos Reyes." He grasped and shook Rodgers hand.

"You sure, man? 'Cause you look just like Felix. We met out in New Jersey about a month ago."

"I'm sure. I must have a common face. I gotta run." Carlos slipped purposely away, leaving Rodgers confused and standing by himself.

Indeed, they had met. Carlos indeed trafficked in drugs to finance his personal aspirations and had sold Rodgers two kilos of cocaine a month ago at a Holiday Inn in North Jersey. Carlos never allowed his true identity to become known. This chance meeting was a serious breach of his otherwise impeccable security regime.

Jack walked over to Carlos as he was fleeing Rodgers and placed his arm around him. "Hey, man, I can't tell you how much we appreciate Manuel's confidence in what we're doing here. It's a shame he couldn't come tonight."

"Yeah, well, he's out of the country this week, but he sends his regards." Among Manuel's many attributes was the fact that he was a world-class metrosexual who wouldn't have been caught within five hundred feet of this dockside rathole. Besides that, Manuel had served his purpose in this matter; it was Carlos's show from now on. Jack made a few comments to the assembled collection of burnouts and fans with Carlos at his side and accepted Manuel's check. Then the crowd got back to what they actually had come for in the first place: the ample bar and buffet of narcotics curated by Jack's numerous grants. If anyone was left standing by the time the sun came up, it would be their own fault. Carlos, on the other hand, didn't intend to follow suit, since this was strictly business for him. Carlos warmly shook Jack's hand and congratulated him on his upcoming show.

"Jack, I like this place. I can only imagine the history that's passed through this old building."

"Really?" Jack replied. "You're into the waterfront?"

"Oh yeah, man, ever since I was a kid in Cuba."

"Oh, man, I could show you things down here you just wouldn't believe!" Jack said, stepping back.

Carlos responded with feigned sincerity, "Hey, I'll hold you to that."

Carlos then made his excuses to leave. Having set the hook, he could now free himself of this collection of free spirits for the time being.

As he walked toward the door, Carlos made eye contact with Eldred Rodgers and beckoned him to follow. When Carlos exited the building, he turned right and walked toward the desolate area at the head of the pier. Rodgers was quick to follow, and Carlos waited for him to catch up.

"Good evening, Mr. Rodgers," Carlos said in a much more cordial tone as he shook Rodgers's hand. "Yes, my friend, I do recognize you, and I must apologize for putting you off back there. I can't allow the businessman I am tonight to be identified with the individual you met with in New Jersey. Please accept my most sincere apologies."

Carlos's sincerity put Rodgers at ease. Carlos clenched Rodgers's hand tighter, pulled him closer, quickly slipping the unfolded blade of a large buck knife between Rodgers's fourth and fifth ribs into his heart. Rodgers's eyes bulged, a shocked expression coming over his face as he desperately grabbed at Carlos's shoulder. Carlos spoke to him as the life drained from his body. "I'm sorry, Mr. Rodgers, but I can't allow you into my world. Good evening, sir." With that, he spun Rodgers around and pushed him off the end of the pier. If his body was found, it would be chalked up as another robbery victim on the dangerous piers of Red Hook.

With the deed completed, Carlos began the short walk back to his car. Alone on the dark streets, the only sounds were those of his own footsteps and the nearby horn of a Staten Island Ferry leaving the Whitehall Street Terminal in Manhattan. At this time of night, the silence of the street had soothing quality to it.

Carlos made his way out of Red Hook down deserted Van Brunt Street. Before heading home, he would stop at a restaurant on Third Avenue for a debriefing. The traffic lights before him obligingly turned green in sequence, and he knew he'd be at the café shortly. Tonight, a glass of hot tea with a like-minded friend would taste especially good.

CHAPTER 2

Orlando Rodriguez was an American enigma. He'd succeeded repeatedly, despite himself, and rose to become a millionaire three times over. If he had not been a degenerate gambler, he might have had to accomplish that feat only once.

Orlando grew up on Manhattan's Lower East Side, a resident of a city housing project on Avenue D and East Twelfth Street, across from a live poultry market. This was the high side of the neighborhood that would later be known as Alphabet City. On a humid summer night, the putrid odor of the poultry market mixed with the stifling diesel fumes of the passing buses. The Lower East Side was the neglected underbelly of the well-heeled Upper East Side, which had seen its fair share of improvements in recent years.

Orlando had been raised by his mother after his father was killed by a junkie for a few bucks and a pair of lottery tickets. On the Lower East Side, death and drugs were a way of life. His mother, Edna, was a nurse's aide at Bellevue Hospital, where she worked excessive amounts of overtime to support Orlando and his younger sister, Sofia. Edna's only goal was to someday get her kids out of the dangerous neighborhood; she worked tirelessly for the sake of her children. Orlando often took advantage of his mother's work schedule to skip school.

Javier Aponte, better known as Flocko, was a skinny twenty-year-old when Orlando was sixteen. Orlando admired Flocko because he always had cash in his pocket and never resorted to drug dealing or thieving. Instead, Flocko was a three-card monte dealer who scammed tourists in Times Square from April to November.

Orlando's job as a kid had been to stand out on the edge of the crowd and look out for the cops. Once spotted, Orlando would scream out "Five-oh! Five-oh!" and the crowd would scatter. Occasionally, the mark would figure out he'd been had and a fight would ensue, but Orlando could always repeat his caution of "Five-oh! Five-oh!" and neutralize the confrontation.

It wasn't uncommon for greed to quickly set in and marks to be down hundreds of dollars in just minutes. In 1974, Flocko cleared $65,000 between April and November. He always compensated Orlando for his troubles with fifty bucks or more for his role in the con. A strong friendship grew out of this working relationship as Flocko treated Orlando like a little brother and always looked out for him. One August night, they took a break and went to a chicken and rib takeout place they both liked over on Eighth Avenue and West Forty-Ninth Street. They got their usual fix of chicken, rice, and beans and ate on the steps of St. Malachy's Catholic Church. If they were lucky, a breeze would funnel down between the buildings and relieve them from the sweltering heat. They plopped down and watched the hurried theater crowd racing to their shows. As they sat, Flocko began to groom his protégé.

"Papi, are you enjoying yourself?" Flocko asked as they devoured their plates.

"Tonight, Flocko?"

"No, like, in general."

"Yeah, man, a lot."

Flocko took a more serious tone as he locked into Orlando's eyes. "You know, man, I'm not gonna to do this forever. You do understand that, don't you? This is what they call a means to an end." Flocko went on to explain his master plan, telling Orlando he had been saving most of his money and intended to be completely legal in five years. He aspired to own a convenience store. He also hoped to one day marry and start a family of his own while opening additional stores. Although he accepted that an occasional arrest was part of his current overhead, he hated it. This was not the life for him.

"Orlando, I could do this until I'm an old man and never realize I'd gotten old before the best things in life had passed me by." Flocko continued, "Papi, Mira, where we live, do you want to live there forever? Do you want your momma and Sofia to live there forever?"

Orlando was absorbed by Flocko's seriousness; he'd never seen him like this. Orlando could only shake his head no.

Flocko went on. "Man, if you don't want to live with the smell of chicken shit for the rest of your life, you gotta have a plan. You have to imagine how things could be, and always use your head, papi. Get a plan!"

The words stuck, and through the years, Flocko's speech greatly influenced Orlando. In 1976, Javier Aponte walked away from the street and turned his business over to Orlando. Then eighteen, Orlando had become incredibly adept at three-card monte. He was a workaholic, conning people through the winter months, long after most other dealers shut down their operations. Because of his persistence, Orlando was able to purchase a house in Brentwood, Long Island.

Through the 1980s Orlando's neighborhood had become a haven for drug dealers and users. Drug dealers were in complete control of the streets to the point where junkies would line up around the block to get their fix. It was complete chaos, a virtual supermarket for users and dealers to roam freely. By 1988, it had gotten so out of control that a cry went up to city hall demanding the law be enforced and the area be reclaimed. And enforced it was, with a vengeance.

A massive police presence moved into the area, arresting anyone coming into the neighborhood to buy drugs. The police removed the demand in the most draconian of ways. You couldn't spit on the street without drawing the attention of police, especially the young cops eager to prove themselves. The area had become a mecca for kids from the tawny suburbs of Long Island and Westchester to score their drugs. When these white-bread kids were caught buying drugs, not only were they arrested and held in the most despicable of conditions, but Dad's BMW or Mercedes was impounded, permanently, with no chance of reclaiming it. This tactic caused a riot back home (and sometimes in the station house).

It took about two years for the demand to dry up as the suppliers and buyers were arrested regularly. Tranquility slowly returned to the neighborhood, but it was a neighborhood in ruins. Block after block of shells of buildings, cinder-blocked and closed. But appearances could be deceiving. While they looked beyond hope for the most part, many of the structures were still viable and could be rehabilitated. Orlando, with approximately $600,000 burning a hole in his pocket, saw the opportunity and jumped on it. This was the beginnings of the Rodriguez Group, controlled by a driven Orlando on the road to his first million.

Orlando's first investment was on East Third Street between Avenues A and B. It was a forty-unit building, and he purchased the abandoned and damaged structure for a song. Because of the long-standing blighted nature of the neighborhood, he was able to resurrect it with a combination of low-cost loans and outright grants. The sturdy structure returned to its previously handsome appearance, and the gentrified tenants helped send Orlando on his way. Six months later, he bought his second building, and shortly thereafter, a third. Orlando was floating along pleasantly on a sea of cash at thirty-two years of age.

He was a responsible businessman, at least initially, but felt entitled to enjoy some of his good fortune. Atlantic City and the horse races were just what the doctor ordered. Money also provided something that Orlando never had much luck with: women. His newfound wealth disproved an old bromide and showed that you could in fact get laid with a fistful of twenties. Excess led to excess, and after some poor wagers, Orlando developed an unhealthy relationship with one Carmelo Fonseca, or "Fausto" as he was known on the streets, a local loan shark and occasional leg breaker.

Orlando, with his uncanny ability to pick losers, was into Fausto for a bit more than $278,000. Orlando had made three large football bets with Fausto, and on each occasion, he had bet with the line taking the suggested points. Orlando owed Fausto $278,000 without including the points on the loan, which accrued weekly. Orlando's remittances had been problematic. Fausto cajoled and threatened but to no avail. The only thing that kept Fausto from killing Orlando was the fact that he would be out a great deal of money. Fausto was at his wit's end.

Carlos Reyes had been a tenant in Orlando's East Third Street building for the last two years. Carlos and Orlando had a casual, friendly acquaintance. While Carlos kept his ear to the street, he was not part of the street. His demeanor, at least outwardly, was typical of a successful young Hispanic that gentrification had brought. He was neither tall nor short but of medium height and build and very confident. Even though he had a nefarious purpose, Carlos always kept his eyes open to opportunity. The evening he turned eastward on East Third Street from Avenue A, opportunity inadvertently fell right across his path.

While Fausto did not like the "leg breaking" aspect of his profession, he realized it did, occasionally, have its place. Orlando Rodriguez had resisted all efforts to make timely payments; he had pushed Fausto to the brink. Orlando was a popular street guy, and Fausto could not allow him to make him look weak.

CHAPTER 3

Fausto was waiting for Orlando on the corner of Avenue A and East Third Street in the shadows of a brown brick tenement building that housed a deli, accompanied by his assistant, Hector Glaves. Hector was 190 pounds of muscle without any discernable neck and possessed the personality traits of a pit bull with none of the inherent charm.

It was 7:00 p.m. and still light out, with many local residents on the street just the way Fausto wanted it. The neighborhood had seen a recent influx in new residents and businesses, but most still lived by the code of the streets.

Orlando had just rounded the corner onto East Third Street when Fausto stepped into his path, smiling but saying nothing. Orlando's blood went cold; he immediately realized what was coming. He could no longer hear the passing traffic, and his throat went dry as adrenaline began to pump through his veins. Orlando turned and attempted to break and run back to Avenue A to save himself, but his situation took a turn for the worst. Hector, who had been waiting in the deli for him to pass, fell in behind him with an aluminum bat in hand.

Fausto spoke first, "Papi, you got what I need?"

Panicking, Orlando made the mistake of trying to charge past Hector. Using the bat like a bayonet, Hector jammed the barrel into Orlando's solar plexus. Orlando jack-knifed up into the air and fell face-first onto the gray pavement. He gasped for air and writhed in pain as Fausto began to speak again.

"Man, I need my fucking money, man." Strutting up to his doubled-over victim, he sarcastically spoke to Orlando. "What's that you say? You can't pay? I'll tell you what then. I'll take it out of your ass, son. You see that first shot. That took a grand off what you owe me, dog. Hector, take another grand off my man's nut." The bat whipped down again, breaking Orlando's left wrist as he raised it to fend off the blow. Orlando screamed in agony while simultaneously puking and shitting himself.

An unsuspecting Carlos Reyes turned the corner onto East Third, walking into the pitiful specter of what was taking place in the gutter. He recognized both Orlando and Fausto, taking only a moment to drink in what was happening. He walked straight into the melee, addressing Hector directly. Hector took two quick powerful kicks to the groin. While Carlos may have looked like a yuppie punk, he was anything but. He'd dealt with many Hectors in his life and knew exactly how to handle the situation. As Hector struggled to regain his footing, Carlos grabbed him by the scruff of his abbreviated neck and drove his face into a brick wall. Hector slumped unconscious against the wall, leaving a bloody smear on the sidewalk below as he dropped, with his forehead split open and nose broken.

Carlos picked up the aluminum bat that was lying in dog shit on the curb and walked over to the now silent Fausto. Dryly Carlos offered the bat by the handle to Fausto, inquiring "Is this yours?" Fausto nodded his head yes. Carlos told Fausto in a measured tone, "We'll talk about this and Mr. Rodriguez's other problems in a day or so," handing the bat to Fausto. "Maybe we can find a satisfactory solution. Until then, would it be possible to cut my man Rodriguez some slack? Would that be okay with you?" Of course it was. Fausto then tended to the unconscious Hector as Carlos saw to Orlando, recoiling as he did at the mess and stench. Carlos hailed a cab and took Orlando to Bellevue Hospital.

Utter chaos. That's the best way to describe the appearance of the emergency room at Bellevue, but it was actually a medical masterpiece within the world of emergency medicine. Any Manhattan cop knows that if you're shot or seriously injured, with your last conscious breath, you say, "Take me to Bellevue."

After a considerable wait, Orlando was x-rayed, examined, and found to have sustained two broken ribs, a broken left wrist and index finger, a bruised spleen, and assorted painful contusions and abrasions. He would be a guest there for at least the next week. After accepting Orlando's gratitude and promising to safeguard his valuables, Carlos left the hospital before the police arrived.

It was obvious to the medical staff that Orlando had been the victim of a vicious assault, so they immediately called the police. Orlando, of course, did not cooperate, and the police investigation went nowhere. For his part, Carlos realized that what had started out as a purely altruistic deed might turn into a blessing in disguise. Carlos knew Orlando was a wealthy man, so he was surprised that he had let his finances get far out of his control. How much was he in the hole for? Were these the excesses of a degenerate gambler, or something else? Carlos began evaluating his gift horse. He had so many questions.

*****

Tuesday morning Carlos was up and out by 9:00 a.m. to begin his research on Orlando. The night before, when Carlos returned from the hospital, he called some local acquaintances on the block to find out what Orlando was mixed up in. Much to Carlos's surprise, the sentiment in the street framed Orlando a local champion to the needy, well liked but not without his problems.

The consensus was that Fausto had allowed Hector to go too far; thus, Carlos demonstrated considerable humility and began to milk his new status as a neighborhood hero. With his newfound esteem, Carlos was able to illicit information from the normally tight-lipped folks on the block.

Among the witnesses was Mrs. Heldi Concepcion, an elderly German war bride and widow of a Dominican immigrant. She lived in Orlando's building on the second floor. Heldi's window faced the street, and she propped herself on the sill daily from morning until night when not cleaning or cooking. She missed nothing, and what she didn't learn by watching the street, she learned in the laundry room or at the bodega. But as quickly as she took information in, she was just as fast to let it out. Heldi's service had often proved to be invaluable to the cops.

Carlos had some leverage with Heldi ever since she had virtually adopted him when he moved into the building. She was the source of many delicious home-cooked meals and equally delectable pieces of information. Heldi told Carlos that Orlando owned seven local buildings in the neighborhood, not including the two he had under his mother and sister's names.

Carlos grabbed a cab on Avenue A and took it up to the public library at East Forty-First Street and Fifth Avenue. Once there, he used the library computer to access NYC.gov and look up the property records for the buildings Orlando owned. He could have used his home computer, but Carlos knew better than to leave a trail. The library's computers afforded him complete anonymity, so no record of his inquiries would exist.

Carlos soon found that Orlando's buildings were operating under the names Monte Enterprises, Three Card Properties, and ABC Realty. All three companies fell under the umbrella of the Rodriguez Group located in an office in the basement of the building Carlos lived in.

Carlos next entered the block and lot number of his own building, which brought up a profile of the property. He was astounded to learn that in 1985, his building had been cinder-blocked shut and abandoned but was now listed in the city as having a 2008–2009 market value of $5.5 million. As he did the same with the rest Orlando's buildings, he became increasingly awestruck. The total listed market value of all of Orlando's properties came in at slightly over $51 million. Carlos was speechless. Orlando's had allowed himself to be compromised for a measly $278,000 gambling debt. This did not make sense to Carlos, but that was irrelevant, since he now had an exploitable situation he intended to take full advantage of.

At about 3:30 p.m. Tuesday afternoon, Carlos found Fausto on Third Avenue near the corner of Avenue A.

Carlos casually leaned against the wall of the pizzeria and asked, "How's your man?"

A clearly distracted Fausto abruptly answered, "He's got a big head, but he'll be okay."

Carlos shrugged and asked, "Do you want to talk money? What does Rodriguez owe you?"

"Two hundred seventy-eight grand, my friend."

"Fausto, have you got a few minutes to sit with me in the pizzeria? I'll make it worth your while."

"Yeah, but not too long."

They sat down in a restaurant on the corner and had coffee brought over. Fausto spoke first. "What's your play, papi?"

"I intend to make a business arrangement with Rodriguez, and I need him undistracted. I want to buy his nut."

"Sure, man, that'll be 278 grand."

"I'll give you one hundred grand."

"Like I said, man, that'll be 278 grand. Listen, I got to get back out," and Fausto started to get up to leave.

Carlos grabbed his arm and sat him down again. Carlos reached into his jacket pocket and dumped a wrapped stack of hundreds on the table. "A hundred." Fausto said nothing. Carlos reached back into his pocket and dropped another stack on the table. "A hundred, right now, right here. No more worries, no more dogging him, a hundred K right now."

After a moment, Fausto finally spoke. "You know, man, I could take your money, say thank you, and Rodriguez would be up my ass again tomorrow looking to play. He's hopeless. I've been doing business with him for years. We've gone through millions. Usually, I eventually get paid. This was the first time I had to tune him up. I don't know what got into him. In the past, he's refinanced on his buildings to pay, but eventually he always paid. You're be wasting your money man, really."

Carlos was seeing a different side of Fausto, his business side. Carlos spoke resolutely, "Look, I understand everything you're saying, but trust me, I can control him, I know how. A hundred K, what do say?"

Fausto thought for a minute; it was too tempting to pass up. "Deal." Carlos had just bought himself a degenerate gambler.

Carlos knew Orlando was going to become a huge asset, but he'd have to properly motivate him first. Carlos understood that he would be faced with the task of explaining his new partnership to Orlando. He had a particularly riveting manner in mind.

*****

Orlando's properties were rich in equity as he'd owned a number of them for twenty-five years. For example, the building Carlos lived in had a market value of $5.5 million, and once it was actually on the market, it might increase in value another 10 percent. Carlos formulated a plan in which Orlando's property was refinanced for a hefty fee that would earn him just short of $2 million. He knew he could convince Orlando that this would be in his best interest.

In many ways, what Carlos was doing was similar to an old Mafia strong-arm routine. Carlos's objective was to earn the maximum profit while remaining anonymous. The unwritten contract he would be forging with Orlando would be sealed in a ruthless manner, but beyond that, he didn't want to smother Orlando's business acumen. He would let Orlando share in the wealth derived from their relationship. It was fate that placed Rodriguez in Carlos's hands, and he intended to use the money to finance many other operations he had planned.

CHAPTER 4

Carlos got an early call from Manuel Pabon.

"Carlos, are you busy this morning?"

"No, I just finished breakfast, why?"

"Could you come up to my office at the gallery? There's something we have to talk about."

"Sure, my friend, I'll be over in a half hour."

He showered, dressed, and caught a cab to Pabon's gallery. He passed through the open front door into the expansive exhibition area and walked toward Pabon's office in the rear.

When he entered, Manuel was at his desk, smiling, with someone sitting in front of him, his back turned to Carlos. He recognized the form even before he turned around; it was his brother Faisal.

Carlos Reyes, as is often the case in life, was a more complex person than he appeared to be. He'd been born in Saudi Arabia in 1976. Physically, he passed for a Hispanic, usually a Dominican or Cuban, as he'd hoped and planned. In reality, he was a Sunni Muslim who spoke Arabic, English, German, Spanish, and Urdu flawlessly, which was a rather extraordinary feat for an Arab. Even more impressive was his ability to adjust his accent to fit the people he was dealing with. Carlos was actually Khalil Ebrahim Wafi.

Carlos's spiritual call came in college, while still in Saudi Arabia. As a young man, he and many others his age were driven by a call of jihad that caused his blood to boil. After graduating in 1998, he slipped into Afghanistan for formal training with his older brother Faisal. Faisal, a manager with Saudi Arabian Airlines, had his own call to jihad a number of years earlier. He'd lost two of his best childhood friends who were involved with Egyptian Islamic martyrdom operations. After the death of his friends, he became acquainted with

18

Dr. Ayman al-Zawahir and eventually to al-Qaeda. Faisal hated the Israelis and their American allies. Faisal and Carlos both held Western society in utter contempt and faithfully awaited the day when one Muslim caliphate would rule over all.

Carlos would have blissfully gone the way of a martyr had his superb linguistic talents not caught the attention of Abd al-Raheim al-Nashiri. Al-Nashiri was Osama bin Laden's lieutenant in charge of naval operations; he had masterminded the attack on the USS *Cole*. It was al-Nashiri who calmed the outraged Carlos when he was told he would not immediately become a martyr. It took nearly two weeks of calming conversation with al-Nashiri to convince Carlos that his language skills were invaluable and he needed to learn how to use them. Carlos's talents proved to be immeasurably important in a number of operations, including the one against the USS *Cole*. As al-Nashiri's wisdom showed itself through results, Carlos began to see the bigger picture. The 9/11 attacks were like an epiphany for Carlos since he could now see the importance of carefully planned operations. After the capture of al-Nashiri in 2002 and Khalid Sheikh Mohammed in 2003, many operational units of al-Qaeda went underground, and a realignment ensued.

In April of 2003, Carlos returned home to Riyadh, staying there until June. When his mother asked where Carlos would be traveling to next, he informed her he'd been awarded another contract to teach in Germany.

It was not the truth, although he would technically be passing through Germany. Through a series of dead drops, Carlos received his orders along with tickets and cash through intermediaries. Authorities in his organization ordered him to fly to Havana via Munich and Canada. His Spanish passport identified him not as Khalil Ebrahim Wafi but as Carlos Reyes of Barcelona and Havana. As a university professor, he'd be teaching Spanish at the National University in Havana. Carlos was being placed in total immersion until in December of 2004 when he would move on to New York City via Mexico City.

Carlos used his Spanish passport to identify himself as a Cuban national with dual citizenship by way of his parents: a Cuban mother and a Spanish father. Cuban officials provided him with the appropriate documentation, and because of his immersion in Havana, Carlos had overcome one of the most challenging portions of his mission. At first, Carlos found it instinctually difficult to speak Spanish without a distinguishable Middle Eastern accent, but his time in Havana allowed him to overcome that liability and perfect his dialect. Khalil Ebrahim Wafi, aka Carlos Reyes, was remarkably thorough and transitioned smoothly into his next role.

Travel had come somewhat easier for Faisal as an employee of Saudi Arabian Airlines. He'd started as a steward and rose to an internal managerial position, both of which allowed him liberal traveling privileges. He managed to have himself transferred to the airline's London office with minimal difficulty.

Carlos nearly pulled Faisal into a joyful bear hug in Manny's office. Carlos's spirit soared as the brothers embraced; his self-enforced solitude in this hostile land had stripped him of what he treasured most: his family. At least for right now, right here, even for a short period of time, all was good with the world. Faisal told his brother how the family was doing. Then, after another couple of minutes of light conversation, he smiled and casually said, "Oh, by the way, the prince says hello." Carlos continued to smile, but that phrase told him Faisal had been sent to him with an operational tasking message. While Manuel understood Faisal's visit had intelligence implications, the message itself was not for Manuel's ears. Carlos and Faisal needed somewhere private to talk.

They chatted a bit longer, and then Carlos said, "Manny, my brother and I have not seen each other in very long time, so please do not consider me rude, but I would like to take him to lunch and catch up."

"I completely understand, don't give it a second thought."

The brothers left, intending to walk down West Broadway to a trendy bistro called Orion on Duane Street. Out of earshot of Manny and any possible monitoring devices, Carlos and Faisal comfortably spoke quietly as they walked toward the restaurant.

As they walked, Faisal got straight to the matter at hand.

"Brother, very serious things have been put into motion, and you should know your name has come to the forefront.

"It has been determined that the time has come to punish the great Satan again. Wisdom dictates that another attack by air would probably be pointless, since the American efforts after the blessed event of 2001 have made a repeat of that particular tactic harder to facilitate. But we still believe a worthy operation can be achieved in New York again."

Faisal continued, "While they have closed the door to the skies, many other doors have been left open. They have become complacent and believe us to be less capable. We will attack their Achilles heel."

Carlos understood that they were talking about an attack from the sea. "You may tell the sheik that I will do honor for the Prince of the Seas." Carlos was speaking of al-Nashiri, who had earned the title of Prince of the Seas as a result of the *Cole* operation.

Faisal asked, "Babur, do you have a preference as far as targets?"

"Yes, I do," Carlos responded. "New York is a maritime center. The American authorities have taken great pains to secure their waterfronts. They have, however, secured themselves from the shore and left the water side open. I believe a martyrdom operation similar to that employed in Yemen against their destroyer could be extremely successful here."

"Do you have a particular target in mind?"

"Yes, the Americans commute through the harbor in large numbers, and the ferry from Staten Island to Manhattan has as many as three thousand people aboard during the peak morning rush hours. A martyrdom operation against a ferry will produce large scale and dramatic results, and the rescue efforts will be extremely difficult, if not pointless. I have an appropriate secondary target."

They arrived at the Orion, but rather than continuing the conversation within earshot of others in the restaurant, Carlos suggested they continue to walk around the block. It was now Faisal who added another dimension to the plot.

"Brother, it is possible to accomplish our goal with something other than a martyrdom operation."

Carlos was both puzzled and disappointed. "I do not know how to respond to that." Once again, he was to be denied the honor of martyrdom.

"Khalil, we may have an ally who can provide us with superior technology that can catch the Americans totally off guard without leaving a trail. Sheik Atef Kahlid Mohammed is being sent to New York to consult with you."

"When?"

"Soon. Can you provide a secure location?"

"I can."

Carlos and Faisal had a joyful lunch at Orion, talking at length about home and family. They laughed as they spoke of their mother's exquisite cooking and shared stories of their youth. It was a respite of normalcy Carlos hadn't enjoyed in quite a while. When they parted company, Faisal announced he was heading to an apartment in Queens. Carlos had a plan for the next day.

"Faisal, I want to meet you early tomorrow and show you something."

"Yes, but it must be early. I'm flying back to London in the afternoon."

"Certainly. We'll meet at 6:30 a.m. in Manhattan. Are you familiar with the New York City subway system?"

"Somewhat. I will buy a map and acquaint myself more thoroughly."

"Good, at the Queens R train station, buy a two-ride Metro Card. You'll notice that all subway stations have more than one entrance. One entrance is usually manned by a ticket agent, while the other entrances are only turnstiles that accept fare cards. Use the unmanned entrance, and it will be easier to determine if you're being followed.

"At the Times Square Station in Manhattan, you'll transfer to the number 4 train, southbound. Take that to Bowling Green. As you exit the station, you'll notice a park in front of you on the right. That's known as Bowling Green Park. The Staten Island Ferry Terminal is at the other end of that park. I will be sitting on a bench near the entrance. Pass me by and enter the terminal. Take the escalator to the main lobby and wait for me there. I will lag behind to see if you're being followed. When I enter the terminal, if I don't come to you, don't approach me. That will mean I've detected surveillance. If that's the case, we'll take the next boat across and stay apart. When you get to the other side, take the ferry boat back to Manhattan. Take a taxi back to your apartment, and I'll contact you through Manny later. If we're not observed, I'll show you a few things. Do you understand?"

Faisal nodded that he did, and they went on their separate ways. Carlos's head was spinning. His time was coming. Allah be praised.

CHAPTER 5

On Saturday morning, Carlos went to Bellevue to take Orlando home. His discharge process was complete by 10:30 a.m., and shortly thereafter, he was wheeled outside by a nurse's aide. Carlos was waiting with a cab.

"Man, I really owe you for everything you've done for me. Now don't think I'm unappreciative, but why? You hardly know me."

"Orlando, how could I walk past you in your moment of need? We'll talk after I get you home. How do you feel?"

"Like I was hit by a truck, but I am much better than the day it happened. The doctor said I'll have to take it real easy for the next three to four weeks."

"That's understandable." There wasn't any more meaningful conversation during the short cab ride downtown in the light weekend traffic. Orlando got out of the cab very slowly with Carlos's assistance. His only welcome home was from Heldi, who was perched at her windowsill.

"Hi, darling, how are you?"

"Better, Heldi. Thanks for asking."

"Call me if you need anything, okay?"

"Thanks, sweetheart."

They made it up to Orlando's sixth-floor apartment, where a clearly tired Orlando collapsed on his couch.

Carlos asked Orlando, "Can I get you anything to make you more comfortable?"

"You're going to host me in my own home?"

Carlos smiled and nodded. "Actually, yes. We have some important issues to discuss. You should be comfortable."

"You're more to the point than I expected, but I didn't think your kindness would come without a price."

Carlos smiled wryly. "I completely understand your problem with Fausto."

"That bastard!"

"Satisfy my curiosity. You did place the bets. You owe him the money, do you not?"

"Yes, but he's sucking the life out me. I...I...I..."

"Stop, you don't need to worry about Fausto anymore."

Orlando looked up at him, bewilderment etched across his face.

"I'm a businessman, Rodriguez. I bought your debt."

"All of it?"

"I'm a successful businessman. I see us making tremendous profits—together."

"Together?" he said with a bit of smile. "I've built this business up from the street alone, and now you just threw us together? I am truly amazed at the balls on you. I can write you a check for the $278,000 and add a substantial amount on top of that to express my gratitude. But a partner? I don't think so, friend."

Carlos listened without showing any outward emotion. He realized then how unrepentant Orlando was about his gambling addiction. He excused himself briefly and made a short phone call and then offered a suggestion. "I'd like to explain myself a little more clearly. I'm sure you'll understand, but first, I have something to show you. Come with me for a few minutes."

"Where?"

"Downstairs, to the basement."

Orlando recoiled.

"No, please, come, I want you to understand me more clearly." He beckoned softly, feigning sincerity. "Please!"

Against his better judgment, Orlando followed Carlos into the elevator and down to the basement through the labyrinth of deserted corridors. Carlos ushered Orlando into a janitor's office at the end of the hallway. Orlando immediately began to regret putting his trust in Carlos.

As Orlando followed Carlos into the room, he noticed a slightly built man, possibly Indian, seated behind a desk. A Latino male stood directly behind him. The seated man was tied to the chair and was struggling to break free. The Indian man was obviously pleading, but Orlando could not understand his language. Beads of perspiration covered his face, and his eyes bulged in fear. As Orlando stepped into the room, the door was shut, revealing a second, younger man standing behind it. Carlos's demeanor changed abruptly.

"Mr. Rodriguez, sit," he said as he pointed to a wooden chair on the opposite side of the desk. Orlando's response lagged as he absorbed what was laid out before him. "Sit! Now." He did as was commanded; his facial expression acknowledged he knew that he had just walked into a world of shit. Orlando's adrenaline began to pump; he saw no way out.

Addressing himself to Orlando, Carlos said, "Let me introduce you to a business associate of mine. He is a colleague in a mutual venture, or at least he was. To make a long story short, he stole from me and then lied about it. I find both of these practices intolerable." The now agitated Carlos had a slight but absolutely frightening smirk on his face.

The gentleman was Aruran Yatthavan, a Sri Lankan whose specialty was credit card fraud, specifically skimming. Aruran had exercised extremely poor judgment and believed he could take a little extra for himself.

Credit card fraud was one of the sources of income Carlos used to finance his operations. A number of people both within and outside his local community, people who worked in restaurants and gas stations, were willing to assist Carlos to supplement their own meager wages. Carlos provided each with magnetic card readers. The portable readers only weighed a couple of ounces and were kept by Carlos's assistants. When customers paid with their credit cards, there was the normal swipe of a card through the legitimate credit card machine and a second swipe for Carlos.

The magnetic strip on a credit card consists of three strips called tracks with the first two strips containing the card holder's name, account number, expiration, and pin number. The card readers can hold the records of two to three thousand swipes. Carlos purchased half a dozen of these little moneymakers at $250 apiece on the internet, along with a card-encoding machine and blank card stock that enabled him to create his own cards using the information he'd gained. The only thing he was lacking was the technical background needed to harvest this windfall. Enter Aruran Yatthavan and his associates.

Aruran was a Sri Lankan national who entered the country a few years ago on a student visa, which had since expired. He remained in the country illegally in the large Sri Lankan community on Staten Island. He was a member of the LTTE, Sri Lanka's notorious Tamil Tigers, known for instigating various forms of naval and non-naval mayhem, including the invention of suicide bombing tactics and, to a lesser degree, as specialists in the art of fraud. Carlos came to an arrangement with Aruran, but apparently, he had an entrepreneurial side that was rearing its ugly head.

Carlos routinely monitored Aruran's work as he methodically manufactured new cards from the skimmed information through an encryption device hooked up to a PC. Aruran, unaware of the hidden camera, was using his own personal skimmer and stealing from Carlos. Carlos watched one day for almost an hour and counted six instances of Aruran skimming. As he watched, his anger built. What vexed Carlos the most was not the loss of a few cards but the break in trust and his authority. Security and survival are based on trust and integrity, and his business integrity was a commodity he could not allow to be compromised. Aruran had shown himself to be a liability.

The Friday night before Orlando was scheduled to be released from the hospital, Carlos confronted Aruran as he left his stash house. Carlos guided Aruran back into the apartment and interrogated him with his two trusted assistants. Aruran claimed innocence, which infuriated Carlos even more, but a single search of his pockets turned up the skimming device. He was also shown a video from the hidden camera, and finally Aruran capitulated and told all. He was working for himself, he confessed, not for his LTTE handlers back on Staten Island. He begged forgiveness, calling himself a greedy, stupid man.

It didn't matter though, and he was quietly removed to the basement to await his fate.

In the janitor's office the next morning, Carlos set the stage for Orlando. "Mr. Rodriguez, I know I've told you I'm a businessman, and I am. I've also told you we're partners now, and you're understandably resistant, but I assure you we are." He drew himself close to Orlando's face and in his most intense tone said to him, "I own you. Never forget that." The room was warm with little ventilation and a slight odor of diesel fuel in the air from the oil burner. Orlando felt extremely lightheaded.

Carlos stood up and glared at Orlando as he pulled pliers from his pocket. With no hesitation, Carlos walked over to Aruran and gave him a heavy backhanded smack across the face. Before Aruran could recover, the man behind him grabbed his lower jaw and forced his mouth open. Carlos opened a four-inch buck knife. He then inserted pliers into the Sri Lankan's mouth and pulled his tongue out to its full length. Aruran's screams were muffled as Carlos cleanly cut Aruran's tongue out. The severed system of the tongue spewed a torrent of blood across the room, leaving Orlando frozen in terror. Carlos again moved toward Orlando and whispered to him, "Fuck me just once, you degenerate gambler, and see where it gets you." He then dropped the severed tongue into Orlando's lap for effect.

Carlos walked behind the restrained Aruran Yatthavan, produced a silenced brush metal Sig Sauer P-220 .45-caliber automatic, and blew Aruran's brains through his face and onto Orlando's face and shirt.

As Carlos walked toward the door, he leaned down to the shaken Rodriguez and whispered into his ear, "We'll talk again soon, partner. And, oh yes, your gambling days are over, if you know what's good for you."

Orlando began to shake uncontrollably and vomit. After being forced to assist in the cleanup of the grizzly scene, he was taken back to his apartment. Orlando was still in a state of shock as he tried to contemplate his new business relationship.

Aruran Yatthavan would be rolled up in a rug and later dumped into the East River. For three weeks, he'd ride the prevailing tides and eventually wash up onto a Staten Island beach, headless. There would be an attempt to identify him by his fingerprints, but to no avail.

Carlos, for his part, was satisfied that he'd made a favorable impression on Orlando and that he would, after thinking about it, fall into line. If Orlando proved himself to be a fool, Carlos owned more than one rug.

As for the LTTE, the video of Aruran's transgressions and confession should at least persuade them to more closely vet the next skimmer they sent Carlos's way.

CHAPTER 6

Detective Brian Devine was a New York City cop all the way down to his marrow. His father, brother, uncle, and grandfather had all worked for the NYPD. The forty-year-old stocky Irish Marine Corp veteran had been assigned for almost all his seventeen years on the job to Manhattan's Ninth Precinct in the East Village. He'd walked foot posts in Tompkins Square Park, on St. Mark's Place, and then down on Avenue B. He'd also worked in radio cars. He'd seen and experienced most of the Lower East Side and knew its people and liked them. More importantly, they liked him. It would be difficult to find anyone who would utter a bad word about Brian Devine.

Brian may not have made hundreds of dollars, but he followed the lessons he learned from his father, especially those stressing compassion. He had taught Brian early in his career to remember that the people he'd meet on a day-to-day basis may one day need him on the worst day of their life.

While other precincts might be flashier or located in more pleasant areas, few provided the grit and professional challenge that the Ninth did. While it was not as wild and crime ridden as it had been, the work still tested you daily. Professionally, the Ninth Precinct represents the gold standard in policework. The fraternity among Ninth Precinct cops, past and present, is legend.

Brian was a big guy, six feet two inches, 180 pounds, and could be forceful when needed but preferred not to push his size around to get people's attention. He was known for his ability to listen to what was being said as well as those that went unsaid. His credibility and popularity in Alphabet City were a result of his compassion.

On a cold December afternoon, Brian and his partner, Louie Lugo, responded to a report of a food store manager "holding one" at a store on Avenue C near East Fourth Street. The manager had caught a small Spanish woman in her early thirties who tried to steal a two-pound loin of pork by concealing it under her coat. Although he was being pounded by theft, the merchant was clearly overplaying the righteously indignant card. The woman in question was found to be a sincerely pathetic soul. She was unemployed, had four kids, and was not making it, not even on welfare. She said her family had not tasted meat in weeks and admitted to the theft as an act of desperation, having only thirty-seven cents to her name. The woman was terrified of an arrest. Who would take care of her children? She had touched a chord in Brian and Louie. Brian asked the manager if he'd be willing to cut the woman some slack and not press charges.

"Absolutely not! These people have to understand they cannot steal me blind!" The manager's lack of sensitivity pissed Brian and Louie off. Still, Brian kept working on the manager, but he just folded his arms and said, "No, absolutely not. Arrest her!"

"That's a pretty a tough stance, friend. How about if we just pay for what she stole?"

"Absolutely not! I insist that you do your job. I'm a taxpayer!"

Brian looked momentarily in Louie's direction, their eyes meeting briefly, and nothing more needed to be said between them. Brian took out his portable radio and said to the store manager, "That's pretty tough, friend. You're a taxpayer, huh? Well, if you want the law enforced, okay, fine with me." He picked up his walkie-talkie and casually reset the frequency from the main divisional police frequency to a short-range local car-to-car tactical frequency that only went a few blocks. He triggered the key, "Nine Boy to Central, Kay. Is the Health Department Emergency Response Team on the air?"

Immediately, an adjoining sector car picked up the ploy and joined in. "Yes, we are, Sector Boy. Where are we needed?"

The store manager's demeanor immediately changed.

"Is the rat-dropping expert working tonight? Kay."

"Sitting right next to me, Boy."

"Good," Brian said, adding some enthusiasm to his voice. "Could you respond to the food market at the corner of Avenue C and Fourth Street?"

"Absolutely!"

It was then that the manager became unglued. "What? Wait, wait, what are you doing?"

"You can stand up to a little Health Department inspection, can't you?"

"Wait a second now. How about if I just ban her from the store?"

"Maybe, but she'll be going shopping first."

"What?"

"Sector Boy, do you still want the Health Department to respond?" the other car chimed.

Brian smiled and held the radio up in the manager's direction.

The newly converted altruist indicated in the negative with frantic hands. "Shopping, sure, sure!"

Brian called off the "Health Department" while Louie grabbed a shopping cart. Brian, Louie, and the formerly accused went shopping. Before they were done, the cart contained the original pork loin, a few chickens, rice, milk, and a host of other necessities. The tab came to about fifty bucks, which Brian paid. He sent the woman on her way after reminding her not to go back to that store, and before leaving, she planted a kiss on both of them. A small knot of people had watched the little show and liked what they'd seen. Among them was Orlando Rodriguez.

Brian's commanding officer, Deputy Inspector John Mercer, appreciated what he saw in Brian and called him into his office one Friday afternoon. "Brian, Kevin Pfelty up in Community Affairs is retiring at the end of the month."

"Is Kevin all right, boss?"

"He is, but unfortunately, his poor wife, Carol, has cancer. He's got to be home, so we've been giving him the time he needs, and we'll continue to do so, but he wants out."

"What can I do to help, boss?"

"Actually, I called you in to ask if you'd like to take his spot when he leaves. You know the precinct well, and people find it easy to communicate with you. If you could see your way to do it, you'd be doing me a tremendous favor."

"Wow, that's a lot to take in! Look, boss, if that's what you need, then sure, but could you give me until Monday to talk it over with my wife?"

"Absolutely, Brian."

"I'm think it'll be fine, but I'd rather talk to Maureen about this than spring a surprise on her."

"I completely understand. I'm working Monday, a ten-to-six. See me then, but I have to know fairly soon."

"Yes, sir, talk to you Monday morning."

Maureen Nash, a nurse at Staten Island University Hospital, had been the best thing to come into his life. They married the previous April. It was the second marriage for both of them and had brought a much-needed stability into both their lives.

Brian married when he was twenty-two, but it hadn't worked out. The boozy relationship lasted a little more than a year before falling apart. Both he and his ex-wife had been foolish and partied excessively, and on one particular night, he walked out the back door of Duffy's on Forest Avenue and found her drunk, screwing around with a female friend in a parked car. In his rage, he tried to get at her in the locked car. Yanking on the door, he ripped the handle off, but luckily, he didn't act further on his impulse. They immediately separated, followed shortly by a mutual consent divorce.

Brian he made his way home with his mind buzzing about the changes he had coming his way. The air on the Staten Island Ferry commute home helped clear his head after his meeting with Inspector Mercer.

Brian preferred to commute by ferry rather than drive his car, which was a habitually cranky piece of shit. Plus, the traffic was a nightmare with people who didn't know how to drive, along with tolls and gas prices that quickly added up. On top of everything, it was nearly impossible to find a parking space near the precinct, since the designated spots were always taken. Public transportation was the best way for a Staten Islander to get to the city. People who regularly take the boat can usually be found in exactly the same place each day. In Brian's case, he and a couple of guys from the Ninth, including Louie, staked out a section of the left rear/front, coming and going.

The ferry, however, was not only a transportation staple but also a social hub. Generations of Islanders have "taken the boat to work." It's a floating town square where people meet to talk and sometimes plan their lives. More than a few personal relationships have blossomed and grown "on the boat."

CHAPTER 7

It was 10:00 a.m. on Tuesday when Brian and Louie turned out for their scheduled ten-to-six tour in the Ninth Precinct conditions car. They were working direct enforcement in response to nonemergency problems that residents of the Ninth brought to the commanding officer's attention. They attended to all manner of situations, including traffic problems, disorderly groups, all types of street predators, and any other quality-of-life condition. First and foremost, they attended to their routine radio assignments. If needed, they would jump into the radio queue and help out.

Brian was scheduled as the operator of the unit, a fairly new Chevy, number 1206 on the roll call that morning. Louie was the passenger, better known as the recorder, who made all the reports: after four hours they'd switch positions. One additional responsibility of the recorder was to go into the bagel shop and get coffee. As was routine, they pulled over on Houston Street and ate. They could only hope for fifteen or so undisturbed minutes to enjoy breakfast.

"Louie, the boss called me in Friday and asked me to move up to Community Affairs."

"Just like that?"

"Sort of. Pfelty's wife has cancer, so he's retiring. What do you think, Louie? Should I do it?"

"What's Maureen think?"

"She's okay with it. What about you?"

Like many police partners, they melded together psychologically when working. Call it what you will, a result of training or exposure to a continual routine, but Brian and Louie were in sync with each other to an extent that was almost scary. It was easy to appreciate the magnitude of the separation Brian was suggesting, almost akin to divorce.

"If that's what you want, go for it. It's not like you're moving to the dark side of the moon. You're only going upstairs." Brian could detect a slightly emotional tone of disappointment.

"Okay, that's settled. I'll speak to the boss when we go in for a meal. What have we got today?"

Louie checked the clipboard and looked surprised. "We've got to see about a friend of yours this morning."

"Really, who?"

"Do you remember that old lady, Heldi, over on East Third Street?"

"Yeah, oh sure, the block watcher. She's nice."

"Dude, she was a block watcher before anybody knew what that was. She's never out of that window."

"Do you know what she wants?"

"No, it just says to see her."

"Okay, then let's do that."

Brian held a special place in Heldi's heart. Heldi's son, a Marine, had been killed in the Vietnam War, and she saw in Brian the son she'd lost.

As they came up on Heldi's building, Brian looked up and saw Heldi at her perch in the window. She saw him at the same time and placed her thumb to her ear and her pinky to her mouth, mimicking a phone to suggest she didn't want to speak in the open. Brian continued past her building and then made a right onto Avenue A. He pulled over and called her number he'd had for a number of years.

"Heldi sweetheart. How are you? Are we being secretive today?"

"I'm fine, baby. Congratulations on your promotion, and yes we are."

"Woman, how did you know that? I haven't even said yes yet."

Louie just laughed; he knew what she'd said. Heldi knew everything that went on in the neighborhood.

"You will, baby, you will."

"What can we do for you today? Why'd you call?"

"Your boy Rodriguez had a problem recently. Did you hear about it?"

"Vaguely. He caught a beating, didn't he?"

"Yeah, but it wasn't from any mugger. Hector, Fausto's man, tuned him up because he went deadbeat on Fausto. He beat him bad, Brian. If the Cuban guy hadn't saved his ass, he could have killed him."

"Cuban guy, which guy?"

"The guy who lives upstairs from me."

She had Brian stumped. He couldn't place a guy big enough to take on Hector; the man was an animal.

"Which Cuban upstairs?"

"Brian, you know who I mean. The artist guy up on the fourth floor."

"Him! That thin dude? He smacked down Hector?"

"That's right. The man's badass."

"Wow." Brian knew whom she meant. He was an average-sized dude and kind of nerdy. He could only think, *I guess you never know.*

"Look, Brian. Orlando deserved what he got, sort of, but shit like that brings back the old days."

"Thanks, Heldi. We'll have a few words with Fausto."

"Brian, you be careful."

"Always, honey."

"Louie, we gotta see some people, but first I have to pick something up." Brian filled Louie in on the way.

Brian made a quick stop at the local church that provided a meeting place for Gamblers Anonymous, where he picked up a reference for Orlando. Up until now, he'd only occasionally lectured Orlando on his habit, but now he felt he had to do something before the guy got himself killed. Brian was conflicted because he was entering a gray legal area. He wanted to protect Orlando; he didn't want to go "official" with him. If he didn't act carefully, his good intentions could expose Orlando to legal problems for not being truthful with the police originally. On the other hand, if he exposed the reality of Orlando's situation, he could place him in a far worse position where he might face retribution at Carlos's hands.

Brian and Orlando had an off-duty relationship that revolved around their passion for fishing. One of the first things Orlando did when he became financially successful was buy a boat. This was not just any boat either, but a thirty-eight-foot Donzi with three beefy three hundred horsepower outboards. It wasn't a great boat for fishing, but damn, that floating rocket ship was fun!

First things first though; a visit to Orlando was in order. Brian's mind ran ahead of him, *Please don't let me slap this dope.*

The minute Orlando opened the door, Brian lost the urge to slap him. His eyes widened as he took in how badly he had been beaten. "Hello, shithead. What in the fuck have you gotten yourself into?" Orlando's appearance was appalling. His head was swollen, and both eyes were blackened.

Orlando had difficulty meeting Brian's eyes. "I fucked up big-time, Brian. I deserved it. I stiffed him bad."

"Let's get something straight. You didn't molest his sister, so no, you didn't deserve anything like this. How much, Lando?"

"$278,000."

"Jesus Holy Christ! Can you cover that?"

"Yeah, man, easily."

"Then why the fuck did you let it come to this?"

"It's hard to explain. Let's just say I got tired of being strong-armed."

"This Cuban guy saved your ass?"

"Oh yeah, my savior," Orlando admitted as he rolled his eyes and expelled a long breath.

"Look, first things first, I'm going to be in your life more than you'd like."

"No, man, not now, please!"

"No my ass. Take this card and call this guy. It's Gamblers Anonymous. I'm not asking you. I'm fucking telling you! Let me find out you don't go to the meetings, and I will personally lock your stupid ass up for hindering the investigation into your own assault! Do you understand me?"

Orlando's head hung down as he meekly nodded yes.

Brian softened and threw him into a consolatory bear hug, causing Orlando to scream in pain. "Ribs, ribs, man, please, broken ribs!"

"Oh, Jesus, I'm so sorry. I forgot, oh shit, I'm sorry. Listen, this will work out, I promise you. Obviously, you're not going to give up Fausto."

Winded, Orlando agreed with a half smile and a shrug. Brian and Louie left with a promise of seeing Orlando again soon.

Brian and Louie walked out into a beautiful day; the sky was a shocking crystal clear blue. The block's present condition always amazed him. Although he wasn't a cop when the area was reclaimed, Brian remembered the piles of trash and burned-out cars in the street. He could close his eyes and see the cinder-blocked windows and doors and buildings in decay. Now it was a tree-lined street with thriving businesses and restaurants, kids playing, and mommies pushing strollers.

As they got back into the car, they both noticed the same thing down the block, near the corner of Avenue A. It was Fausto and Hector taking bets. The two reminders of the old days caused Brian's face to harden. Louie smiled; he knew what was coming. Louie said aloud, "Shall we?"

Through tightened lips, Brian replied, "Yup."

Brian pulled the RMP beyond Fausto and Hector and then walked back toward the two. Accordingly, the two began to walk away, but Brian stopped them in their tracks.

"Fausto, if I have to chase you, I am going to beat your head down into your shoulders."

As they stopped, Fausto feigned innocence. "What, I didn't know you wanted us to stop."

"Right, scumbag. Officer Lugo, will you entertain Mr. Glaves while I speak with Mr. Fausto privately?"

"Absolutely." Hector tried to go with Fausto, but Louie blocked his path with a smile. Fausto signaled Hector to stay. Louie had to remember that Hector was under the control of Fausto and was capable of incredible viciousness.

Brian led Fausto into the lobby of 181 East Third Street. There was a second door that led to a second rear lobby. It was poorly lit with too many coats of paint on the walls and missing tiles on the floor. Brian closed the door, and it began. "I saw what you did to Rodriguez. Let me ask you a question Who owns this street?"

It was then that Fausto made his first mistake and smirked.

Brian gave him a backhand slap to the mouth, then a forehand, and then another backhand, causing him to bounce off the wall. Grabbing him tightly by his throat, Brian raised him up onto his toes. Holding him against the wall, Brian took out a folding knife with a serrated blade and plunged it into the wall next to Fausto's head. He began to read him the riot act.

"Scumbag, I own this fucking street, and I know about the .25-caliber in your right-hand pocket, so why don't you go for it and let me put a nine-millimeter round into your small brain!"

Fausto declined, a good move on his part. Had he moved in that direction, they would have found him with a nine-millimeter bullet hole in his head and the gun in his hand. As it were, Brian had him remove it from his pocket with two fingers and placed it on the floor. Brian then kicked it away.

"Understand this, hump, if I ever find out you've done anything like what you did to Orlando again, I'm not going to lock you up 'cause there won't be enough left of your worthless ass to throw in a cage. Do we understand each other, fucko?"

"Absolutely. But there isn't going to be a problem. The Cuban took care of everything."

"What do you mean?" Brian's eyes narrowed.

"He bought Rodriguez's nut. He said he had his reasons."

"He bought all of it?"

"Every bit. The guy took out stacks of hundreds like he had a printing press in the basement."

Brian suddenly got a bad feeling about Orlando's problem. "Get the fuck out of here, and remember what I said."

"Done. Can I have my gun back?"

"No, you fucking idiot, get the fuck away from me!"

When Brian got back to Louie, he said, "Louie, we should meet this Cuban. There's something more to this."

Heldi saw a disheveled and somewhat agitated Fausto precede Brian out of the doorway. Heldi, looking down from her window perch, just smiled as she thought to herself, *There's the law, and then there's justice.*

CHAPTER 8

Orlando had been attending Gamblers Anonymous meetings a few times a week for the past three months. Some days were harder than others, but he was determined and had the support of friends, like Brian and Louie. With their encouragement and that of others in his program, Orlando began to take hold of his addiction. He was ready for change in his life, but it was a daily struggle, and Orlando missed the comfort a blackjack table used to bring him. Orlando strived to regain the respect of his sister, mother, and the neighbors who had watched him spiral out of control. Most of all though, he wanted to return the patience and kindness Brian Devine had shown him.

He was also ready to recover control of his business, or as much as he could. His biggest motivation to seek help, though, was his fear of Carlos. Orlando did not want to share the same fate as the Sri Lankan. There were times when he would find himself suddenly in a tearful state of panic, unable to understand how his life had gotten so far out of control. Orlando often found himself thinking, *God, I've fucked things up so badly,* and he even considered suicide. Now with the help of other members in GA, Orlando learned his affliction was beyond his control, and he gave himself up to a greater power.

St. Emeric's on Avenue D and East Thirteenth Street was his mother's parish, where she had found the inner strength to live through the hard times as she worked endless hours as a nurse's aide to help support her family. He often marveled at how she had never missed work or Mass. He remembered the day, as a child, that it snowed so hard that bus service stopped. He couldn't believe his mother walked more than twenty blocks in that blizzard to and from Bellevue Hospital because, as she put it, sick people depended upon her and she wouldn't let them down.

Nowadays, Orlando did a lot of walking to keep his head clear and just to think. On this particular day, he found himself in front of St. Emeric's. He sat alone on the steps of the old church, named for some long-dead Hungarian saint. He thought about his mother's sacrifices and compared them to his miserable life choices. He soon became embroiled in his own misery. He couldn't bring himself to go inside, feeling somehow that he was unworthy to set foot in the church. After he had calmed himself, a sense of inner peace came over him. Call it an epiphany, introspection, self-therapy, or the voice of God, but peace was beginning to edge its way back into to him.

*****

Orlando sat quietly in the living room of his apartment, taking stock of his situation. Once again, he'd been suddenly jarred from his fitful rest by the same recurring dream, his bed soaking wet with sweat. Night after night, Orlando relived the Sri Lankan incident in slow motion. Carlos stood directly behind his victim as Aruran's head exploded onto Orlando's face. Carlos stood there glaring at Orlando with a sinister smile on his distorted face.

Orlando's apartment was the only sanctuary where he could think nowadays. He got out of bed and put on his warm terry cloth robe and tried to get the chill out of his bones. He grabbed a towel out of the bathroom to wipe off the sweat as he paced around his living room. The soft lighting, subdued colors, and soft leather arm-chair and couch set a soothing mood. The framed photographs on the wall reflected much of Orlando's life. There were the photos of his smiling mother and sister, pictures of his boat, the thirty-eight-foot Donzi *Sofia*, and other photographs of deep-sea fishing trips with his raucous friends. The most prominent was a large black-and-white photo of Times Square looking downtown from West Forty-Seventh Street on the west side. It was a remarkably well-framed photo by Orlando, which held a deep sentimental value to him. The block between West Forty-Sixth and West Forty-Seventh Streets was where he'd spent years dealing monte on the street and made his bones. He walked over and opened the street-side window. Orlando sometimes just couldn't think without the cacophony of the street.

On one hand, the mere thought of Carlos scared the hell out him. Carlos seemed to be a reserved individual, almost kindly, as odd as that might sound. Whatever had been the sin of that poor Sri Lankan, it had surely brought out a schizoid side in Carlos. If Carlos's conduct was meant to warn or threaten Orlando, he'd succeeded. But Orlando now had to admit that Carlos had become instrumental in the two raking in money. In the last few weeks, they had refinanced two of Orlando's properties, worked out a sixty-forty split, and had already made enough profit to pay off Orlando's debts with enough left over to consider reinvesting in another building. Whatever Carlos's game was, excessive greed wasn't part of it, as he showed no intention of killing the golden goose. Orlando found the whole thing perversely disturbing. He could not put their puzzling relationship into a rational perspective.

Who was Carlos Reyes, and what exactly did he do? Orlando had assumed he had something to do with drugs, which wouldn't be a first for this old neighborhood. Carlos was cagey and never did anything overtly on the block, at least nothing that could be seen publicly. There was certainly no parade of people to and from his door; in fact, just the opposite was true. He kept his office in one of the apartments, but again, nothing suspicious went on. One curious thing was that since this agreement, Carlos had started keeping a few apartments for his own use. The occupants came and went over various time periods. They were white, black, Spanish, Europeans, Middle Eastern. Again, all the travelers were quiet and respectful and brought little if any attention to themselves. Carlos was probably using the apartments as safe houses of some kind, but safe from what, who, and why?

Ultimately, Orlando couldn't brush aside the fact that Carlos Reyes was a stone-cold killer. He had no idea what had set this obvious nut off. More importantly, whatever it was, he didn't want to inadvertently fuck up and trigger Carlos's dark persona. He had considered telling Brian what had happened, but what exactly was that? The man Carlos had killed wasn't local; he'd never seen him before.

There had been nothing made of the killing. He'd seen nothing in the paper or on TV. What could he tell Brian? Where was the body, who was he? If he told Brian, there'd obviously have to be an investigation, and that, in and of itself, could be dangerous. Carlos would immediately know how that started. The investigation would probably go nowhere without a body or motive. In short order, Carlos would be free and clear, and there would be no hole dark enough to hide Orlando. He would do well to keep his mouth shut, at least until he better understood where Carlos was coming from, and he was nowhere near that point yet.

Then there was a spiritual component to his predicament. How the hell did he justify, in his heart and soul, working with this evil bastard? How much longer would he cower and look the other way to protect his own worthless ass? Even more disturbing was his deep suspicion that partnering himself with Carlos's business meant his involvement in other unknown evil. This was certainly not making kicking his gambling problem any easier. Oh yeah, the life he had built for himself was the gift that just kept on giving.

He mixed a water glass of Jamison's and tea. It wasn't long before he felt drowsy, so he went back in the bedroom to give sleep another try.

*****

Brian sat in the solitude of the dining room table in his suburban home late Tuesday evening, pen and paper in front of him, hashing and rehashing Orlando's rather odd situation. At face value it would appear that Orlando had been rescued by some type of Clark Kent who had morphed into a superhero. It was even more difficult for Brian to identify the milquetoast he knew as Carlos Reyes to be as the crime fighter Heldi had described to him. Orlando's obvious lack of enthusiasm for his newfound relationship with Carlos said volumes, but Orlando's silence said even more. Then there was the money. What art gallery employee has access to wrapped packs of one-hundred-dollar bills? It was all very strange.

As vexing as it all was, Brian realized he would start with the basics and formulate a plan to unravel Orlando from his problem. Brian had completed all the discreet checks he could into Carlos's background. He'd run Carlos through the Organized Crime Control Bureau. Carlos was unknown to them. Devine had spoken with his friends in the First Precinct who knew of Carlos's place of employment on Spring Street. Again, nothing.

It was not in Brian's nature to idly stand by and knowingly allow another person to endure an abusive situation, never mind a close friend. As a child he had endured endless bullying. There was no tolerance in his heart for "strong-arm artists," as bullies were known in police circles.

The baseline of his plan was to convince Orlando to tell him the complete truth about his involvement with Carlos, something that was missing. Brian called Orlando and set up a lunch meeting for the next day at a local Cuban restaurant.

CHAPTER 9

Café Cortadito was located just east of Avenue B on East Third Street. Its existence was one of those pleasant bonuses that occur when a neighborhood experiences a successful urban renaissance. The small café was a red-hot item on the Manhattan restaurant scene for good reason. Reservations, even for lunch, were a good idea.

Brian arrived first and sat at one of the half dozen or so tables in the small front dining room. Orlando arrived a bit late but with a smile on his face. They settled in over a glass of wine and placed their orders. Brian zeroed in on camarones enchiladas, shrimp in a spicy Creole sauce, while Orlando opted for pollo plancha, grilled chicken. As the food arrived, small talk subsided and Brian made his point.

"Orlando, I worry about you a lot."

"I know, Brian, and believe me, I appreciate that you're there for me."

"Well, I'm not completely there for you. I know you're holding something back."

What had begun as a casual meal between friends took a different tone.

"Orlando, do you know how this guy Reyes bought your nut from Fausto?"

"No, do you?"

"Well, as a matter of fact, I do. He met Fausto and handed him stacks and stacks of hundred-dollar bills. He doesn't look like the kind of guy who would have access to that type of cash. Orlando, what's this guy really about?"

"Truthfully, I'm not sure. What I do know about him…"

Orlando began to start hemming, hawing, and stammering.

Brian gently prodded, "Orlando, how bad is this guy?"

"As bad as they come." His voice was reduced to barely a whisper. "I can't let you get involved in this. Believe me. I have my reasons, and you wouldn't like them."

"Pal, you're into something that's way over your head with no happy ending."

"If you become involved, it could get very nasty for me."

"That's what I do for a living. I know what the job wants me to do and not to do, and I know how to dance on the line between all of that. How about letting me decide what can and can't be done? I wouldn't let you get hurt. You know that, don't you?"

There was no answer.

"Orlando, this is way beyond what you can deal with. Talk to me, man. Let me help." Orlando's head hung down, but Brian could see tears welling.

His voice breaking, Orlando whispered, "Brian, I'm so fucking scared, man."

Brian consoled, "I know, man, I know." He sensed that he'd made a breakthrough.

"No, no, you don't. You have no idea."

Brian let the conversation sit for a moment, and Orlando made a quiet suggestion. "Let's finish up, pay the tab, and take a walk."

They did just that. While walking slowly eastward on East Third Street, Orlando began to open up.

"Reyes killed a guy in front of me."

"Who was he?"

"I don't know, never seen him before. Carlos said he'd doubled-crossed him in a business deal, and he wanted me to see what happened to people who did that to him." He then described in graphic detail what had happened.

"Did you know who the other two guys with him were?"

"I've never seen them before."

"What happened to the body?"

"They wrapped it in a rug and took him out of the basement. I don't know what happened after that. I was forced to stay behind and clean up the mess. Me and one of Carlos's thugs cleaned the place up with oxygenated bleach with hydrogen peroxide until there was no trace of what had happened."

Brian smiled and thought to himself, *Sly son of a bitch is no art dealer. We can't even use Luminol to check for blood because of the oxygenated bleach.* Carlos Reyes was apparently a meticulous professional, but what was that profession?

"Has Reyes ever done anything that gave you a hint as to what he might actually do?"

"No, he's quiet. I can't explain the difference in the person I saw in the basement and the person I now see day to day. He's never mentioned that morning in the basement again. It's like dealing with Jekyll and Hyde. He keeps an apartment on the fourth floor for business under another name that I let slide as long as the rent is paid."

Brian mused, "I'd love to see what's in there."

"I'd be careful there. He's got that place alarmed and cameras set up inside. My maintenance man saw it all installed."

"Does he remember the name of the installer?"

"I'll ask him."

"Okay, I have to digest all this and figure out how I'm going to deal with it. Believe me when I tell you we are going to get through this—together. You haven't done anything wrong. You're the victim of an extortion. Don't do anything you wouldn't normally do. Just keep your eyes and ears open and keep me informed."

"There's one thing I forgot to tell you about. He keeps three apartments set aside for his own use. People stay there from time to time in some kind of transient situation."

"Like a safe house," Brian said with a slight smile.

"Yeah."

"Could you get me some information on those people?"

"I'll try, but he keeps that stuff to himself. I feel like such a piece of shit for causing all this to happen. If I wasn't such a degenerate, self-serving gambler, none of this would have happened."

Brian brought him up short. "Wait a minute, you can't believe that. This guy is about exploiting opportunities, which you provided. If it hadn't been you and your situation, he would have victimized someone else. Don't go overboard beating yourself up. We'll get through this."

Orlando asked, "Would you mind if I continued on by myself? I want to clear my head a bit."

"Sure, we'll talk in the next few days."

"Thanks again, man."

"Not a problem." Brian walked back toward his car, which was parked near the restaurant. His head was swimming with the task in front of him.

By the time they parted company, they'd reached the corner of Avenue C and East Sixth Street. Orlando continued north on Avenue C, lost in his thoughts. He was in his old neighborhood and looking for answers to the questions spinning in his head.

Orlando arrived at the corner of East Twelfth Street, across from his old building in the housing project. He could almost see himself and his friends playing on the walkways and grounds.

The years had brought much change to the old neighborhood. The building that housed the fresh poultry market had been turned into a school, and the area in front of St. Emeric's Church was now blocked by a construction site, though the church was still there. It was then that he heard a voice from behind him.

"Orlando my boy, how nice to see you!"

It was old Mr. Polanco, his former next-door neighbor from the projects. He was almost like family when Orlando was a kid, always trying to keep him on the straight and narrow, especially when he was running with Flaco.

"Son, look at you. You've done so well! I'm so proud of you!" The old man was genuinely filled with joy at meeting him. They had a short but pleasant conversation about his and Orlando's families and life in general. As they parted, Mr. Polanco pumped his hand and clapped his back again, saying, "I'm so proud of you!"

He couldn't help but think, *If Senor Polanco only knew.* Orlando lived only a few blocks away on East Third Street, but it seemed a world away. He had over $50 million in assets to his name but was nowhere near as content as old Polanco, who lived in a bare-bones four-room apartment in the projects. It stung as he realized Polanco had everything and he had nothing.

CHAPTER 10

"Carlos, Jack O'Connor here. How are you?"

"Fine, Jack. To what do I owe the call?"

"I remembered you telling me that you enjoyed harbor-related events. Well, I've got one you might be interested in."

"Really, what's that?" Reyes's curiosity was piqued.

"I've received an invitation from the Prall's Marsh Harbor Conservancy to sail with them on an environmentalist cruise around Staten Island this Saturday morning. Would you be interested in joining me?"

"Yes, I would. How did you score the invite?" Carlos perked up as he sensed an opportunity coming his way.

"I met one of their directors at my last show. He had an interest in my work, which has developed into a mutual project. The guy's name is Don Peterson. The more we spoke about the shoreline, the more his ecological concerns seemed to converge with my historical and artistic interests. The Staten Island waterfront is a unique place. It can be very mysterious in some places and modern in others. Among the most interesting locations, though, are the ship graveyards, in particular an obscure abandoned island known as Shooters Island. It was an active shipyard before and during World War I, after which it closed and was abandoned to nature."

"Interesting, what's it used for now?"

"Well, not much other than a very active bird sanctuary protected by the New York City Department of Parks. There have been some rumors of homeless folks living there, but those are only rumors. The building ways and piers have long since rotted into the harbor, but the buildings are supposedly still there."

"Supposedly?"

"Yeah, the place is so completely overgrown you can't see anything from off shore, even looking on Google Earth, nothing. It's completely overgrown."

"I'm impressed by your expertise. What's your interest in all of this?"

"The conservancy would like me to do a show based on the shoreline of Staten Island. They feel it can be hugely beneficial ecologically speaking and, in my case, artistically. By doing a show with a positive environmental twist, I get access to explore these little jewels and get clearance to go out on that island. Without the conservancy's assistance, that would be nearly impossible. And then there's the elevation of my credentials in the ecological community."

"I admire your dedication. Honestly though, Jack, where do I fit into all of this? I also get the impression I should bring my checkbook."

"I'll be honest with you. If you feel so inclined, please do. I'm sure a financial gesture like that would be appreciated by the conservancy and by me. As I said, I hope to do a show based on this area. You told me that you have an interest in this kind of thing, and I frankly thought it could be a project of mutual interest. I think the trip can give you a valuable insight into little known areas of the harbor."

Carlos realized that he'd stumbled into an opportunity—he'd found another asset.

"When and where do I have to be?"

"The boat leaves from Staten Island at 9:00 a.m. I'll pick you up at your place at 6:45 a.m."

"I'll be ready, see you then."

*****

A group of environmentalists, some maritime buffs, Jack, and Carlos Reyes boarded the boat at the Great Kills Harbor Marina on Staten Island's south shore. She shoved off promptly at 9:00 a.m.

Once on the boat, one of the environmentalists acted as the narrator as they worked their way northward along the shoreline. Carlos tried to hide his disinterest as they passed the long dormant quarantine stations of Swinburne and Hoffman Islands. After they passed under the Verrazano Bridge, the Staten Island waterfront began to reveal itself. This looked like it could be a wealth of tremendous commercial promise located alongside considerable opportunity squandered. The audience got a thumbnail sketch of Fort Wadsworth, formerly the country's oldest army post, which had since been given over to the Department of the Interior as parkland.

Just beyond the Verrazano Narrows Bridge was the former Naval Station New York. Opened in the mid-1980s, the facility was state of the art, costing $450 million. It had been doomed almost as soon as it opened. While the majority of the population of Staten Island supported what became popularly known as Homeport, many off-island politicians and antiwar activists opposed it, nicknaming it the Nukeport. It was, however, its own original mission of support to battleship strike groups that brought about its end. By 1994, the age of the battleship had come to an end, and with it the logic for the Homeport. Thirty-seven acres of prime harbor-side real estate had not been used until recently for commercial and residential real estate development.

Just past the navy base was the transportation hub of St. George and the Staten Island Ferry Terminal. At least a dozen city bus routes and a train line terminate in St. George, discharging their passengers into the newly reconstructed terminal and onto the ferry boats. As the *Laura M* approached the terminal area, they were forced to give way to an arriving Staten Island Ferry. The large 310-foot orange vessel, the *Barberi*, had the right of way as it glided into its final approach to its slip. The smaller conservancy vessel slowed and turned to her right, her bow pointed toward midstream, allowing the two vessels to pass safely port side to port side. The charter boat slowed practically to an idle, rolling sloppily in the wake of the larger vessel. Carlos was impressed at how gracefully the large vessel glided into its mooring and came to a smooth stop.

"Jack, how often does the ferry make its crossings?" Carlos mused.

"This time of day, they leave every half hour or so, carrying tourists and people working odd hours. In the morning and evening rushes, they cross every fifteen minutes."

"They're fairly large. They must carry several hundred passengers."

"That boat can carry 6,000 but usually carries about 2,500 a trip during the rush."

Carlos was having a moment. He was temporarily speechless, realizing he'd picked the right target. Carlos noticed the chop of the water had reduced as they entered into the Kill Van Kull. What caught his attention more was how they approached within fifty yards of the crowded ferry completely unchallenged.

After the ferry passed, the *Laura M* turned to port and continued on, following the island shoreline into the next waterway.

Don Peterson, who was narrating for the tour, described what they were seeing. "We are now entering the Kill Van Kull. This waterway separates Staten Island and New Jersey. The Kill Van Kull and the next, the Arthur Kill, reflect Staten Island's Dutch heritage." The chop on the surface quickly dissipated, and the slack water assumed a greenish-gray tint. On the right, New Jersey was a continual line of commercially thriving refineries and industrial facilities. To the left was Staten Island and dilapidation mixed with marine industries, like the huge rock-salt piles of the Atlantic Salt Company.

They continued another half mile farther into the Kill, passing port to port to give way to a huge outbound Maersk container ship. Again, no Coast Guard, police, or other sign of any waterborne security. Carlos's eyes once again saw an opportunity calling.

Carlos's interest in the Kill Van Kull was growing exponentially. As they continued on, he failed to see any concern for security. His attention became more riveted. As the boat moved on through this four-and-a-half-mile-by-500-yard-wide maritime artery, they passed active shipyards, tug and barge companies, and thriving commercial enterprises. There was not an inkling of security. Carlos was a bit confused; how could a people who are as dependent on their maritime heritage as their commercial life's blood be so negligent?

The boat approached the arch of the Bayonne Bridge and was again forced to give way to a large outbound oil tanker. They passed the tanker and then under the bridge with an option to go either left or right; they went left and followed the contours of Staten Island's north shore.

"Jack, where does that waterway to the right go?"

"That's Newark Bay. Up to the left there, you can see Port Elizabeth, and beyond it, Port Newark. Both are huge container facilities. There is some industry beyond that, but those two are the major players in the bay."

They again had to give way. A tug was heaving around another outbound container ship that came out of the left-hand channel.

"Where do you think that ship is coming from?"

"Probably from the Howland Hook Container Facility, farther on up the Kill on the Staten Island side."

"They seem to be having a difficult time."

"It's a difficult transit for some of the larger vessels, but they do it regularly. The tug crews and pilots are very competent. They'll be out of the way shortly."

Carlos looked to the left and saw a deserted island.

"What is that over there?"

"That is Shooters Island, all forty-three acres of it. That's the island I told you about."

"Now I see what you meant—that's really some dense foliage. I can't see anything, and we're close by. Have you ever been on that island?"

"No, but hopefully this project can get me there. We're still waiting for permission from the NYC Department of Parks. We may also have to get permission from Bayonne, the New Jersey town where that bridge is located, and possibly the town of Elizabeth, New Jersey. The place is jointly owned. I want to get there, but I have mixed emotions."

"What do you mean?"

"The place is infested with mosquitoes, and there's been no control of them whatsoever."

It sounds like a real nasty place, Carlos thought to himself. *It would be a great safe site.*

As they continued, Carlos saw the large container ship facility at Howland Hook and found himself asking about the petroleum facility in Linden, New Jersey. Jack explained, "Farther on to the right over there is one of the largest petroleum production facilities in the country. It processes 269,000 barrels of crude oil delivered by tankers and converted into 145,000 barrels of gasoline and another 110,000 barrels per day from other distillates. This is all shipped out through pipelines, barges, rail, and trucks throughout the East Coast."

The cruise pressed on out of the Arthur Kill and began to head back toward the marina they'd departed from. Don Peterson of the conservancy approached and asked Carlos's impression of the tour. Carlos did not have to feign a favorable impression. Carlos asked if his organization could contribute, rather substantially, to the conservancy's efforts. Peterson could not have been more pleased.

CHAPTER 11

Carlos and Faisal met the next morning as planned, without detecting any surveillance. The entire trip to Staten Island and back was not a tourist event but a reconnaissance.

They waited in the terminal as the morning commuter crowd built around them. The growing throng gathered in the newly reconstructed main hall, dominated by high ceilings and forty-foot glass walls that offered a spectacular view of the harbor. Two huge side-by-side saltwater tropical fish tanks were the centerpiece of the main entrance hall.

They made note, both mentally and photographically, of the adjacent bus and train terminals that fed into the ferry. Carlos was surprised how quietly this large group of people queued up; there was barely a conversational hum. Faisal said it for both of them: "They're like a quiet flock of sheep."

Carlos snapped a series of digital images of the scene unfolding before him. Police were present standing near the rear entrance at what used to be the turnstiles from back when there was a fare. They had a dog that Carlos correctly guessed was a bomb sniffer. Once Carlos and Faisal passed the police checkpoint, the police paid them little mind as they mixed into the crowd.

They stayed and observed two successive boatloads of commuters passing through the large glass doors leading to the boats. Their photography wasn't noticed by the police, but it did draw the attention of a municipal ferry worker who confronted them. He politely reminded them that photos taken within the terminal and on the boats were prohibited. Carlos lamely claimed that they were tourists and didn't realize they were in violation. The worker smiled, accepted their explanation, and returned to the attractive woman he'd been speaking with. No intelligence report would be made of who or what he'd seen. Neither did he ask that they delete what they'd photographed, assuming they were legitimate tourists.

Somewhat unnerved by the challenge, the two boarded the 7:30 a.m. boat, the 310-foot *Andrew J. Barberi*. Carlos and Faisal boarded after positioning themselves near the end of the rambling queue and had difficulty finding two seats together.

As the *Barberi* continued across the harbor, the brothers noted the relaxed and almost congenial atmosphere among the passengers. Faisal agreed with his brother. "I have to agree with your choice of objectives. It seems almost too easy."

When the boat docked, everyone disembarked. Instead of immediately leaving, the brothers bought two cups of tea from the concession stand and spoke about what they'd seen and their plans in general, as Faisal led them to the street. "While there is an appearance of security, in reality I have to say that it is shockingly superficial. This is a very lax situation here," Faisal said.

"I agree. Security seems far from anyone's mind. I could have easily walked into that terminal area wearing an explosive vest and not come within fifty feet of that bomb dog and its handler. On the boat itself, the atmosphere seems relaxed, if not cordial."

Faisal continued, "As I said, the sheik believes he can make advanced technology available to us. But before we commit to a course of action, we should wait to speak with Atef." Atef, or more formally known as Sheik Atef Kahlid Mohammed, was Carlos's immediate superior and international liaison.

"That would be prudent," Carlos agreed.

"Brother, how will Atef join you in New York? He cannot readily travel." Atef was in Canada where he had political asylum. Faisal continued, "He has become engaged in cross-border human trafficking of foreign nationals. He is a person of interest to the Royal Canadian Mounted Police in a scenario where it is extremely difficult to find individuals who would be willing to provide corroborative evidence."

"I know. I'll devise a plan. I have been using the American artist Jack O'Connor to help me. He is unaware of our actual purposes. He merely believes we're engaged in a criminal endeavor. I'm going to meet with him, and I'll judge whether he can be of further use to us. I pay him well, so he will probably suit our needs. He lacks any sense of values."

"Are you sure he doesn't know who you actually are?"

"Oh yes. He thinks I'm a Cuban entrepreneur of dubious purpose. He views me as a more than adequate payday. He may have his limits, but we haven't arrived at that point yet. Right now, he's useful to me."

"Then, of course, there is his most valuable quality: a remarkable knowledge of maritime issues involving the New York Harbor, which he is completely willing to share."

"I'll speak with Atef. You must prepare for his arrival. Call me if I can assist you."

"Of course."

They walked down to the front of the terminal and embraced, and Carlos made sure Faisal knew how to get back to his hotel in Queens before they parted ways.

CHAPTER 12

The village of Whitley sits on the Canadian border, nestled in the rolling hills of northeastern Vermont. It's a peaceful rural town that shares a border with the equally picturesque Canadian community of Montcalm, Quebec. The pastoral streets are divided with one side of a residential block in the United States and the opposite side in Canada. Even the local library and opera house are shared by both countries with a visible line drawn right down the middle.

Unfortunately, illegal immigrants took notice of the sparsely guarded side streets of Whitley and took advantage of the situation. After September 11, 2001, it became painfully apparent to authorities that their intervention was necessary, much to the chagrin and displeasure of the locals who had coexisted for generations.

The folks of Whitley/Montcalm are native locals, sprinkled with a few city transplants who would be quite content if all change could pass them by. Even so, after 9/11, Homeland Security regulations placed these border towns right in the middle of modernity. Neighbors living opposite each other for a lifetime were, as of the last few years, unable to walk across the street for a visit. Instead, they must proceed to their respective border station, present their passports, and then continue to their destination, even if it's just to a neighbor's home for a cup of sugar.

Once a quiet New England town, post 9/11, a substantial border patrol presence attends the line. An unintended or casual crossing of the line brings an immediate response from authorities, causing residents to bristle. The quiet residential side streets are monitored from the town's border patrol station on Route 5 in Whitley. To be fair, the border patrol presence was warranted, since it wasn't uncommon for a carload of illegal immigrants to run the line and attempt an escape on nearby I-91. Pro- and anti-immigration groups often used the town for protests, all at the cost of the treasured peace and quiet that now eludes northern Vermont.

Atef Kahlid Mohammed sat comfortably at his regular table at the Laughing Fox, a small local bistro located within Auberge Dumont, a charming country Inn in Montcalm, one hundred yards from the Canadian border with Whitley. Atef had arrived in Canada in July of 2002 from his native Saudi Arabia and was granted political asylum by Canada. He tried to maintain a low profile, since he brought quite a bloody past with him. A member of the hierarchy of al-Qaeda, he had been a contemporary of Abd al-Raheim al-Nashiri, architect of the attack on the USS *Cole* and the French tanker *Limberg*. When al-Nashiri was captured and taken into custody at Guantanamo Bay, Mohammed went underground in Canada.

Now in charge of the North American operations of the loosely knit terrorist group, he attempted to live as quietly as possible in Montreal with the exception of purchasing three taxicabs. He hadn't bought them in hopes of making his future in transportation, but instead to establish himself as a coyote, a human trafficker. In doing so, he was able to facilitate more than his share of illegal entries, along with moving weapons and explosives across the US border.

Even with his relatively low profile, Atef realized his tenure in Canada needed to come to an end. Police informants had identified him to the Royal Canadian Mounted Police who were now watching him, and he had recently been put on the terrorist watch list. Informants who had been placed in positions within the Canadian government were literally worth their weight in gold. The proverbial wolf was at the door, and Atef knew he had to get out of Canada as soon as possible.

He and his girlfriend and partner in his affairs, Nina Gerard, a Canadian, left their Montreal apartment and moved into one of his safe houses. They began to scrupulously avoid old haunts in Montreal, leaving his cadre of coyote associates to operate his cabs, communicating through disposable cell phones, standard mail, and encrypted emails. He was fortunate enough to have enough money stashed at various locations to keep him operating.

Atef's time in Canada had allowed him to accomplish vast reconnaissance along the border. After taking his illegals, money, he would send them over the border into areas he suspected were protected by electronic sensors. By recording the success or failure of his clients, he was able to build up quite the database of hot and soft spots along the border. He also spent many weekends along the border, probing and observing under the guise of an ornithologist, a common sight in the area. Armed with his bird books and binoculars, he would fit right in amid the woods and farmlands of the Quebec-Vermont border.

Atef operated in plain view when observing potential crossing sites. When he could identify the owner of the property, he would approach him and identify himself as a bird watcher and ask permission to walk the property. He was almost always allowed access. Atef used the pseudonym of Anthony Phelps, posing as an Englishman of Pakistani heritage who'd changed his name in order to meld into his new homeland.

Atef and Nina spent increasing amounts of time in the vicinity of Montcalm, which was about an hour and forty-five minutes outside of Quebec. They found Auberge Dumont to perfectly fit their needs. Atef easily blended into the mix at the bistro, as "bird watcher Anthony Phelps from Montreal with his girlfriend, Nina." He was accepted at face value and admired for his alleged naturalist calling.

With Montcalm as his base of operations and through the associations he'd made, Atef freely roamed the border countryside. Locally, he'd become a social afterthought; at times, he might have well been the proverbial fly on the wall. Binoculars around his neck, birding books and Moleskine notebook in hand, he made detailed border observations.

Strangely, after a period of staged bird-watching operations, Atef actually developed an affinity for birds and became fairly proficient in his observations, rather enjoying his studies. Few who may have seen him at work would believe that while his glasses were focused in the trees, he was actually identifying border-sensing devices and not yellow-rumped warblers. His notebook featured illustrated maps of wooded areas and farms, annotated to show where he'd spotted each bird, but a closer examination would have revealed the location of possible paths through nests of border sensors.

He could have remained longer at Auberge Dumont, enjoying friends and food at the Fox, but both he and Nina realized that their time there was limited. His forged papers, while excellently crafted, were not infallible, and his driver's license as Anthony Phelps might link him to his problems in Montreal.

Messages from New York City alluded to the favorable progress of the operation he'd envisioned. He was fully conscious of his responsibility to this task, which dictated that he now belonged in New York City. It was getting to New York itself that was the problem, since being on the terrorist watch list made a legal crossing out of the question. He did have a plan though, a deception on a grand scale. The chaos it would create, typically, would only benefit him.

Atef took out his cell phone and dialed the number of a phone that Carlos kept for only one purpose: this call. "Mr. Reyes, good evening. How are you?"

"I'm fine. It's so good to hear your voice. How's the weather?"

"Unseasonably warm, very warm."

Atef had communicated a list of codes to Carlos in the box when he sent him the phone. He indicated to Carlos, in this discussion of weather, that his departure from Canada had to be hastened.

Moving Atef south would entail some planning and a face-to-face meeting. Wisdom dictated that Carlos going north on his Spanish passport was too risky, so enter Jack O'Connor. Carlos explained how he would use Jack to Atef as a useful tool, ignorant of their actual plans. Atef immediately strongly resisted the use of "this infidel," as he referred to Jack. Although Atef disliked the idea, he finally relented to Carlos. Jack would go north to finalize Atef's move south. Perhaps, if Atef's situation were less desperate, he would have vetoed Jack's use, but that was not the case. Carlos maintained the ruse by not telling Jack any more than necessary. As far as Jack knew, Atef was simply a rogue who needed to move south because of his criminal liabilities. Jack was a useful idiot. More importantly, though, he was an American traveling on an American passport.

"Might I still be expecting Jack for dinner next Wednesday?" This meant he would be there on Saturday. The actual date was always three days after the stated date.

"Absolutely, he's looking forward to it."

"Very good, I'll see him then."

CHAPTER 13

Jack's ride through the Vermont countryside was beautiful but seemingly endless. Eight and a half hours in a car was painfully tedious, and the pit stops hadn't relieved the feeling that he had a spike stuck in his backside.

He left Route 91 just short of the Canadian border, choosing to drive the last four miles to the border along local Route 5. As he approached the quaint rural community of Whitley, he purposely slowed down to absorb the bucolic surroundings. The business district of Whitley consisted of a sleepy two-block zone with a gas station and restaurant that opened when the mood suited the owner, along with a beauty salon and drugstore. All these were located across the two-lane road from the US Border Patrol station. A wye intersection marked the northern edge of the business district. To the left and one hundred yards up was the Canadian border station, and to the right was Casale Avenue, which ran roughly parallel and at points comprised the physical border. Jack drove left and continued across the bridge above the rushing Black Maple River to the Canadian side.

Following posted instructions, he pulled to the right after crossing the bridge and stopped at the swing-down gate of the border station. A Canadian border agent in a blue utility outfit came out and greeted him in a pleasant but firm tone.

"Monsieur, bonsoir. Est-ce que je peux voir votre passport? Parlez-vous francais?"

In a bumbling display of international savoir-faire, Jack responded with a resounding, "Huh? Excuse me?"

The agent patiently smiled and answered in perfect but accented English, "No, apparently you don't speak French. Good evening, sir. May I see your passport please?"

Jack fumbled through his pockets and produced the passport stammering, "Oh sure, absolutely."

"Why are you here, monsieur?"

"I'm vacationing in the area. I'm meeting friends at the Laughing Fox for dinner." He gestured generally ahead to the Canadian side.

After a few more routine questions, the agent bid him, "Tres bien, amusez-vous. Conduisez sans risqué." Seeing Jack's bewildered expression, the agent smiled and added, "Proceed, Mr. O'Connor. Enjoy yourself and drive with care."

After passing through the crossing and the diminutive Montcalm business district, Jack pulled into the driveway of the beautifully rustic Auberge Dumont. All he could say to himself was "Wow," as he peeled himself out of his car.

Jack felt some excited anticipation at the prospect of meeting Anthony Phelps. He was oddly proud of the fact that Carlos had selected him to handle this responsibility. Jack was certain that some of the errands he'd run had involved some illegalities but found the notion thrilling. *So what?* he thought. This stuff was exciting and nicely supplemented his spotty artistic income. This assignment with this Phelps fellow, who was integral in Carlos's business, was a step up.

Jack walked through the small vestibule of the Laughing Fox and into the main dining room. He smiled as he took in the eclectic choice of artwork in the restaurant; he was going to like this place. The owner, Algerian native Alec Levant, had created a very pleasant avant-garde culinary and artistic surprise. Earth-tone walls were adorned with a varied and attractive collection of paintings by fledgling local artists. Jack immediately noted that his own work would look very good here.

It was a smallish place, with at most a dozen tables, each with a vase holding freshly cut flowers. The room was dominated by a large stone hearth. A naked-blade fan blew a cooling breeze down on the four seated diners. There was a small bar to the rear of the room with a natural rough-hewn quality that added to its warmth.

Jack stood awkwardly on the wide oak-planked floor at the entrance, waiting to be recognized. A man seated at a table to his left accompanied by a woman put down his paper and smiled up at Jack.

"You must be Jack O'Connor." As he spoke, he rose and offered his hand.

"Yes, I am, and you must be Mr. Phelps?"

"Tony, please."

Jack had expected a somewhat more staid individual, but instead, his hand was being pumped by a tall, thin, dark man with a graying ponytail, dressed in jeans and a short-sleeved Hawaiian shirt. Tony's appearance said school teacher. Tony, or more properly Atef, would have been pleased by that misconception.

Phelps introduced his girlfriend, Nina, a smallish auburn-haired woman in her early forties. A bit on the pudgy side, she used no cosmetics but had a natural beauty about her.

"Nice to meet you, Jack." As he shook her hand, he noticed they had known manual labor.

Jack sat opposite Tony and Nina with his back to the door. Tony got right down to business. "Jack, my ventures have run afoul of the Canadian authorities, and it has come time for me to move on."

Jack respectfully interjected in the same muted tone being used by Tony. "Sir, is it wise to speak publicly about this?"

"If we keep our voices down, it shouldn't be a problem. The locals here are neither nosy nor judgmental. If necessary, we'll go outside and take a walk. But as I was saying, I have to leave Canada as soon as possible, and Mr. Reyes has graciously invited me to New York. My manner of leaving, however, will be unconventional."

As he said that, a couple came in and sat at the table across from them. Tony took notice. "Jack, it's time to take that walk. Nina, we'll be back in ten minutes." She simply nodded as she continued to read her paper and sip her iced tea.

Jack followed Tony out the rear door through the backyard garden directly to the rear gate. A few yards past the gate, they came to a sturdy metal fence above the Black Maple River, which rushed over a series of small falls. Tony turned to Jack.

"I can't just show a passport and walk or drive across the border. I'm wanted. So I intend to create a huge diversion here in Whitley so I can cross roughly fifty miles away from here." Gesturing broadly across the river with his hand, he continued, "I need to create a big enough distraction to draw law enforcement from all over the area, on both sides.

"Jack, the border area is peppered with detection devices that are monitored from border patrol consoles at central locations not far from here, as well as other border patrol facilities in the area. The area where I've chosen to cross has minimal devices deployed and is close to a road on the American side. It's called Morse's Line Road, just west of the town of Franklin, Vermont. I may trip a device when I cross, like that camera on that tree over there. What I'm hoping is that the people manning the central station console will be so occupied by what's happening in Whitley that even if I'm detected, they won't be able to justify pulling resources away to capture one man. That's what I hope will happen."

Jack asked curiously, "What kind of diversion are you talking about?"

"That is no concern of yours. I have a packet that you must deliver to Carlos. The contents are for his eyes only. I also have a packet for you. I want you to drive back to New York following the route I've laid out. Remember what you see and have seen and what I've told you. You'll be doing reconnaissance for Carlos for when he comes to pick me up. You need to brief him when you return to New York. Can you do what I'm asking?"

An engrossed Jack could only nod, thinking to himself, *In for a penny, in for a pound.*

Tony simply smiled and said, "Good, let's go back in and have dinner. Do you like Pakistani food?"

"Sure."

"You must try the *kheema*. It's superb."

"Sounds good."

It was an enjoyable evening at the Laughing Fox. Jack judiciously managed his alcohol consumption by mixing Mooseheads with a reasonably tasty nonalcoholic beer. The last thing he needed was to get bagged for a DWI at the border crossing. At about 1:00 a.m. he retired back to a Super-Eight Motel in nearby Newport, Vermont.

Jack was up and out the door by 10:00 a.m., taking Route 105 along the Canadian border out of Newport, past Lake Memphremagog, over Jay Peak, through half a dozen farming communities. He could see why Tony had chosen this portion of the border area. It was mostly desolate with homes few and far between.

The biggest obstacle Atef faced was the local citizens, who were traditionally suspicious of outsiders and would not hesitate to report a stranger to authorities. Tony's pickup would have to be timed in order to expose him and the vehicle for as short a time as possible.

Atef found the ideal location outside of the northern Vermont town of Franklin. The rarely traveled Route 235, known locally as Morse's Line Road, ran west out of the small rural community. A fallow farmer's field with loamy soil on the north side of the road joined North and South Dandurand Roads. A stand of trees sat about a hundred yards back from the road with an animal track along its western edge. The woods were thick but only a half a mile from the Canadian border and Canadian Route 235 on the other side. It would be here that Nina would drop him off on the morning of his crossing.

She would then rush back to Montcalm to report via text message as events unfolded. When mayhem was at its zenith in Whitley, it would be Atef's time to go.

Jack parked his car at the corner of Morse's Line Road and Dandurand Road. He liked what he saw and thought aloud, "Yeah, this can be done." He took some digital pictures and made mental notes about the tree line.

Jack had gotten a little too immersed in his thoughts when a young man in his twenties wearing jeans and a T-shirt suddenly appeared at his window.

"You lost?" The guy had rolled his Ford 150 up behind him and was right in Jack's face at the window.

Jack didn't have to fake being startled as he jumped in his seat. "Jesus Christ, are you fucking crazy! You just scared the shit out of me!" Jack took a deep breath to regain his composure and another to think quick on his feet. "No, I'm not lost. I'm from *National Geographic* magazine. I'm doing some research for my boss. I've been at it for a while, and I'm just taking a break to get my thoughts together. You live around here?"

"Yup, just down the road in that blue house over there. Why's *National Geographic* interested in us?"

"I don't know, they just sent me out. I'm fine though, just a bit tired. Thanks for stopping, really." Jack was still speaking when the guy suddenly turned and walked away with a blank expression on his face, got into his truck, and drove off. Really, he seemed to just want Jack to know that he'd been seen.

A still-jangled Jack yelled at the rear of the departing truck as it sped eastward on Route 235, "You bet, see ya now, you take care now." He added for good measure, "Ya fucking nut!" He'd just experienced what many before him had: the unfriendly relationship between "Flatlanders" (out-of-state folks like Jack) and "Wood Chucks" (Vermonters, like truck boy speeding off in the distance).

Jack noted to himself that they needed to tighten the timing of Atef's movements to prevent another similar encounter. As he moved away from the area, Jack realized something else. He should be present on the day of the crossing rather than rehashing his experiences to Carlos. Jack made his way across Lake Champlain and then got onto Route 87 for his long trip back to Manhattan.

*****

Joseph Babatunde was a Nigerian immigrant who'd come to Canada in 2005 and overstayed his visa. He dreamed of moving to America but lacked the funds for the move until his best friend, Tokunbo, met Achmed, a Montreal taxi driver, who suggested a possible solution to Joseph. Achmed, who was Atef's employee, had been instructed by Atef to find an immigrant to further Atef's escape plan. Desperate and gullible, Joseph seemed to be the perfect candidate.

Achmed scheduled a meeting with Joseph and explained that he had a connection to a human rights group that was interested in addressing the plight of immigrants like Joseph. Achmed explained that the group was in need of a scapegoat, whose role it would be to provoke the US Border Patrol to an ugly response to prove the group's thesis that US border policies were based solely on racism.

Achmed spoke to Joseph in fatherly tones with his arm around his shoulder. He assured Joseph that he would not be injured if he did exactly as he was told.

"Mr. Babatunde, I will take you to within a few meters of the American border. I want you to calmly just walk across the border. You will be challenged by the American border patrol." It was apparent to Achmed that Joseph's nerves were getting the better of him. "Please feel at ease. What I'm suggesting is purely a theatrical event, but we need the occasion to be as realistic as possible. When they attempt to take you into custody, I want to push and shove the officers. We will be filming the event in demonstrate our point."

Babatunde for his part was less and less sure if this was a course of action he either wanted or should be a part of. "I do not think it is so good of an idea, sir. The policemen shall surely beat me severely. I do not think I should do this."

Joseph's eyes bulged, his fear clearly showing. In his home country, raising of one's hand to a policeman could easily be the cause of one's demise.

Achmed reassured Joseph. "My friend, these are professional police officers. At worst, they will merely handcuff you and you will be taken away into America." For Joseph's trouble, he was promised he would not be charged the customary crossing fee, and in addition to having a free top-notch attorney handle his case, he would be given $1,000 for his trouble after he was arraigned. Joseph was skeptical of the offer but couldn't resist the money and accepted the offer. Of course, everything he'd been told was utter bunk, but Atef had his fish, and Joseph Babatunde would serve more than adequately in the role of a sacrificial lamb.

Wednesday morning broke cool and crystal clear as Achmed drove into Montcalm a few blocks north of the border. Maps reviewed, Joseph got out of Achmed's cab and walked over to LeFevre Street, turned right, and began walking southward toward the border four blocks away. Joseph was determined to do the job as best he could, but his nerves were beginning to fray. Achmed parked his cab on LeFevre Street near the border to observe what was about to unfold.

Border patrol officer Danny Landroux was on duty on LeFevre Street and Casale Avenue, opposite the library. He was absorbed not in his patrol duties but with the fight he'd had with his wife the night before. His wife, Cindy, hated almost every aspect of his job. For months, Cindy had complained of the frigid winter and her absolute hatred of Danny's friends and the town in general. Recently, she began threatening to leave Danny and take their two-year-old daughter with her to live with her parents in Georgia. Danny couldn't give two shits if Cindy left him, but the thought of not seeing his daughter every day was unbearable. Danny was wound tight as a drum, but the sight of a young black man walking up LeFevre Street directly toward him brought him quickly back to reality. The man showed no sign of slowing his purposeful stride and crossed the border, ignoring Danny, who was standing directly in front of him.

Danny immediately challenged him and ordered him to halt. Not only did he not comply, but he broke into a run, heading down Casale Avenue toward the highway in an obvious attempt to evade capture. Danny was on him after a one-block foot chase, colliding into him with enough force to cause them both to crash into the ground. Rather than submit to the arrest, Joseph, in a complete panic, overplayed his role and fought with vigor, attempting to gouge out Danny's eyes. It was then that Joseph made a fatal mistake.

Joseph continued to fight as Landroux attempted to draw his weapon, a Beretta nine-millimeter automatic. He realized the situation was getting out of control and grabbed Landroux's gun hand in an attempt to prevent him from drawing the weapon. Unfortunately, Danny and the half dozen witnesses watching this desperate struggle interpreted Joseph's action the opposite way, as an attempt to take Danny's gun from him.

Danny Landroux, adrenaline pumping, tried to get to his hand-cuffs or Mace but was unable to and used all his strength to over-power Babatunde. He rolled Joseph over on his back, lifting him and then slamming his head into the ground in an attempt to stun him into releasing his pistol. He slammed the still-struggling Nigerian's head down again and again.

Joseph Babatunde's body went limp as he lost consciousness. His skull had been fractured, and he began to bleed from his ears, eyes, and scalp. Achmed and his camera on the Canadian side cap-tured the grisly sight of the lifeless body of a bleeding black man lying in the street, with a much larger white man straddling him. Atef Mohammed had his blood sacrifice. Joseph lingered in a coma for another month, dying without ever regaining consciousness. It wouldn't be long before enraged demonstrators would converge on Whitley, Vermont.

Atef Mohammed observed the incident from the Canadian side of the border. He made a mental note to reward Achmed for a job very well done.

CHAPTER 14

Brian and Louie walked down East Third Street toward Carlos Reyes's building. Brian keyed his portable radio and told Central what he was about to do.

"Nine Conditions Car to Central, Kay."

"Go ahead, Conditions."

"Central, we're going to be out of the car, signal 10-61, at 181 East Third Street, apartment 6A."

"Ten-four, Conditions."

"I just want to get a feel for this guy."

"Okay," Louie agreed, "let's go a calling."

Brian wanted their visit to be a surprise; he wanted to see Reyes's reaction. Brian had accumulated keys to a number of local buildings over the years, including Carlos's. He got the keys from landlords seeking to enhance their security by allowing the cops to come in and do vertical patrols, random roof-to-basement searches with their consent. These really put a crimp in the street junkies who would use the stairwells and roofs as shooting galleries.

They took the elevator to six and rang the bone-colored buzzer. Carlos answered the door without asking who was there. His surprised reaction was palpable.

"Good morning, Mr. Reyes. May we speak with you?"

"Ah, yes, certainly, Officers. What's the problem?" Carlos's heart was racing. He felt awkward, and his stomach tightened. As Brian's and Carlos's eyes met, Brian saw shock and a momentary loss of composure. Brian saw a fear that these two rather large well-armed police officers were not the docile infidels Carlos had expected to wage war on. He was most definitely unnerved.

"There's no problem, sir, at least not for you. May we talk?"

74

"Certainly. Please, please come in." He was now a tank of boiling adrenaline. He motioned them to his living room couch.

"What's the purpose of this visit, gentlemen?"

Louie led off. "Gracias tanto para invitarnos en."

"Es mi placer."

"Permitanos hablar en ingles, yo no quiero sergrosero a su amigo."

The conversation switched to English to avoid insulting Brian.

"Mr. Reyes, my partner Louie and I have reason to believe we should be thanking you."

"Why might that be?"

"There's no need to be evasive, Mr. Reyes. We know how you rescued Orlando Rodriguez, and for that we thank you. You did a great service to him and to the community. I don't suppose you could identify the criminals who assaulted him?"

"No, I don't think so."

"I see," Brian responded with a smirk on his face. "A lot of that seems to go on around here."

Carlos offered, "Can I get you something to drink? Coffee, tea, juice?"

They agreed on orange juice, and Carlos walked off to fill the order. When he was out of their sight, he steadied himself against the kitchen counter. He silently scolded himself, *Compose yourself, man.*

"Is there anything else I can help you with?" he called as he opened the fridge.

Brian chimed back, "I've heard you've gone to work for Mr. Rodriguez."

"Yes, I have. He offered me a position in his real estate business. I've wanted to learn the ways of that business for years, and he's allowed me to apprentice under him."

Carlos came back into the living room with two large glasses of orange juice. He gave one to Brian and the other to Louie with a smile, saying, "Aqui esta su zumo de naranja, senor."

Louie smiled and said, "Gracias."

"Do you have another job, Mr. Reyes?"

"Yes, I do, and please call me Carlos. I'm a project coordinator for an art dealer in SoHo. I wish the salary were as impressive as the title."

Louie asked, "Your accent, Carlos, I'm trying to place it, but I can't."

"I'm Cuban. I come from Havana. I taught languages at the National University before I came up here a few years ago."

Brian brought it to an end; he'd seen and heard what he'd wanted. "Well, Carlos, you're a hell of a guy, and I thank you for saving Rodriguez's ass. As you may have guessed, he's a friend to me even with all of his faults, and I'm very protective of him." Clearly there was more going on with Carlos than Brian knew, but Brian also knew more than Carlos realized.

"Carlos, you're an asset to the community. Thanks for doing the right thing. I hope to be seeing you around."

"And I you, Officers."

Carlos showed them to the door. On the way down, nothing was said, but Louie had that smirk on his face again.

When they got back into car, Brian said to his friend and partner, in a monotone, "You know, of course, that this guy was as full of shit as the Christmas goose."

"Oh yeah, and not for all the reasons you think."

"What do you mean?"

"I don't know what type of Spanish that was, but it's definitely not Cuban. I can tell you that."

"What do you mean?"

"His inflection is all off. The rhythm is wrong. I'm Dominican. We speak fast, much faster than, say, Puerto Ricans. Cubans speak fast too, but Cubans speak more distinctly. This guy was off. Plus, when he gave me the orange juice, he said *zumo*. A Cuban would have said *jugo*. He definitely didn't learn his Spanish in Havana. If I had to take a guess, I'd say somewhere in Europe, like Spain."

Brian's voice dropped an octave, as he said very gravely, "There's something very odd here."

"There certainly is, but what, Sherlock?"

"Fausto said Carlos paid him over $100,000 in stacks of bills. Did that apartment look like it belonged to a guy who had that kind of money?"

"Not really."

"Where'd he get it? What's this guy's con?" Brian wondered aloud. "It's almost like an old Italian mob shakedown, but who's the mob here? If there is a mob. What's this guy's angle? He hardly comes across as a strong-arm artist. I think we should run him through the Organized Crime Control Bureau when we go in for lunch and see if they know him. The guy is way too slick."

"What reason are you going to use to justify the check, bro?" Louie cocked his head to one side and peered at Brian skeptically.

"I'll use the original '61' from Orlando's assault, and I'll submit supplementary 5s along the way to cover our ass."

Louie thought to himself, *Our ass? Here we go again. You've got that fucking look in your eye.* He knew once Brian sunk his teeth into something like this, he wouldn't let go easily—the sign of an instinctively good cop.

"Okay, what's next?" Brian asked, obviously distracted. He toyed with the radio controls, looking absently out the window.

Louie played with him. "We've got to go down to the East River and harpoon Moby Dick."

"Okay, let's go," Brian blankly responded.

Louie was still laughing and shaking his head when Brian just looked back and finally said, "What the fuck did you just say?" Louie just laughed harder.

CHAPTER 15

Brian knew from the beginning that maintaining Orlando's safety would make for an unconventional operation. On the other side of the ledger was the fact that the police service, as a fraternity, can operate in gray areas that offer alternative solutions. The police department's bible, the Patrol Guide, was a document of dos and don'ts that rivaled the Manhattan phonebook in size. It delineated almost every conceivable law enforcement and nonenforcement situation, from the appropriate time limit assigned to taking a crap, to how to properly manage a crime scene. The main flaw with the guide was that the department attempted to pigeon-hole every conceivable situation. Young cops inevitably learned to improvise and most often followed simple common sense.

On the same afternoon he'd met with Orlando, Brian got on the phone in his office and called his old friend and fellow former Marine, Bill Wadley. A talented investigator, Bill had taken an early retirement to form a private investigation firm. Brian had first met Wadley back when they both served in the First Marine Division. It was on a liberty in Barcelona, Spain, that Wadley's prolific and often creative sexual appetite earned him his lifelong nickname.

After his next day tour, Brian made his way over to Wadley's office on West Twenty-Ninth Street. Wadley, who was impeccably dressed, rose to meet his old friend with a smile and an outstretched hand. "How you doing, pal?"

Brian was equally as pleased to see his old friend. "I'm fine, Piggy. How've you been?" he said as their hands clasped. After pleasantries were exchanged, they sat down, and Wadley's secretary, Rosemarie, brought in coffee.

"What brings you over here, Brian?"

"I've got a friend in a jam. He's bitten himself off a son of a bitch of a problem." Brian went on to tell Orlando's story.

When he was done, Wadley responded without hesitation, "How we gonna get him out of it, Brian?"

"I knew I could count on you."

"Hey, *semper fi*, buddy. So what do we have, pal?"

"Piggy, I don't know if that guy will ever take a collar for that homicide. Actually, I suspect not, but there's obviously something bigger here, and I can't put my finger on it."

"Agreed. This Carlos guy appears to be an evil fuck. It sounds like drugs."

"You're probably right, but I just don't know. Carlos doesn't fit the tough-guy mold. He comes across as a real milquetoast, actually."

"Brian, I have a whole bag of tricks at my disposal." Wadley possessed the latest in surveillance electronics and computer databases, which could cull vast sources of information. Even more importantly, he was privy to a vast network of security professionals who worked in all areas, from credit card companies to phone companies. He had also attended the FBI Academy, a symposium offered by the FBI, which broadened his networking capabilities exponentially.

"Let's do this. Are there people in the neighborhood who have had closer contact with this guy that you can talk to?"

"Yeah, actually there is someone. This woman in his building, Heldi, is kind of close to him."

"Good, talk to her about it, but lightly around the edges, you know, any discretionary information you can get. Any of his likes, dislikes, what he talks about, you know what I mean."

"Got ya."

"Your friend Orlando. He's the guy's landlord?"

"Yeah."

"Good, get me a copy of the Cuban's rental agreement. If I have any luck at all, it will have a Social Security number and a date of birth attached. I can do wonders with that."

"What have you got planned, Piggy?"

"Well, a number of things, actually. You're right for coming to me. I think you've taken this as far as you can within the system. I'm going to begin to paint a picture of who this hump really is. First of all, get me that rental agreement."

"Okay."

"Then, if you have it, his phone number. Does he have a car?"

"I don't know."

"What I'd like to do is a triple *I*."

"What's that?"

"It's an interstate investigative inquiry, triple *I*. I'll run his name in four surrounding states."

"Okay."

"I have friends at the Credit Union that'll help find out how our boy spends his money. I'd also like to take a shot at getting his LUDs and MUDs and find out whom he talks to on the phone."

"Listen, Piggy, Maureen and I are having a barbeque next Sunday at our pool club on Staten Island. Why don't you bring the family and come out? It's a nice place. There's a pool and a picnic grove, and it's all enclosed and private. The kids can run free without you worrying. Louie and his family will be there, and so will my friend Orlando."

"You know, that sounds good. Let me check with Lisa and I'll get back to you. But it sounds good."

*****

It was midmorning when Brian let himself into Heldi's building and quietly went up to her second-floor apartment. As she opened the door, a smile grew across her face. While she was at least seventy-five years old, it was still possible to picture her as she must have appeared in her youth. If Heldi was slowing down a step, it certainly was hard to detect.

"Sweetheart, do you mind if I ask you a few more questions about the Cuban?"

"No, not at all, please come in, please, sit."

He leaves me curious every time I think of that mousy guy laying out Hector Glaves. It just doesn't fit right. As a cop, I'm confused."

Heldi sat him down in her kitchen, padding around, making him breakfast, talking as she went. She lovingly prepared his eggs Dominican-style, a delicious combination of eggs, peppers, tomatoes, ham, onions, and vinegar. Heldi possessed a strong mothering nature and an even stronger reputation as an exquisite Dominican cook. Brian dutifully sat down and scarfed down the breakfast laid down before him.

When Heldi was sure Brian was comfortable, she finally took a seat. "He sort of confuses me too, son. I met him when he first moved in a few years ago. He's quiet and very polite. I first spoke with him in the laundry room. He seemed so alone. I invited him to dinner one night and cooked him *pescado con coco*—that's snapper in a coconut sauce. You should let me make it for you one day."

"Twist my arm real hard. It sounds delicious."

"He was nice. He brought flowers."

"Did he say much about himself?"

"Not at first, but I had him over a few more times, and he began to talk more freely about Cuba and where he taught and his family. He's a bright young man. He said he taught foreign languages at the University in Havana. And misses his family terribly."

"How did he end up coming to New York?"

"He said he met the guy he works for here down in Havana through a friend. He made Carlos an offer, and he took him up on it. His boss works with young artists."

While he didn't mention it to Heldi, Carlos's circumstances seemed a bit contrived to Brian, if they were to be taken at face value. Carlos had been a citizen of a totalitarian communist regime; people in that situation don't just get up and move on when a business opportunity arises. Maybe Carlos was something other than what he appeared to be.

Brian was beginning to wonder if Carlos might have been some sort of Cuban agent. All he had was a gut feeling, but the mystery of Carlos Reyes continued to grow.

Brian smiled and slowly shook his head. "Heldi, I don't know why the CIA doesn't simply maintain an office in the laundry room with you in charge. Is there anything that goes on around here that you don't know about?"

She thought that was hysterical and roared back, "Not really!"

Brian had enjoyed a great meal, but now he had even more questions than answers and his curiosity was running wild. As he was leaving, he asked Heldi very earnestly, "Sweetheart, I guess I don't have to tell you not to mention any of our conversation to Carlos. All right? Please?"

"Absolutely, son, don't worry about it," Heldi said with a wink.

*****

Hillside Swim Club is a vestige of a quieter, more peaceful time, when Staten Island's population was a fraction of what it is today. Five acres of picnic groves, swimming pools, bathhouses, play-grounds, ball fields, tennis courts, horse shoe pits—it was the perfect place on a summer day. The memberships, for the most part, were families with legions of children running amok. The place was secure from the street with sufficient staff to provide kids with a perfectly safe place to be kids, leaving adults to conversation and a guiltless adult beverage.

Orlando arrived with Brian and Maureen early, around 12:30 p.m., and sat down in the maple-tree-sheltered picnic grove. Maureen walked away from the two to have a cup of coffee at a close-by table with a girlhood friend. For their part, Brian and Orlando were left to start the first fire of the day by discussing the merits of charcoal versus gas, and offer vivid descriptions of the greatest cheeseburgers ever, all over the day's first cold Bud. This was a pure pleasure for Brian but was a godsend for Orlando, who'd just about forgotten about all his problems.

"Brian, this is great, man! This isn't even like being in New York City."

"I know it's a little slice of heaven."

The fire was lit and blazing, with Brian tending it like a pyro-maniac using his can of igniter fluid like a flame thrower. When he was satisfied the fire would burn properly, he finally sat down and got a little serious with Orlando.

"Let's get down to business. Any updates?"

"Well, after I agreed to our partnership, Carlos said he'd need a couple of apartments set aside for what he called 'special tenants.' He told me not to ask too many questions and we'd be fine, so I went along. It wasn't too long before he moved three guys into a vacant apartment on the third floor. At least one guy is an Egyptian. I don't know too much about the other guys, but I think they're Arabs also. The rent is always paid on time, and they're quiet, keep to themselves. The only really odd thing came to me from one of my maintenance guys. The toilet in the apartment got clogged up, so he went up to fix it. He told me there was barely any furniture in there. They had a kitchen table and two chairs. There are three guys supposedly living there, but there must be half a dozen mattresses stacked against the walls and no other furniture."

It was about then that Louie, his wife Marie, and his three kids, two boys and a girl, arrived at the top of the grove.

"Louie! Marie! How the hell are you?"

They made their way over, toting coolers and other picnic gear. Maureen came back to the group and exchanged hugs and kisses. The kids wanted none of it, only caring about getting into the pool immediately. Marie took them off to the bath house, helped them change, and let them go after making them promise not to be wild.

Maureen suggested that the coals would not be ready for a bit and the kids might need some supervision in the pool. With shrugs and a smile, the men loped off toward the pool area.

While Orlando enthralled Louie's kids with his ability to stand on his head underwater, Louie and Brian leaned comfortably against the wall in about five feet of water, watching the show. Louie smiled as he observed Orlando's daring do, feet thrashing in the air, and noted, "Behold, the Puerto Rican Michael Phelps."

Brian laughed, "That's okay, it'll take his head out of all that other shit."

"How's that going?"

"So-so, at times it's hard to make heads or tails of it all."

83

Louie matter-of-factly asked, "How's the new assignment?"

"Not bad, it'll take some getting used to. It gives me time to do other things I want to do. At least I have my own phone and office."

Brian launched off and did a few laps. On the fourth lap, he heard a familiar call from above him at the edge of the pool. It was Bill Wadley.

"Hi, hump, how's it going?"

"Hey, Piggy, nice to see you!"

Brian hopped out and grabbed Wadley's hand and pumped it. Wadley's kids joined Louie's, and the men rejoined the women in the grove.

Later, after they'd decimated all the meat and most of the beverages, the group settled back into lounge chairs and enjoyed the late afternoon sun that filtered through the trees. Bill asked Brian if he'd made any progress with "the other thing," as he referred to it. Brian turned toward the ladies.

"Would you girls mind if we went off to ourselves and talked business for a bit?" They didn't. Their being asked to leave drew waves of dismissive hands as the women continued in their conversation about a joint dinner party they were planning.

The men grabbed a few cold ones and walked off toward the now vacant tennis court bleachers. Brian addressed himself to Wadley.

"You come up with anything, Piggy?"

"Piggy?" Louie laughed incredulously.

"Yeah," Brian responded, offering an apologetic nod to Wadley, who blew the comment off. "That's another story for another time, guys."

Bill gave his accounting. "LUDs and MUDS didn't show all that much. What few calls he makes and receives are to the same places. Most of them seem to be business calls. He speaks with an art gallery up on Prince Street fairly regularly. Only once did he speak to somebody out in Flushing. He really isn't that chatty at all, so he's probably using a cell."

"He works at the art gallery, but I don't know who's out in Queens," Orlando responded.

"I have a way of finding that out," Piggy chimed back.

"Bill, did any other of your checks come up with anything else?"

Brian grimaced in disappointment. "Not yet, I'm still waiting on the triple *I*, but I have a feeling I would have heard something already if something came up." He recalled what Heldi had told him about the Egyptian sailor on the third floor. Thinking out loud, Brian said, "Maybe we've got a drug smuggler?"

Wadley just shook his head no. "Nah, there's something about this guy we're not seeing. Orlando, is he giving you any problems day to day?"

"No, it's like nothing ever happened. He's actually given me a couple of business ideas. The refinancing has made us a tidy buck." He added, gesturing broadly. "I just want you all to know that I really appreciate everything you guys are doing for me."

"Yeah, yeah, we're not out of the woods yet though," Brian said.

Brian wrapped it up. "Orlando, you got to keep your eyes and ears open and let us know what's going on."

"Okay."

"Guys, other than that, let's go back to the table and have some coffee and cake."

They walked back to their families, sharing a of sense unanimity.

CHAPTER 16

Although he'd driven all day and night, Jack went directly to Carlos's apartment to report. Seeing how tired Jack was, Carlos ordered him to go home and rest and report in the morning so that he wouldn't overlook any crucial details. He took Atef's information packet before Jack left.

Atef's notes were voluminous and comprehensive with photos and maps detailing what would occur. He was relying on Carlos to ensure that the planned demonstration decrying the Nigerian's fate would trigger the appropriate levels of spontaneous violence among demonstrators.

As much as Carlos wanted to go to Manny for his logistical and organizational help, he needed to restrain himself. After all, Manny, was a nonbeliever. There was no need for Manny to know any more about the nature of Carlos's plans than was necessary, especially the relationship between him and Atef. When the time came to initiate Carlos's plan, there would be many conspirators involved, most unknown to each other, creating a web of security. For now, Carlos had to handle this personally.

Before he retired for the evening, he sat down at his computer and brought Atef's crossing point up on Google Earth. He studied and restudied the winding country roads and wooded hills.

The next morning, Jack was at Carlos's door at 8:30 a.m. Jack's enthusiasm preceded him like a rush of air from a speeding subway train arriving at a station. Jack jumped right in. "I have to speak seriously with you about my experiences during the trip. Actually, I'd like to speak to you about my role."

Carlos responded carefully to his excited underling, not wanting to dampen his enthusiasm but knowing already that the return trip was not going to be Jack's. "Jack, I truly appreciate what you've done to this point, but this is something I have to do myself. When Tony and I get together for the ride back to Manhattan, we're going to discuss some things that, quite frankly, you can't know about. This is as much for your protection as it is for mine."

Jack's eyes widened as he stammered his indignant response. "Carlos, you're going up there not only based on Tony's information but also based upon what I've seen. I've got to tell you that the signage on those country roads up there really sucks. I also became really familiar with the pickup area, and it's really not someplace you can just dawdle along trying to find your way. You will be noticed and reported. The locals hate outsiders. The bottom line is that I know the area, and if the objective is a one-shot deal at trying to pick up Tony, you need me with you."

"Jack, everything you've said is valid, but I still can't have you with me."

"And that's because of what I'm 'not privy to'?"

"Yes, it is."

"If I'm not mistaken, Tony is a foreign national, and by that, I mean somewhere beyond Canada, correct?"

"Yes, he is. Look, where is this going?"

"Do you speak his language?"

"I do."

"I only speak English. If you have to speak securely with him on the way home, speak in another language. I would have no idea what you were talking about."

Carlos was amused at Jack's stubborn insistence and that he'd raised an interesting point about the language barrier. "That's an interesting proposal. Let me think about it."

Ultimately, Carlos knew Jack was right. He knew he would only have one chance at picking up Atef, and Jack's assistance would considerably aid his chances of success.

But what impressed him most was Jack's initiative and dedication to the operation. It occurred to Carlos that he might do well to gently probe the heart of this godless soul for harvest by Allah.

*****

In his early sixties, James Kelly, known to most as Jimbo, was a brusque Runyonesque anachronism—hard drinking, cigar smoking, former longshoreman who'd rubbed elbows with many a West side tough guy. He was a hardcore street fighter, and depending on what he'd been drinking on any particular night, he could have been a cop's best friend or worst nightmare.

After two wives and innumerable arrests for assault and alcohol-related offenses, the only faithful relationship he'd maintained through the years was with the longshoreman's union. There was nothing he wouldn't do for the union.

Needless to say, no one scabbed any picket line he stood on, whether it was a longshoreman's strike or any other action they supported. Jimbo was a natural leader, often by the simple virtue of his presence. He could be, and usually was, very intimidating.

Back in the midsixties, Jimbo used to drink at the Red Lion, a pub in Greenwich Village where he'd listen to Irish musicians belt out his favorite IRA tunes. It was on one of his binges there that a union brother introduced him to a group of journalists and writers.

One boozed-up reporter from *Newsweek* recognized his name from a story he'd done and began vicariously touting him as "the legendary Jimbo Kelly," followed by buying him rounds. Kelly thought them all to be a bit full of themselves and a bunch of assholes, but what the fuck? If they were buying, they could sling all the bullshit about him they cared to. The tales woven that night, however, led to the genesis of a book focused on Hell's Kitchen, with large portions written about Jimbo Kelly and his compatriots. Years later, that book would come to the attention of Manny Pabon.

As he read about Kelly, Manny realized he could utilize such talents. Manny had connections at *Newsweek* and asked if any of them frequented the Red Lion. They did, and it came to pass on a summer evening in 1982, amidst copious quantities of Guinness and Irish music, that Manny Pabon and James Kelly became acquainted.

For all his shortcomings, Jimbo Kelly was far from a fool. What he lacked in formal education, he more than made up for in an uncanny, intuitive common sense and survival skills. It usually didn't take Kelly long to take the measure of a man over a couple of pints. The culling process was further simplified by Kelly's personal standard that if you didn't drink, he didn't trust you.

Kelly, by virtue of his associations, traveled in circles where political persuasions were solidly grounded in the radical left. He was involved in most of the left-wing antiwar demonstrations of the 1960s and 1970s. When he marched with the Students for a Democratic Society, he assisted by generating physical conflict, which came as second nature to Jimbo. James I. Kelly was a pathological ball breaker and rough-hewn narcissist who, at any given time, could provoke the pope.

At most protests, you had your average folks, special interest groups, and kids interspersed with Jimbo Kelly and his ilk. The crowd was urged on by the impassioned exhortations of ideologues, while Jimbo and his friends would taunt the police. Agitators tried to focus particular attention on rookies or cops who allowed the insults to get under their skin. If young cops weren't properly mentored by wiser heads, the physical situation could deteriorate badly early on. It was usually up to the more experienced cops to hold the line.

As the tempo of a demonstration reached just the right pitch, it came time for Kelly's magic. Kelly and the ideologues would fade like ghosts into the rear of the crowd. Once out of harm's way, Kelly would toss a bottle, rock, brick, bag of urine, or excrement on a high arc from the rear of the crowd toward the assembled cops. On one occasion, he actually tossed a full-size police barrier at the cops, crowning a police captain.

The brawl was typically on by this point, with union workers and kids taking the brunt of the beating as they faced the cops, falsely assuming that Kelly and his cohorts had their backs. Instead, Jimbo and his associates were always long gone, allowing the gullible to get the shit kicked out of them.

For his specialized talent, Manny Pabon had paid Kelly handsomely in the past and was about to call on his services one more time.

*****

After the first media reports of the incident in Whitley, Carlos caught a cab on Avenue B to Manny's office. Always congenial, Manny offered a cup of dark coffee and asked what had brought him there.

Carlos had solicited Manny's assistance by liberally salting his request with half-truths. Manny had long accepted the mutually parasitic nature of their relationship, since there were many aspects of Carlos's business Manny didn't want to know anything about.

"Manny, I have had to engage myself in a rather elaborate ruse in order to come to the aid of a relative of mine who has unfortunately run afoul of the Canadian authorities. If you've listened to the news today, you may have heard of a situation that occurred in Vermont."

Manny had not and curiously asked what had happened.

"American border authorities have brutally beaten to death an African fellow who was attempting to cross into the States. I'm sure as a result of the barbaric conduct of the Americans that people in the human rights movement will undoubtedly march on that location."

"If what you say is true, the chances are good that will happen. Would you like me to verify that?"

"Yes, I would. I do have one additional request."

"And that would be?"

"If and when that demonstration or event occurs, do you know anyone who might be able to maximize the fervor and passions of those people and cause them to act out?"

"My friend, are you suggesting that we instigate a riot?"

"Well, crudely put, but yes."

"May I ask why you require these theatrics?"

"A sufficiently energized situation at one location will draw a large proportion of local law enforcement to it."

"And away from the location where your relation will cross the border?"

"Exactly."

"I think I have just the right man for the task. Why don't you have another cup of coffee while I make a few calls?"

"Fine, thank you. I will pay your man $2,500 to attend the event and an additional $2,500 if he is successful in creating the desired effect." He continued while reaching into his coat pocket, extracting a white envelope. "This, my friend, is for you and your efforts on my behalf." It was fifteen one-hundred-dollar bills. As he handed Manny the envelope, Carlos continued, "And of course, I will reimburse any further costs."

"Thank you, that is most generous of you."

Manny called a local number and had a short conversation with the person on the other end. James Kelly would come right over.

"Carlos, my man will be here shortly. I understand your needs, so there is no need for you to meet him."

Carlos nodded. "One more thing. Could you call your friends and find out when and where the demonstration will occur?"

"Absolutely." Manny dialed his phone again, this time to a friend in Burlington, Vermont. After a short conversation, he hung up and turned to Carlos, "My colleague is sure there will be action within a week or so. He will be back to me with particulars shortly. I'll call you when I have more detailed information, and coordinate our efforts with them. But please, my friend, leave this to me. You have arrangements to make with a long trip ahead of you. Good luck."

It would be a long trip, but he'd have Jack with him for company. He would use the time for them to become better acquainted.

CHAPTER 17

When the human rights community, New York radical collegiate, and Marxist community heard about Joseph Babatunde's misfortune, the result was an outpouring of general outrage. The same reaction occurred in New Jersey and Connecticut. The general consensus was that this criminal fascist act must be confronted directly.

Among those answering the call for confrontation were two busloads of students and community activists, including James Kelly, who were all headed to Vermont on the following Friday. The service employees and civil service employees unions had also enticed members to make the long trip to Vermont by the promise of a meal ticket and a fifty-dollar chip to the Mohegan Sun Casino on the return home from "The March for Justice," as it had been billed.

To further the chaos, Atef ordered Achmed to organize a Canadian contingent to participate from their side of the border. That would no doubt result in an additional twenty or so folks on the scene.

All arrivals were coordinated to converge in Whitley at 11:00 a.m. on the designated day. At most, the American authorities would be able to muster ten or twenty men to immediately respond to the assemblage. A general mobilization of area law enforcement, a Code 100, might swell their ranks to sixty or seventy within an hour. The police position was going to be precarious; even after re-enforcements arrived, they'd be outnumbered four to one. The first hour would be frightening. Over four hundred angry people were going to converge on this a hamlet.

*****

Jimmy Russell had gotten his life back on track, which had been no small task. In his sophomore year, as a prelaw student at New York's Columbia University, he'd been arrested for the sale of ecstasy at his off-campus room in Morningstar Heights. He'd become the prisoner of Detective Chris Roland of the Manhattan North Narcotics Division. When Jimmy saw his life going down the shitter, the detectives made him a proposition they commonly used in this type of situation. Jimmy was a small fish in a bigger pond, and he was about to allow the police access to his world. Chris sat down with Jimmy Russell and began to run his pitch. If successful, it would result in him becoming a police confidential informant, or CI.

"James, I guess you understand, you're in a world of hurt. We've made five buys from you with one of our undercover cops. You, my friend, may end up doing considerable prison time."

Jimmy felt as if he was about to pass out. His mind raced to comprehend what he was hearing.

"What's your major, kid?"

"Prelaw!"

"Well, that's over. You understand that, don't you?"

He was absolutely horrified, alone, and on the verge of losing control. "I only did this for walking cash," he blurted out.

Roland knew he had him.

"Let me make you a proposition that may help your situation. Are you interested? Jimmy, this doesn't have to go any further than today."

Jimmy just kept his mouth shut and let the cop do the talking.

"While what you've done is serious, we'd much rather have one of our undercovers meet and buy from your connection."

"What's that going to do for me?"

"You work for us for a period of time. Introduce us to the right people, provide us with worthwhile information, and eventually the charges against you will be dismissed and disappear from your record."

"Just like that?"

"Yup."

"I haven't got many other options, have I?"

"Actually you do, but they all involve Riker's Island."

"Okay, what do I do?"

Jimmy was taken to the Twenty-Sixth Precinct for the formality of appearing to be booked. In actuality, he was taken to a private office and debriefed in order to determine what he might provide. Jimmy had some credible narcotics information, but to the detective's amazement, he also had information pertinent to issues outside of narcotics.

As a prelaw student at Columbia University, Jimmy associated with a nest of student radicals, political extremists, and Marxists. The more he spoke of Columbia, the more Detective Roland understood he had a rare bird in his cage. Roland politely stopped their debrief for a moment and called a friend at the NYPD's Intelligence Division, Detective Steve Ambrosio.

Steve came up to the Twenty-Sixth and debriefed Jimmy Russell personally for over two hours. It became apparent that while he may have been able to supply credible drug information, his ability to engage with the radical community was considerably more valuable. It was a few days later that Jimmy Russell became confidential informant 07/341 working for and reporting to Detective Steve Ambrosio.

That spring, Jimmy had heard of a bus trip to Vermont being planned for the following week. He dutifully called the Intelligence Division to report his information.

"Intelligence Division, Detective Battle, how can I help you?"

Russell, as was procedure, only referred to himself by his CI number.

"This is CI number 07/341. Can I speak to Detective Ambrosio?"

Detective Battle checked Ambrosino's schedule and immediately informed Russell, "He's on vacation, and he'll be back next week, Wednesday afternoon for a 1500 by 2300 tour. Can I take a message for him?"

"Gee, can you get a message to him on his cell?"

"What's this all about, anyway?"

"I've got information that certain people from my school are planning to go up to Vermont on Friday to demonstrate about that black guy who got beat up a few days ago up there."

"I hate to bother him on his vacation, 341. He's coming back Wednesday—that's plenty of time. I'll leave him a message that you called, and he'll get back to you."

This wasn't the first time that he'd been put off like this. He resigned himself to allow whatever would happen, happen. In his mind he said, *Fuck it, I've done what I'm supposed to.*

He further added, "Fine, Detective. Please make sure my serial number and phone number get on the message."

Detective Anna Battle assured Russell again that Ambrosio would get the message. She appropriately routed the message and went about her business.

What Detective Battle could not have known was that the schedule she had in front of her had not been updated. Steve Ambrosio had been granted an additional two days off and would not be back to work until the Friday afternoon of the scheduled demonstration. Chris Russell's information would fall between the cracks and lay on Ambrosio's desk.

Law enforcement in Burlington, Vermont, got wind of the small contingent of Vermonters planning to be in Whitley on that Friday and informed the state police in Newport, Vermont. They made a note of it and planned for a demonstration of fifty to sixty people. They had no idea what was actually coming their way.

CHAPTER 18

The following Thursday morning, Carlos and Jack hopped into Carlos's Jeep and headed up to Vermont. In addition to Jack's clever suggestion that Carlos and Atef talk in a native tongue that distinguished Jack from the sheepish men Carlos was used to working with, Jack's considerable maritime knowledge easily justified his cultivation.

The two were an unlikely pair. Carlos was neat as a pin, with short brown hair, pressed blue jeans, and a maroon Perry Ellis sweater. In contrast, Jack had a just-rolled out-of-bed look with his ripped blue jeans, Metallica shirt, and jean jacket. His hair, even under a wool watch cap, gave the impression that it had been coiffed with the assistance of a lightning rod.

Conversation was limited at the beginning of the trip as they listened intently to the GPS directions to ensure that they made it out of New York City and onto the Taconic Parkway. Once safely on the Taconic, the mood eased. They sat back into the comfortable bucket seats and settled in for the ride.

Jack broke the ice. "Thanks for bringing me along. I appreciate it."

"My pleasure, Jack. I assume you're comfortable with your participation."

"I am."

His reply lacked the degree of enthusiasm Carlos had hoped for. "You seem tentative?"

"No, not really."

"Jack, it must be apparent to you by now that some of my dealings transgress the boundaries of the law. Does that bother you?"

"Yes and no. I obviously have no desire to get myself locked up. Like I've said to you before though, man, this shit is exciting, and you're generous too."

Carlos smiled and nodded.

"In an odd way, I feel like I'm getting something accomplished. It's hard to explain," Jack offered.

"I understand exactly. If I'm not being too personal, you seem to be ambitious. What's your motivation?"

"A boat, man. I want and need a boat for my maritime artwork."

"Such dedication. How did you find this profession?"

"Carlos, have you ever heard of an artist by the name of John Noble?"

"No, I can't say that I have. Who is he?"

"An artist from mid-twentieth-century New York City. He was possessed by a love of the sea, sailing vessels, especially the aging ones, and the New York Harbor. He had an eye for the harbor and an exceptional sense and reverence for its history. His drawings and lithographs are highly prized. But how he went about his work is probably the most interesting part of his story."

The GPS broke into the conversation. "Exit to the right in one mile."

Jack interrupted himself and concentrated on the road. "We're coming up to the Mass Pike."

They slid onto the Massachusetts Turnpike and headed eastward. The conversation between them was as close as Carlos was ever going to get to an employee interview. Jack's story about John Noble had Carlos enthralled. His contacts with Jack to that point had led him to think of Jack as an intellectual lightweight; now he was beginning to rethink his assessment.

"So how did your artist follow his passion?"

"In the early portion of the twentieth century, sailing ships rapidly became obsolete. Noble took a job as a watchman at a ship graveyard where these obsolete ships were stored on the Kill Van Kull. While working there, he removed the cabin from a European yacht and constructed a barge to marry it to. He created a studio out of the cabin on the barge." Jack smiled and continued.

"The barge had no power and could not move on its own. Noble, however, was a man of the people. He and his work were held in such high regard within the maritime community that tug boat companies towed him from site to site within the harbor, free of charge. If he had to get down a narrow or shallow creek, he'd get in his rowboat, sometimes with his wife, Susan. He knew every nook and cranny of the harbor, and his art proves it.

"Carlos, do you remember during the conservancy boat ride I told you that Kaiser Wilhelm's Yacht, the *Meteor*, was built on Shooters Island?"

"I believe I do."

"Well, the shipyard where Noble worked on Johnston Island is where it ended up."

That caused Carlos to arch his eyebrows and cock his head. "How interesting. And you, Jack, you see yourself as the modern-day John Noble?"

"To even be mentioned in the same sentence as Noble would be an incredible honor! That's why I'm working toward that boat. Something with a shallow draft so I can get down those back channels. Unfortunately, even small boats are incredibly expensive, but everything comes in time. I appreciate the grant money, but that only covers the expenses of the shows I do. It doesn't honestly leave a lot for me. And as for your work, well, your business is your business, Carlos. I try not to be judgmental."

"Jack, I feel like I'm seeing an entirely different side of you."

"Hey, I know I can be a huge asshole at times. I like to party a bit too much, but I try to hold it down while I'm working."

As the trip continued, Carlos spoke of his family affectionately, though always referring to them as Cubans. Jack said little about his family, as he'd been estranged from them for quite a while. Jack also took some time to educate Carlos on all he knew about the border. It would be a busy day tomorrow, and they could leave little room for error.

*****

At 2:20 in the morning on Friday, three large buses were loading at the curb on Morningside Avenue in Manhattan as a light rain fell. The only audible competition to the droning hum of the idling engines was a nearby garbage truck. Word had been passed to those attending that the buses would leave promptly at two thirty. They were getting a good turnout, albeit a sleepy-eyed one.

Jimbo Kelly, by contrast, was wide awake and on the bus early. This was not the beginning of his day but nearer the end of it. He'd spent most of the night before at a favorite pub of his, McGarrity's, on Tenth Avenue. On the way up to the bus, he made a quick stop home and grabbed a large ice chest full of beer and wine coolers along with a bag of joints to loosen the kids up. He couldn't help thinking, *Kelly's the name, and party planning's the game!*

The bus driver, a pleasant man by the name of Tyrell Gaines, saw Jimbo wheeling his beer cooler toward the bus and was immediately up in arms.

"Whoa, whoa, stop right where you are. There will be no alcohol on my bus!"

"Oh, geez now, this is just a little something to take the edge off a long ride." When Jimbo was anywhere near three sheets to the wind, even though he was born on the West side of Manhattan, he developed an inexplicable subtle Irish brogue. "Friend, the name is James, James Ignatius Kelly, and it's my pleasure to meet ya."

"Hi, Tyrell Gaines and I am responsible for this bus." Tyrell hadn't wanted to take this run, but he needed the overtime money and was now regretting it. He hadn't even left the curb, and he was already dealing with heartaches.

"Tyrell is it, may I call you Tyrell, my friend?" There was no response from the obviously upset and glaring driver.

"Tyrell lad, are ya a union man such as myself?"

"I'm a union man, all right, and I'm a union man that wants to keep his job! No alcohol on the bus!"

Jimbo could be persuasive in a number of ways. "Tyrell, this trip is being sponsored by a number of unions. We're going all the way to frosty old Vermont to protest the brutal treatment of one of our own by the police."

Gaines was beginning to soften a little, but he still firmly held out, "No alcohol on the bus!"

"Tyrell, the truth is, I'm supposed to be acting as sort of the hospitality host on this long trip, you know, to put these folks in the right frame of mind. But I can see what a dedicated man you are. The company should be proud to have such a responsible fellow in their employ." As he spoke, Kelly rummaged through his right front pants pocket.

"I can see that it's a practical man that you are, Tyrell Gaines. Let me shake your hand!"

Kelly extracted his right hand from his pocket and clasped it in Gaines's right hand, pumping it vigorously as he exchanged the contents of his hand into Gaines's. Gaines tried to hide his surprise while looking at the contents of his hand. There was a joint neatly folded within three crisp one-hundred-dollar bills. Before him stood a white-haired older gentleman, Gaines, his hands folded over his protruding belly with a pixy smile.

As he stepped out of Jimbo's way, he only said, "Welcome aboard my bus, my union brother! Make sure none of these drunken fools bother me while I'm driving, and if they puke, they clean it up themselves!"

"Done and done!" Jimbo boarded the bus and took a seat behind the driver. His cooler took up the entire seat behind him. Jimbo got comfortable and briefly nodded off.

Mark Finestein was assigned as a "bus captain." It was his responsibility to organize the occupants of the group toward a productive goal. The bus captains were all members of Ken Langston's Marxist group, the Liberation Front for Immigration Justice. Finestein agreed with Langston's premise that all borders—and this one in particular—were fascist and racist in the extreme. Their thesis on national sovereignty was somewhere way to the left of wildly anarchistic. Their goal was to destroy the concept of organized borders, whatever the cost.

Shortly before the bus left the curb, Finestein took his position in the aisle toward the front of the bus. "Could I have your attention please? My name is Mark Finestein and I'd like to thank you for coming on this most important bus ride, especially on such short notice. Last week, a Nigerian immigrant by the name of Joseph Babatunde merely tried to walk across the border from Canada at a small Vermont town by the name of Whitley. Normally, if captured, he'd be jailed and probably eventually returned to his home country. Unfortunately, Mr. Babatunde had one thing working against him that would seal his fate: He was a black man. He was attacked because of the color of his skin and nearly beaten to death by the racist, fascist border police of the United States! This criminal act cannot be allowed to stand!"

Those gathering on the bus responded as one would expect with loud cheers and applause. Jimbo Kelly woke and added for effect, "The bastards, those miserable murdering bastards," as if on cue.

Finestein continued, "We will protest vigorously and loudly in Whitley. I cannot guarantee that we will not be set upon by police thugs, but our voices must be heard. If anyone finds the risk to be beyond what they are prepared to assume, I'll open the door and let you out now, no hard feelings. Other than that, the next stop is Whitley."

Two fifty-something-year-old women raised their hands and left the bus. The others appeared to be fairly steadfast, and a general buzz of indignation circulated the bus as they left.

*****

Atef and Nina Gerard prepared for the next day quietly with the coming separation weighing heavily on her. They reviewed their plan for the next day, and Tony made sure he gave Nina the cell phones she would need, one primary and one backup.

"I will call you when things stabilize in New York, and we'll make our plans to meet."

The normally impassive Nina's eyes welled with tears. She knew. She knew this would be their last night together. He pulled her close, but she pulled free, a look of indignation on her face. A Nina he'd never seen before smacked him across the face with enough force to cause him to lose his footing and fall clumsily against the dresser. She was now sobbing uncontrollably, but it did not mitigate her rage in any way. He rose again, and she stunned him with a second blow that caused him to fall backward onto the bed. A now hyperventilating and sobbing Nina stood over the stunned Phelps. Then she was on top of him, pinning him to the bed. She ripped the boxer shorts from his body in one motion. She rose briefly to shed her clothes and mounted him. This night, he would understand the magnitude of his loss.

The ride to Atef's drop-off point, about a mile north of the American border, was quiet. Nina pulled her car to the side of a gravel road opposite a farmer's field shortly after 7:00 a.m. After a prolonged silence, Atef flatly said to Nina, "Don't forget, I'll be waiting for your text when things start in Whitley."

Nina nodded icily, and after another blank look between them, Atef departed with nothing further said. He climbed over the fence and entered the field on the other side, purposefully walking between the furrows and through the corn stalks toward the tree line on the southern side. As he did so, he was met by the farmer on a dirt road that divided the field.

"Bonjour, monsieur. Do you speak English?" Atef asked.

"I do, sir, and this is private property."

"I beg your pardon, sir. My name is Phelps, Tony Phelps. I'm a bird watcher. Would you mind if I walked across your property to look at some birds?"

"No, not really, go right ahead. I've seen you around here before, haven't I?"

"Probably. I've set up in Monsieur Renner's field in the past to do the same thing."

"I thought so. If you go in those woods over there, be careful. Don't go too far south and to the west. There's a depression in the ground down there. The border people have sensing devices on the western side of my property. My land goes right to the border area. Otherwise, enjoy yourself. How long will you be?"

"I should be gone by noon."

"Well, have a good time."

"Thank you, sir."

Following the farmer's caution, he set up his gear near the trees in the center portion of woods, about a hundred yards north of the border. He sat down and poured himself a cup of tea from his thermos. He would wait there for Nina's text. The wind rushing through the swaying fir trees was incredibly soothing. Having slept very little the night before, he sat and propped himself against a tree to take a nap. Before he did, he took out his cell and called Achmed to give him explicit instructions on how to take care of Nina in his absence. That done, he leaned back and closed his eyes.

*****

Jimbo Kelly had made himself the center of attention on the bus as it raced north in the early morning sunlight. He'd gotten three and half hours of good rest and was then quite ready to face the day. Jimbo soon won over a cadre of kids who thought he was the best thing since canned beer. At least a quarter of the bus had a good buzz on as Mr. Gaines looked back, shook his head, and hoped for the best. The group leader, Finestein, had all but ceded spiritual control of the bus to Kelly, who had been galvanizing the group thus far. Finestein had no idea what he was in for.

CHAPTER 19

It was shaping up to be a beautiful day, and near the metal barricades, there was no indication that this day would be unlike any other. Three troopers manned the barriers, while the rest remained in a command vehicle. There was no need to alarm the locals by putting everyone out on the street, at least not just yet. Two border patrol agents were chatting with their Royal Canadian Mounted Police counterparts when a mobile unit trailing the bus from Burlington called Lieutenant Mike DeNovich.

"Lieutenant, the bus is about five minutes out on 91."

"Ten-four unit, thanks. Freddy, stay out on the perimeter by the highway in case I need you for anything else."

"Ten-four."

As predicted, the bus turned off Route 91 onto Casale Avenue with the welcoming party waiting down the hill at the library.

DeNovich walked over to the command bus and smacked the side of the police bus. "Okay, let's go, everybody out!" It was showtime.

Ten of the twenty-five troopers filed out and stood at the barricades, while the remainder formed ranks between the barriers and the border. The border patrol officers formed a line across the border next to the library, while the Canadians formed a line on their side. The bus stopped across the way on Casale Avenue. DeNovich waited for the demonstrators to disembark, or at least for Ken Langston to step forward so he could let the protesters know what was permitted.

DeNovich waited ten minutes before anyone stepped off the bus. Suddenly he heard the sound of another approaching bus. DeNovich turned and, to his surprise, saw another bus coming down Main Street from the opposite direction.

Just then a border patrol agent called out, "Lieutenant, my office in town says there are more buses coming!"

There were indeed three more buses coming from that direction, and Mike DeNovich soon realized he'd been set up. He didn't have time to completely digest the situation when he got a call from his mobile unit standing by at the highway.

"Lieutenant, I've got two more buses getting off the highway from the other direction."

Moments later, he saw the two slowly moving buses from Boston coming down Casale Avenue toward him, while another bus approached down LeFevre Street on the Canadian side. A slight panic crept into Mike DeNovich's mind. The original permit was for sixty-five, not five hundred, which left DeNovich and his men seriously overmatched and in dire need of reinforcements.

While the law enforcement agencies scrambled to adjust to the new situation, the bus captains were patiently waiting for Ken Langston to call and allow the passengers to disembark the buses. Langston had been holding back the bus occupants to enhance the dramatic impact of the large crowd on the unprepared police and border patrol. Langston smirked, thinking, *How's it feel, scumbags?* In a few minutes, he spoke with all the buses and told them to release the demonstrators and have them form up opposite the police line on the other side of Casale Avenue. He remained on the bus, allowing his captains to line everyone up and start the chants.

"Hey, hey, ho, ho! Border racism has to go! Hey, hey, ho, ho! Border racism has to go!" As the chants grew louder, Langston stepped off the bus and made his way to the head of the crowd.

DeNovich saw Langston approaching and stepped out from behind the barriers to confront him. "Good morning, Langston. You have a permit for sixty-five, making this an illegal gathering."

"Yeah, how about that." His response dripped with contempt. He knew he'd eventually get locked up, but he could do the time, and his lawyer would have him out quickly. Langston's lofty ego kicked in. He knew the people he was leading would take the brunt of the police response, while he would be able to boost his street cred.

"Langston, I'll give you ten minutes to put these people back on the buses and start leaving."

"Or what?"

"I'll start enforcing the law."

Langston looked right at him and laughed. "Yeah, right. Fuck you, DeNovich." He turned and walked back to his line, leaving DeNovich standing in the middle of the street.

The even-tempered DeNovich marched back to the barriers and called his assistant, Corporal George Hastings over. "Georgie, get Major Rice on the phone, now." He called his border patrol and RCMP counterparts over and told them what he was about to do.

As Hastings dialed the phone, Langston ordered his captains to arch the ends of the crowd around DeNovich's position, while the Canadian protesters did the same. DeNovich was now flanked and almost completely surrounded.

Lieutenant DeNovich asked Major Rice to call a signal one hundred, which would alert all federal, state, and local law enforcement agencies in Vermont and New York to the situation in Whitley. If things deteriorated, Major Rice could also ask the agencies to send assistance immediately. Until help arrived though, Mike DeNovich would have to survive on his wits.

"Georgie, I need ambulances and a fire department pumper to stand by in town and another pumper up near the highway. And, Georgie, make sure you tell both the ambulances and fire fighters to stay out of sight with no lights or sirens." Hastings went about his task with a quick nod.

Ken Langston faced his constituents and went on a long-winded diatribe about racism and border inequities, while the protesters hurled vile obscenities at the police line. The loudest members of the crowd were easily Kelly and his surly group of bus compatriots. Kelly saw that his window of opportunity to accomplish his objective was limited.

Langston came off as a living tribute to the legacy of Saul Alinsky, but to James Kelly, he was just a real pain in the balls. It was becoming apparent that Langston had no intention of carrying this occasion to the next level and the potential for chaos was going to be wasted on Ken's ideological blather.

Much to Kelly's surprise, he realized he'd developed an ally in Mark Finestein. As it turns out, young Finestein was a real firebrand. He stole Langston's thunder by changing the crowd's chant to "Babatunde! Babatunde! Babatunde!" in an increasing pitch and rhythm, urging the protesters to move toward the police. The irate Finestein turned to Kelly.

"This cocksucker Langston is going to blow this by never getting off his fucking soap box and getting down to business. He's just framing himself against the cops like some kind of fucking demagogue. This is fucking bullshit, man! We need to be down in the pigs' faces making our point!"

"Fucking aye, laddie! What should we do?"

"Let's take it from him and bring it to the pigs. Follow my lead."

The intensity of the moment had wrapped the crowd into a fevered pitch. The emotional intensity of the surging cry "Babatunde!" was rapidly changing the gathering into a mob.

Finestein, now in the front ranks, began to slowly move forward toward the troopers. Kelly did the same farther down the crowd line. What had been a well-organized crowd began to snake and distort. Kelly taunted the troopers and border agents, "We're coming for you, pigs!" He turned to the demonstrators around him who were moving forward at his command. "Let's bring it to them, people!" The line of demonstrators had passed Langston, who was shocked that his moment had literally passed. All he could do was shut up, turn around, and move with them. The line was now even more distorted and ragged. Individual demonstrators, normally law-abiding citizens, lost themselves in the anonymity of the mob and, following Kelly's lead, began tossing rocks, bottles, and anything else available at the police.

The mob, invigorated by what appeared to be their apparently dominant position, closed the distance with the police and came within ten feet of the law enforcement line. Kelly moved laterally and began to extricate himself from the main body of the mob as the oppressive weight of the protesters continued to move forward.

Now at the rear and slightly above the surging formation of the crowd, Kelly was able to get a clear picture of what was happening. Screaming demonstrators were in contact with the police barriers on the right side, swinging their placards that were supported by pine two-by-fours. Police and demonstrators were now toe-to-toe, beating each other bloody. The irregularity of the line had inadvertently formed a wedge; the mob's weight knocked over the metal police barriers, separating half a dozen troopers from the main police formation.

Kelly picked up a loose piece of paving stone and caught Finestein's eye some fifty yards away. Kelly held up his stone for Finestein to see, and Finestein did the same with a comparable stone. Kelly walked into the rear of the mob and let his missile fly through the mob, hitting the police command bus and shattering a side window, while Finestein's hit the ground behind the troopers and border agents. On their second throw, both Kelly and Finestein nailed two troopers.

Others in the crowd followed suit, and the sky above the troopers mimicked a cloud of arrows from medieval archers. The left side of police barriers fell, but the police line behind them did not falter. From amidst the crowd, Kelly heard four sharp popping sounds. There was no mistaking them for anything other than gunshots. He looked over to the right but could no longer see Finestein. Kelly knew his mission had been accomplished, so he slowly but purposefully withdrew himself down Casale Street toward downtown Whitley. As he left, he passed by a fire truck heading up into what was now a full-blown riot.

*****

Mike DeNovich watched as the demonstration dissolved from an organized event under Ken Langston's control to a seething mob moving closer and closer to him. It was difficult to ascertain what had instigated the chaos, but he was now focused on the flying debris being hurled from the rear of the crowd. As the protest continued to deteriorate before his eyes, he chastised himself for waiting too long.

"Georgie, call for assistance now, and tell the major what the hell is going on here. Tell them to get us all the assistance they can as quick as possible!"

As the crowd began flinging debris and using the lumber of their signs as weapons against his officers, DeNovich realized that the tide had turned. Restraint while making arrests by the troopers and border agents was no longer an issue. The only thing that mattered now was survival. A tall kid, maybe twenty-two, came directly at DeNovich, swinging a piece of lumber. DeNovich parried his swing with nightstick, striking the kid in the side of the head resulting to a spray of teeth and blood. The kid went down, but others kept coming.

The front ranks of troopers squeezed off bursts of Mace at the lead demonstrators, reducing their numbers as they writhed in agony from the chemical spray. Still, the demonstrators behind them continued forward, over and around their stricken comrades.

On the right side of the line, demonstrators picked up a barrier and used it laterally as a battering ram to push back the troopers and agents. The line continued to hold, but one trooper, John Golino, was knocked down and pinned under the barrier.

The crowd stampeded over the metal barrier with Golino underneath as they brawled with troopers and agents. As the tremendous weight of the crowd squeezed the breath out of Trooper Golino, he drew his nine-millimeter Smith and Wesson and fired four rounds into the mass above him. Two rounds lodged into the legs of two demonstrators. Another miraculously missed everything and passed through the mob, landing harmlessly in the bushes across Casale Avenue. The fourth round ricocheted off the horizontal metal of a barrier and deflected leftward into the crowd. The shock of the gunfire and screams of those injured caused the demonstrators to slow down. Officers were able to pull the shaken Golino back into their ranks and regroup as the demonstrators faltered.

Strangely, the Canadians on the other side were having fewer problems compared to what the Americans were enduring. The Canadian demonstrators may have ranted and raved, but they did not resort to violence.

Finestein, after having caused the right side of the crowd to breach the police line, experienced a sudden burning sensation under his left armpit. He'd momentarily thought he'd been stung by a wasp, but this pain was much more severe. There was a crushing pain in his chest. He grabbed where he felt the pain, and his hand came away soaked in blood. Suddenly, his legs gave out, and he fell on his back as began coughing up blood. His last thought was, *What the hell is happening to me?* Trooper Golino's fourth errant round had found its mark.

Tim O'Reilly, chief of the local volunteer fire department, stood with his crew and their fourteen-ton Seagrave pumper truck, *Felicity*, and it's even bigger supporting tanker truck, the *Walrus*, sequestered safely on Main Street. Stationed out of sight and awaiting orders, the firefighters could only sit and listen to the chaos taking place two blocks over. To get a better idea of the unfolding situation, O'Reilly walked around the corner to Casale Avenue. What he saw horrified him.

The surging crowd was hurling rocks, bottles, and other missiles into the air as they swarmed the splintered police line. O'Reilly had seen enough; it was time for him to take action and aid the police any way he could. He went back down to his truck, gathered the twenty volunteers under his command, and briefed them on what he intended to do.

"Guys, the cops are in over their heads up there, and they're getting their asses kicked. Looks like they're on their own with no backup coming anytime soon. I want to take the trucks up there, run lines, and start hosing these motherfuckers down. Hopefully, we can take some of the heat off the cops, but I've got to be honest, it could get ugly. These assholes could, and in fact and probably will, turn on us, so we'll have to defend the truck. You guys good with this?"

The firefighters responded in unison, "Yeah, let's do it!"

O'Reilly then radioed the firefighters on the other side of town to tell them what he was planning to do, and they agreed to help by moving in from the other side.

As they headed down the street, O'Reilly turned to his driver, Mikey Bresnahan, and said, "Mikey me boy, let's make some noise and let the cops know they have some friends. Lights and sirens now please!"

The truck barreled up Casale Avenue and stopped at LeFevre Street with the sirens blaring. Some of the firefighters jumped off the truck and got the hose stream on and working, while the rest armed themselves with Kelly tools, gaffs, fire axes. O'Reilly and his crew were big boys, even by country standards. Armed with the tools of the firefighters' trade now raised high as weapons, they took a belligerent stance in front of their trucks. Anyone who came near the trucks would feel their wrath.

Just as they hooked up and stretched the lines, two police cars from the nearby town of Hutton pulled up. They agreed to protect both fire trucks, which freed up the firefighters to assist with their assault.

All four of the two-and-a-half-inch lines came alive and took down anything near them. As the firefighters made their way ahead, a group of demonstrators tried to flank them, but they didn't even get close. The water stream from the deck gun operated by O'Reilly on the roof of *Felicity* knocked them down and then sent them flying into the air. Then O'Reilly had an idea and called to Mikey on the ground.

"How many cans of foam do we have with us?"

"Not much, Tim. Three or four cans." The foam came in five-gallon cans that could be siphoned off through the main line and put down in a thick white bed of viscous foam. Each of the cans would only last a few minutes, but O'Reilly thought that might be sufficient.

"Mikey, use whatever you have and lay it down between us and them. Let's see their ice-skating skills."

"You got it, boss, absolutely," Mikey chimed back.

As Mikey sprayed the foam, the upslope between them and the demonstrators turned into an ice-skating rink. On top of the slippery conditions, the foam produced noxious fumes similar to engine coolant. The sight of demonstrators slipping and falling everywhere was only accentuated by the nauseating effect of the foam itself.

On the police line, DeNovich and his troopers saw the firefighters in action and finally found a reason to smile, even though they were far from out of the woods.

*****

Nina Gerard was shocked by the scene at the border as she sat in her car three blocks away on the Canadian side. The mayhem in Whitley was clearly overwhelming, so it was time for her to text Tony and Carlos. Just as she was about to, Achmed knocked on her window with a broad smile on his face.

"Ms. Gerard, this is wonderful, is it not?"

"Yes, it is. Get in the car," she replied as she opened the back door. He climbed in behind her and leaned back, taking in the view.

Nina's first text message was to Tony: "Whitley in chaos, police have lost control. Good luck!" Her second message was to Carlos: "Tony will be moving, be alert."

She put the phone back in her pocket and sat back. "That's it, I've done my job. It's over for me."

Achmed agreed as he grabbed her by the hair and pulled her head forcefully back on the headrest. He quickly took a six-inch buck knife and slit her throat. Nina Gerard bled out with a look of stunned disbelief on her face as she grasped at her throat. While she sat dying, Achmed removed the cell phone from her pocket and calmly left the car. Atef did not like loose ends.

*****

Meanwhile, Atef sat on a hill, anxiously overlooking the border. It was after 11:00 a.m., and he still hadn't heard anything from Nina. At 11:20 a.m., his cell phone vibrated in his pocket; her text eased his angst.

The drop to the gravel border strip was a steep thirty feet. He looked up and down the open strip, seeing nothing at all. The pristine wooded area was peaceful, with birds singing and crisp fresh air. Using the protruding roots of trees along the hillside, he made his way down. When he was within five feet of the bottom, he jumped and landed on a bed of soft earth and fallen leaves. Atef got up, looked up and down the road, and proceeded across the border.

The Blackberry in Carlos's pocket vibrated. "Within ten minutes of the pickup point, move in five." No more needed to be said. With the stream of police cars speeding through town, the locals paid little attention to Carlos and Jack. While neighbors gathered at a store and deliberated over what was happening, Jack and Carlos quietly slipped out of town, westbound toward the pickup location.

Atef stole toward the edge of the farmer's field that bordered Route 231 and stayed within the cover of the trees to the west of the field. He followed the line of trees fifty feet from the road, knelt down, and waited.

Carlos and Jack slowly passed Durand Road when Carlos's phone vibrated again. This time it was from Atef.

"I can see you. I'm in those trees just east of that blue house."

"Got it, come on out to the road."

They pulled up just as Atef was vaulting the fence at the road's edge. He was in the car in less than ten seconds, and they were on their way. It had gone off perfectly, creating a mood of absolute elation in the Jeep. Atef was appreciative beyond words but also a bit confused by Jack's presence. Carlos jumped in before he could say anything about it, gravely stating, "Tony, Jack has been of invaluable assistance to me, and I doubt I could have done this without his help. Jack thoroughly understands that he cannot be privy to our business-related conversations, so he suggested that if we find it necessary to discuss business, we speak in your native Urdu. He won't have the foggiest notion what we are talking about, and frankly, he doesn't care. It's my very sincere belief that Jack could be extremely valuable to us in the future."

Atef caught on but was not too pleased. Jack had some valuable attributes they had to encourage. He'd play along for now. "Okay, Carlos. Okay, Jack."

Atef switched to Urdu briefly and said to Carlos, "He knows nothing of us in reality, does he?"

"Not a thing. He thinks we're some kind of organized criminals. He's just with us for the money."

"All right, we'll talk more of this later when we're alone. Let's speak in English so we don't insult him."

"Well, Jack, I thank you for all you've done, but I have to rest now. I'm exhausted." Atef crawled up into the back seat and was asleep in minutes. He slept that way for the next three hours.

*****

Within the hour, state, local, and border patrol units were streaming into Whitley. The local volunteer fire department had finally been successful in breaking the back of the riot. With the help of the high-pressure hoses, they had easily dispersed the demonstrators into smaller groups.

After reinforcements arrived, the troopers were able to move out of their defensive pocket. Armed with plastic zip ties, they gathered up the dazed and injured rioters, rear-cuffed them, and contained them on the very buses they'd arrived in.

The border patrol agents began scouring the surrounding areas for any protesters trying to escape, when a woman who lived in the house on the corner of LeFevre Street stopped Mike DeNovich.

"Excuse me, Officers, I live over there." Pointing to her corner house, she whispered, "I have one of those people hiding in my backyard shed."

DeNovich thanked her and asked her to stay in front of the house.

He took two troopers with him to check out the shed. Everything appeared to be in order except for a fifty-five-gallon drum upside down in the corner. Looking closely, he noticed a shoelace protruding from under it.

DeNovich motioned to his officers with his finger over his lip and pointed to the shoelace with a broad smile. "Okay, fellas, I think this guy must have gotten out of here before we came in. Let's move out." He then motioned for the other two to leave and slam the door. DeNovich took a seat on a wooden crate near the wall and waited.

It took about ten minutes until the drum moved and then moved again. DeNovich had finally had enough and kicked the drum over. Crouching before him was none other than Ken Langston.

"Well, good afternoon, Mr. Langston!"

Langston was as white as a sheet and quite meek, finding himself all alone in the shed with DeNovich.

"Let's see, Mr. Langston, what was it you said to me last time we spoke? Oh yes, I remember. It was 'Fuck you, DeNovich,' wasn't it now? You scumbag!"

Langston said nothing. Any vestige of swagger was gone.

"Get up, you worthless piece of shit!"

Langston apparently did not get up fast enough to suit DeNovich, who grabbed him by his ponytail and lifted him nearly off his feet. He placed him in zip tie cuffs and told his officers to haul him off.

The body of Mark Finestein lay in the street under a yellow tarp with the area taped off as a crime scene. John Golino knew by now that the guy under the tarp had been killed by one of his rounds. Devastated by the man's death, he was reassured by his brother officers that extraordinary events had caused him to fire, and he would probably not face any charges. Their words fell on deaf ears as grief filled Golino's being.

A Canadian retiree who lived on LeFevre Street across the border in Montcalm found Nina's bloodied body in her car. Just one more fatality.

While the town of Whitley grieved, James Ignatius Kelly had successfully escaped. He called a local car service in downtown Whitley to take him to Newport, Vermont. Once there, he checked into a motel and spent the evening at the only Irish pub in town, charming the shit out of the locals. In the morning, he rented a car and headed home unscathed.

CHAPTER 20

Carlos, Atef, and Jack arrived back in Manhattan around 9:45 p.m. after a long, draining trip that was exacerbated by heavy traffic outside the city. There was only small talk among the three, which Carlos took as a personal rebuke from Atef for allowing Jack to come. Time would tell how angry Atef was, but for now, Carlos decided to keep his mouth shut. When they finally reached Carlos's apartment, he ushered Jack and Atef inside.

"Gentlemen, please come inside and make yourselves at home. Can I offer either of you a cold drink? Tony, I have an additional bedroom you can sleep in. Jack, would you like to take the couch for tonight?"

"Actually, I'd like to get home," Jack replied.

"Fine, take my Jeep. I'm not going to need it tonight or tomorrow. I'll talk to you tomorrow about bringing it back."

"Thanks, it would be nice to avoid public transportation tonight."

"That's understandable. Please park it in a safe area."

"Absolutely, good night, gents."

After he left, Atef made minimal conversation other than asking, in a dismissive tone, "I'm very tired, please show me to my room." As Carlos showed him the room, Atef turned to him and said, "We will talk tomorrow," closing the door with no further conversation.

*****

The following morning, Jack awoke and wandered into the kitchen to set up the coffeemaker and flip on the radio. It was a routine he'd gotten into after 9/11, seeing if everything was okay before starting his day.

The lead story was about some contentious flap the new president was having with a member of the Senate minority. He heard the run-up to the story, and after that, he only heard, "Blah, blah, blah, and blah." It was the second story that caught his attention.

"Peace has now been restored to the US-Canadian border area in the small town of Whitley, Vermont, after yesterday's bloody riots. It now appears that one additional death, mysterious in its circumstances, has been attributed to the demonstration. Royal Canadian Mounted Police in the neighboring Canadian border community of Montcalm report that a woman was found murdered in her car mere yards from the border conflict. The woman, now identified as forty-year-old Nina Gerard of Montreal, was found by a local resident with her throat slashed. The RCMP will only say that the death is under investigation."

Jack's immediate reaction was to think, *Whoa*, and then he sat in stunned silence. He was cool with causing a riot, but people getting killed, *That's fucking sick, man!* He could only wonder if Tony knew.

*****

Carlos rose shortly before noon and walked out into his living room where he found Atef fully dressed, enjoying a cup of coffee.

"My brother, you're a late riser."

Carlos was annoyed with himself; he'd allowed Atef to catch him at a disadvantage yet again. Worse, he hadn't offered appropriate hospitality to a guest in his home, especially one of Atef's stature.

"I'm terribly embarrassed. Please forgive me."

"Don't let it trouble you." Inwardly, Atef gloated. "We have a great deal to discuss."

"I could make dinner here for us."

"No, show me your city. Can we dine out, say tonight?"

"I imagine so. I'll make reservations."

"Very good."

Before he could begin to do so, his phone rang. It was Jack. "Carlos, have you been listening to the news on the radio?"

"No, should I have been?"

"Tony's girlfriend was found murdered in her car. Her throat had been cut. Does he know?"

"No, no, he doesn't, at least as far as I know. I'll take care of it. Are you coming over this afternoon?"

"Yeah, I'll be there in an hour."

"Fine, but don't plan on staying long. I'm sure he'll be very upset."

"I understand."

Atef flatly asked, "Who was that?"

"That was Jack. He had some bad news, I'm afraid."

"Really?"

"Yes, my prince. Nina is dead. I'm so sorry. Did you know?"

"Allah be praised, she is martyred." Then without missing a beat or exhibiting a wisp of emotion, he asked, "Have you spoken with Faisal recently?"

The point had been made regarding Nina.

"No, we usually speak only when necessary. Please come with me. I have something to show you."

"Certainly."

Carlos left his apartment with Atef in tow, taking the elevator to his business office.

Near the end on the left side of the hall was a double-locked apartment door.

"I keep two apartments in this building, sometimes more, depending on circumstances. I have a working arrangement with the landlord that allows me this apartment as an office and the one we came from as my home. I do not like to cross my worlds."

Atef noticed his computers and SAT phone. "Secure phones?"

"Yes."

Atef noticed some other electronic instruments whose functions he was not familiar with. Carlos ignored the curious look on his guest's face and led him into the adjoining, very conventional bedroom. He walked toward the closet at the rear. "I believe I told you in a previous conversation that I've managed to become self-sufficient. I've engaged in a number of lucrative endeavors."

Carlos unlocked and opened the closet door. "This, my honored guest, is the fruit of my labors." Within the closet there was a wood freight pallet stacked with US currency four feet high, four feet wide, and four feet deep.

Atef was visibly floored, and after an extended period of silence, he looked at his subordinate, smiled, and embraced him, "Praise be upon you! How much have you accumulated?"

"Approximately five million. Atef, there is no reason for you to remain in my apartment, so take this apartment for your own. I don't have to tell you how critical it is that this apartment be properly secured every time you leave."

"I completely understand."

"Also, don't take this the wrong way, but I am going to lock that closet and keep the key. I do it only as an overriding security measure and nothing against you."

"I completely understand. You have done a magnificent job!"

Outwardly, Carlos presented a very proper, placid appearance, but internally he was high-fiving himself.

Atef suggested they go back to Carlos's apartment for the time being. He would return here later in the evening.

Carlos reminded Atef that it was Jack who had informed him of Nina's death and that he was coming over to return his car keys. Carlos suggested that it might be appropriate for Atef to "grieve" out of sight in his room and allow him to deal with Jack.

Shortly after they reentered Carlos's apartment, the lobby bell rang. Carlos answered through the intercom, "Yes, who is it?"

"Jack."

"Come up, please."

Carlos let him into the living room as Jack asked, "You've told Tony about Nina?"

An appropriately demure Carlos responded, "I have, he is grieving in his room."

"How is he?"

"He is understandably inconsolable. I will see to him, but now I have to ask you to leave. I will call you in a day or two."

Jack just nodded and returned the car keys, shook his hand, and left after telling Carlos where he'd parked his car.

Later that night, Carlos and Atef headed to Brooklyn for dinner at El Sirocco. Atef softened. "My brother, I have imposed myself on you, and you have not flinched in your graciousness. I am most appreciative, thank you. Let me get to the point that causes us to be together. The time is coming upon us, the faithful, to act. The Americans and their crusader allies have gone all over the world to confront our brethren, and it is now time that we take the fight to them in their homeland. We are going to strike at the heart of Satan and cripple his economy. You might think I've created an overly optimistic goal for us, but in reality, it is not. The Americans have allowed themselves to become dependent on the rest of the world to support their economy. Their dependency on seaborne commerce shall be their downfall."

Atef had Carlos's complete attention as he explained further. "In 1980, there was a longshoremen's strike on America's west coast. That strike lasted for approximately ten days and brought commerce to a halt. You must understand that the US maritime industry is only one part of an intricate commercial chain. Products arrive from overseas ports on a definite and continuous line and schedule: ports overseas to merchant vessels, then to US ports, and then to the railroads. Eventually, the goods reach distributors and consumers. The strike I mentioned, during the ten days it lasted, nearly brought the US economy to its knees. This event, with its known parameters, cost the US economy $1.9 billion a day! Imagine, if you will, another event in one of their ports, a much more chaotic incident, unexpected and violent, to which their government has no credible defense. Then try to imagine the commercial and financial ramifications of such an event."

"What are you proposing, Atef?" asked a spellbound Carlos.

"I understand that you have some definite ideas about targets for our operation. You feel that the local passenger ferries would provide the effect we are looking for. I agree with you, at least partially.

My hope is to cause an event that would result in more of a commercial catastrophe. The window in which to achieve our goals may be of limited duration."

Carlos politely but assertively interjected, "My prince, I believe we can achieve both goals."

"Please explain?"

"An explosive device or devices detonated on a ferry boat has the potential of killing hundreds of infidels if done at the proper time. If it is detonated in the right place, an appropriate charge could heavily damage the vessel. After I've accomplished that, I could then attack a previously chosen secondary maritime target a short time later."

"How would you do that?"

"The northern shore of Staten Island, near where the ferry terminates, is bordered by a body of water, a strait, known as the Kill Van Kull. It is about four miles long and approximately five hundred yards wide. This narrow body of water is the gateway to most of the area's huge maritime receiving facilities. The vessel traffic in the Kill Van Kull is as vigorous as that of a city street. I propose attacking a merchant target of opportunity in that area while the Americans are still reeling from the attack on the ferry boat."

"What manner of attack would you employ?" asked an engrossed Atef.

"I would act very much as we did in Aden against their destroyer the *Cole*. I would employ small boats, which I will obtain."

"My brother, I fully approve of your plan." Atef clapped Carlos on his back, while Carlos demurely nodded.

Atef put down his fork and dabbed his mouth; he leaned closer, lowering his voice. "Please allow me to modify your plan somewhat. In my position, I have access to resources you're not aware of. I have been in contact with an ally in Venezuela where they have embarked on a modernization program of their Navy. In doing so, they have acquired a number of advanced weapons such as torpedoes and naval mines. My contact is able to provide us with two extremely advanced mines. My brother, we are not going to damage that ferry. We are going to obliterate it!"

Carlos immediately felt a fever of emotions washing over him. He could only quietly utter, "Allah be praised," as tears welled in the corners of his eyes.

Atef began to sum up his presentation. "My brother, we have a great deal to prepare. It is getting late and I want to enjoy my dinner, but we must meet again soon to set events in motion."

"If I may interject, my prince?"

"Of course."

"I would like to physically show you the areas I have spoken of. I have access to a boat through my landlord, so let me check the weather for the next week and pick a day that I can take you through the waterways. I think the visualization will be extremely helpful during the preparation phase of the operation."

Atef nodded approvingly and, in an almost fatherly fashion, said, "I agree, please arrange that for us."

After dinner, Carlos found his morale to be the highest it had been in months.

CHAPTER 21

Carlos called Jack the next morning to get the wheels in motion for their maritime excursion.

"Jack, I need a favor."

"Name it," a willing Jack came right back. There was always a tinge of excitement that ensued when Carlos asked a favor.

"Jack, could you operate a thirty-eight-foot Donzi with three outboard engines?"

"Sure, no problem."

"Are you available all week?"

"When do you need me?"

"I'm not exactly sure. I'll call you back later."

"Okay, later."

As soon as he'd gotten off the phone with Jack, he walked up to Orlando's apartment, where he was invited in.

"Orlando, I hate to keep making requests of you, but as it happens, that's what I'm here to do. You have a boat, do you not?"

"I do."

"I need to use it."

"Where do we have to go?"

"I need the boat, not you."

"What do you mean? You just can't take off with my boat. It's a complicated piece of machinery that you just don't jump into and drive off like some sort of Toyota."

"I'm not piloting it. I have a professional mariner to do that."

"Why not me?"

"Mr. Rodriguez, this is one of those occasions we've spoken of, when it would be better that you were not involved in my business."

Orlando began to feel ill at ease. He detected that slight change in both Carlos's tone and attitude. The thought of where it had taken him before terrified him. Still, this was his boat.

"I don't know, man. I really don't. I can't just turn *Sofia* over to a total stranger."

Carlos anticipated reluctance and had a solution in mind. "Mr. Rodriguez, may I suggest that I have you meet my man on your boat? You can test his skills, and if you are completely satisfied, then you can lend me your boat. And if not, we will find one elsewhere. I will pay you very well for the time I have it."

"It's not about the money. It's about my boat. Who is this guy? Have I ever met him?" It almost seemed as if Carlos was asking permission to date his daughter.

"I'm not sure. It's Jack O'Connor, an associate of mine."

"No, the name doesn't ring a bell. Where are you taking the boat?"

"We're just going out locally with some friends. That's all I can tell you."

"I'll tell you what, I'll check your man out. I'll bring *Sofia* from the marina on Staten Island over to the East Twenty-Third Street Marina on a day and time of your choosing. Let me put him through his paces on the river, and if I'm satisfied with his performance, we'll then talk again about me lending you the boat."

"An equitable proposal." Carlos allowed Orlando his moment.

Early on the following Friday morning, Carlos and Jack waited on the landing at the Twenty-Third Street Marina for Orlando. The marina was located next to an apartment building that housed the exclusive UN International School in the shadow of FDR Drive. As the sun rose, Carlos and Jack waited patiently while Orlando slowly maneuvered the sharply raked blue-and-white form of the *Sofia* toward the landing. The deep rumble of her three-hundred-horsepower outboards gave restrained testimony to what the beast could do when unleashed. Jack took Orlando's lines and secured *Sofia* to the landing. The lines weren't necessary, but Orlando was going to have Jack do it all from the get-go. He shut the engines down and welcomed them aboard.

Jack sincerely complimented Orlando, "Really nice boat, man!"

"Thanks. You got any experience with anything like her?"

"Not like her exactly, but my dad had a twin Evenrude."

For some reason, Orlando found his honesty refreshing. He walked Jack through the startup procedure. Once he'd started the boat, he turned to Jack. "Okay, take her out."

That he did, and much to Orlando's satisfaction. Jack moved *Sofia* gently away from the landing, walking the stern out first. The grumbling of her powerful engines seemed to be a protest from the boat for having to move in such a restrained fashion. Once clear of the landing, he applied a little more power, moved out into the main stream of the river, and wheeled her bow south. He applied less than half power and proceeded downstream in the direction of the Williamsburg Bridge. Jack found that not only could he handle this powerful lady, but he was loving it.

Also present that morning, in a vacant fifth-story apartment of the adjoining apartment building, were Brian and Louie. As soon as Carlos had approached Orlando with his request about the boat, he had contacted Brian. Brian borrowed his brother's Nikon D-90 Digital SLR camera to use for surveillance.

Brian snapped frames as fast as he could as *Sofia* left the landing. "Louie, have you ever seen John Doe Paddy Boy sitting next to the wheel with Orlando?"

"Can't say I have. Does Orlando know him?"

"Nope."

"Louie, isn't that a fucking beautiful boat!"

"Sure is, man. How fast is it?"

"Orlando says he's gotten it up to forty knots!"

"Damn!"

"Well, they're out on the river, so we might as well hang out until they come back."

About a half hour passed before they could see the *Sofia* coming back.

"Louie, they're coming back in booking it."

Orlando approved of Jack's skills and allowed him to open her up at about a third of her power on the way back to Twenty-Third

Street. Jack maneuvered a bit north of the marina and slowed down to make his approach in a rapid outgoing tide. He made a good approach, and Orlando told Jack and Carlos he felt confident in lending his boat.

"Okay, you can have her for a day. When do you need her?"

"Now." Orlando did a double-take.

As they got closer to the landing, they could see Atef waiting. "Now?"

"Yes, we're taking my associate out for a few hours."

Brian had been engrossed by the boat when Louie brought the man on the pier to his attention. "Brian, who the fuck is he?"

Brian swung the camera onto the man waiting on the landing and snapped away. He appeared to be Middle Eastern, if he had to take a guess. "I have no idea who he is. We now have J. D. Ponytail."

"Kind of nerdy looking, isn't he?"

"Yup."

"Sounds good, J. D. Ponytail it is. What's going on here?"

"I only wish I knew, but it just gets stranger and stranger."

"That it does."

The boat was now idling next to the landing while Orlando held it to the pier, and Atef climbed aboard. No introductions were made, and as fast as he came in, they were going out again. Carlos called out to Orlando on the pier, "I'll call you a half hour before we come back in." All Orlando could do was watch them leave. As they pulled into the main stream, Atef joined Carlos in the seating area at the front of the boat. He handed Carlos binoculars and casually said, "Take these please." The comment was barely audible over the engines, but Jack had heard it. Jack sat at the wheel, stunned, thinking. He felt oddly anxious as he processed what was in front of him; he called out, "Where to, Carlos?"

"Let's do the same tour we did on the environment cruise around Staten Island."

"You've got it."

As soon as *Sofia* was out of sight, Orlando called Brian's cell and was directed to the vacant apartment.

Once there, Brian asked, "Orlando, do you have any idea who the other guy is?"

"I've seen the guy who's at the wheel in the building before. I've seen the other guy too, although I don't know his name. Carlos seems to treat him very respectfully."

"All right, Louie and I have to get to work. You're obviously staying until they get back."

"Absolutely!"

"I need you to do something for me."

"I seem to be in the business of doing favors. What do you need?"

"Don't clean up the area they were sitting in. I have a fingerprint kit I use at work, and I want to see if I can get any prints off these guys."

"Aw, come on, man. No, please!" Orlando had seen enough crime scenes in his day to know print powder is an absolute pain in the ass to get off a clean surface.

"I will personally clean the boat until I get every bit off. I'll only use as much as I need to do the job. Hopefully, we can find out who these assholes are."

"Okay, just make sure you get it all off."

"And don't dump their trash, any of it. I'll meet you back on the island after work, and we'll go over it."

"Okay."

"Call me after they leave."

"Gotcha."

*****

Sofia made her way down the East River, passing under the Williamsburg, Manhattan, and Brooklyn Bridges on the way. Carlos and Atef sat in the bow so the growl of the engines would block Jack out of the conversation. Speaking exclusively in Urdu added a precaution, and it also had a side benefit. Not having to guard his every word had allowed Atef to relax; he was having difficulty not playing the tourist. As they passed the South Street Seaport on the right, Atef wondered out loud about the cluster of buildings behind the seaport. "What are those buildings over there?"

"That's the financial district, Wall Street," Carlos responded.

"Ah, yes, the heart of Satan. A very worthy target in its own right."

Just beyond that, Carlos described the Whitehall Terminal to Atef. "Just ahead on the right is what's called South Ferry." As he spoke, a large orange ferry in the slip sounded its horn and slowly began moving out into the channel. Jack slowed somewhat and gave way.

Atef noticed the narrowing of the channel between the southern end of Manhattan and the former Coast Guard base, Governors Island, about four hundred yards farther south across the channel. "An inviting choke point," he said under his breathe to Carlos.

"Yes, but it doesn't have the volume of traffic that other areas of the harbor have. Forty or so years ago, it would have been a different story. Now, there isn't any worthwhile volume of traffic that goes through here. The only exception would be on the other side of Governors Island toward Brooklyn. There is a passenger ship terminal over there that supports the English ocean liner *Queen Mary II* when it's in port."

They left the East River and passed into what is referred to as the upper bay. Beyond Governors Island, the bay opened into a large several-mile-wide anchorage, with Brooklyn on the left and New Jersey to the right. They couldn't help but notice the Statue of Liberty on the right. Equally obvious was the NYPD police boat standing guard directly in front of it. Still, Atef wondered to himself what he might be able to do with an RPG round or two.

Carlos continued in the role of tour guide as they moved toward Staten Island. "This is the beginning of the area I want to show you."

He shifted to English effortlessly, "Jack, could you go to the right over there and stop for a while?" Jack nodded and put the boat into a right turn. He went another hundred yards and idled just outside the north side of the channel.

Shifting back into Urdu, Carlos said, "Where we are at right now is arguably one of the most critical junctures and waterways in the harbor. The river goes off to our right into what is known as the Kill Van Kull. At the top of the Kill Van Kull is the ferry terminal, as you can see. The traffic in and out of the terminal is brisk at this time of the day." He took a quick look at his watch. "It's 8:10 a.m. You'll notice a boat will soon leave, carrying commuters to work in Manhattan. Between approximately 7:00 a.m. and 9:00 a.m., boats leave every fifteen minutes. They can carry thousands of passengers."

Atef listened intently and simply stated, "This is where the mines will be placed."

"Mines are not something that would have occurred to me! That is an ingenious idea!"

Atef felt as if he'd just delivered an unanticipated present to a child. "The mine's parameters can be set when we choose to strike and what size target we choose. If they do not detonate under a ferry, they will destroy something of equal or greater size. Looking at the traffic volume in this waterway, I do not doubt we will have a spectacular result." He referred to the large car carrier that was passing their position as they spoke.

"My prince, I have a second target in mind, if I may?"

"Certainly."

"Jack!"

"Sir?"

"Let's continue on up toward Shooters Island, please."

"Absolutely!"

Jack throttled up and moved off toward the right, into the Kill Van Kull. While the engines were idling, he could hear the conversation as it became increasingly animated, and it began to unnerve him. There was almost an air of enthusiasm between them. He thought, *For a Cuban, Carlos speaks that stuff way too comfortably, and for guys who know nothing about shipping, they're awfully interested in shipping.* Jack began to seriously reconsider the situation he'd become a part of. He sensed Carlos's and Atef's objective to be something way more sinister than he wanted to be part of. If what he was thinking were true, he would be of limited use to them once these guys no longer needed his abilities as a seaman. Jack fought to keep his composure; he wanted to finish the day and get the hell away from this pair.

Jack passed under the Bayonne Bridge and closed in on Shooters Island. Carlos called out again from the bow, "Jack, could you give us a slow pass outside of the island? Don't go between the island and the shipyards over there on the Staten Island side."

"Understood."

Jack did exactly as he asked and passed very slowly along the north side of Shooters Island.

Carlos once again briefed Atef, "This is Shooters Island, an abandoned bird sanctuary. You'll notice that the waterway separates here, and the containership terminal at Port Elizabeth is to the right over there, by those cranes. If you look beyond that, you can see the even larger container facility at Port Newark. There are least three large vessels moored there. Can you see the two bridges farther on to the left?"

Atef nodded.

"There's another giant container port on Staten Island just before the two bridges known as Howland Hook, which we will pass shortly. Past those bridges on the right side resides a large petroleum terminal in Linden, New Jersey, where large tankers routinely moor and discharge flammable cargoes. The intersection of waterways at this small abandoned island could provide a wealth of targets."

"I propose we quietly preposition ourselves and our equipment on this abandoned island prior to our attack on the ferry. Our people will have a number of small kayaks at their disposal, some loaded with explosives. Once we have successfully destroyed the ferry, each manned kayak will tow an unmanned kayak filled with explosives to a second target. We must plan this part wisely and cautiously because after the destruction of the ferry, this harbor is going to come to a standstill until the Americans can determine whether anything else is lying in wait for them."

A pensive Atef offered the observation up, "My brother, I sense a mood of finality in your operational plan."

"My prince, may I make a proposal?"

"Certainly."

"I am willing to completely finance all aspects of this project in return for consideration of a request for a personal favor."

"Go ahead."

"Please allow me the privilege of martyrdom."

"I thought that was what you were going to say. I know you have made this request before and were refused. You have been denied because of the value of your intellect. You are brilliant and have done all that has ever been asked of you, so I can deny you no longer. Allah be with you, brother. How will you complete your mission?"

"As I have said, I will have my people on the island before the beginning of that phase of the operation. I will join them that night after making observations in preparation for the attack. I will not know which target we will attack until I find out what vessels are in port on the evening we strike. While the authorities scramble to prevent entrance into the harbor, we will already be in position. I hope, if possible, to strike a large tanker at the petroleum facility in New Jersey. But I will ultimately have to adjust my plans based on the situation. We will paddle out from the island and pick our target from what's available."

Jack was acting as casual as he could. He couldn't help but notice Carlos's gesticulations as they slowly moved past Shooters Island. It was obvious to him that something in the vicinity of this waterway, specifically near New Jersey, was important to Carlos. When Carlos finished speaking, he looked over at Jack and said, "Continue on, and make your way back to Manhattan." With a wave, Jack took the boat down the Arthur Kill.

As they calmly moved along, Atef began to explain what he needed to happen in the attack. "I need your assistance with a couple of issues."

"What can I do?"

"I need a means to transport the mines into the country. Do you have any connections in the Caribbean Sea or Bahamas?"

"As a matter of fact, I do. I have an associate who is currently down there with a boat doing commercial charters."

"A large vessel?"

"Sixty or seventy feet, I believe."

"Perfect, just perfect! The mines are to be delivered via a vessel posing as a cargo ship. If I give you the particulars, could you make the arrangements for the transfer?"

"Absolutely. Let me speak with my people and determine their availability. How much time will your delivery vessel need in order to rendezvous?"

"They'll have to get underway from Venezuela and could get almost anywhere in that area within a week, but let's give it two weeks to be sure."

"Good, that's done."

"Secondly, your mariner here, Jack. You do realize he is a liability, don't you?"

"Yes, unfortunately, I do."

"How are you going to address the problem?"

"I need his talents for now. I will deal with him as soon as I can. Now let me ask you a question."

Atef nodded positively, showing his understanding.

"My prince, I am going to need reliable people for my mission. Preferably younger men with some knowledge of boating and the water. You understand the nature of the mission and that their devotion to Allah must be beyond any question."

Atef assured him that he understood every aspect of the mission. "My brother, as I have said, I have access to many other sources. I have a location and people who will fill your needs very well. I'll reach out, but for now I believe we have touched on all the major issues and can deal with the smaller ones as they arise."

CHAPTER 22

Sofia slowly slid back into the landing at the Twenty-Third Street Marina shortly after 11:00 a.m., as Orlando waited impatiently on the pier. Orlando jumped on board immediately to give his boat a quick inspection for damage while the passengers began to disembark. Carlos walked over to Orlando and palmed five one-hundred-dollar bills into his right hand, saying, "Thank you very much. Please allow me to refuel your boat."

Orlando pocketed the money and bid Carlos and Atef goodbye as they walked off, but Jack lagged behind at the boat. Orlando couldn't help but notice the disconnect between Jack and the others, observing how he seemed a bit quieter than he'd been when he had arrived. "Jack, how did she handle? Was everything okay?"

"Fine, absolutely fine. It really is a beautiful boat."

"Would you care to stay while I refuel her?"

"Yeah, sure, fine."

As the boat was refueling, Orlando casually asked, "Where do you live, Jack?"

"Brooklyn, over in Red Hook. Do you know where Van Brunt Street is?"

"Oh sure, down by the Gowanus Canal near the Warehouse Pier."

"Exactly. Do you know that red brick warehouse with the iron shutters on the left?"

"I know it well. How'd you get here this morning?"

"Bus, train, and another bus."

"Jeez, that really sucks. I'm taking *Sofia* back to Staten Island. It wouldn't be a problem for me to just pull in next to your building and drop you off at the pier on the way, if you want?"

"That would be great, thanks."

After he fueled her, Orlando took *Sofia* out into the mainstream of the East River and opened her up. Jack's tension seemed to ease as his concentration now revolved around the surging boat. They both spoke easily now that Carlos and Atef were out of the picture, sailor to sailor, both stopping short of inquiring about each other's relationship with Carlos.

*****

Nadal Ibn Youssef's phone rang in his office at the Safi Islamic Academy in Warrenton, Virginia,

"*Salaam Alkhem*, my brother, how are you?"

"Atef, is that you?"

"It is."

"Where are you?"

"New York City," answered Atef.

"But I thought you were in—"

"I was. That's a story for another time, old friend."

"How can I be of service to you?"

"I have a major project for two of the older boys. They must possess upper-body strength and unquestionable dedication. Do you have a crew team?"

"No, but it's apparent where this is going. We do have a lake with canoes. Would it be useful if we trained a few of our best in them?"

"Yes."

"What is the training period?"

"A month or two, maybe a bit more."

"They will be ready. If you have the time, you should visit me. You would approve of what we're doing here."

"That would be nice, I'd like that. I will stay in contact."

Nadal Ibn Youssef was the headmaster of a madrassa, a very private Muslim cultural school. It is one of several in Prince William and Fairfax Counties, Virginia, outside of Washington, DC. The Safi Islamic Academy was one of a number of Muslim institutions that could be found in and around Fairfax County, Virginia; the area came to be known as Wahhabi Alley. These madrassas were funded through a variety of Islamic charities, some with questionable sources. The Islamic Safi Academy had been clearly shown to be an organ of the Saudi government. The school strictly adhered to the stringent tenets of ultraconservative Wahhabism.

The Fairfax County residents had raised hell over what they perceived as a foreign entity radicalizing local Muslim youth and promoting a seditious agenda. The SIA curriculum fostered hatred and intolerance of nonfaithful Muslims, along with inciting jihad among its faithful. The valedictorian of the class of 1999 was currently doing thirty years in a federal prison for engaging in terroristic activities.

On a particularly pleasant May afternoon, Ted Lohse, a freelance writer, stood at the gates of the Safi Academy. Lohse had covered the local hearings in Fairfax County relating to the SIA's estrangement from the local community and wanted to do an interview to get madrassas' side of the story.

The actual gate to the 105-acre facility was located up a winding road bordered by a railed fence. Ted made it only as far as the guarded front gate before he was told there would be no admission without a prior appointment. As he walked back to his car, he passed a red Volvo with a woman inside. When he glanced in, he noticed that the slightly built, brown-haired woman was sobbing.

The woman's cry was so pitiful and deep that he stopped and leaned in the window. "Excuse me, can I help you, madam?"

She unsuccessfully attempted to control herself, shaking her head, saying, "No, no one can."

Partially driven by compassion and partly a professional curiosity, he persisted. "No one? What do you mean?"

"The bastards in this school have taken my son from me."

Somehow the vulgarity didn't fit the soft image he saw in front of him. "I don't understand. Could you explain that to me?"

"Who are you?"

"My name is Ted Lohse. I'm a reporter."

After a long pause, she threw her caution to the wind. "Do you have children, Mr. Lohse?"

"Yes, two daughters."

"I have one son, Anthony, who's seventeen years old. He's a student here. They've taken him from me."

"Is he being held here against his and your will?"

"Mr. Lohse, I don't know where he is."

"What do you mean?"

"All his father will tell me is that he has gone on a senior trip. By the way, Mr. Lohse, my name is Miriam. Miriam Thaci."

"My pleasure, Miriam Thaci."

"Mr. Lohse—"

"Please, call me Ted. Miriam, would you mind if I recorded this?"

"No, not really."

He flicked on a small digital recorder and placed it in his shirt pocket.

"Anthony is my son, my only child. My husband Fatmir and I migrated to Alexandria from Kosovo, just outside of Pristina, in 1996. He and I are Muslims, but we're more secular, as are many Kosovars. We left Kosovo for safety while the country was fighting for its independence from Serbia.

"Fatmir has always been a wonderfully caring father to Anthony. He decided after we arrived here, and I agreed, that it would be appropriate for Anthony to become acquainted with our faith. Fatmir became affiliated with a local mosque and took Anthony with him. Initially, it seemed like a beautiful bonding for the men. Soon after, though, my naive husband was seduced by his new friends, and it was all downhill from there.

"A few years ago, Fatmir announced he was taking a trip back to Kosovo to visit his family. He returned to us briefly and announced he'd be going back overseas but wouldn't tell us where he was going or how long he'd be gone. He was away for almost a year, and when he returned home again, he had a new name, Youssef Bin Hasid. Since he's come back, nothing has been the same.

"He changed from a relatively benign accountant who took great pleasure in gardening, to a hateful and actively violent individual who would beat me or my son at a whim if it pleased him.

He is not the same man I married. The most disturbing part is how he treats Anthony. Anthony was supposed to attend our local public high school, but Fatmir suddenly insisted Anthony embrace this frightening strain of Islam. He enrolled him in this damned academy against his will and my wishes, where he is now abused by the instructors."

"Can you elaborate on the abuse?"

"If Anthony doesn't answer his instructors properly, they sometimes hit him. He has come home from school with welts on his legs and back where he's been beaten."

"Have you confronted them about this?"

"I can't. I'm a woman, and it's not my place, at least according to Fatmir. I'm not even supposed to leave the house without an appropriate male escort. If I get insistent, I don't fare much better than Anthony."

"He beats you?"

"You look as if you don't believe me."

"No, no, I take your word for that."

Miriam looked at him and smiled wryly. "Ted, please understand. I'm not trying to make you feel uncomfortable, but I want you to see something." She turned away from him in the front seat and raised the back of her sweater. Her back was bruised with purple and red welts in a diagonal pattern. "Pretty, isn't it? Do you now have a better idea of what I'm dealing with? Fatmir was never like this!"

"Miriam, why are you here now?"

"I tried to confront the school authorities, but they won't speak with me."

Lohse was moved. "Have you gone to the authorities?"

"I have, and I wanted to report my son missing, but after they investigated, the police returned to me with a permission slip signed by my husband."

"Where is your son?"

"All Fatmir would tell me is that he's in a school-affiliated camp in North Carolina. The police said there is nothing they can do."

"Did you tell them about the instances of physical abuse?"

"No. Then what would happen, an investigation, an order of protection? Mr. Lohse, Fatmir and his current cohorts are dangerous men, and I have no doubt whatsoever that if I continued with my complaint, even if Fatmir was arrested, he would eventually get out and kill me or my son."

"Miriam, if I got someone from protective services to speak with you, would you try to work with them?"

"I'd have to think about it. Do you have a business card?"

He gave her his card, and she left with the promise of a call.

Lohse stood there a moment, organizing his thoughts. He realized he might have bitten off a bit more than he could chew.

*****

Two days after a fairly mundane weekend, Lohse was running a few local errands for his wife when his cell phone rang.

"Hello, Mr. Lohse, this is Miriam Thaci. We should talk." There was a fierce urgency in her tone.

"Miriam, are you all right?"

"Could you meet me at the same place where we met the other day?"

"Sure, what time?"

"At 11:00 a.m. We can go somewhere from there."

"I'll be there. Are you all right?"

"No! We'll talk soon."

Lohse immediately headed over to Warrenton. He arrived about ten minutes early, and Miriam was parked there already, seated behind the wheel. He walked over to the car and immediately understood the reason for her call. She had a swollen left eye and a bruise on the corner of her mouth.

"Follow me, Ted."

He did, and she led him to a back road in a nearby park. She stopped her car and sat mutely in the front seat. He thought for a moment that she might break down, but it became apparent that the trembling was in fact a building rage.

"This morning, I demanded Fatmir tell me exactly where Anthony is. He went into a screaming rage and completely lost control of himself. He took off his belt and beat the shit out of me. Ted, this is not the man I once knew. Can you help me?"

"Yes, yes, I can. I have a protective services agent who would like to speak to you, if are you willing."

"Yes, but I have to get myself far away from Fatmir and his friends."

"I believe she can arrange that. Where is Fatmir?"

"He went to work. I'm done with him, Mr. Lohse."

Lohse looked down at Miriam's right side and could see that she had a carving knife clutched in her right hand. She was holding it so tightly that her knuckles were pure white. "Miriam, we'll work this out. Why don't you put that down before you accidentally cut yourself."

"Huh? What? Excuse me?"

"The knife, Miriam. Please." Ted gestured with his hand toward the front seat.

She looked down at the knife, let out a long sigh, and plunged the blade into the passenger seat with enough force to bury it to the hilt as she let out an impassioned scream. "Bastard!"

Lohse wanted to take her to the emergency room, but Miriam wouldn't have anything to do with that.

As she began to rant about how controlling and abusive her husband was, it became very apparent that had Fatmir somehow been present, he wouldn't recognize the cowering woman he had beaten. As they waited in the park, Ted slowly calmed Miriam down.

She was adamant about not returning to Fatmir, even for the night, to gather her things, so Ted called Cathy Moore, his connection at the Fairfax County Domestic Violence Crisis Center. Miriam and Ted went to the crisis center and began the intake process. Ted was allowed to observe and document the proceedings.

Only Miriam could decide whether or not she would press charges against Fatmir. The authorities could pursue the basic case against Fatmir, but without Miriam's willing participation in the prosecution, it would be an exercise in futility. Ted felt as though he had developed an uncharacteristic bond with Miriam in the short time since he met her. His article began to shift from balancing out stories of the contentious public hearings in Fairfax County to a personally charged journalistic pursuit. He had a contact in the FBI who might help him better understand Fatmir Thaci's radical leanings. Perhaps the time had come to give him a call.

CHAPTER 23

Who's got a better life than me? Gary Morris thought contently to himself. He was sunbathing in his lounge chair, on the fantail of his converted sixty-five-foot shrimp boat, the *Bayou Rose,* pulling out yet another Sam Adams from the ice bucket next to him. The ice-cold brew bit deliciously at his throat on the way down. His partner and co-owner, John Rexson, stepped out of the cabin and looked down at him with a wry smile on his face.

"You know, you really should try to loosen up, pal." He laughed as he grabbed a cold one for himself and sat down next to Morris. The island of Rum Cay could actually render an individual incapable of a negative thought.

"I know, I know, but this is the best I can do for right now," Morris clowned. "Look at this place, John. Is there anywhere more beautiful on God's earth than the Bahamas?"

The island's dive sites had brought the two of them to Rum Cay for the past few weeks when a documentary film crew chartered them for a shipwreck dive expedition. They'd be heading home Tuesday morning, but until then, the weekend was theirs, which would include some excellent spear fishing off the southeast coast of the cay, followed by a couple of nights of fine dining at a damn good restaurant in town called Out of the Blue.

Their weekend in paradise was rudely upset by the ridiculous ring tone of Morris's cell. He'd been meaning to reset that damned thing to a manlier ring tone and one that didn't sound like a soft-ice-cream truck.

"Hello, *Bayou Rose.* Gary Morris speaking."

"Mr. Morris, good morning, this is Carlos Reyes. How are you today?"

"I'm beyond fine, Mr. Reyes. What can I do for you?"

Morris understood that this phone call was about to alter his weekend plans. Reyes and the *Rose* had a history that left Morris and Rexson uneasy. Reyes paid well, but he did so for a reason.

"I've been vacationing in Fort Lauderdale and thought I might be able to get together with you for some fishing out there."

Gary began to get that ill feeling that always accompanied a Reyes call, but Gary had expenses, fuel, food, child support, and alimony to take care of.

"Sure, why not. When are you coming out?"

"I'll be arriving on a Cat Air flight arriving at your location at 11:30 a.m. tomorrow morning from Nassau. Could you possibly arrange for transportation from the airport?"

"That shouldn't be a problem. It's a scheduled flight, so I'll see you tomorrow when you land."

*****

The Cat Air Bandeirante E110 twin-engine turboprop from Nassau set down promptly at 11:30 a.m. Gary met Carlos, and the two took a taxi back to Port Nelson, where they boarded the *Bayou Rose* and set out to sea. Gary got two miles out and cut the engine, allowing them to drift. The three sat in the wheelhouse, while Gary and John opened beers and Carlos had an iced tea.

"What's up, Carlos?" Gary dryly led off.

"Mr. Morris, that's what I admire about you. Even amid all this magnificence," he gestured widely to the outside, "you're still a cold businessman."

"Business is business, and I've got bills to pay. What can I do for you this time?"

Carlos raised his eyebrows and smiled. The last three transactions he'd had with Morris resulted in enough of Carlos's marijuana moving up the coast to pay Gary's ex-wife's alimony and child support for the next five years.

"I have two rather large packages to be moved up to a location on Chesapeake Bay. You were planning to go back up soon, weren't you?"

"How much?" Gary said flatly.

"Twenty-five thousand up front and another twenty-five when you successfully deliver my packages."

"What am I moving?"

"Never mind that. Are you interested?"

"Yeah. Now what am I moving?"

"Two packages, one containing a washer and the other a dryer."

"Fifty grand to deliver washing machines. Yeah, right."

"Look, do you accept or not?" Carlos was beginning to get irritated. "I understand it sounds unusual, and it is, but that is not your concern. Now, can you do this without questioning me any further?"

Morris relented. That fifty thousand was too good to resist.

"Yeah. What's your play?"

"We're going back to Florida this week. Could you possibly delay another week or two at my expense?"

"Here? Absolutely!" he said, giving a wide grin to John.

"Good." Carlos grabbed his athletic bag and took out an electronic device. "I'll give you three days' notice to get underway. More than likely, it will be the Wednesday after next. Here's the GPS unit you'll use." He handed Gary the small rectangular device. "It has a preprogrammed destination in it, about twenty-five miles off to the east of here. Plot a course and make what allowances you have to in order to assure you arrive at those coordinates by 11:00 a.m. on the day you leave. You will rendezvous with a small Liberian cargo ship, the *Azure Star*. You have surface radar, right?"

"Yeah, we do."

"Good. The *Azure Star*'s radar is probably a little more powerful than yours. Check the area before you approach her. Unless there is another vessel in sight, you will pull alongside the *Star*. They will winch over the two factory-wrapped packages to you." He reached into the envelope and gave Gary a bill of sale for a commercial Maytag washer dryer combination purchased in Miami. "Do not tamper with the wrapping or packages in any way. Is that absolutely understood?"

Gary and John both nodded.

"Once the boxes are secure on your deck, continue on course for Virginia. The transfer shouldn't take more than fifteen minutes at most. Toss the GPS device over the side before you continue on. Your destination is a place called Blue Claw Point, midway up the Chesapeake Bay on the Delmarva Peninsula near Bloodsworth Island. I've included the particulars in this envelope. Your navigational plans should get you there by designated time."

Carlos produced a cell phone. "Mr. Morris, this is a disposable cell phone with one number saved in its memory. When you get past Thimble Shoal, call that number, and it will hook you up with the people who will move the packages off your boat. Tell them what time to expect you. After you make the transfer, leave immediately and dump the phone. Is all that clear?"

Again, they agreed.

"There is one more thing. Should you be approached at any time during the trip by the authorities and it seems you are about to be boarded, dump both packages and everything I've given you immediately. Under no circumstances can these items or documents fall into the authorities' hands!"

"Understood. Can you tell us what these things actually are?"

"No, as I said, you do not have the need to know. I'm sure you're familiar with the concept."

"Are these things a danger to my boat?"

"Do we have a deal?"

Gary looked at John and then back at Carlos. "We do."

"Good, gentlemen, then let's enjoy the weekend on this beautiful island."

Carlos was in an especially good mood knowing that the odds of this operation's success were relatively high. There are 326 ports spread through 3.4 million square miles of the US oceanic economic zone ranging over 95,000 miles of US coastline. An estimated seven hundred commercial ships, thirteen million registered and eight million nonregistered US recreational vessels, one hundred thousand fishing boats, and other miscellaneous vessels arrive at US ports on any given day. Among all those vessels would be the nondescript *Bayou Rose*.

Also helping the odds was the fact that the *Rose* wouldn't pop up on any watch lists. For all of Gary Morris's shortcomings, stupidity was not one of them. His ability to remain below the radar was one of the attributes that had originally attracted Carlos to him. The *Rose* was in compliance with all the appropriate Coast Guard regulations. Her diminutive thirty-three gross ton size and often ambiguous trips afforded her an additional benefit. She was too small to be affected by many of the ISPS regulatory provisions for cargo or passenger vessels. She was not obligated to be fitted with the automatic identification system transponder that could pinpoint her location at any time. In many ways, nautically, she was neither fish nor fowl.

Before the three went out for the night, Gary had one more task to take care of.

"Let's just stop at the marina office for a minute. I have to send a fax to the Coast Guard sector at Hampton Roads and cancel my notification of arrival that I sent before we knew about all this."

"Will you tell them of the new date of arrival?"

"No, not yet, I won't do that until ninety-six hours before I leave."

"Will the cancelation cause any suspicion?"

"No, not at all. It'll probably have just the opposite effect."

After he sent the fax, all three set off with nothing more than a good time in mind.

*****

In the following two weeks, the boys would become the toast of Port Nelson, holding court at the Green Flash, one of the port's less formal, friendlier bars. Their decisions were limited to which beer or rum to drink and whether to have lobster or yellowtail for dinner. Even Carlos loosened up with a respectable brace of Cuba libre.

Among the regulars at the Flash's bar was Anthony Waite, a British Army retiree who owned a small home on the outskirts of town. Waite had been a captain in the First Battalion of the Duke of Edinburgh's own Gurkha Rifles. They had served in the Falklands War under his command.

A thoroughly charming fellow, Waite had traveled extensively in South and Central America, both before and after his retirement. The peace and solitude of Rum Cay were a perfect fit for his retirement, and he frequently spent his afternoons and evenings drinking his favorite rum at the Flash. He had met Gary Morris at the bar where they became acquainted with each other's military background and spent their time ordering each other rounds.

Arriving on the same plane that would take Carlos back to the mainland were Gwen Sims and Roxanne Anderson. The two co-eds from the University of Maryland were arriving for a dive vacation and, as they would say, "whatever." Gary and John met Gwen and Roxanne on the cab ride back to Port Nelson. The rest of the week consisted of spectacular reef diving, spear fishing, and wildly memorable nights of whatever. The only reaction Gary could muster after his first rum-fueled night with Gwen was "Whoa!" He could understand the voraciousness of her sexual appetite, but at twenty-two, he wondered how she could have developed her level of skills.

On Sunday night, Waite joined Gary, John, and the girls on the fantail of the *Rose* for an American-style barbeque and seemingly unlimited quantities of beer. The tropical night wore on, and John provided some entertainment, taking out the banjo and demonstrating his considerable bluegrass talents.

As things mellowed out, Waite found Gary sitting on the fantail railing nursing a Sam Adams.

"You throw a proper soiree, Yank!"

"Well, thank you, Anthony. I felt it important that I do something to reciprocate the wonderful time John and I have been shown here."

"Well, thank you, Chief. It's been a pleasure. Too bad your other friend, the Middle Eastern chap, couldn't stay longer."

Gary was immediately raised up by this rather odd statement and wanted Carlos out of the conversation.

He quickly countered, "Carlos? No he's actually of Cuban descent, Anthony. And yeah, he's a good guy, but he had to get back to the mainland."

Gary's sense of ill-at-ease was well founded. Waite was a British pensioner, but he was also a paid informant on the island for MI-6, the British equivalent of the CIA. The island's proximity to Cuba allowed him the chance to earn a few extra bucks to keep an ear out for anything suspicious. Carlos's presence had piqued Waite's interest.

Gary casually went into bullshit overdrive in order to prevent fucking up his deal with Carlos.

"Yeah, Carlos was actually responsible for the introduction that got us the Discovery Channel job that landed us down here. We thought it would be at least proper to host a weekend for him. Yes, he's a decent sort."

Gary had combined just the right balance of lies and truth to create a plausible story. Carlos's passport could be verified, as could his employment, if necessary, and the Discovery Channel shoot was common knowledge. Gary's gregarious nature sealed the deal; Waite's curiosity was deflected. He shrugged off his original suspicions and opened another beer.

*****

The following Monday, the party came to an end. Gary woke up with one of the worst hangovers of his life and realized he needed to start slowing down. They were leaving Wednesday, and a clear head was essential for a successful smuggling operation. They said their goodbyes to the girls and Waite at the marina and began to prepare for what was ahead.

Wednesday morning came early. The *Rose* was powered up with John and Gary prepping by 5:00 a.m. At 5:40 a.m., they took in the stern and bow lines, and the *Bayou Rose* started slowly out of the channel into an igniting sun on the eastern horizon. The Cat 3412's diesels had recently been overhauled and sounded great running in sync. At 6:00 a.m., the *Rose* cleared the channel. Gary set a course of 090 and brought the *Rose* to a cruising speed of ten knots. While cruising, Gary and John ate breakfast and silently gave thanks that the sea was their stock-in-trade. When the depth dropped off sharply and the water abruptly changed from azure to deep blue, they knew it was time to get back to work.

"John, get the straps and pallets out for the deck cargo. I want everything set when we get to the meet."

"You got it, Gary."

Morris turned on their Furuno radar and set it to the thirty-five-mile range. He wanted to have a good surface picture up till the meet. He was picking up a few local fishing boats and a scattering of boats to the north in the direction of San Salvador. He expected those contacts to fade out as he moved farther east and the *Azure Star* to appear toward the southwest. He'd set the latitude and longitude from Carlos's GPS into his navigation system. They had a five-hour steam to the rendezvous site.

*****

The *Azure Star* rendezvoused right where they were expected. The smaller *Bayou Rose* maneuvered carefully alongside the 550-foot Liberian-registered cargo ship that towered over them.

Gary called over to the larger ship, "I understand you have a delivery for us?"

On the main deck of the larger ship, a black man who appeared to be a mate called back, "We do, are you ready to receive them?"

"Yes, sir, we are."

"Come alongside, stop, and put out your fenders, and we'll be finished in no time." There was a distinctive British twang to his voice. The fenders were a good idea as Gary noticed the *Rose*'s lurching roll; Morris didn't need his hull being holed.

The larger ship's crane effortlessly placed the two boxes on deck. The exchange took just fifteen minutes, and after securing the boxes and covering them with blue tarps, Gary and John were on their way.

CHAPTER 24

The *Rose* arrived off Cape Henry at dawn on a gray Saturday morning. The trip had been generally uneventful. John Rexson came up into the wheelhouse with two cups of hot coffee.

"Morning, John, how's it going?" Gary said as he accepted the coffee from his partner. "It's going. I'm bushed. Thanks for the joe." Gary was obviously fatigued. On the last night, Cape Hatteras had been typical, pushing them along on the lazy four-to-six-foot swells of a following sea. The *Bayou Rose* was light and rode high in the water, which caused her to have an unpredictable and irregular lurching motion, making her difficult to steer. The tedium of making constant course corrections was mentally exhausting.

"John, stay with me. I could use an extra pair of hands and eyes. There's a lot of traffic coming out of the bay."

"You want me to take the helm for a while?"

"No. That's a temping offer, but I would appreciate it if you could go out on deck and check the tie-downs on our cargo and come back in. I can't wait until we get into Annapolis, where I can stand on steady flooring in a room, preferably a bar, where there isn't engine noise and it doesn't reek of diesel fuel. Until then, however, heads up."

Gary passed by the Chesapeake Channel and Thimble Shoal, continuing on to the less-traveled north channel in order to navigate their way under North Channel Bridge, which was part of the Chesapeake Bay Bridge Tunnel.

Gary brought the *Bayou Rose* slowly under the North Bridge at 8:30 a.m., when he asked John to take the helm, allowing him time to take a shower. After his shower, he decided to nod off for an hour.

Before he did lie down, though, Gary took out the disposable cell and called the only number in its memory. Evan Dandridge picked up.

"I have a package to deliver. Are you ready to take it?"

"Yup, what time?"

"I figure 7:30 p.m. Will you be ready?"

"Yup, see you then."

"Right." Gary turned off the phone and, as instructed, tossed it over the side.

The trip, while it had been somewhat trying at times, had some quiet moments of introspection for the two as they had traveled northward. On the last night, Gary came on deck to take his watch at the helm. Rexson briefed Gary on his course and speed and what had transpired on his watch, including the location of local traffic. John went into the small galley, got a cup of coffee, and returned to Gary.

"Gary, I guess you know how much this trip has me worried."

"I know, John. I'm not all that comfortable with it myself."

"Gary, we have no fucking idea what's in these boxes. For all we know we could be transporting explosives or some type of biological shit or something! Do we really need the money that badly?"

"Actually, we do. All the nifty electronics we've installed on the boat cost us a ton of money. As of now, we're keeping our heads above water, but we've got to keep the cash coming. We have everything invested in this boat. I'll do whatever it takes to keep her afloat."

"Gary, I never liked this Carlos guy. There's something off about him."

"I know. I hope not to have to deal with him again in the future. Shit, I'd love nothing better than to only deal with film companies and dive trips. Maybe eventually that's all we'll do. But for now, we're stuck. I'm going to get some sleep."

"Yeah, see you in a little while." It felt had good to get that off his chest. Both men felt strangely that this had to be the last trip for Carlos.

*****

After spending most of the day passing through the Chesapeake Bay and the Tangier Sound, Gary slowed as he approached their final destination, the sparsely populated Bishops Head, Maryland, at Blue Claw Point.

Blue Claw Point was a twelve-hundred-acre property owned by John Pennington of Annapolis, Maryland, who was an absentee landlord for the most part. The property included a comfortable seven-room main house that was used as a hunting lodge during the duck and goose hunting seasons. In the off season, it was attended by a local caretaker, Charlie Meriweather, who worked on the property on Thursdays and Fridays. On Saturdays, Charlie visited with his daughter in Baltimore, and on Sundays he went to church. Charlie strictly maintained his schedule, which Evan Dandridge had made it his business to know.

Evan and his close friend and business partner Richie Butler came from the eastern Maryland shore town of Cambridge. It was a working-class town that survived on light service industries and tourism. Evan owned a small gas station and auto-repair shop.

There was a time, however, when things weren't going along so well for Evan. His business had fallen on hard financial times, and he was forced to make a hard decision.

A customer he'd known a long time had some connections to questionable financing sources and introduced Evan to a loan shark from Baltimore. Evan took a loan but was having a difficult time making the payments, so when the same customer asked Evan if he would be willing to do a favor or two for him that might result in his debt being decreased or forgiven, he was tempted. Once he agreed, he asked what the favor was. The customer asked if he would mind picking a package up from a boat arriving on Hooper Island later that week.

Evan asked right out, "Is this drugs?"

"Would that freak you out?"

Drug smuggling along the bay was not unheard of, but Evan had never dealt with it or been in much trouble before.

"Why are you asking me to do this?"

"You've got a reputation of having a level head on your shoulders, and you might be able to help yourself out. I'd understand, though, if you don't want to. Nobody's forcing you."

Surprising himself, Evan said, "What would I have to do?"

"You'd merely have to meet a boat, take a few bales off, and move them to this customer's truck on a local back road. We'll set everything up for you."

Evan and Richie were more than qualified to navigate the mazes of back oyster shell roads and the Jimson Marshes, having towed numerous hapless motorists back onto the local raised roadways.

With Richie's assistance, Evan did that job and then five more and was eventually told that his loan was forgiven. But now he found, he'd never be able to completely sever his ties with his former patron. His debt was only "forgiven" after he agreed to give the man from Baltimore a "taste" of any future profits. This was actually a small price to be paid for the references he would get, and most importantly, his and Richie's personal safety was now guaranteed. Eventually, he learned to appreciate the new income source.

Evan and Richie were both quiet family men, and none of these dealings changed that. Their wives knew nothing. Cash was kept in a stash in the garage and not flashed in any way. Evan kept one cell phone exclusively for business. No one in their private lives had that number, just as his new "business clients" didn't have his private number.

Most importantly, Evan's attention to detail approached an obsessive level, and all his clients loved him for it. He and Richie both had a reputation for integrity and discretion that allowed them to prosper in their increasing business. That reputation led Carlos to them. In Carlos's circle, names of people like Evan were usually prefaced in a conversation with the phrase "I know this guy..."

Evan Dandridge and Richie waited patiently in their rented step van at the foot of the pier, just past the lodge on the oyster shell road. They had remained in the air-conditioned cab with the windows shut tight to ward off the wrath of the mosquitoes outside. Evan was in the driver's seat, lost in thought and devising plans for every possible scenario they might encounter. Richie also kept watch, casually munching on a bag of pistachio nuts between his legs.

Suddenly Richie tapped him on the shoulder.

"Evan, lights out there to the left."

He could see the *Rose*'s running lights about a mile out.

With about a foot of draft under the boat, Gary slowly maneuvered the *Rose* perpendicular to a small pier on Blue Claw Point. John put out a bow and spring line to the cleats and was ready to unload.

Gary and John uncovered the two crates as soon as they arrived at the pier. They rigged the first crate and swung it out onto the pier and then onto a dolly in ten minutes flat. While they were rigging the second crate, Evan and Richie ran the dolly down to the head of the pier, where they had the step van affixed with a magnetic slap plate advertising a local seafood-processing company on the door. It took a bit of work, but they hefted the crate onto the lift then into the truck. Both of them were sweating profusely and getting eaten alive by the mosquitoes.

When they got back down to the *Rose*, Gary already had the second crate rigged and waiting to go. Gary swung the crate out onto the dolly and retrieved the boom. He immediately secured the boom and briefly and almost cheerfully bade the fellows facing him on the pier goodbye. "It's been great doing business with you, see ya." He headed back to the wheel as Evan and Richie cast them off.

Gary slowly backed away from the pier and swung around facing out into the channel once again. He was losing light and didn't want to stay in these backwaters any longer than he had to. He eased out back toward the main channel. Gary felt sure that this would be his last trip for Carlos, at least until the next time he found himself on his ass. The *Rose* moved away quietly and left Evan and Richie wheeling the last crate down the pier. The quiet was broken by the rhythmic thumps of the dolly's wheels rolling down the pier over the planked surface and then a crunch as they rolled over the crushed oyster shells. The second crate was loaded on the truck in short order. The *Rose* was well on her way when Charlie Meriweather casually strolled up and said in his high-pitched voice.

"Hello there, what ya doing here?"

A startled Evan struggled to think on his feet. "Oh, hi there. One of our boats had something to drop off to us. I asked him to pull in here briefly. I spoke with Mr. Pennington the other day, and he said it'd be okay."

That was a blatant lie, but Evan just wanted to get past this guy as easily and as fast as he could.

"I probably wouldn't have minded either had ya asked me."

"I tried to, but I couldn't find ya."

"Ah-huh." Charlie dead-panned.

"I'll shut the gate, and we'll be on our way."

"No, leave it, I have to go down to the house. I'll shut it on the way out."

Evan smiled and apologized again as he drove off the property. Under his breath, all he could say was, "Shit! Damn it!" He'd just lost this great site. He had to stay away from Blue Claw Point now that he'd been seen.

For his part, Charlie Meriweather wrote down the name of the fish-processing company from the side of the truck but didn't bother with the license plate number. He checked the lodge and found nothing was out of order. He made a mental note to put a lock on the gate and check out the guy's story the next day, but he forgot.

*****

A few days later, he called the company whose name was on the truck. Charlie called the Chilly Crab processing plant at Wingate and got Cal Ringel, the plant manager. Cal was an old-timer, a Smith Islander. He was one of a decreasing number of bay men who spoke their own peculiar local dialect. Steeped in English and Welsh traditions, their patois was often impossible for an outside ear to understand. Fortunately, that was not the case today.

"Cal, Charlie Meriweather here."

"A-low, Charlie, what can I do fer ya?"

"I had a couple of fellas down on the hunting lodge property the other night. They had a truck with your plant name on the doors, you know, with those magnet signs? They said they had to make a pickup from a boat. Do you know anything about that?"

"No, Charlie, we only use those signs when we have to rent an extra truck. But we've been missing a couple of them lately, now that you mention it. What did the two guys look like?"

"Two white guys in their late twenties to early thirties, big boys. I didn't know 'em."

"What color were the trucks?"

"White."

"Nope, ours are blue."

Charlie hung up the phone and thought about calling the police but did not. Charlie allowed his laid-back attitude to get the best of his judgment. He rationalized the house was locked and undisturbed, and he felt it was just as well Pennington didn't know that he'd allowed trespassers on the property. He vowed to himself to be more attentive in the future.

Later that night, Evan and Richie secured the crates in a Salsbury U Store-It facility. The key to the facility would be mailed to a Manhattan post office box, and in return, Evan and Richie would receive two postal money orders two weeks later.

CHAPTER 25

Jack sat at the broad-planked kitchen table in his Brooklyn loft, trying to calm himself. What he'd seen and overheard on the *Sofia* left him greatly distressed. He was beginning to realize that his greed might have made him complicit in some type of foreign intrigue, or worse, once Carlos and Tony had no use for him, they'd get rid of him.

He was feeling increasingly paranoid and in need of protection. He went to a nearby housing project in Red Hook and paid $350 for an illegal .25-caliber Beretta automatic. Jack's new piece did little to alleviate his anxiety, but it was the best he could do. It had been over a week since he and Carlos had last talked. He had been left to agonize over what Carlos's next move would be.

None of this was lost on Carlos, who understood that Jack was a liability who was likely growing suspicious and would have to be dealt with. But Jack had information they needed. For now, Carlos had to attempt to smooth over any rough waters. He called Jack.

"Jack, where have you been, my friend? I have some money for you."

"Carlos, good to hear from you." Jack cringed.

"Could you come by my place and get it this afternoon?"

"I have a few things to get done today…"

Carlos reiterated, "Jack, this afternoon, at two, please."

"Two, yes, sir."

*****

Brian sat in his precinct office, sifting through his caseload. He really had a bottomless pit of work. Although his new hours allowed him a lot more latitude in his time management, he had to be judicious about the amount of time he allotted to work on Orlando's situation.

He had gleaned some interesting tidbits from Bill Wadley's efforts, but it wasn't enough. Carlos had omitted both his Social Security number and date of birth on his rental application, which limited the possibility of any startling revelations.

Piggy had a postal inspector friend in Queens who tracked the single nonbusiness phone number he'd gotten through the LUDs and MUDs. It led to a two-family house in Flushing, owned by an absentee landlord. The home rarely received mail addressed to anyone other than "occupant." The carrier knew the house in question was frequently occupied by members of a local mosque. As long as the rent continued to be paid on time, the landlord didn't care who lived there, so the occupants were constantly changed. Recently, he said, the place seemed to be occupied by a man in his forties with a dark complexion. Wadley's investigation was able to discern that the guy rarely used the house phone and probably had a cell. Carlos's misstep on his landline phone had revealed his safe house.

Wadley said that he had asked a few people about Carlos's employer and learned about his connections to Manuel Pabon and his associates. A check with a friend of Piggy's at the state department revealed Carlos's multiple citizenships in Barcelona and Havana. The check also showed that Carlos was traveling on a Spanish passport.

The clandestine cruises on *Sofia* caused more concern as it reminded Brian of John Gotti's "walk and talks." Rather than speak of confidential mob business inside his headquarters to avoid audio surveillance, Gotti and his underlings would walk around the block where it was less likely that their conversations could be bugged. A sensitive conversation on a random boat in the harbor presented an even more secure scenario.

Brian called Wadley to mull over a couple of his concerns and ask him if he had any ideas.

"Brian, I don't know about that stuff on the water, but I know a guy who does. Al Calcaterra, a retired sergeant from our job, works in maritime security. Let me give you his number. He knows his stuff."

"Bill, one other thing, I took some pictures of these guys while they were at Orlando's boat. Do you know if this new facial recognition equipment we've got could make an ID off a photo?"

"I don't think so. You'd probably have to take the picture with that gear in order to make the match, but I could be wrong. I'll ask somebody who knows about that stuff and get back to you. You know, Brian, you may have to go official with this. It may reach beyond your capabilities."

"Yeah, it's starting to look that way."

"You talk to Calcaterra, and I'll work on this other stuff. I'll talk to you tomorrow."

Al Calcaterra was a retired sergeant from the detective division who had served in the Navy as an intelligence specialist and remained in the reserves after he was finished with the regular Navy. Once retired, he'd devoured anything that was written about terrorism, especially maritime terrorism. With his background in both naval intelligence and detective work, he decided to start his own maritime security firm, which had quickly turned into a profitable business.

When Brian hung up with Wadley, he called Al's number.

Al Calcaterra answered almost immediately in what turned out to be his typical energetic style, "Hello, Calcaterra here!"

Brian introduced himself and mentioned that he'd been referred by Bill Wadley.

"Piggy! How is that hump? We worked together at one point. Good man."

After the requisite professional pleasantries, Calcaterra broke through the side conversation and asked, "What can I do for you?"

"Al, I'm working on a case that has an odd maritime component that I really don't understand."

"What do you mean?"

Brian went on to briefly describe Carlos in the broadest of terms and his use of Orlando's boat.

"Brian, I have to interview a guy in Manhattan tomorrow. You want to do lunch so we can talk?"

"Sounds good. When and where?"

"Do you know the diner on the corner of Twenty-Third Street and Second Avenue?"

"Very well."

"How about 12:30 p.m.?"

"Sounds good."

Brian hung up feeling like he'd just caught up with an old friend.

*****

Jack left shortly after he spoke with Carlos. He packed his newly acquired Beretta in his jean pocket, just in case. When Jack arrived at Carlos's apartment, Carlos invited him into the kitchen and asked him to sit at the table. He began making small talk, attempting to loosen up an obviously uncomfortable Jack. Carlos then sat down opposite him and said, "Jack, I know why you didn't come over or call since the boat ride. It was fear."

At first, Jack didn't reply—he avoided his glance.

"Tony's icy attitude toward you is an unfortunate situation. But you have to understand something. Tony comes from a culture that finds it very difficult to interact with those outside of his community. He was not pleased with my decision to bring you along. That, however, was my decision, and it's my problem, not yours. I will try to persuade him to be more tolerant. He may be a bit difficult to understand, but you needn't be fearful."

Jack eased up a bit, but a tension lingered in the room. Still Carlos was reaching out with an olive branch, and Jack knew it would be inappropriate to slap that hand away.

"Jack, you do believe me, don't you?"

"I guess so, but he's a scary dude, man."

"Are we okay? You've become rather important to me."

"I guess." Jack offered a half smile.

"Good. I need you to do something for me. Just do it and don't ask how or why." Carlos was all business.

"What do you want?" Jack eyed him warily.

"Here is a list of sporting goods places that specialize in kayaks. I need six that can each support at least a two hundred-pound man.

I'm planning a trip with some friends down the Delaware River in a few weeks, and I already have two kayaks but I need six more. I also want you to see if you can find a trailer to transport them. You can take my car to shop, but after you decide which is the best to buy, come back to me before making the purchase. Try to get this done today or tomorrow."

"Yup," Jack replied in a compliant but reserved tone.

Carlos gave him a smile and a slap on the shoulder. "Good man!" He was actually able to extract a smile from Jack.

"By the way, here is your fee for the boat trip." He handed Jack a hefty plain white envelope, which made Jack smile widely. He flipped Jack the keys to the Jeep. "Now go."

Jack nodded and left without further conversation. Carlos couldn't help but marvel at the gullibility of Americans.

Jack, on the other hand, was still not fully convinced that he was out of the woods. He did feel a little better thinking that Carlos would be running interference for him.

*****

Brian had two official meetings Wednesday morning, the last one at Borough Headquarters, just upstairs from the Thirteenth Precinct on East Twenty-First Street. His third, unofficial meeting would be with Al Calcaterra for lunch just two blocks away.

He finished up at Borough Headquarters shortly after noon and headed to the diner. As he walked north on Second Avenue, Brian realized he was meeting with someone he'd never seen before. He felt a silly apprehension at the possibility of seeming foolish. As he walked into the restaurant, his fear passed. There was no one there who could have been Al Calcaterra except a portly fellow at one of the front tables on the right side of the diner. He saw Brian and immediately waved with a broad smile. The positive connection they made on the phone continued in person.

"Brian? Brian Devine?"

"That's right, and I guess you must be Al?"

They shook hands and sat down at Calcaterra's table to order lunch. Brian described, line and verse, everything that had transpired to that point He didn't want to omit any detail that might be important to Calcaterra.

"Al, I may have steered myself into a problem by not reporting the original homicide, but I couldn't put my friend's neck on the block."

"I am not here to judge. I'm retired and no longer obligated to report anything. Tell it like it is."

"I'm curious about all these connections to boats. Am I seeing stuff that's not really there?"

"At face value, this guy sounds like a smuggler, probably drugs if I had to take a guess. That said, there are other possibilities. Your friend's boat could be used as a weapon. You've heard of the USS *Cole*?"

"Sure."

"Your friend's boat could be used in the same manner. The targets in the harbor are almost countless. The boat could be used for both smuggling and terrorism. Smaller boats might be a little more difficult to use for smuggling, but they could definitely be used for terrorist activities. If this is a terrorism situation, you're going to need the resources of your job. You may have to suck it up and take the hit. You shouldn't hoard this kind of information."

"I know. I hope I haven't wasted your time."

"What you're doing is where actionable intelligence comes from. It's never a waste of time."

Al and Brian spoke for over two hours before parting company. Calcaterra assured Brian he was available to him at all times. Brian walked back to the department vehicle on Twenty-First Street, engrossed in thought. When he turned the key, he found that the starter was dead.

"Great, just fucking great!" He called the precinct to tell them of his situation and then dialed up Louie's cell.

"Hey, it's me. Where are you?"

"What's the matter?"

"The starter in the car died. I'm stuck at the Thirteenth."

"I'm down on St. Mark's Place. I'll be up in ten minutes."

"Thanks."

As promised, Louie was there in just that. "Taxi, sir?"

"Yeah, I guess so. Thanks for coming up."

"No problem, bro."

Brian climbed into the caged back seat of the Nissan Maxima. He never did like sitting in the back seat; it was extremely restricted and rather uncomfortable. "Hi, Bobby." He greeted Louie's new partner, Bobby Ferguson, a Ninth Precinct veteran.

"Hey, Brian, a little tight back there?"

"Nah, it's okay, I appreciate the ride." They went back around the block and began their trip south down Second Avenue.

*****

It had been a long day. Jack's shopping trip had taken him to a few Manhattan sporting goods stores, but he eventually found the best deal at Brick Township, New Jersey. He'd liked the price on a twelve-foot polyethylene kayak that could hold a three-hundred-pound payload. The salesman was quite willing to offer a better price since Jack was talking about purchasing six boats and paying cash at $570 each. The salesman further piqued Jack's interest when he told him that while he did not sell trailers for the kayaks, he did know of someone locally who was selling a trailer that would suit his needs. He'd told the salesman he'd run it past his boss that afternoon and call him later that day.

As he picked his way through traffic eastbound on Fourteenth Street, going toward Avenue A, he was again mulling over what Carlos would need these kayaks for. He'd put the salesman's number on one of the brochures that he'd laid on the seat next to him. As he moved through the right-hand lane approaching Second Avenue, he reached over and looked through the pile of papers on the passenger seat for the number. Fatigued after the long drive, his foggy thought process caused him to roll right through the red light at the intersection of Second Avenue.

Brian was seated, relaxed in the rear of the radio car, when he heard Ferguson yell, "Louie, look out!" Almost simultaneously, Louie stood on the brakes and launched Brian forward into the cage, hitting it face-first.

Louie's instant reaction allowed him to just barely miss the Jeep Cherokee that had blown past him.

Louie's first reaction was rage. "You stupid motherfucker!" This wasn't an uncommon event for people who drove in Manhattan for a living, but it didn't make it any less excusable. "Brian, are you all right?"

"Yeah, I think so. Get that stupid bastard."

"Absolutely!" Louie flipped on the roof lights and siren and lit off after the offending vehicle, pulling the Jeep over about halfway down the block between Second and First Avenue, just past the New York Eye and Ear Hospital.

Louie and Bobby got out. While Louie approached the driver with his hand on his weapon, Bobby approached from the sidewalk side, also with his hand on his weapon. Louie spoke to the driver, a white male in denim jeans and a well-worn plaid button-down shirt and with a shaggy head of hair.

"License, registration, and insurance card please!"

"What's the matter, Officer?"

"The matter? What's the matter? You don't know what you've just done? Have you been drinking? You just sailed through the red light back there and nearly killed us, caused me to jam the brakes on hard enough to throw the guy in the back seat forward and injure his face. That's what the matter is, you brain-dead fuck!"

The driver got out of the car and handed Louie his license, stating, "Here's my driver's license, but I haven't got the registration or the insurance card. It's my boss's car, so he's got them."

Louie looked down at the license and said, "Well, Mr. O'Connor, you've got a problem then. Turn the vehicle off and hand me the keys and sit in the car." Louie went back to his car with Bobby.

Brian had seen all this going on and immediately realized who the driver of the other car was. It was the guy who had piloted Orlando's boat! He tried to get out of the car but was unable to do so; the rear seat automatically locked and could only be unlocked from the front.

When Louie got back, Brian was barely able to contain himself. "Louie, do you know who that guy is?"

"He looks familiar. Who is he? Oh, man, your cheek is all bruised up. Does that hurt?"

It hurt a little bit, but he was more interested in Jack O'Connor. "Louie, this is the guy from Orlando's boat, man!"

"Oh, yeah, wow, he is. I guess that old saying is true. There's no luck like dumb luck. Are you sure you're all right?"

"Yeah, don't worry about it."

"Well, Brian, we've got him by the balls. He's got no registration or insurance card. You want me to take him into the house?"

Since Jack had no way of proving ownership, they had the right and obligation to take him and the car into the precinct until ownership was established. "Yeah, Louie, let's do that. You take him and I'll drive his car." Brian couldn't wait to get a look in the car and speak to Jack.

They all got out of the radio car and approached the Jeep. Jack appeared quite shocked to be rear cuffed and put into the back seat of the Maxima. He did have a quick moment of relief, however, when he gratefully recalled that he'd left his Beretta home this morning.

Brian got into the Jeep to drive it to the precinct. As he belted up, he looked to his right and saw the kayak pamphlets on the passenger's seat and smiled as he thought to himself, *Well, how about that? This car is getting a thorough toss before we call anyone.* This was turning out to be a good day after all.

Louie and Bobby got back into the radio car after placing Jack into the rear seat. "Officers, really, the car isn't stolen. It belongs to my boss, really!"

"When we get to the precinct, we'll call him. If he can come down with the registration and insurance papers, you'll be off the hook. Until then, you're with us." Louie called in their catch on the radio.

"Oh man, he's going to be so pissed. This sucks so bad," Jack whined.

Jack being off balance definitely played to Brian and Louie's advantage. Louie asked him, "Who's your boss, Jack?"

"My boss is Carlos Reyes. He lives on East Third Street."

"Have you got a phone number for him?"

He did and gave it to Louie.

It was a short ride down to the precinct on East Fifth Street between First and Second Avenues. Bobby and Louie took Jack in to the desk officer and explained what they were doing. They then logged him in an arrest-room holding cell. Bobby stayed with Jack, while Louie went back outside to scour the inside of the car with Brian.

"Brian, didn't Orlando mention something about kayaks?"

"He sure did. He said this guy Carlos had bought two, and what do we have here but brochures for even more kayaks. Interesting."

He looked through the stack and found the business card for the New Jersey sales representative attached. Brian took down the information from the pamphlet, while Louie looked under the seats. Nothing. He then looked in the console glove box. "Hey, Brian, look at this." They were receipts for a three- or four-day period a few weeks prior for highway tolls and gas. One of the receipts placed him in someplace called Newport, Vermont. Brian took every piece of paper in the car into the precinct and made photocopies and returned them to where they had been found. It took them all of ten or fifteen minutes, then he and Louie returned their attention to Jack.

"Okay, Jack, let's call Mr. Reyes."

Brian dialed up his cell, and Carlos answered, "Hello."

"Hello, this is Detective Devine at the Ninth Precinct. Sir, do you own a 2004 Jeep Cherokee?"

"Yes, yes, I do. What's the problem?"

"We stopped a young man driving it. He does not have the registration or insurance papers for the vehicle in his possession."

Carlos loudly exhaled, said something unintelligible, and then inquired, "Are he and the vehicle all right?"

"They are, but we're holding him at the precinct. Could you come over here with the vehicle's papers so we can release the car and Mr. O'Connor to you?"

"I'll be right over."

When Carlos arrived at the precinct, he presented himself to the desk sergeant, telling him he was there to see Detective Devine. Brian came down to the desk and met him.

"Good morning, Mr. Reyes. We meet again. Unfortunately, this time at my place."

Carlos immediately recognized Brian and smiled as he shook his hand. "Yes, Detective, I am so sorry to have inconvenienced you. Jack was using my Jeep to do errands for me around town. I forgot to give him the papers. This is all my fault."

"Well, the papers may be your fault, but his driving is not. The reason we stopped him was that he went through a red light and very nearly collided with us."

Carlos couldn't help but notice the nasty bruise on Brian's cheek. "Officer, was that a result of the sudden stop?"

Brian smiled coyly and nodded. "It's not that serious. Don't worry about it, Mr. Reyes. This is finally an opportunity to show my thanks for what you did for my friend Mr. Rodriguez." He handed Carlos the keys after a too casual perusal of Reyes's documents. "There will be no charges or repercussions from this incident, but please have a word with Mr. O'Connor about his driving habits. You don't want him bringing you, himself, or anyone else any grief. I'll send Mr. O'Connor out to you in a few minutes."

"Thank you, Detective. I'd appreciate that."

Brian went back into the detention room. "Jack, Mr. Reyes is outside. We're going to give you a break. Well, not you, but him. Your boss once rescued a friend of ours who was in trouble."

"Did he seem pissed off?" Jack bit his lip nervously.

"Hard to say, he's kind of reserved. He accepted responsibility for the papers and said he forgot to give them to you. We told him about your driving, but that's not his responsibility. You, my friend, drive like shit."

"I apologize for that. I should have been paying attention."

"Ya think? Listen, your boss, he's quite a guy. Do you know Orlando Rodriguez?"

"Yeah, he's his landlord."

"Mr. Reyes rescued him from a street beat down by a couple of really rough guys. Reyes seems to have a decidedly rougher side himself."

"Yeah, that's what I've heard. Never seen it personally."

"Well, Jack, here's your license back, and here's my card. I put my cell number on there. If I can do anything for you, don't hesitate to call. I often ask people in the neighborhood to call me if they see anything strange going on. Stay in touch, Jack."

"Thank you, Officer. I will. Take my cell number too." Jack wrote it down on the backside of one of Brian's papers. It occurred to him that someday he might need a safety valve.

"Thank you, Jack. Let me walk you out." They walked down to the desk area. When Jack and Carlos saw each other, there was no outward reaction by either. After another round of thank-yous and handshakes, they were gone. Brian and Louie looked at each other after Carlos and Jack left with self-satisfied smiles.

"Good day," reprised Brian.

"Yeah, not bad, and it's about time to go home." *Some days you eat the bear, and some days the bear eats you,* Brian thought.

CHAPTER 26

Brian knew his motives were pure, but he wasn't sure he could convince the job of his intentions. After agonizing, he realized that Al Calcaterra was right; this thing he'd taken on was rapidly moving beyond his capabilities. He had to come clean with his CO, Deputy Inspector John Mercer. Mercer had always been fair and had a great reputation for being a heads-up boss. It wasn't appropriate to keep Mercer in the dark and have not only himself but also his command face negative repercussions. In all his years on the job, there had never been a negative word said about Brian. He recited his private cop's prayer: *Please, God, get me through this and I'll never do anything like this ever again. Well, I probably won't do it again.* After all, it's not right to bullshit God.

Brian found himself mulling around outside the door to the inspector's office, trying to get his nerve up to knock. Mercer relieved him of his indecision.

"Hi, Brian, how's it going? Is there something you need?"

Mercer was a stocky man in his midforties with a ready smile and easy disposition.

"Actually, there is. Have you got a few minutes, boss?"

"Sure, come on in and sit down."

"Boss, I think I may have involved myself in something that's more than I can deal with."

"Sounds ominous, tell me about it." Mercer's tone was even, as he sensed it took some courage for Brian to walk into his office.

Brian went on to relay everything he'd kept from his superior, while Mercer sat back and listened, showing no reaction. When all was said and done, Brian quietly awaited the guillotine until Mercer spoke up after a few tense seconds.

"Brian."

"Sir?"

"It took a lot of balls to come in here and tell me all of this."

He could only think, But here comes the ax.

"Brian."

"Sir?"

"Let's figure out how we're going to straighten this mess out."

"We, sir?"

"Did you think you were handing me this bag of shit and not bearing some of the responsibility for setting it straight?"

"You mean I'm not being suspended or something?"

"Only if you ever get involved in something like this again and don't come to me immediately and allow me to help. We'll figure this thing out."

Mercer called the commanding officer of the detective squad and asked him to join them.

Inquisitively and meekly, Brian ventured, "Boss, no charges?"

"No, Brian, relax."

Relax? He felt like he'd just been reborn.

Lieutenant Bill Sykes, the squad boss, came into the room and sat in on the conversation. He sat his lean six-foot frame opposite Mercer and next to Brian, who briefed him to the point he'd taken Mercer. Brian then continued and told them about the maritime connection he'd noticed. Sykes interjected his opinion in his typically slow, deliberate manner.

"Gents, while I generally agree this Carlos may very well be into drugs, this may be something Intelligence should take a look at."

Mercer chimed in, "I agree, but this doesn't explain the kayaks. Look, for now, let's do a few things. First, Bill, reach out to Narcotics and see if they've got anything on this Reyes guy. Then reach out to Intelligence and see what they think about all this. And one more thing, Bill. Call the DA's office. If you've got somebody in the Homicide Bureau you're comfortable with, speak to them. Explain the sensitive nature of the situation, and see if we can work together. Get together with Devine here and craft a 'sixty-one' for the homicide and the unlawful imprisonment of Rodriguez. Make it out, get it a number, but I do not want any copies floating around anywhere but in my office and yours, Bill. Make sure all supplemental reports are done and then locked up. I do not want any chance of this being seen by the wrong eyes. Is that understood?" Brian and Bill nodded in agreement. "Brian, tell Rodriguez I want him to come in and speak with Lieutenant Sykes. Make him understand how serious we are about his safety. As for you," Mercer got up and walked directly to Brian, placing his hand on his shoulder, "you are my eyes and ears out there. Do discrete canvasses. We need an ID on that homicide victim and the other two guys who were in that room. Do what you have to find out what this Carlos guy is about. I'll talk to the boss in your office. You're off the chart and working directly for me until this thing settles down. Do you need anything else?"

"Yeah, boss. I need to bring in Louie Lugo."

"Done. Use your head. Now get out there, and beat the bushes."

*****

Carlos and Jack had not spoken since Carlos freed him at the Ninth Precinct on Tuesday of the previous week. Carlos retrieved his Jeep and left Jack at the curb with a terse, "We'll be speaking about this. Were you able to find the kayaks?"

"Yes, I was. Here's the dealer's business card and his brochures. I wrote down the prices on the card. He'll come down further for cash."

"Good, I'll take care of it myself." He was curt, and his displeasure was apparent.

"Carlos, I'm sorry."

Carlos just glared, spun, and walked away without a further word. He returned home and called Atef to set up a meeting. Atef came right up to Carlos's apartment and listened to his report over a glass of mint tea. Atef made no attempt to hide his considerable displeasure. "My brother, if you do not kill this idiot, I am going to go after him with my bare hands. Now do you understand the liability this fool represents?"

"Yes, but I still have the same problem. No one is as qualified or is approved to operate Rodriguez's boat. We will need his services at least once more."

Atef responded with a guttural cry and a dismissive wave of his hand. "You have spoken with this American policeman, Devine, twice now. On both occasions, he has reminded you of what a good and personal friend Rodriguez is. Your relationship with Rodriguez has obviously been compromised. Devine speaks with Rodriguez, and we must assume he has told him about using his boat. I doubt these American police are fools, so with their interest in you escalating, we should expect surveillance. I think we should move to a secondary location. If they don't know you're leaving or have actually left, all the better. I am going to quietly transfer myself to the Queens safe house."

"I completely agree. One solution would be to eliminate Rodriguez, but it would rain police on us."

"My brother, why is it so essential that we use Rodriguez's boat to begin with?"

"It's not essential, but it was a timely solution to an immediate problem."

"I think we're going to have to find another boat. Do you have an alternative solution in mind?"

"I'll have to think about particulars, but I believe, my prince, you are correct about moving the operation. To stay here is to invite disaster."

"Your work computer is probably a target. You should transfer the information on the hard drive to a laptop and destroy that hard drive. Leave nothing on that computer."

"Understood."

"Secondly, your funds have to be moved."

"I have a storage facility on Staten Island I can move it to."

"That is going to be quite a physical process. It may attract attention."

"It could, but it is essential and must be done. I'll pack as much as I can into suitcases and move it at hours when I am unlikely to be observed. If I am seen, I will say I am leaving on a business trip."

"Do you know where you may relocate to?"

"I have one location I keep available in Staten Island close to our areas of interest. It is considerably more austere than my current lodgings, but that is irrelevant. I will have to make some security modifications there before I move."

"Good, we should move quickly. We are on borrowed time with the authorities." Atef continued, "Now, back to the other thorn in our side, Jack O'Connor."

"Yes, he will be dealt with very shortly. Manhattan's streets breed violent crime. He has outlived his usefulness."

*****

Carlos's new digs were in the Tompkinsville section of Staten Island, a few blocks from the ferry terminal. His second-floor rear apartment was located in a distinctly less gentrified neighborhood than the Lower East Side. The front of his building was across the street from a small triangular park whose centerpiece was a statue of a soldier from the Spanish-American War. The rear-facing windows looked over a parking lot of a fast-food restaurant and a number of low-end store fronts. His building was one of ten in a row of three-story wood-frame structures. It was a diverse neighborhood where he could blend in anonymously.

Carlos immediately upped the security in the apartment by changing the locks, barring the windows, and installing an alarm system. Also, there was minimal contact among the neighbors in the building, which helped to preserve anonymity.

Once he had established himself in his new home, he called Jorge Astero, one of the Dominicans he'd employed to deal with the Sri Lankan in Rodriguez's basement. Astero was a cold and efficient killer, and Carlos found his degree of professionalism refreshing. His assistance was needed to clean up one last loose end.

Carlos called Jack on Friday the next week. There was little in the way of salutation in his tone. "Jack, I need to meet with you at my apartment, tonight at ten thirty. Do you understand?"

"Yeah, look, man, I'm sorry..." Carlos set down the phone.

Jack took the Van Brunt Street bus to the subway and then the A Train to Second Avenue and Houston Street. He then had about a four-block walk to East Third Street and Carlos's building on what was turning out to be a beautiful early summer evening. He thought of a club he might hit if Carlos didn't destroy his mood. He was a bachelor again, since Thea, his former live-in girlfriend, wandered off weeks ago, addled by drugs and alcohol.

Jack got to East Third Street and Avenue A and turned eastward, when he caught sight of someone leaving a building to his right. The paranoia that now consumed Jack kept his head on a swivel, and he turned just enough to see who was in the doorway.

There wasn't a word exchanged as Astero charged at Jack with a large folding knife in his right hand. Jack saw him but not the knife, and he sidestepped the lunging Astero just as the knife came into view. Jack tried to twist away and avoid the blade but failed. The blade, which should have caught him high in his back, penetrated clear through his left side just short of his kidney. Jack felt an immediate burning sensation, but his adrenaline kicked in, and he reached for his Beretta. He tried to take aim at Astero as he lunged toward him once again but realized he had never chambered a round. He left enough time for Astero to be on him, and they rolled over each other on the sidewalk. As Jack desperately kicked Astero in the face, he was finally able to jack a round into the chamber, but as he did, Jorge broke free and plunged the knife into his left shoulder. He screamed out, pointing the Beretta in Astero's direction and began firing wildly. Out of the eight rounds, he fired, six flew wildly in all directions, impacting walls, windows, and trash cans. As he shot aimlessly, Astero slipped the knife into Jack's abdomen. Two of the eight rounds, however, made contact, hitting Jorge Astero in the chin and fatally through his left ear. The automatic was actually in contact with Astero's head as he fired. He died instantly. The last thing Jack heard as he lost consciousness was an odd whistling sound.

*****

Bill Thatcher and Frankie Pirro had a fairly calm shift up to that point. It was almost over, and they were looking forward to going out with friends after work. Then a voice crackled through their radio, "Nine Adam."

Thatcher picked up the mike and answered, "Adam/Boy kay."

"Adam, a report of shots fired and two men down F/O 107 East Third Street."

"Adam/Boy, 10-4, on the way." The roof lights snapped on, and Pirro threw the car into a U-turn on Avenue A, about a minute away.

Before the dispatcher could say it, other responses popped back, "Nine Charlie, on the way."

"Nine Frank too."

"Sergeant!" The spirit in the Ninth and other places like it has always been "One goes, we all go."

When Pirro and Thatcher's car swung onto East Third against traffic, they saw a throng of people halfway up the block. Pirro stopped right next to them; he and Thatcher both jumped out. They were greeted by a group of locals who were attempting to aid a white man who was bleeding heavily from his upper and lower torso. He seemed to be semiconscious, clutching a small automatic pistol in his right hand. One of the civilians was applying pressure to an abdominal wound. Behind the wounded man, closer to the building line was another man, who appeared to be Hispanic and very dead. A bloodied folding knife was near his right side.

Thatcher grabbed up his portable radio, "Central, is the bus on the way?"

"It is, Adam."

Thatcher and Pirro returned their attention to the wounded man and tried to wrestle the gun from his hand. They weren't primarily concerned for their safety; the slide was locked back, indicating all its ammunition had been expended. It was just evidence now. The man, apparently in considerable pain, faded in and out of consciousness. The woman tending him, Heldi, lifted the towel from the wound and revealed a puncture that had sliced deep. The wound gushed a pulsing flow of dark blood. Thatcher realized he was looking at the guy's intestines and had Heldi replace the towel and hold it down hard. Thatcher and Pirro then secured the gun and knife from the scene to retain for evidence. While they began to secure the area, the wounded man regained consciousness and weakly held his arm out, beckoning Thatcher to come closer.

Thatcher knelt down and got closer to the man, who reached out, took his hand, and pulled him in. Thatcher asked, "What is it? What do you want to tell me?"

The injured man said through his pain, "The motherfucker set me up."

"Who?"

He was having difficulty speaking but managed to reach into his front pocket and produce a business card. It had Brian Devine's name and phone number on it. He pulled Thatcher close again and could only say before passing out again, "Tell him!"

Thatcher walked over to Heldi and asked, "What happened, Heldi?"

"I saw it from my window." She told him the complete story. "I began blowing my whistle as I dialed 911. Then I heard gunshots, a lot of them. The guy with the knife collapsed. I guess the stabbed guy shot him."

All that Thatcher could say was an appropriate, "Nice job, sweetheart, nice job!"

Soon the ambulance arrived and removed Jack. Thatcher rode with O'Connor in case he revived and said anything else. Pirro led the way for the ambulance toward Bellevue Hospital with flashing lights and sirens blaring.

The ambulance pulled to the rear of Bellevue at the bay that led to the ER and backed in. Jack would be heading directly into emergency trauma ICO, located to the right of the main room. As the gurney broke through the ICU doors, the overhead speaker announced their arrival, calling out, "Trauma in the slot!" Almost instantly, the trauma team swarmed into the room. Within a minute, Jack was stripped and stabilized. Eight minutes later, he was on his way to the operating room on the tenth floor.

It would take at least two hours to repair the damage to Jack's large intestine and he'd spend another few hours in the recovery room with his future in doubt. During that time, Bill Thatcher and Frankie Pirro rifled through Jack's effects to identify him. Thatcher then honored Jack's request and called the number on the card.

*****

Brian and Maureen were cuddled up on the couch, watching Bill O'Reilly when the phone in the family room rang. Maureen took the call and turned to Brian. "It's for you. Work."

"What the hell do they want?"

Maureen shrugged her shoulders and held the phone out to him.

He took the phone and tersely asked, "Who is this?"

"Brian, this is Bill Thatcher."

Brian could tell from his tone that something was out of whack. "What's up, Bill? What's wrong?"

"Sorry to bother you at home with work stuff, but I thought you'd want to know about this one. We caught a job on East Third Street about forty-five minutes ago. A guy got stabbed."

Immediately, Brian thought out loud, "Orlando? Bill, what's the name?"

"O'Connor, John O'Connor."

"No shit! How bad?"

"Bad, multiple stab wounds, but the one in his gut is the worst. They're working on him now, but they just don't know. The reason I'm calling is because when we got to him, he regained consciousness briefly and insisted that I call you."

"How did it happen?"

"There was a witness who said he was jumped from the rear by the guy that he shot."

"Shot?"

"Yeah, he may have a bit of a legal problem if he recovers. He had a .25 Beretta that he screwed into the other guy's left ear and blew his brains out. Listen, Brian, while he was conscious, he told me something. See if it means anything to you. He said a couple of times, 'The motherfucker set me up.' Does that mean anything to you?"

A shocked Devine quietly said, "Yeah, maybe so. I'll be in as soon as I can. Bill, has the duty captain been notified?"

"Yeah, he's on his way."

"Is the squad there?"

"Yeah."

"Listen, Bill, if the duty captain gets there before me, please tell him I'm coming and that Inspector Mercer would probably appreciate a notification."

"Sure, no problem."

"Where is O'Connor now?"

"They took him to the OR."

"Do we know who the perp was?"

"No, nothing yet, just a male Hispanic in his late twenties with a newly installed breezeway between his ears. Never seen him before."

"I'm on my way."

He hung up and explained what was going on to Maureen. He went upstairs, changed, and was on the road in ten minutes. At this time of night he'd be at Bellevue in thirty-five or forty minutes. He called Louie from the car and told him what was going on. Louie's response was a predictable, "I'll meet you there."

"Naw, Louie, not necessary. I'll keep you informed."

"I'll be there."

Just to be on the safe side, he called Orlando and told him to stay inside and not to answer his door that night unless it was him. This thing reeked of Carlos.

Thirty-five minutes later, Brian's Ford F-150 pickup slid into a parking space outside Bellevue Hospital's emergency room. He identified himself to the hospital security officer.

As he walked through the sliding doors, he saw people gathering with anxious expectation. Bellevue Hospital lay within the confines of the Thirteenth Precinct and had an officer permanently assigned as a liaison at the hospital. That night, it was Detective Frank McGowan. Brian had called Frank's cell to tell him he'd be there soon. Five minutes later, he walked up to Frank with his hand stretched out.

"You must be Devine. You made good time."

"Yeah, I did. Call me Brian. How is this guy?"

"Not good. They can't say which way he's going to go. He's in the OR, and they're listing him in critical condition right now. Come with me and we'll go in the back and speak to Dr. Blumen."

McGowan led him into the inner emergency room through a labyrinth of corridors and treatment rooms where they found Dr. Alan Blumen, a thirty-two-year-old ER resident, at the nurse's station. "Doc, this is Detective Brian Devine of the Ninth Precinct. That stabbing that came in earlier, O'Connor, it's his case."

"Didn't I talk with the detectives about him already?"

"Yeah, but Brian has a unique relationship to the people involved in this case."

"Hi, Doc. What's this guy's situation?"

"Well, he has a number of stab wounds, but the major issue is a stab wound to the abdomen. From what I can tell, the blade significantly lacerated his large intestine. We were able to somewhat control the bleeding, but he had to go up to the OR to attempt to completely stop it, if that's possible. He could still bleed out. And even if we're able stop the bleeding, there's still the danger of sepsis."

"How long will the surgery take?"

"It shouldn't be much longer, but he's going to be out for quite a while. I don't know when you'll be able to speak with him."

Brian addressed McGowan. "Security has got to be set up on this guy. They might take another shot at him."

"That's already been done. An MOS is with him outside the operating room door. He gets whatever he needs."

"Good. I guess now we just wait."

"That's it."

Just then, Bill Sykes and Louie arrived together.

The three stepped into the privacy of the parking lot. Brian brought them both up to speed.

Sykes added, "Brian, we ran those prints you gave us from the boat. When we ran them through NCIC, nothing came back immediately. Then we ran them through Interpol. One of those guys, the guy with the ponytail, he popped up. He's Atef Kahlid Mohammed, aka Tony Phelps, and get this. He's supposed to be in Canada. They didn't even know he was here. Brian, he's got major terrorist ties."

"No shit, really?" Brian was not totally surprised. Louie, on the other hand, did a double take.

"As it turns out, his specialty is maritime terrorism."

"I guess that answers the interest in the boat."

"Brian, we've notified the Joint Terrorism Task Force. They want to be notified the minute John regains consciousness and interview him."

"Fine, but they'll have to get in line."

"You know, Bill, they may take another shot at him. I've got to make a point of telling the desk in the Thirteenth that whoever they assign to sit in with him shouldn't think this is some piece-of-cake post."

"Agreed."

"I guess we'll wait around and see how he makes out."

"Not a bad idea. I saw a coffee stand in the front. Let's get some." They got coffee and sat down when Brian's cell phone rang.

"Brian, John Mercer. I just got here. I'm at the ER. Where are you?"

"At the coffee shop, we'll be right back."

"No, no, I'll come to you." In five minutes, they were all seated at the same table. Mercer was up brought up to speed on what was going on, and he had some ideas of his own.

"Look, guys, I'm not really happy with the situation as it stands. Before I called you, I went up to the tenth floor by the operating room to check on this guy's condition without a shield out. I walked past the uniform guy a number of times. No challenge, nothing from anybody. That's unacceptable."

All Brian could utter was a disgusted "Shit!"

"Brian, have you got Frank McGowan's number?"

It didn't take long to locate McGowan. They met in a temporarily vacant treatment room. First, Mercer told him about the security lapse outside the operating room, and McGowan got equally upset.

"Like these other guys, I really worry about somebody coming up here and doing this guy in. Let me ask you a question, Frank. What if this guy were already dead? There wouldn't be any further interest in him, would there?"

"He's not out of the woods yet, so that may end up being a moot point. I think I know where you're going with this, but I'll let you say it anyway."

"Okay then, would it be possible to fake his death?"

"Well, boss, I can't say that it hasn't ever been done before."

"Would the hospital go along with it?"

"It would have to come from levels above us."

"We might be able to arrange that. I'm going to need an area I can work in."

CHAPTER 27

Carlos sat listening to the news report of Jack and Astero's altercation on his kitchen radio. The news report left Carlos with mixed emotions. He was disappointed that Jack had not died, but Astero's passing was an unexpected plus. It provided Carlos with one more layer of insulation from the murder of Aruran Yatthavan in Orlando's basement. Jack's survival was non-negotiable though, and Hector Herrera, Astero's partner, would have to finish the job.

*****

Mercer left Bill Sykes in command at the ER, with the promise of a call if and when the situation changed. By 6:30 a.m., they'd almost lost track of time, waiting to find out how Jack would fare. Security had been augmented, first outside the operating room and then at the recovery room.

Sykes was interrupted by two representatives of the Joint Terrorist Task Force. Special Agents Scott Burton and Bill Krieger of the FBI introduced themselves. Burton, a stocky former Notre Dame fullback with a crew cut, spoke for both of them. "Your boss spoke with our boss and sent us down to talk with your guy. He's apparently got some heavy-duty friends."

Sykes closed his phone and rose, extending his hand. "Bill Sykes, Nine Squad, have you two been sent to take this case from me?" As much as he hated to admit it, the Terrorist Task Force was much more capable of using Jack's information.

Burton responded flatly, "Maybe. We got a call about what happened to your guy. The boss is really concerned, but let's see what we can do for each other." There was a history of acrimony between local and federal authorities based on the perception that the Feds used their considerable financial assets to wrench cases away from the locals. Since the formation of the task force, though, the tension had eased.

"I appreciate that. Listen, if this guy dies, it's all a moot point. You fellows should sit down with me and my people. There's quite a story to be told here."

"Sounds good. By the way, the guy whose prints were lifted from that boat is a major player for al-Qaeda. He's apparently here and wandering somewhere in the city. Quite frankly, he's what brought us here. If the others are marching to the beat of his drum, they're just as bad as he is. You're not cleared for all we know, but trust me, he's a real bad character."

"Were you guys able to identify any of the people from those photos we provided?"

Krieger chimed in, "Well, yeah, but it was a little difficult. We used the facial recognition software we have to enhance what you gave us. The pictures were taken by a recreational photographer, weren't they?"

"Yeah, was it a problem?"

"Well, yes and no. We got one good ID from the enhanced photos, but it's not useable in court. But it's better than not having any info. Hopefully, we'll be able to get you guys appropriate clearances that will allow us to be more open. I apologize for being so secretive."

"Don't worry about it. For now, that's all I have to know."

"Where are the rest of your guys?"

"They're up on the tenth floor standing by O'Connor. He's out of surgery and in the recovery room but still hasn't regained consciousness. It's touchy, but they think he'll survive."

"Why are they sitting him? Didn't the precinct provide somebody?"

"Yeah, they did, but I feel better with my guys there too."

"Yeah, these are some vicious bastards," Burton chimed in.

Sykes interjected, "Listen, instead of just talking among ourselves, why don't we go up to the tenth and let my guys share their information?"

They joined Louie and Brian at the door of Jack's room, where Sykes made the introductions. Louie stood on the door while the others stepped into a nearby vacant room to talk. Sykes asked Brian quietly, "Any change?"

"No, the nurse said he's holding his own, but she can't predict when he'll wake up."

"Brian, give these fellows the rundown, beginning to end. Let's all get on the same page."

It took a while, but Brian did as requested.

Burton and Krieger found it all very interesting. Scott Burton turned to his partner with a curious tone and said, "It filled in some of our blanks," but he mused, "Who the fuck is Carlos Reyes?"

After he'd finished his debrief, Brian turned to Sykes. "Lou, is the precinct sending somebody to sit on Jack? Louie and I have been here since last night and we're falling-out-our-ass tired."

"I expect so, starting on the day tour. That's about two hours from now. Hang out until you're relieved. They'll be sending two guys, not the usual one. The patrol sergeant has been notified to give them a scratch every two hours. When you get relieved, go back to command and crash in the dorm. Get a few hours rest, and make sure the desk knows you're up there in case anything changes."

"Okay, will do."

They were relieved shortly after 8:30 a.m. and beat feet back to the command and a soft bed in the dorm.

*****

Brian's cell phone jarred him awake. "Devine, this is Frank McGowan over at Bellevue. Are you up?"

"Huh? Oh yeah. Frank, what's up?" Brian did his best to fight through the grog.

"He's awake. He opened his eyes about a half an hour ago."

"Oh, great, great. What time is it?"

"It's five thirty."

"Morning or night?"

"It's nighttime, Brian. Are you coming up?" McGowan was somber.

"Yeah, we'll be right up."

Brian and Louie grabbed a quick shower and a change of clothes and were off. When they got to the floor, they met Burton and Krieger, followed ten minutes later by Bill Sykes.

They were reminded by Nurse Manager Nancy Clements that they could only speak with Jack in twos and only for short periods of time. Sykes delegated the responsibility for the initial interview to Devine and Burton.

"Gentlemen, he needs his rest. I'll give you ten minutes every three hours, and make sure to keep him calm," Nurse Manger Clements told them kindly but firmly.

Brian and Scott nodded compliantly as if they were being told to tow the line by their parochial schoolteacher. Brian politely interjected, "Nurse, please don't put any information out on him."

Before he could continue, she returned, "It's Nurse Manager. We understand his protected status and will take care of our end. I hope your security folks can do their jobs and keep the dregs that want to kill him off my floor. Try not to send up any more doofs like that first potsy you sent last night. He was a near narcoleptic for Christ's sake!"

"Yes, ma'am, thank you very much."

"Can we see him now?"

"Sure, come with me." The nurse manager left them alone with a last piece of advice. "Look, he's had a vent in his throat for the last six hours. We just took it out, and his throat is very sore. He's not going to be able to speak very loudly or clearly, so be patient with him."

Jack had been placed in a private room to make security a more manageable affair. When they got into the unit, the extent of Jack's injuries was abundantly clear. His right shoulder was heavily bandaged, and he looked completely washed out. There was a nest of multiple IVs, monitor wires, urine tubes, and his colostomy connection. Burton gestured with his finger to Brian to begin the brief interview.

Brian got close to Jack's face and asked, "How's it going, Jack? Can you hear me?"

His response was a barely audible "Yes."

"Jack, can you speak with us for a little while?"

Jack nodded yes.

"Jack, this is Special Agent Scott Burton from the FBI."

Again, Jack nodded.

Scott Burton jumped in. "Are you in much pain?" Jack's eyes just bulged in reply. "Jack, can you very briefly tell us how this happened?"

"Carlos set me up."

"Carlos Reyes?" Brian queried.

Again, Jack nodded yes.

"How did he do that, Jack?"

"He called me and told me to come to his place. The way he said it though and how quickly he hung up had me spooked. That's why I had the gun. I'm sorry, am I going to be in trouble?"

Brian and Scott could only smile. "Pal, don't worry about that right now. It's the very least of your problems at this point. Why did he do it to you?"

The short, labored response was a brief "I know too much."

Brian and Scott shot each other a knowing look.

"Jack, are you willing to work with us?"

Jack motioned for Brian to come closer as he seemed to be fading. He labored to say, "Anything you need, just get this scumbag." Jack then directed his attention to the two representatives of the Joint Federal Task Force. "I'll cooperate with you as long as these other guys are included," gesturing toward Brian and Louie.

Nurse Clements came back into the room. "Enough for now, gentlemen."

Brian finished with a last thought. "We're going to do everything we can to protect you, Jack."

Jack responded with a thumbs-up and fell back to sleep.

As they left the room, Brian turned to Scott. "I think we should have a conversation with Mr. Reyes."

Scott responded with a concise, "Oh yeah! But I think we should learn a little bit more from Jack before we do."

Brian agreed.

*****

Hector Herrera sat for almost an hour in the enclosed front terrace area of Bellevue, watching the comings and goings. He paid special attention to the security staff and was relieved to see none were apparently armed. Carlos had requested his services after reminding him of his partner's fate, but it hadn't really fazed him. He knew he was more cunning than Astero.

Once satisfied with the conditions in the lobby, Hector began to look inward toward the elevators. He called hospital information and asked about Jack's condition, posing as a friend. Hector was told that Jack was listed as critical and visitation was restricted. There was a station at the elevator bank manned by one guard, who was checking everyone. He figured that the best time to slide through was in the middle of the day, when the guard would probably be overwhelmed by the pedestrian traffic. For now, he studied the guard's habits, working up a plan to gain access to Jack. Once past the elevator guard, he knew how to handle the other officers he'd encounter at O'Connor's room. He'd use his silenced 9 mm Walther PPK to take out the guards and then give Jack a nice double tap to the face, escaping in the always predictable confusion.

One major flaw in Hector's plan, though, was that he had not taken into account the eagle-eyed security guard Henry St. Jean. Henry noticed that Herrera was loitering and appeared to be staring at St. Jean, which made him uncomfortable and suspicious. He couldn't leave his post to confront Hector, so he did next best thing and called Frank McGowan.

"Mr. McGowan, this is Henry St. Jean down at the elevator bank."

"Hi, Henry, how are you?"

"I'm fine, sir. I have a guy who's been loitering next to the elevators for a couple of hours now. I can't leave my post to check him out, but there's something not right about him. Could someone come over and see what his deal is?"

"Sure. In fact, I'm coming down in a few minutes. I'll take a look myself."

"Thanks a lot, Mr. McGowan. Sorry to bother you. It's probably nothing."

"No bother at all, Henry. I'll see you in a few minutes."

McGowan was at St. John's station in minutes. "Henry, which guy are you talking about?"

"Mr. McGowan, right after I spoke to you, I turned around and he was gone."

"What did he look like?"

"He was about thirty, midsized, in blue T-shirt and jeans, kind of scruffy looking—a Spanish guy."

"Okay, Henry, I'll keep an eye open for him. Tell hospital security about him too, all right?"

"Sure, Mr. McGowan. Thanks for coming down."

"That's okay, Henry. Call me if he comes back."

*****

Krieger turned to Brian across the table. "You want to call that nurse and find out what his status is?" The lead topic of discussion was the uneasiness they all had with Jack remaining at Bellevue. Brian broke off the talk and called the floor.

"Hi, is Ms. Clements there?"

"Who's calling please?"

"This is Detective Devine."

At that, he got a friendlier response, "Oh, hi, Detective. Nancy is on break now, but we moved your fellow. He's doing a little bit better. He's in 1027A now, by himself."

"Is he awake?"

"On and off. He's still pretty washed out."

"The security moved with him, right?"

"Oh, yes, they're here now."

It took only a few minutes to get to the floor, and as they passed the nurse's station, they could see the two officers in front of the door. One was seated on a straight-back chair, and the other stood next to him. Two sets of eyes locked on Brian and the others as they walked down the corridor. As they came closer, the seated officer stood next to his partner. Brian thought, *Good, very good!* They closed the distance between them and took their shields out and hooked them over their outer garments. Brian and Scott quietly went into the room, where Jack appeared to be sleeping. "Brian, do you think we should try and wake him?"

A quiet voice rose from the bed, "I'm awake. I've been waiting for you."

Both Brian and Scott smiled as Brian responded, "Hey, pal, how you doing?"

"I hurt."

"You sound a little better."

"Well, I might sound better, but when I try to move, the pain is murder."

Scott joined in the conversation as he produced a small digital recorder from his pocket. "Jack, would you mind if I recorded our conversation?"

"No, go right ahead."

"Good, just let me head the tape. The date is Sunday, June 30, 2010. The time is 9:15 p.m. I'm Special Agent Scott Burton of the Federal Bureau of Investigation, Southern District of New York, assigned to the Joint Terrorism Task Force. I'm present at Bellevue Hospital, room 1027A with Detective Brian Devine of the New York City Police Department, Ninth Precinct. We're about to interview John O'Connor."

"Agent Burton, only my mother called me John, and she's dead. The name's Jack."

"Jack it is."

"Jack, to stay on the safe side of legal propriety, we're going to do a few things to accommodate the law. I know you've already said that you're willing to cooperate fully, and for that, we're really appreciative. What we want to do is register you as a confidential informant with the police department and government. It's better for the case in general and actually beneficial for you specifically if you're registered. If you continue to work with us truthfully, your weapons offense will eventually go away. Doing that will take a little time—not a lot of time, but a little more than I, *we*, want to wait through. Keeping that in mind, in order to cover the interim while the paperwork is being processed, I'm going to read you your rights to ensure that whatever you say would be usable in any future prosecutions that arise out this case. Do you understand what I've said, Jack?"

He simply replied, "Yes."

"Okay, Jack, I'm going read you your rights. Just answer my questions and don't let this stuff stress you out, okay?"

"Okay."

Scott finished the Miranda rights reading and asked, "Jack, do you understand each of these rights I've explained to you?"

"Yes."

"Now that I've read you your rights, are you willing to speak with us freely?"

"I am."

"Good. Thank you, Jack." Burton had him sign the sheet he'd just read his rights off.

"Okay, now a few questions."

"All right."

Brian continued, "The last time we met, you said that Carlos wanted to kill you because you knew too much. What did you mean by that?"

"I'm an artist. I get a lot of funding from an organization known as the Pabon Group located over on the west side. The owner is a guy by the name of Manny Pabon. Carlos Reyes works for Pabon and distributes grant money for him. Pabon's organization gave me a grant for $75,000 that I needed for a project of mine. Reyes administered it.

"Because of the grant, Reyes and I got to know each other. All of my works deal with the harbor. That's what I'm all about. It's my medium. He told me at one point that he was interested in the harbor and its workings. This was after I'd known him for about a year.

At first, he'd call me up and ask me to do him small favors, like pick up a package here, take it there, and so on, and I did it. Hey, I didn't want to insult the golden goose. When we got together, he'd always have questions about the harbor, boats and such, stuff that was easy for me to talk about, and I did."

"Jack, did you know what was in these packages?"

"No, but honestly, it couldn't have been very legit."

"How much did he pay you on the side, Jack?"

"Sometimes hundreds. And then toward the end, I was doing things that brought me thousands."

"Did you ever actually see the contents of what you delivered?"

"No."

"What else did you do for him?"

"Like I said, he had this interest in the harbor. There was this one day when I told him I'd been invited on an environmental cruise around Staten Island, and I asked him if he wanted to come along. He did."

"Where did this cruise go?"

"All around Staten Island."

"Did anything unusual happen?"

"Happen? Not really, but he showed different levels of interest during portions of the ride."

"What and where?"

"Well, he asked questions all around but seemed particularly interested in that area around the Bayonne Bridge where it goes off in one direction toward Newark Bay and in the other direction around the island in the Arthur Kill. Do you know where I mean?"

Burton replied, "Not really," but Brian interjected quickly with, "Yeah, I do."

It was then that the nurse stepped in and cut them short, "Fellas, it's time to give it a break. He's got to rest."

All present including Jack expressed their disappointment in having to stop, but the nurse was gently adamant.

Brian shook Jack's hand. "We can continue this tomorrow, we've got all the time in the world. You just relax tonight. You've done good."

Jack sunk back in his bed as they left the room. As they got to the hallway, Brian's cell rang.

"Devine, this is Frank McGowan."

"Oh, hi, Frank."

"Listen, Devine, it's probably nothing, but lobby security just told me about a guy loitering near the lobby elevators. Again, probably nothing, but I just thought I'd tell you."

"Thanks, Frank. What did he look like?"

McGowan filled him in and ended the conversation.

Brian turned to the two uniforms as they left the room. "Guys, keep your eyes open. There's a very real possibility that the people who did this to him may be in the building. Jack and both of you are in very real danger. By the way, nobody should be visiting except us."

Brian provided the uniforms with the description he'd just gotten. "Guys, be careful. If anybody from the job comes up whom you don't know or don't feel right about, make them show you their ID. If they don't like that, fuck 'em. They don't get in."

"You got it, don't worry."

As they walked to the elevator, Brian turned to Scott Burton. "Now I think I'm beginning to understand why they want him dead." Brian told Scott of the conversation with McGowan.

"Yup, I completely agree. He's a target now."

"I'm not comfortable leaving him here."

"Neither am I. If you and your people agree, my office has a site we can remove him to."

"Where?"

Burton confided, "It's here in Manhattan, but I'd rather show you than tell you."

"Okay, when?"

"When we leave here."

"No, I mean him."

"As soon as possible. I'd like to have him out of here early tomorrow."

"How?"

"Brian, early tomorrow morning, Jack O'Connor is going to pass away of something the doctors consider appropriate for his condition. Jack's going to be removed from here and be taken to our other site before the sun comes up. We'll place an unidentified DOA in the morgue that looks something like him and who we are sure has no next of kin. We'll then create a bogus next of kin who will identify the body as Jack, and after the obligatory autopsy report, the body will be released to that person. The remains identified as Jack will be quickly cremated—well, not really, but on paper. After that, the unidentified DOA will be given back his anonymity and eventually be buried in potter's field. Jack will disappear. I really doubt Reyes or whoever is trying to kill him will figure us out. Let's use my car, and I'll show you guys what we have in mind."

They got into Scott's blue government-owned unmarked Dodge Challenger and headed across Manhattan to West Street and turned north, with neither Brian nor Louie having the slightest idea where they were going or what constituted the Feds' idea of unique safe house.

At West Forty-Fifth Street, Burton pulled into the driveway of the USS *Intrepid* Air and Space Museum. With a self-satisfied grin, Burton theatrically announced, "Fellas, I give you the grand old lady of the US Navy, the aircraft carrier USS *Intrepid*. She was saved from the scrap yard in the 1980s and now serves as one of New York's premiere tourist attractions. Recently, she was given a yearlong facelift and renovation. She came out looking as good as new, ready for another fifty years of service to her country, but some of the renovations that took place don't show up in the museum's brochures."

Scott guided Brian and Louie across the gangway that led to the *Intrepid*'s hangar deck. There was virtually no one around; the place was quiet as a tomb. When they boarded the ship, they were met by the watchman who just smiled knowingly. Scott led them along the hangar deck on the starboard side, past the beautifully restored aircraft museum. Three quarters of the way down on the starboard side, they came to an inconspicuous watertight door. Scott undogged the door, revealing a compartment that acted as an anteroom roughly eight feet wide and lit by vintage period lighting. They walked twenty feet farther down the well-worn green-tiled passageway to a door secured by a keyed lock. Scott opened the door and entered yet another anteroom. It was similarly lit, but the door at the other end of this space had a modern cipher lock on the bulkhead at chest height. Scott fingered the switches in the lock's panel and opened the door. They stepped out of the museum and onto new rugs and a suite of rooms as luxurious as any of Manhattan's new hotels.

Brian could only look incredulously and say, "Well, I'll be goddamned!"

Burton smiled, saying, "What do you think?"

"I don't know what to say. I thought we weren't cleared for this type of stuff."

"That's been taken care of. You, Louie, Sykes, and Inspector Mercer have all been granted limited clearances that will cover your current needs."

"Thanks, I think."

"Fellas, this space has a large parlor and meeting room, a clerical office, a fully stocked kitchen, two heads, and two bedrooms. When Jack arrives tomorrow, his room will be able to handle any of his medical needs, with medical personnel on duty 24-7. We'll also have a security officer on the door, again 24-7. The kitchen exhausts and waste lines use those of the ship itself and will not be noticed. The relief occurs at three o'clock in the morning. When this place is in use, the staff on the ship at the time of change are actually federal officers. Until Jack comes aboard in the morning, the watchmen, like the fellow at the gangway, are our people. Very few people from the museum staff even know this place exists."

"Wow!"

"You guys will have to rearrange your hours to accommodate the facility."

"Sure."

"Listen, let's get out of here. The staff will get here before Jack. Let them get Jack set up tomorrow. Believe me, he'll be just fine. We'll feed the media an appropriate bullshit story. Let's see how Carlos or whoever reacts when they think Jack is dead. And I really don't have to remind you that no one, and I mean no one, learns about any of this, right?"

"That goes without saying."

As they left, Louie could only smile and shake his head. He turned to Brian and said, "My tax dollars at work. I think I love it!" They shared a good laugh.

CHAPTER 28

Upon returning to the hospital, Scott called the administrator, Dr. Fabian Ferrara, who had been informed of the threat to Jack.

"Doctor, this is Special Agent Burton. We're going to have to act on our plan regarding John O'Connor."

"I see. I'll be over to you in fifteen minutes. Could you meet me at the nurse's station?"

"Certainly."

Dr. Ferrara had been told that there was an active threat to Jack's life and probably anyone else in the way. While Scott could not place a time and date to that threat, Ferrara understood that he expected it to happen sooner rather than later. Beyond that, Ferrara was not told why Jack had been targeted, nor did he care.

Nancy Clements was surprised to say the least when Fabian Ferrara appeared at her office opposite the nurse's station.

"Good evening, Nancy."

"Dr. Ferrara, how nice to see you. What can I do for you?"

"May we speak with you privately?"

She was able to look beyond him and see Scott standing behind him.

"What is this about, sir?"

"Nancy, may we step in?"

"Certainly, please." She gestured toward the door.

Ferrara and Burton stepped into her small office and closed the door behind them. Scott began to explain the plan.

"Nancy, we've decided to remove Jack O'Connor to a more secure facility tonight."

"I can appreciate that, sir, but I don't think he's ready to leave our care."

"Your care has been superb, but he's being removed to a facility that will also provide an excellent level of medical care—perhaps not to your fine levels, but it will be dedicated to only him around the clock. The success of what we're planning, however, depends on the employment of considerable amounts of guile and deception. Tonight, at about 3:00 a.m., Jack is going to suffer a fatal heart failure and pass away." She was filled in, line and verse, in regard to the coming theatrics.

"Now, I notice you seem uneasy, and I can't blame you," Ferrara said in a soothing tone.

Clements splayed her palms skyward and rolled her eyes. "Well, yes, you're asking me to falsify documents. I don't know if I can participate in this."

Ferrara, again gently, injected himself into the conversation. "Nancy, we—you, I, and the authorities—will participate in this bit of necessary deception in order to ensure not only the safety of Mr. O'Connor but also that of our fellow workers and patients."

Scott added, "Nancy, we must create the illusion of Mr. O'Connor's death in order to nullify the threat against him. You must maintain secrecy, since no one outside this room knows of this plan."

Ferrara added, "I will be here tonight with you, and I will sign the death certificate. The police will provide the transport team to remove Mr. O'Connor from the hospital."

"Does Mr. O'Connor approve of all this?"

Scott answered, "Jack has authorized us to do whatever is necessary on his behalf. He is also dedicated to the arrest and prosecution of everyone responsible for what has happened. I assume Jack is resting now?"

"Yes, he is."

"Good, let's leave it like that. We haven't told him of the exact plan yet, so we'll wake him just before we're ready to start in order to brief him. Nancy, will we have your cooperation and silence?"

An obviously troubled Nancy inhaled deeply, looking at the floor, and said, "Yes."

Ferrara asked, head tilted in toward her with his eyebrows raised, "Nancy?"

"I understand. Okay, I'm in."

Ferrara added, "Shortly before we're ready, send the staff at that end of the floor on break. Tell them you'll cover. It will be just us."

"And if they have any questions?"

"They know he was there under special circumstances and attended to with extraordinary security measures. Simply tell them the police procedures required that he be removed and autopsied as rapidly as possible to maintain the continuity of their case. If your staff nurses return while we're doing this, just tell them you're handling it. If they see him being removed, all the better. Have them remake the room afterward, but leave it vacant for now."

*****

As per the plan, Scott and Bill arrived at Jack's room at 3:00 a.m. and were greeted by the two uniforms by the door, who were sent on their way. The floor was dark and extremely quiet with the exception of the continual chirping of multiple monitors. The staff nurse sat at her desk, updating charts until Nancy sent her quietly on her way. Scott stepped into Jack's room and approached the bed. He put his hand on Jack's left forearm, gently squeezing it, and in a low tone called, "Jack. Jack."

Jack awoke and looked at him. "What's up? What's going on? Christ, what time is it?"

"Three a.m. Sorry to wake you like this, but we're going to have to move you to a safer location."

"Now? Where?"

"Now, yes. Where, you'll see when we get there. I'm afraid you're going to have to put up with some theatrics in order to get these people off your back." Scott explained the plan.

"You're going to put me in a body bag? Now you're starting to freak me out!"

"The zipper will be left open so you can breathe. All you have to do is lay absolutely still for a while. Can you handle it?"

"Well, actually, I prefer waking to orange juice, coffee, and an attractive blond, but sure, wake me at three in the morning to tell me you're going to kill me, throw me in a body bag, and spirit me off to God knows where. Oh sure, I can deal with that. I guess that just goes to show where my fucking life is at!" He threw his arms up in dramatic fashion. Then he continued on in a much more solemn tone. "Guys, they're going take another try at me, aren't they?"

"I'm afraid so, Jack."

"Let's get it done then." He frowned with resignation.

Both Dr. Ferrara and Nancy played their roles perfectly, and Jack was in the black Yukon heading uptown in less than twenty minutes. Jack O'Connor had died.

Jack was quite comfortable on the rollaway stretcher in the back of an oversize unmarked black Yukon, fully awake, alert, and extremely curious.

"Would it be out of order to ask where you're taking me?"

Brian answered, "No, but how about we wait, you know, like for dramatic effect?"

"So is this what's called a black op?"

Scott playfully responded, "You could say that."

Scott made a right onto the pier that was the home of the USS *Intrepid* and parked near the elevator that led to the gangway. They wheeled Jack out. Jack's mouth hung open in awe at first then broke into a broad smile.

"Here? This is it?"

"Yup," confessed Scott with a smile.

"Oh man, this so sick!"

"What do think, Jack?"

"If you had told me you were taking me here, I would have never believed you. This is so fucking cool!"

The elevator door opened on the hangar deck as they spoke. Brian and Scott pushed the stretcher in as Scott added, "Well, I'm glad you approve. Get used to it. You're going to be here awhile."

Jack had one request of Brian as they rolled him aft on the hangar deck. "Do you guys think you could get me some art supplies? You know, like a sketch pad and some pencils, stuff like that?"

Brian chimed back pleasantly, "Not a problem, not at all."

The sooner Jack settled in, the sooner they'd all get some much-needed rest. They could start their interviews in the morning.

*****

Hector Herrera was back at Bellevue the following afternoon and carefully reconnoitered the lobby area near the elevator bank. He had been a bit unnerved by the security officer on duty the previous day, but today was a different story. There was a different officer who appeared to be thoroughly engrossed with the pedestrian traffic near the elevators. Hector seized his opportunity.

He made his move and walked past the security desk at the elevator where he was immediately challenged and asked where he was going. Hector reached in his rear jeans pocket and pulled out a facsimile of an NYPD detective shield and a stolen NYPD ID card with his photo taped over that of its original owner.

"Detective Pontero. I've got to relieve the guys on ten." The guard waved Hector to the last elevator. He was in.

When he exited the elevator, he turned left and walked down to the nurse's station. "Excuse me, nurse, I'm here to relieve the police officers guarding John O'Connor."

Nancy was standing behind the staff nurse Hector was speaking to and interjected herself into the conversation. "Excuse me, I'm the nurse manager. Aren't you aware that Mr. O'Connor is no longer with us?" She immediately noticed that Hector was in plain clothes, while all the other police who had guarded Jack had been in uniform. Something was off.

"Has he been transferred to another unit?"

"No, didn't they tell you what happened?" she asked in an incredulous tone.

"No, they just sent me up here for relief."

"Mr. O'Connor passed away last night." She found this man's lack of information and clumsiness odd, especially since the police operation she'd experienced to this point had been so precise. Hector, realizing he was failing badly in his role, attempted to gracefully remove himself. "Well, you'd think they'd tell me that, wouldn't you know it. Oh well, sorry to bother you. This was a wasted trip. Take care now." Hector smiled, waved, and left.

Nancy quickly got on the phone and called Frank McGowan to explain what had just happened. Frank agreed that her fears were founded and asked, "Where's he heading?"

"He just got to the elevator. He's a Spanish guy wearing jeans and a red Izod polo shirt, longish hair."

McGowan left the treatment area and ran toward the elevators. Just as he got twenty feet from the elevator bank, he saw Hector walking toward the corridor. Frank called out, "Excuse me, sir?" Hector ignored him and kept on walking but picked up his pace. Hector was obviously ignoring him, and his hands were out of Frank's line of sight, a fact that greatly concerned him. Hector exited the elevator corridor and headed toward the lobby. Frank set aside subtleness and decided to just go legit.

"Sir, police, don't move! You in the red polo shirt, police, don't move!" As he said that, his weapon came out in his right hand and his shield in his left. On the word *move*, Hector broke into a sprint toward the lobby with Frank in close pursuit. Frank might have been a little on the chunky side, but he kept up, and Hector could not shake him.

Frank called out again, "Stop, sir. Stop where you are!"

Hector tried to cut the last turn on the way toward the lobby and ran head-on into a young black woman walking toward him. The woman was sent sprawling into the adjoining wall. The collision set Hector on his back, sliding in the direction he'd been going but now facing Frank, who was rapidly closing the distance between them. Hector raised his silenced 9 mm Walther. Frank saw the weapon and fell down to his knees in horror, sliding into a kneeling position to provide a smaller silhouette. Hector let loose with a fusillade of 9 mm rounds from his unbalanced position. Every round went to the right over Frank's head and impacted the wall behind him. Frank answered by firing ten rounds from his kneeling position, but he didn't miss. The rounds struck Hector in both legs, his abdomen, and chest. The round in his leg severed the femoral artery, the gushing wound rapidly staining the antiseptically clean marble floor. The round in the chest struck his heart dead-on. Hector Herrera lay dead on the corridor floor, eyes open in final shock while Frank sat on the floor, spent and shaking. All those in the hall remained motionless, except the woman Hector had knocked to the ground. She had lain in the middle of the gunfight. As she surveyed the scene of carnage in front of her, she attempted to rise but sat back down and began quietly weeping.

*****

The news station cut into its regular programming. "We're getting reports from Manhattan's Bellevue Hospital of a wild shootout in the hospital's first-floor hallways. At this time, police are only saying that an officer assigned to the hospital challenged a suspicious male. A firefight ensued with almost a dozen shots being exchanged between police and the unidentified male assailant. The gunman is reported to be dead. The officer was not injured but is being treated for shock at Bellevue. We will update this story as more information becomes available."

Carlos heard the initial reports and remained glued to the TV. He was furious to learn that the gunman was Hector Herrera but mollified later by the small article in the paper that reported John O'Connor of Brooklyn succumbed to stab wounds he'd suffered days before. With that news, Carlos sat back in his sparsely furnished kitchen feeling very self-satisfied. Apparently, all his albatrosses had flown off. This day, after all was said and done, had been a very good day—after all was said and done. "Inshallah," he said to himself.

Orlando Rodriguez had heard the same news reports. As he monitored the news, his fear of Carlos magnified tenfold. It seemed that every time he felt he had measured the depth of Carlos's evil nature, his expectations were exceeded. He felt a sense of loss in Jack's reported passing. He hadn't known him long, but he had grown to like him. Orlando had no doubt Carlos was somehow responsible.

CHAPTER 29

Ted Lohse chose a relatively neutral venue to meet his FBI contact, Frank Quinn. Both had daughters on the same lacrosse team, and over the past two years, they had often shared transportation duties for the girls. Neither, however, had ever approached each other professionally.

On this particular Saturday morning, along the sidelines, Lohse clumsily broached the subject to Quinn. Quinn sensed his discomfort.

"What's the problem, Ted? You seem a little tongue-tied."

"Well, I don't know about that, but I've run into a situation that may be more in your bailiwick, and feel a little odd about it."

Quinn guided Lohse away from the other parents, holding him gently by the arm as Ted unloaded his burden. He revealed the story of Miriam, who was now safe within the social services system. He explained about Anthony and Fatmir. Initially, Quinn couldn't help but be more interested in Fatmir's travels overseas, so after considering Miriam's information, he tried to extract more details.

"Ted, does this Thaci woman know exactly what this project 'up north' is?"

"No, not really. Is that type of conduct common at these madrassas?"

"I'm afraid so, Ted. Many of these places are hotbeds of radical Islam. Do you think the mother would be willing to speak with either me or someone from the bureau?"

"I'm sure that wouldn't be a problem."

"Good. Here's my card with my work number. We can get together again in a week or so speak more about it this week. Let me know as soon as you talk to her, and we'll put something together on my end. I'd really like to hear a bit more of the dad's travels overseas and his friends."

"Okay, sounds good. Thanks for taking the time. I wasn't sure what I should do with the information."

"You did the right thing. We'll vet it and determine what the approach or course of action should be. Most importantly, the mother was removed from that dangerous atmosphere. Has the kid been taken out of the school in Warrenton?"

"Well, yeah, but the father signed him out of school for a trip to this camp. The mother's frantic. She's lost all contact with her son."

"Okay, we'll talk this week. Meanwhile, let's get back to the kids."

*****

Ted arranged a meeting with Miriam and Frank Quinn for the following Wednesday at her Herndon apartment. Miriam spoke freely, but initially, Quinn mostly asked about Fatmir and his trips. It became abundantly clear that Fatmir Thaci, or whatever he was now calling himself, was about to receive the concentrated attention of the American government. When Quinn's curiosity about Fatmir was satisfied, he turned to Anthony's situation.

"Did Anthony ever speak of the camp he was being taken to?"

"Only that he was going to a place called 'the farm' in North Carolina."

"Have you ever heard about this place before?"

"Yes, but it's not something anybody said to me directly. I'd overhear things, you know?"

"Was anything said about where it was? Or about what they'd be doing there?"

"No, nothing in particular."

"Do you think you'd recognize the name of the town?"

"Maybe."

Quinn ran through a number of names of towns throughout the eastern portion of the United States where radicals had established communities. Her eyes lit up when he mentioned Redfern, North Carolina. "I think that's the one! Redfern, that's it."

Quinn knew all about that particular facility, operated by an organization known as Muslims in America. That camp and a number of other facilities like it were under the control of Sheikh Ali Azzi, a violent extremist. His camps were purchased in backwoods areas where real estate costs to their organization were minimal.

The heavily wooded forty-acre camp provided privacy where Muslims could practice their faith; unfortunately, it also provided a barrier shielding seditious conduct. It was located in the sparsely populated, remote northwestern hills of North Carolina. Gunfire was not uncommon in this part of the country, but sustained fully automatic gunfire was, and it had been heard recently in the area.

*****

A few miles outside of Redfern, rural Route 5 wound its way into the wooded hills. Around a sharp right curve, you could easily miss the gravel road on the right that intersected Route 5 and climbed out of sight. About a quarter of a mile onward, the gravel road deteriorated into a rutted, nearly washed-out track only suitable for four-wheel drive and ended at an old wire fence supported by old wooden posts. Before any visitor could reach the trailers, they were greeted by an elderly man seated casually in a plastic white chair in front of a decrepit gate hanging on one hinge. This is as far as the uninvited got. If a visitor became persistent, the old man at the gate would make a phone call, and glaring armed men would emerge from the nearby trailers.

For public consumption, this was a private religious community where Muslims could attend services and contemplate their faith. In reality, this and all other facilities that the sheik ran provided small-arms and automatic weapons training, terrorism tactics instruction, and training in explosives.

Anthony Thaci and Syed Remmalli, recently of the Safi Islamic Academy in Warrenton, Virginia, sat quietly in their dormitory trailer deep in the center of the complex. Committing themselves to jihad had seemed somewhat more palatable at home when Facebook, phones for texting, and Mom's cooking were available. Much to their disappointment, all phones and other electronic devices were confiscated upon arrival. There was no radio, no television, and no contact with anyone outside the facility.

Physical workouts at sunrise were taking their toll on the two. Their PT instructors, Ali and Razi, made their headmaster back at the Safi Academy seem like Mr. Softee. Both of them found firearms training enjoyable, but their introduction to explosives was an eye-opener. During that portion of the syllabus, they realized that to reach those seventy-two virgins, they would actually have to die in a pretty horrific way.

They had not been told what their mission would be, if any, but they knew it had something to do with the boat training they'd been receiving. Both were smart enough not to flinch in their efforts, as this would result in a caning from their brutal instructors. Even though Anthony and Syed desperately wanted to leave, they would remain at the site and be exposed to the Shariah dogma. Sheikh Ali Azzi felt his staff would bring these two around in time.

*****

Frank Quinn filed a report about his conversation with Ted Lohse and Miriam. The intelligence was filtered to the FBI field office in Winston-Salem, North Carolina. Special Agent Dan Philips read the report at his desk and let out a long sigh of frustration. He fully understood that without a source inside the camp, Miriam's information would be difficult to act on. Still, it was something that could eventually fit into a larger puzzle and get them the search warrant they so desperately wanted.

Until such time, they were collecting every bit of intelligence they could get on the compound. While the passage of a UAV or intelligence satellite over the location was a possibility, it was a very expensive option.

A UAV in-flight over the location last year had found what looked like a children's summer camp; that's what the site had been prior to its purchase by Sheikh Azzi. There had been some notable changes, though. The new additions included an obstacle course, a firing range with twelve firing points, and the enlargement of the administration and housing areas. The summer camp had taken a decidedly militaristic turn, but just this picture by itself couldn't really establish intent. Dan Philips would have to remain vigilant.

CHAPTER 30

"How are you feeling, Jack?" Brian asked as he came aboard *Intrepid* to begin a twenty-four-hour tour with Scott.

"Really not so bad, guys, considering everything." He smiled as he waved his hand to indicate a visual guided tour of his medically modified body. His morphine pump, colostomy bag, IVs, drains, Foley catheter, and other medical paraphernalia made him appear worse off than he actually was. Considering all he'd endured, he was doing remarkably well. It had been a week and a half since his arrival aboard *Intrepid*, and he was keeping up his end of the deal, telling investigators every detail of his story. Today Jack initiated the conversation. "What do you guys want to talk about today?"

"You told us the other day that you made two trips to Canada."

"I did. I was a go-between for Carlos."

"Why were told you were going up there?"

"I was helping set up Tony's crossing."

"Why did he have to leave Canada?"

"I was told that he had run into some problems with the Canadian police. He had to get out."

"Were you told what those problems were?"

"No."

"What did you think the sources of his problems were?"

"Do you mean Tony or Carlos?"

"Both, but I was thinking of Tony."

"Well, yeah, drugs."

"What brought you to that conclusion?"

"I delivered a lot of packages and ran a lot of errands. I was paid way better than someone who works for FedEx or UPS. The people I delivered to were definitely into drugs. Trust me on that one."

"Did you know what was in each package?"

"For sure? No, I just guessed. I was repeatedly reminded not to be overly curious."

"Did you find anything wrong with that?"

"Sometimes. Hey, I thought this was going to be a nonjudgmental thing."

"It is, I don't care if you were a drug mule personally, but I have to get into Carlos's head, and currently, yours is the nearest portal I have to it. So for now, I'll be picking your entrepreneurial brain. Is that okay with you?"

"Ah, yeah." *Cold,* he thought, *but to the point.*

"These people and places, they have names and addresses?"

"Yeah." Jack related a number of people, addresses, and locations. Scott said he'd run them past the Drug Enforcement Agency later.

"So you went up first in April, and that's when you met Tony?"

"Yes."

"When you met with Tony, what did he tell you?"

"That he had to leave and he was going to cause some kind of huge diversion to lure the police away from where he wanted to cross."

"He told you that?"

"Yes."

"Okay, and what was your part on that first trip?"

"I went and scouted out the area he wanted to cross and reported back. I also brought back a packet of information to Carlos."

"You realize by now that he did cause a diversion, a huge one. It resulted in a riot where one person, maybe two were killed, scores injured and arrested, and an incredible amount of damage was done."

"Yeah, I know that now, but I had no idea it would come to that. You know that woman who was killed in Canada, Nina Gerard?"

"Yeah."

"That was Tony's girlfriend. Did you know that? He definitely wouldn't have wanted that to happen. Maybe these Carlos and Atef weren't in control of all that."

"Yeah," Scott deadpanned. "That's all informative and interesting, but that's still not a viable excuse for your conduct. You could at least be charged with conspiracy in all those actions and events."

"Yeah." His voice had a palpable tone of hopeless contrition. "So much for being nonjudgmental."

"Jack, you're not looking too good. Are you okay?"

"I guess. This is all kind of overwhelming. I never would have gotten involved if I knew that it could end the way it has."

"Try to relax a bit. If you're honest with us, you'll walk away from this." Scott patted jack's arm sympathetically but shot a covert grin to Brian. They had him.

"Jack, Tony Philips isn't Tony's name. His real name is Atef Khalid Mohammed. He's an al-Qaeda terrorist. He's a real bad guy."

"Aw no. Sweet Jesus Christ, no. Oh shit! I guess that means Carlos probably is too." The shocking news had the effect Scott had hoped for.

"Probably, Jack. Do you need a rest?" He wasn't faking his concern; Jack's physical reaction was sincere and overwhelming.

"Would you mind?"

"No, not at all. We'll be back a little later on. Take a rest. Jack, we'll work through this, I promise."

Scott and Brian stepped out of Jack's room and went to the lounge. Scott commented blithely, "You're good."

"Thank you, I like to think so."

Scott confided, "We've got enough for indictments on both Atef and Carlos. At least conspiracy, manslaughter, inciting the riot, and a whole slate of immigration violations. We're not going to grab them right now, though. Remember, these two humps think Jack is dead. They'll continue on with what they're up to, whatever that is. I need to know if they're alone in this plot and exactly what their intentions are. The when, where, and how are very important. We'll set up surveillances after we determine their locations. Jack can help us with that. We will have to set up protection for your friend Orlando now too. These guys are some cold-hearted motherfuckers. Nina Gerard's death is not coincidental. We've really got to speak to Orlando soon. I understand Orlando saw Carlos kill someone."

"Yeah, it happened in the basement of his building, but he sanitized the location afterward."

"Let's have my crime scene people take a look at that room. We can't lose anything in trying."

"Okay."

"I'd love to get a print on Reyes, and I think I have an idea on how to. When it gets a little later, I'll call Krieger and have him try something for me."

They figured they'd allow Jack a decent rest and time to absorb what he'd been told. Brian followed Scott into the galley and poured two mugs of coffee before taking a seat at the table.

Scott told Brian that he would start the process of obtaining federal indictments against Carlos and Atef in the morning. Their physical arrest would follow at an appropriate time of their choosing.

"Scott, while he's chilling, let's flake out on a couple of the couches. It's four fifteen in the morning. We need some rest."

"Good point."

Brian hit the soft leather couch; as he sunk in, he could only think, *Two hours, just give me two hours and I'll be set for the rest of the day.* He was out in thirty seconds.

*****

It was one of those Manhattan summer days that was so torrid you felt like you were wearing the humidity like a coat. Orlando was reluctant to leave his air-conditioned office, but he had to. He'd left a flash drive in his apartment, and he needed it to complete a report he was doing.

The elevator stopped on the main floor, and when it opened, Louie Lugo and Bill Krieger were standing there.

"Hey, Louie, how are you doing?" Orlando grinned, and they exchanged firm hand shakes. It was the first time in a long while that Louie felt like he was speaking to the old Orlando. It made all the twists and turns he and Brian had taken on his behalf worthwhile.

"Not bad, my friend. Orlando, this is Bill Krieger. He's a special agent with the FBI. Do you think you could spare us some time?"

"Sure, I was just going up to my apartment. I'd say let's bullshit awhile, but you sound serious."

"Actually, I am and it is."

As they rode the elevator up, Orlando's curiosity got the best of him. "What's this all about?"

"Let's not talk here. It can wait."

"Sure." The rest of the ride was silent, which was good.

Once in the apartment, Louie led off. "Have you seen Carlos lately?"

"Yeah, I saw him a couple of days ago. He stopped by and picked up a few things. He said he was going out of town for his boss, that art guy, you know the one I mean."

"Yeah. Did he say when he was coming back?"

"No, he didn't and I didn't ask either. He does that occasionally. What's the FBI want with him?"

"Well, we're not completely sure what he's up to, but things have taken an interesting turn. You're aware of that guy that got stabbed down the block recently."

"Yeah, it was Jack, that guy who worked for Carlos. What a shame. I read in the *Post* that he died."

"Yeah. Look, pal, that stabbing may not have been so random."

Krieger chimed in at that point, "Mr. Rodriguez, we believe Reyes may be responsible for that."

"You know I kind of figured that. Holy shit, he's one psycho bastard. Look, glad to meet you, Agent Krieger. The name is Orlando."

"Likewise, I'm Bill. Would you look at some photos and tell me if you recognize the people in them? These are pretty graphic pictures. I just want to warn you." Krieger reached into the attaché case he was carrying.

Orlando turned to Louie. "Now do you believe what a sick fuck this guy is?"

"Yes, I do."

Bill took an eight-by-ten photo of the recently deceased Jorge Astero and showed it to Orlando. All Orlando could say as soon as he looked at it was, "Oh wow!" He turned pale and sat back.

Bill asked, "You recognize him?"

"I sure do. He was one of the guys in the basement when Carlos forced me to watch the Indian guy get killed. Louie, does Bill know the story?"

"Yeah, he does."

"He held that guy on one side. That's him, no doubt about it."

Krieger took out a second photo of an equally dead Hector Herrera and presented it. "How about him?"

Orlando smirked. "And that's the other piece of shit that held him on the other side. He was the guy who forced me to help clean up the mess."

"You've got no doubts?"

"No, none at all. I'll never forget those two bastards."

Krieger probed gently, "When you handed your boat over to Jack, did you recognize any of the guys who went out with Jack?"

"Well, there was Carlos and another guy I've seen here a few times, and then another guy who arrived in the building just before the boat ride. In fact, Carlos had him staying here in his other apartment."

"Other apartment?"

"Yeah, didn't you tell him, Louie?"

"No, I didn't remember that." Louie winced. "Reyes keeps two apartments here. He lives in one and keeps another as an office. A very hush-hush place with extra locks and alarms and such."

"You guys still haven't told me what this is all about."

Louie tried to ease into it, but there really was no way to put it mildly. "Orlando, Carlos is as bad as you ever imagined."

Orlando was now hanging on to every word.

"We're beginning to think he may have some type of connection to terrorism. The other guy in the boat, the guy with the ponytail, is an al-Qaeda operative."

"Whoa, no shit!"

"Yeah, I'm afraid so." Louie shook his head.

Bill jumped back in. "I understand Reyes controlled a number of other apartments in your buildings?"

"Yeah, he'd bring people in. Some left fast, others stayed. A couple of them are still here."

"Safe houses?"

"I imagine."

"Could you provide us with their identities?"

"As much as I can, but Carlos kept the detailed information to himself."

Bill's demeanor became more intense. "Orlando, there are a couple of immediate issues I'd like to address, most importantly, your safety. Mr. Reyes doesn't appear to have any problem killing his loose ends. You, Orlando, are just such a loose end. I can't be sure he won't make an attempt on your life. If I were to make arrangements to bring a team in to ensure your safety, could you very quietly provide them with an apartment in the building? You know, without anyone else's knowledge?"

"That wouldn't be a problem. In fact, currently there's a vacancy on my floor."

"Good. Secondly, I'd like to learn more about Carlos Reyes."

"Can't you just arrest him?"

"I'd rather not just yet. There are a lot of things I'd like to learn about Mr. Reyes and his friends. I have no doubt I'll be able to get a proper search warrant for his apartments. But right now, as far as I know, he thinks the people who can be a danger to him are dead, except for you. We'll nullify that threat as best we can. What I'd like to do is try to figure out what his intentions are—what he and this Atef are up to. I don't know how many other people are involved with him. I don't want to move on them and scare them away. Plus I have to know what it is they're up to."

"What would you like me to do?"

"Show me his apartment door."

"Okay. Why?"

Scott opened his attaché case containing a fingerprint kit. "I don't want to go into his apartment, but I do want to dust his door and the knob. I'll bet I can get a good print or two."

"Probably."

"I'll be back early tomorrow morning."

Louie turned to Orlando. "Are you in?"

"Kinda up to my neck. Let's play it out."

In the early hours that Sunday morning, Bill Krieger came back to Carlos's apartment. He lifted a number of smudges and partials around the door, but he did get two good prints off the brass of the knob.

CHAPTER 31

Atef had recently relocated to one of Carlos's safe houses in Flushing, and although it couldn't compare to the apartment he'd been staying at in Manhattan, it had certain advantages. The streets bustled at almost all hours with a diverse population, allowing Atef to hide in the open. In his anonymity, Atef found that he was even able to attend the local mosque a few blocks away. He did, however, make sure to always keep his eyes peeled for anything out of the ordinary.

Returning from the mosque on a warm June morning, Atef turned onto his block and was alarmed by the presence of a sedan with two white men in it parked at the curb on the opposite side of Main Street. It would have been a mild concern if he had not seen a second vehicle similarly manned. Atef went into full evasive mode.

Atef was correct in his assessment of the situation. Scott Burton had asked the Joint Terrorist Task Force to set up surveillance on Maple Avenue. Armed with copies of the photos taken from Carlos's and Atef's boat ride, they patiently bided their time. Detectives Skip Schroeder and Mike Nelson of the NYPD were seated in the black Chevy Malibu on Main Street. It was Schroeder who first noticed Atef and radioed Special Agents George Montrose and Mike Cirvilas.

"Mikey, coming toward you on the north side of the street, the guy with the ponytail and glasses. What do you think?"

"Could be, yeah, could be. Let's see where he goes."

Atef could feel their eyes on him. He could only think to himself, *Calm, stay calm and walk. See what they do.* Wisely, he decided not to approach the house but took a pass around the block and performed some surveillance of his own. As he approached Kissena Boulevard, he noticed the third car with Scott and Brian in it. He was sure now. He could not go back to the house, and he had to get out of there quickly.

Brian called out, failing to subdue his excitement, "That's him, that's him, J. D. Ponytail!"

Scott called out to a fourth car on Kissena Boulevard manned by Bill Krieger and Louie Lugo. "Okay, Louie and Bill, you've got J. D. Ponytail coming up the block toward you on the north side of the street. Get out on foot, Louie, on the west side of Kissena. Bill, on the east, tail him. Skip and Mike, get out and get ready to parallel when we see which way he goes."

They waited. It was only a minute or two before they saw him. Louie added, "Yup, that's him. We're on him."

Atef was fighting the urge to run but kept his composure. He was in trouble, and he knew it. *Think! Think! You can get out of this.*

When he got to corner of Maple and Kissena, he picked up on Louie and Bill but did not look in their direction afterward. He made a right and began walking north toward the 7 train subway station.

Louie turned so his radio transmission could not be seen and simply instructed, "North on Kissena toward Sanford."

Atef headed for the subway three blocks away. When he got to Forty-First Street, he turned toward Main Street.

Dutifully, Louie reported, "East on Forty-First Street. Skip, he's coming to you."

When Atef got close to the subway, he threw both teams a curve. Instead of walking to the end of the station that was served by the token booth and agent, he slipped in where the station was unmanned.

Louie was on it. "Guys, he's headed for the dead end of the station. I've got a Metro Card, I'll follow."

Atef got to the gated turnstile and swiped his card. Once in the station, he kept moving without turning around.

Louie got to the gate fifty feet behind Atef. He took his card from his pocket and swiped. Nothing. He swiped again. Still nothing. Panic set in. He couldn't lose Atef, not when they were this close. Louie, unfortunately, had placed his card in his pocket where it had come in contact with his cell phone. The electrical field of the phone had nullified the magnetic strip of the card and made it unusable. He'd lost him. By the time he was able to get back up to the street and communicate with the team, Atef was out of sight. Murphy's law had raised its ugly head yet again.

Schroeder and Nelson ran down the subway stairs on their end of the station, flashed their credentials, and vaulted the turnstiles. As they raced down the platform, they saw a train waiting in the station. Flushing was the last stop of the 7 line, and trains lay up there while waiting to make the return trip to Manhattan. As they approached, the chimes rang, signifying the doors were about to close. Skip ran ahead and jammed himself in the door, holding it open for Nelson. Both were sure that Atef was on this train that was about to leave.

Instead, Atef had calmly walked down the platform but did not board the waiting train. He had stepped behind the staircase he'd just walked down. He was out of the line of sight of almost everyone in the station except the motorman of the waiting train, who paid him no mind whatsoever. Shortly after, the doors of the train shut and slowly left the station, carrying Schroeder and Nelson. As it left, Atef placed the staircase between himself and the train, making himself invisible to anyone on the train.

When the next train arrived, Atef did not board it immediately but stayed behind the staircase, watching those who got on. Nothing seemed out of order. As the door chimes rang, he darted aboard the train just as it was about to depart. He sat in the nearly vacant car, breathing hard, feeling lightheaded. He dared a look around and realized he'd done it. He'd burned the cops.

*****

Atef contacted Carlos for directions on how to get to Staten Island. Once Atef disembarked the ferry in Staten Island, he was met by Carlos. The two had a ten-minute walk down Bay Street that provided a useful time for a walk and talk.

Carlos could not avoid asking the obvious. "Are you sure you weren't followed?"

"Yes, I lost them back in Queens. They picked me up in the street as I was coming back from the mosque. I never went back to the apartment, but we must assume they know of the house. How else could they have found me? Is your new place secure?"

"For now."

"We must alter and accelerate our plans."

"Agreed."

They arrived at Carlos's apartment. "Can your people facilitate the delivery of the packages from Delaware?"

"We'll have to speak to them, but I think it would be better for me to drive down in this instance."

"I would like to come with you."

"If you wish."

"Another issue. You have to buy a boat."

"I know. I've thought of that and have an idea."

"What is it?"

"The authorities seem to know a great deal about us. You were right. Rodriguez has provided them with some information, and I believe they may have gained additional knowledge from Jack O'Connor before he died. I believe, however, their understanding of me, us, is limited to Manhattan and Queens. For now, this place is safe. I am going to buy a boat but use Manny Pabon as a surrogate buyer. I must assume that my identity is compromised, even if it isn't."

"I don't completely understand what you're proposing."

"I am going to give Manny the money to buy the boat."

"You just can't walk into a boat dealership with a suitcase of cash and buy a boat. You'll arouse too much suspicion."

"Absolutely, but I'm not going to do that. I will give the cash to Manny, and he can launder it through his organization. When we make the purchase, the transaction will be made with a simple wire transfer of funds. There is nothing suspicious about a successful businessman making such a purchase."

"Brilliant, brilliant!"

"We should also bring our young assistants up from the facility in North Carolina. Our time is coming soon."

CHAPTER 32

Captain Greg Mason's 125-foot *Triton* was a hardworking, beefy four-thousand-horsepower tug that he'd inherited from his father. Mason ran a one-boat business mainly dealing with subcontracting to take the pressure off larger maritime companies that occasionally found themselves overcommitted. A stocky, even-tempered man, Mason was an established member of the local waterfront and had developed a solid reputation for reliability. His *Triton* was a common sight in its homeport of Wilmington, Delaware, and along the East Coast and could be found towing or carrying almost any conceivable load as well as handling occasional salvage work. Mason maintained her in order to stave off the ravages of age. She regularly had her bottom sandblasted and repainted and her zinc anodes changed. They also performed engine upkeep, replacing worn parts such as pistons, heads, bearings, and so forth.

Mason's crew was his family. He had kept the same first mate and chief engineer for the past eight years. Wally Kurri was a tall olive-complexioned forty-year-old man, with dark deep-set eyes and a brooding persona to match. He was a thoroughly professional and impeccable first mate. Kurri had also introduced Mason to the second pillar of his crew, Chief Engineer Charlie Gonsalves.

A loner, Walid "Wally" Kurri, a naturalized American citizen, emigrated from deadly Beirut in late 1982. It was not an immigration born of new hopes and dreams, but one of survival as he and his mother, Rania, fled for their lives during the Lebanese civil war.

Wally's father, Bashir, had been murdered in the Phalangist massacre at the squalid Shatila refugee camp in front of his young son and wife. Rania knew that she needed to leave the country in order to protect her family. Once she and Wally arrived safely, they received political asylum and were taken in by Rania's brothers, Albert and Maurice Malouf, in Ridgewood, New Jersey. When Wally was in high school, his uncle Albert got him a summer job working on a tugboat in nearby Newark Bay. He started as low as anyone might. He was just an ordinary seaman, but he loved working on the water. Wally had found his life's passion.

A few years later, despite the protests of his uncles who wanted him to attend Columbia and study law, Walid Kurri enrolled in New York State Maritime College in the Bronx, New York.

The first half of his college experience was successful and without incident. In his junior year he developed a friendship with a native-born Egyptian student, Nasir Ibn Torok, or Nicky to his friends. In spite of the fact that Nicky came from a family of wealthy Egyptian fabric merchants, he thought of himself as a champion for oppressed Muslims. Through their conversations, Nicky became aware of Wally's experience in Beirut. Nasir Ibn Torok saw in Wally the chance to cement his own credibility among his radical Islamic circle of friends. Wally Kurri was soon introduced to the strata of jihadists.

*****

Increasingly, Wally began to spend his weekends on leave with his newfound friends in the city as opposed to going home. When he did travel home and brought his new friends with him, his uncle Maurice found them to be both rude and arrogant. On one occasion, a scruffy, wild-eyed young man actually had the audacity to accuse Rania of dressing immodestly since she had not covered her head "properly." The fact that she was a Maronite Christian did not seem to alter his opinion.

By the beginning of Wally's junior year, he began to reconsider Islam under the persuasion of his new friends, one of those being a fellow mariner, Charlie Gonsalves. Charlie's career path had not come through college but through the ranks as an engineer on tugs and barges. Among his new friends, Wally was fed anti-Israeli and anti-US propaganda. He became convinced, through his naiveté, that the Zionists were the cause of all evil in the Middle East. He now believed that Americans and Israelis were responsible for his father's death.

At the end of his senior year, against his family's wishes, Wally joined a "student" trip to Lebanon with his new Muslim friends. Once there, the group was guided to radical meetings in one refugee camp after another. Harangue after harangue ensued as local militia leaders all delivered the same message: the social and economic ills of the Arab world were being perpetrated by the Israelis and their American masters. It was time to seek revenge.

By the time he returned home, Wally had become an angry young man. Very little of the person Rania and his uncles had sent off remained. They had hoped his trip might purge some of his zeal, but just the opposite happened. Among his Muslim friends, on the other hand, he had gained a great deal of stature and a bit of a swelled head. Wally and Charlie Gonsalves were being groomed to become sleeper agents in the maritime community. After his graduation, Wally was guided to the Philadelphia area and eventually to Wilmington and Greg Mason's *Triton*. He became estranged from his family, and after a few months of working, he convinced Mason to bring Gonsalves aboard.

At first, reintegration into the culture of the infidel was vexing for Kurri and Gonsalves. While they'd been told to be open in regard to their faith, they were also counseled not to be so enthusiastic as to draw attention to themselves. Neither Kurri nor Gonsalves openly prayed, nor did they do anything else that would make Mason uncomfortable or overly conscious of their faith.

Over the years, the crew of the *Triton* developed a mutual respect for each other. Wally and Charlie were always prepared for the phone call that would activate them, but until that time, it was tug work up and down the East Coast. Then that June, the call came. It was Carlos.

"Mr. Kurri, this is Mr. Reyes. Would you be interested in some part-time work I have?" It was the activation code he'd be told would come.

"Why, yes, I would. Can we possibly get together so you can explain what you need from me?"

"Absolutely. Would Saturday afternoon be okay?"

"Yes. Does 2:00 p.m. work?"

"Good, then Saturday at two at your home. Oh, by the way, I'll have my brother-in-law Tony with me. That will be okay, won't it?"

"Absolutely, that will be fine. See you then."

After they hung up, Wally had to take a deep breath and settle down. He realized his life was about to take a drastic turn.

*****

The disposable phone Carlos had given Manny Pabon startled him when it rang in his desk drawer.

"Hello, Manny here, is this you?"

"Yes, it is. I have to meet with you. Can you spare some time for me this afternoon?"

"I have a lunch meeting until one, but I'm free after that."

"Very good. I'll meet you on the 2:00 p.m. Staten Island Ferry. Don't approach me, I'll approach you. Do you understand?"

"Yes."

"Good, I'll see you later."

As planned, Manny got out of the taxi at the Customs House at 1:45 p.m. and began to walk toward the ferry. Carlos was seated on the park bench to Manny's right. They both got on the 2:00 p.m. ferry, employing the same tactics Carlos and Faisal used to meet.

"Hello! How are you?" Carlos said cheerfully.

"Never mind, are you in trouble?"

"Possibly, I'm not quite sure."

"Did your friend's problems follow him down from Canada?"

"That's quite possible. Manny, I apologize if I must speak cryptically, but it's for both our benefits. The less you know, the less you'll be accountable for. I imagine you've read in the papers about poor Jack's death."

"I did. What a tragedy for the artistic community. He was such a talent!"

"Manny, I couldn't care less about the artistic community. What a loss for me! He was like my right hand when it came to his abilities with boats. Because of Jack's death, I need a new boat right away."

"Certainly, what do you need?"

"You are a tried and true friend. I can't buy a boat myself right now as my situation is somewhat tenuous. I would like you to buy it for me."

Manny reacted with a wry grin and arched eyebrow. "Really!"

"I will provide you with the cash. You will make the actual transaction through your business."

"You want me to launder your cash."

"For lack of a better term, yes."

"Where would we do this transaction?"

"I've been shopping online with a yacht sales business on the Jersey shore near Barnegat."

"Ah yes, I know it well."

"Ideally, we'd pick a day within the next week to make the purchase."

"Just like that?"

"Yes, as I said, I am under time constraints. From what I've been able to determine, if we make the transaction then and there with a wire transfer, it will not seem unusual. Our rationale for the purchase is that 'you've always wanted to take up deep-sea fishing and want to start with a used boat to decide whether or not you really enjoy the sport.'"

"Actually, I really have always wanted to try just that."

"Well, we're only going to need the boat for one, maybe two occasions."

"What will I do with the boat after your need passes?"

"You'll enjoy it. It's yours."

"Really?"

"Really. It's just my way of paying back a loyal, true, and proven friend."

Manny drew back his head as a sincere, full smile broke over his face. "What can I say?"

"That you are available to go shopping." Carlos grinned.

They set the day for the Friday after he and Atef were set to return from Delaware.

A sincerely grateful Manny Pabon ended the conversation with a proposal of his own. "Carlos, please allow me to express my gratitude as well."

"That is not necessary."

"Yes, it is. I am in good stead at one of the larger casinos in Atlantic City. Let me host you and a friend for the weekend with me."

"That is very gracious of you, thank you." Carlos felt in his heart of hearts he was not unlike a gladiator being allowed one last bacchanal before battle.

*****

Jack found himself feeling remarkably better only a couple of weeks after his brush with death. He was just about weaned off his morphine drip and had a few of his tubes removed. He was no longer bedridden but was still restricted to his quarters. Even so, just being able to walk about was a treat. Besides that, he looked forward to his sessions with his debriefers, especially Brian and Scott, whom he'd built a bond with them since the hospital.

On this particular day, Jack was visited by Brian, Scott, and a newcomer, Coast Guard lieutenant Todd Robles. After introductions and some small talk, Scott told Jack that Lieutenant Robles had some questions.

"Sure, anything."

"Jack, I understand on your boat rides with Reyes and his friends, Carlos expressed an interest in the Staten Island Ferry. Did he ever indicate what their intentions for the ferry were?"

"No, not really, but he specifically took notice of it on both the environmentalist cruise and on Orlando's boat. On the environmental cruise we had to slow down and alter course to let the *Barberi* pass by. He was immediately curious about the passenger load. On the cruise on Orlando's boat, he specifically had to show his friends a ferry passing by."

"What did he say about it?"

"Well, the thing of it is, I really don't know. He and his party were seated up in the front cockpit, and I was up at the wheel. They didn't even speak English among themselves—it sounded like Arabic to me."

"How do you know it was Arabic? Do you speak Arabic?"

"No, I don't, but one of the guys was the fellow I brought down from Canada that I knew as Tony. You guys say he's somebody else. I was told he was Pakistani. Maybe that was a lie too."

It was nearly impossible to hide Scott's and Robles's look of concern. Robles spoke up, "Pakistanis speak Urdu, not Arabic."

"Urdu, Arabic, it's all Greek to me."

Todd Robles let out a long sigh. "This is not good at all. When you took them out, did they show interest in anything else?"

"When we went up the Kill, Carlos asked to stop alongside Shooters Island. He pointed out the container ports in Newark Bay, and they all seemed interested in the oil refinery at Linden and Howland Hook."

Scott spoke up this time. "It just gets worse and worse, doesn't it?"

Brian was beginning to feel a little left out and jumped in, "Guys, you're making me nervous. How bad is this?"

"Bad enough. These guys are doing more than an amateurish initial surveillance. They're definitely pros. Jack, are you sure you couldn't make anything else out that they were saying?"

"Sorry, nope. Tony probably thought I knew too much even then. I was surprised he didn't try to kill me sooner."

Scott probed now. "Tell me about the kayaks again."

"Carlos told me he was organizing a kayaking trip to the Delaware Water Gap. He said he had two kayaks and needed six more. He gave a list of places to try. I ended up getting a good price on them in Brick Township, New Jersey. I was coming back when I nearly smashed into Brian and Louie's car. After Carlos picked me up at the police station, he asked me for the information on the kayaks and said he'd take care of the rest himself."

"Do you remember where the place was where they found the kayaks?"

"Sure, give me a piece of paper and a pen." Jack wrote down the information. "The salesman was a kid named Dan. He said he had a friend with a trailer, and Carlos wanted to buy one too. That's where I left off."

"You know, a year ago we had a solution for situations like this," Robles lamented.

"What do you mean?" asked a curious Brian.

"We've had to make cut backs to our Maritime Safety and Security Teams. But there were guys in rib boats who did intense harbor security, escorts, and boardings. They were like our Green Berets."

"What you mean by 'had'?"

"They transferred some of the MSST units to Boston in an economic move."

"So what protects the harbor now?"

"Whatever remains of the Coast Guard presence, both regular and Coast Guard Auxiliary, the New York City Police, the New Jersey State Troopers, and Port Authority Police."

"Well, what about the Coast Guard helicopters?" Brian asked.

"They were transferred out of New York years ago. The nearest helicopters are in southern New Jersey and Cape Cod."

"That sucks."

"That it does, Detective. That it does."

"Jack, how knowledgeable of a seaman is this fellow Reyes, or for that matter, any of the fellows he was with?"

"I think that was the reason I was around."

"Do you know where Carlos stored his kayaks?"

"No idea."

"Scott, we've got to speak to that kayak dealer and see what he remembers."

"Good point."

*****

"Good morning, gentlemen, I'm Brett Blasingame. Welcome to Garden State Boat Sales. How can I help you?"

Manny Pabon was his most gracious self as he introduced himself and Carlos. "Good morning, Mr. Blasingame. I'm Manny Pabon, and this is my brother-in-law Peter Santiago. We spoke last Thursday about my interest in purchasing a boat."

"Yes, Mr. Pabon, how nice to meet you. You're the gentleman who called wanting to entertain your ambition for deep-sea fishing. Good for you!"

"Yes, I've spent some time since we last spoke investigating your online site. I've decided to purchase a used boat. If I find I have no ability or boating does not meet my expectations, well then, I haven't made an exorbitant investment."

"What price range would you like to stay in?"

"Approximately $80,000, give or take a few thousand."

The veteran salesman seamlessly suppressed his enthusiasm and moved to close his sale. "You mentioned you've investigated our online site. Did you see any vessels that caught your interest?"

"Yes, I did. It came down to three. A thirty-one-foot Maxum 3100 SE, a thirty-four-foot Sea Ray I/O Sundancer, and a thirty-eight-foot Luhrs 380 convertible."

"Which boat do you favor?"

"I'm not completely sure. Which do think would be the most suitable for my purposes?"

"Well, all three are good choices in your category. What is your level of ability as far as seamanship goes?"

"Mine is limited, very limited. Peter here has had some exposure to boating though."

Carlos offered a wan smile.

"That's all right. I can do two things. First, I'm going to suggest something I really hope you'll consider. Take the Coast Guard boating safety course. Boating can be a terrific pastime, especially when you understand the intricacies of it. Secondly, if you purchase from us, I will throw in lessons here at our facility. Now then, about your choices. At this stage of the game, the Maxum and the Sea Ray, while both fine boats, are probably more than you can handle or need. The

Luhrs, in my opinion, is perfect for you at this point. It is a reliable craft, and this particular one is in excellent condition. Would you like to see it? It's right here in the yard."

"Yes, we would."

Blasingame took them out into the yard and to the white cabin cruiser. Manny and Carlos were now caught up in the moment and enjoying themselves. They climbed up onto the boat and were surprised at the level of luxury inside the cabin. They hemmed and hawed for an hour and a half while Blasingame entertained their every question. Then came the time when the question had to be asked.

"The website listed the price at $83,900. Can you do anything with that?"

"Will you be financing?"

"No, we'll be making the payment in full, if the price is right."

"$82,000."

"Would you do anything more if I paid via wire transfer today?"

"I can bring it down to $80,000 and throw in the lessons. That's the best I can do."

"Does it have to be registered?"

"We'll take care of that."

Before lunch, they'd bought a boat. Manny was sincerely thrilled, but a sadness was eating in at Carlos, though he managed to hide it well.

Blasingame asked if they might be staying over since they were close to Atlantic City and if they'd like to take a lesson on Saturday. They could learn enough to get the boat safely to and from the slip and would pick up enough basic navigation skills to not be a menace to other boaters. Carlos was able to schedule a couple of additional lessons on the following Thursday and Friday for an additional fee, which they gratefully paid. Carlos would continue on to Delaware Saturday that week as prepared as possible. Carlos walked out of the dealership very satisfied with both their display business acumen and having patched the gap in his operational situation. Manny, for his part, walked out feeling as if he'd just won the Lotto.

CHAPTER 33

Jack's health was improving every day, but his psychological state had taken a turn for the worse. Finally having realized the consequences of his actions, Jack had developed a sense of guilt that was pushing him to the point of self-loathing, if not outright depression. He was overcome with remorse.

To bide his time and help with his depression, Jack put his newly acquired art supplies to work. He sketched most of the *Intrepid* but seemed most fascinated by the cavernous hangar bay, a repair and storage area under the flight deck that was one hundred feet wide, sixteen feet high, and approximately six hundred feet long. First, he sketched it as it was, a kind of present-day museum, but then he attempted to visualize and sketch it as he felt it must have appeared in the Pacific in 1944.

Jack wanted to capture the *Intrepid* in all its progressive variations, a difficult task. Since the ship's operational days, the flight deck had been modified to accentuate and accommodate the display aircraft. The arresting wires that had brought so many aircraft to a stomach-churning halt in just a fraction of a second had long since been removed as a safety hazard to clumsy tourists. The hangar bay had likewise been remodeled in order to support the *Intrepid's* current mission.

Describing a working warship like the *Intrepid* to someone not acquainted with service at sea is difficult. It's not unlike a son trying to completely understand a father's wartime experiences. The old warrior can provide selected vignettes that are almost always thoughtfully censored. Veterans always keep certain memories to themselves, too personal and painful to relinquish. A warship carries the life force of the thousands who lived, worked, and died within her hull.

One can board the *Intrepid* and be witness to the displays of her gallantry, but full comprehension is difficult. As Jack walked the hangar deck in the solitude of the early morning hours, he willed his imagination to take him beyond the static displays, back to the time when life on the *Intrepid* was a 24-7 operation. Twelve hours on watch and twelve hours off, there are no days off and no weekends, and this routine can go on for months on end. Life at sea is a place where time is rendered irrelevant. It's about flight operations, standing watch, working, eating, sleeping, and then doing it all over again. It's about the work, the fight, the life, and the relationships among the crew.

He forced himself to see beyond the cleanly swept deck and well-lit displays of this now properly retired lady back to the day when her hangar bay area was a beehive of sweat and activity, with a pervasive smell of lubricants. There would have been the din of a hundred voices, blowers, and tools. The monotone of voices would occasionally be punctuated by a raised voice as some petty officer barked at someone not moving fast or purposively enough. Then at sea, there were flight operations.

Jack contemplated the massive human sacrifices that had been made throughout her illustrious career. Young men his own age had put their lives on hold and thrown themselves wholesale into defending their country, the same one he'd disregarded until now. A goodly number of *Intrepid*'s sailors never returned home, going to their rest over the side, buried at sea in a weighted shroud. All in all, from her commissioning in 1943 to her final service in 1974, 272 men died on board. The thought made him feel very small. In his soulful quest to be absorbed into the ship's history, he could not imagine, however, where the search might take him.

On a night that he was not scheduled to be interviewed, Jack set up shop with his pad and pencil, seated on the platform that displayed the ship's bell in the second fire zone of the hangar bay. He was trying for a panoramic view of the area looking toward the bow. Bathed in theatrical lighting, he went about his work until he was startled by a presence there behind him. A fifty-something-year-old man in worn officer's khakis was standing behind him.

"Geez, you gave me a start. I didn't hear you come up."

"I'm sorry, Jack. I didn't mean to scare you."

"You know me?"

"Oh sure, I'm part of your protection. The name's Dom Langianella."

"You're one of my government guys?"

"In a way. I was a crewman on board the ship."

"Really! When, in Vietnam?"

"Actually no, I was on board during World War II."

"Wow, God bless you. You look great. Time has been very good to you."

"Thanks, God's allowed me to age well. I'm lucky, I guess."

"So you're not only a former crewman, but you're also part of my security detail?"

"That's right."

"Well, how cool is that. Listen, thanks for all you did in your time. I'm flattered to have you on my side."

"My pleasure, Jack. Now let me ask you, what are you drawing there, son?"

"I'm trying to get an in-depth view of the hangar deck. Then I want to show what it might have been like in your time, but to tell you the truth, I'm having a hard time visualizing it all."

"Well, maybe I can help. You see that area up forward, just behind where that TBM Avenger is parked?" He pointed to the World War II torpedo bomber that had been restored to pristine condition.

"Yeah."

"Well, on November 25, 1944, we were off Luzon in the Philippines. At about 1250 hours, we were struck by a kamikaze. Its bomb did terrible damage. It hit and penetrated into a ready room where members of the crew were waiting on standby. Damage control was working fires when we were hit by a second Kamikaze. It and its bomb came through the flight deck and detonated right there. All in all, sixty-nine people died that day. Everything was on fire. Armed and fueled planes being worked on went up. Gasoline and debris were all over the place. You couldn't see or breathe through the smoke. The screams and smell—it was unbelievable, Jack. Smells of burning gasoline, oil, wood, paint, and bodies. It was nasty, nasty stuff. Most of the men were much younger than you. They did what they had to in order to protect the country, like you are. Does that help at all, Jack?"

"Yes, sir, it sure does, thanks very much."

"Very good, I'm glad. I'm going to leave you to your work. I'll be seeing you around."

"Thanks, Mr. Langianella. It's been good talking to you. I look forward to seeing you again."

"Jack, please, it's Dom."

Jack returned to his sketch as Dom Langianella walked off and disappeared into the passageway that led to the fantail. It had been a short visit, but Jack's mind now raced. The old sailor's description seemed to open a door to the past for him.

*****

Two days later, Jack was receiving visitors again. Events had taken a serious turn. Brian, Louie, Al Krieger, and Scott Burton were accompanied by Lieutenant Robles. In addition, Scott and Al's agent in charge, George Denby, as well as Inspector Philip Halvorsen of the Joint Terrorism Task Force were there. They all set up in the conference room. Scott Burton took the chair of the meeting and did the introductions all around.

"Good evening, or more accurately, good morning, gents." That brought a few subdued smiles. "First of all, Jack, how are you feeling?"

"Much better. The last of my tubes is coming out this week. They say I'll make a complete recovery."

Burton's game face vanished, and a broad smile spread across his face. "Jack, that's the best news I've had all week. That's great, I'm happy for you. That's great news, dude, great news!" Scott addressed his next comment to the gathered group. "I've got to tell you all. I didn't think Jack would make it. I've seen many victims similarly injured who wound up wearing toe tags. Unfortunately, that's the last of the good news."

Jack asked, "Scott, what's going on?" The mood took a somber turn.

"Jack, gentlemen, we have a credible terrorist threat on our hands. The print that we lifted from Carlos Reyes's door came back. It matched a print that was recovered from Yemen in 2000 at a house used by the crew that attacked the USS *Cole*. It was unidentified then, but we now know it was Carlos's. We will now proceed under the belief that there is an active terrorist cell in New York well into the process of plotting some type of attack on this harbor. We don't know when or exactly how, but it is coming. Brian, has Orlando Rodriguez seen Reyes recently?"

"No, not since shortly after Jack was attacked."

"We have a search warrant for his apartments, so we can get a more accurate picture of what's being planned. We can't sit idly by waiting for events to unfold. We now have arrest warrants for both Carlos Reyes and Atef Khalid Mohammed. We have more than enough in immigration violations alone. Unfortunately, we don't know if there are any other co-conspirators at large. Jack, do you know of any other possible places they could hole up?"

"No, I only knew Carlos as living at the place on East Third Street."

Denby threw in, "Guys, we're way behind the curve on an act of maritime terrorism, and it could be more than one. Their interests seem to be in the waterways near and around Staten Island. The Staten Island Ferry seems to be on their agenda and maybe something else involving the use of kayaks. Lieutenant Robles, I assume we can count on the Coast Guard's participation in shoring up our defensive posture?"

Todd Robles stood up. "Yes, sir, our resources here, while fairly diverse in type and number, are now limited in respect to the expertise the MSST units still present. I'll take the report of this situation back to the district, and we'll act accordingly. The Coast Guard will probably elevate the MARSEC level to at least Orange. That would be MARSEC level II. If we come up with more evidence or additional threat information, I wouldn't be surprised if that level weren't raised to one. Inspector Halvorsen, can we count on the participation of your marine units?"

"Yes, and our aviation assets. Shall I liaison with the port authority and New Jersey State Troopers?"

"Yes. I'll also engage the services of the New York State Naval Militia."

Denby summed up. "Gentlemen, the APB goes out on Reyes and his buddy immediately. I believe they're still somewhere in the metropolitan area. They're going to know we're on to them as soon as we hit the house in Queens. We've got to find them, but it's going to be a helluva job. If you've got informants, squeeze them. Let's also keep one other thing in mind though: we can't panic the population, so let's keep them informed only as much as we have to. If people get spooked and refuse to go to work, we've given the terrorists a freebie. In the same respect, if we come up with concrete information confirming that something is imminent, we shut the harbor down. Safety first. Scott."

"Yes, sir?"

"This guy Reyes, he worked for that Pabon guy in Manhattan. Have we spoken to him yet?"

"No, sir, we didn't want to raise him up unnecessarily."

"That's understandable, but it's time to have a word with him. Let's feel him out. Scott, you and Al take care of interviewing him. We know he's a scumbag and not real likely to cooperate, but let's see what he'll tell us about Reyes. Before you see him, get an order and put his phone up. If he's got a cell, see if you can get it. Put that up too. Let's see how he reacts to your visit. Mr. O'Connor, have we got your attention?"

"Yes, sir."

"I understand you have a great deal of knowledge about this harbor's nooks and crannies along with small boating in and out of them. Can we tap your knowledge?"

"Certainly, it'd be my pleasure."

"Good man. Scott, Lieutenant Robles, see to providing him with what he needs."

"Done, sir."

Brian raised his hand. "Agent Denby, Inspector Halvorsen, if I may?"

"Certainly, Brian, what's on your mind?"

"We may have another asset worth taking into the fold."

"Who's that, Brian?"

"Orlando Rodriguez. Seeing as we're short on maritime resources, well, he owns a rather fast boat, has exceptional skills and excellent knowledge of Reyes. We should use him."

"Okay, Scott, you figure out how to integrate him."

"Yes, sir. One other thing, Staten Island has repeatedly been Reyes's focus. We might do well to consider the possibility that he might want to take up residence closer to his work."

"Good point, Brian. I'd rather not bring the local precinct cops into the fold just yet. I'll give that information to the Intelligence Division people out there. What kind of car does he drive?"

"A dark-gray Jeep Cherokee."

"Do we know his plate number?"

"No. I've run his name through the system to see if it's registered to him. Nothing."

"Brian, stay with that effort." They both knew that finding a dark-gray Jeep Cherokee in New York was like trying to find a needle in a haystack.

"Gentlemen, I think I'm speaking for Inspector Halvorsen: let's get it done. I want these two guys in the can soon." Denby didn't say more, but he was scared down to his soul that he might not be able to stop whatever was being planned. What if they were only able to react after the fact? It was a sober group that quietly left the *Intrepid* that morning.

*****

Scott and Krieger were at the Pabon Group first thing the next morning. They found their way through the exhibit spaces to the interior business offices and Manny's trusted secretary, Abigail Prince.

"Good morning, Miss. FBI." Both Scott and Al exhibited their credentials.

A very businesslike Ms. Prince smiled and shot back, "And a good morning to you, Officers. What can I do for you?"

"We'd like to speak with Mr. Pabon."

"About what?"

"We'll explain that to him. May we speak with him?"

"Sure, if he were here."

Burton was having that uneasy feeling again.

"When will he be back?"

"In a week or two. He's on vacation."

"Where did he go?"

"Didn't say." She didn't appear to be kidding.

Scott took out his business card and gave it to her. "When he gets back, ask him to call me." She was smug and had a great poker face. Scott couldn't help but think, *Is she just a good secretary covering her boss's ass, or is she something more?*

She took the card, and with the same disarming smile, and she said, "I'll do that."

They left and got in their government vehicle outside. As they did, Scott placed a call to the van down the block from the gallery, which was marked as belonging to a plumbing company.

"Any calls placed?"

"No, nothing."

"Stay on it and let me know immediately."

"Gotcha."

There would be no damning calls placed. Abigail was completely involved with Pabon, on multiple levels. She knew that you don't say anything on a phone you wouldn't want to say before a grand jury. Any calls she made that day were purely legitimate business. The call from her apartment that night was not. Manny took the news poorly.

CHAPTER 34

Manny Pabon made a beeline to confront Carlos and Atef in their room down the hall from his own at their plush Atlantic City hotel. He'd set them up in rooms decorated in a New Orleans motif that was just short of tacky.

Enraged, Manny barged into the room. "The fucking FBI was at my place looking for me this morning! What the hell have you gotten me involved in?"

Carlos and Atef had two working girls in the room. Carlos motioned to Manny to shut him up. "Manny, please! Ladies, could we meet you down at the casino in a short while?" He gave them each a hundred-dollar bill. They gladly accommodated him.

Once they'd left the room, Carlos turned to Manny. "What did I get you involved in? No, what did you get yourself involved in!" Even as he said it, he knew he had just said the wrong thing. He needed to calm Manny down. He couldn't afford to lose his cooperation.

"Shit, Manny, I apologize. That was wrong of me to say."

"You bet your ass you're wrong. You're not gonna play me!"

"No, Manny, I'm not. Tell me what happened."

"My secretary just called me. She told me that the FBI was in this morning and they wanted to speak to me."

"Did they say about what?"

"No, they wanted to speak to me personally."

"Did she tell them where you were?"

"She couldn't. She doesn't know." While still agitated, Manny seemed to be regaining his self-control.

"That's good, Manny, very good. It's time that we carefully consider our actions. Things are beginning to come to fruition. I believe I am their item of interest. We're not going to be imposing on you for much longer. My business interests will conclude sooner rather than later. Let's reevaluate the situation. I don't believe the authorities know where we are," pointing to Atef and himself, "at least at this point. And that, my friend, is how it shall stay. Gentlemen, we're going to have to be much more conscious of our security, especially with our cell phones. Only make calls that are absolutely necessary and keep them short and to the point. We have to conduct ourselves as if we're being observed and monitored at all times. The authorities can monitor a call by triangulating between cell towers. If, however, you or I are in a large apartment building or busy public area, it would be considerably more difficult to find precisely where the call was coming from or going to. Manny, do you have some money left of what I gave you for the boat?"

"I do."

"The cops know I drive a dark-gray Jeep. I think it's time that changed. Let's take a ride to Pennsylvania this afternoon and purchase a new car. We can register it in the name of your front business. The car dealer will temporarily register the vehicle on thirty-day Pennsylvania paper plates that are totally ambiguous and buy us time."

All a reluctant Manny could say while rolling his eyes was, "As the American saying goes, I guess, in for a penny, in for a pound."

After exchanging his dark-gray Jeep Cherokee for a green Volkswagen Passat, Manny and Carlos returned to Atlantic City that afternoon. The FBI visit had caused them to reconsider returning to New York, but prudence caused them to remain in Atlantic City, close to their newly purchased boat. It would be boat-handling lessons during the day and the casino at night. Saturday they could continue on to Wilmington for their meeting with Kurri and Gonsalves.

*****

Jack sat on a backless metal stool at a chart table on the flag bridge aboard the *Intrepid*. He was poring over New York Harbor charts that had been provided by Lieutenant Robles. A two-tiered control area resides within the upper decks of the island structure of most aircraft carriers, *Intrepid* included. There is the navigation bridge, from which the ship is actually controlled. The commanding officer, a captain, controls his ship from there. Aircraft carriers, because they are the hub of a naval task force, usually act as a flagship under the command of an admiral. He controls the operations of the entire task force from the flag bridge, which is one deck below the navigation bridge.

Jack quietly sat alone, studying and absorbed in his thoughts. *This particular area of the ship that most accurately portrays* Intrepid *as she was.* The decks still sported the same tired green linoleum tiles they had forty years ago, and the bulkheads had the same boring flaking pea-green paint.

Jack took the responsibility he'd been given by Special Agent Denby dead seriously. It was apparent to him that Carlos had some intention of attacking shipping in or from the Kill Van Kull area with kayaks probably carrying explosives. He knew there would most likely be at least six kayaks involved, but he didn't know how and from where and, most importantly, when. If Carlos and his compatriots were fast, they could launch from at least a half dozen locations along Staten Island and Bayonne, depending upon the distance to their targets. The Staten Island shoreline was porous and undefended with no guard rails or fences at most locations, and roads just ended at the water.

Jack was once again startled by a voice behind him. "Good evening, Jack."

Jack sat up straight. He turned to see Dom Langianella standing there. "I wish you wouldn't do that! You just about scared the shit out of me! Again!"

"I'm sorry. I didn't mean to startle you. This is where I worked as a navigator. What have you got there, charts? Can I help?"

"Harbor charts. I was asked to give my insights."

"What do you think?"

"Well, we know they have a number of kayaks, but we don't know where and how they will be used."

Langianella took a seat next to Jack and looked at the chart, which depicted Staten Island's north shore and the Kill Van Kull.

"Jack, didn't you say that this Carlos fellow took special interest in that area where the Kill Van Kull separates into Newark Bay and the Arthur Kill beyond?"

"I did say that, but not to you."

"Sure you did, how would I know otherwise? Anyhow, I'd take a close look at this place over here. This island, what's it called? Shooters Island. Look here, it's in the middle of everything. Shooter's Island is a key location, but there's probably nothing on it but bird shit and mosquitoes. Look at the tidal tables for the area around the Bayonne Bridge, right next to Shooters Island. The flow doesn't exceed more than a knot and a half on flood or ebb tides. Kayaks, they're those canoe-looking things, aren't they?"

"Yeah, but they're a little less stable."

"Kayaks could be feasible there. The waters off it could be a control point of some type. Jack, I have to continue my rounds. I'll see you again."

"Okay, Dom. It's been nice talking to you. Take care." Jack turned around to bid Langianella good night, but he was already gone.

Damn he's quiet, he thought to himself.

He couldn't help but wonder how the hell Carlos's people were going to approach a ferry undetected. There was just too much open water. Were they going to attack the ferry and something else? And in what order? It was all very frustrating. Every question seemed to lead to another question.

*****

Saturday morning, June 12, Carlos and Atef drove south in their new Passat on the New Jersey Turnpike toward Wilmington and their meeting with Kurri and Gonsalves. The week had been most fruitful. The boating lessons had helped both Carlos and Manny to become marginally competent in being able to control Manny's new purchase. Carlos and Atef had, in fact, left Manny at the boat that he'd named *Mariel*. Carlos made sure he also had his own set of keys for the boat. Manny and Carlos were very satisfied in the fact that they were able to comprehend the GPS and radar; they felt sure he could do what he had to with the boat.

Atef wisely told Carlos as they were driving, "We're going to have to have minimal contact with Manny from now on. It's good that he doesn't know where we're currently residing in New York. The American authorities are going to be on him when we get back to New York."

*****

In the meantime, Manny seemed to understand what was going to happen when he got back and had already contacted his attorney. He would steadfastly refuse to cooperate with the authorities and let his attorney do all his speaking for him. Even if he had to answer questions directly, he could not tell them what he did not know.

"Atef, you said you could get us technical support for these devices we're going to use?"

"I've already attended to that. The Syrians have an expert available to us. He is a retired naval officer trained in using these devices. He will arm them and show us the proper settings."

"We also must determine whether the two brothers we are meeting today can provide transportation for the devices and what their availability is. I believe we agree that the time factor has become limited. Our schedule will depend on conversations this afternoon. Once we speak to them, I can make my final arrangements."

After crossing the Delaware Memorial Bridge, it took another fifteen minutes to reach the Wilmington suburb of Newport. Kurri heard them arrive and met them on the front lawn with Charlie Gonsalves at his side. They continued on into the house.

"As sala'amu alaikum," Kurri welcomed Atef and Carlos to his home, and Carlos replied, "Walaikum as sala'am wa rahmatollahi."

They sat in the small dining room as Kurri served them iced tea and initiated the conversation. "Your call has left me with mixed emotions. I was thrilled that the time to make our contribution to the struggle has come, as was Charlie. I am apprehensive, however, about what might be asked of us."

Atef addressed them both. "First, thank you for your hospitality. All that is expected of you is jihad."

This roused Kurri and Gonsalves, who replied quietly but piously, "Allahu Akbar! Allahu Akbar!"

Atef continued, "My brothers, the moment to punish the great Satan has come, but we must be cautious. The Americans are raised up. This could not be avoided. They are aware of us as of now, but I believe they have not put their puzzle together. Their intelligence people, the police, and the FBI are not fools, and they will find a way to work around any bureaucratic constraints they may run into. In the meanwhile, Mr. Kurri, we have our devices secured in a storage facility in Salisbury, Maryland. Do you have a means of transportation to move them?"

"Yes, sir. If I have to, I can borrow an appropriate truck. If I may, what are these devices?"

"They are explosive devices that, in their current form, are inert. They can be activated at a time and place of our choosing."

"Are they obvious?"

"No. They're concealed within the empty frames of a washer and a dryer and packaged as new appliances."

There was a long silence as Wally and Charlie thought deeply of what had just been said. Atef patiently sipped his tea. Wally asked, "What will we be doing with these devices?"

Carlos calmly explained, "We need you to take them aboard your vessel and deliver them to New York Harbor."

Wally broke the silence after a few moments. "Allah is good, he has provided a scenario. At first, when you mentioned what we have to accomplish, I thought we would be faced with a physical confrontation with our captain and the remainder of his crew in order to gain control of the *Triton*."

"That very well may be the case."

"When you mentioned the washer and dryer, Allah handed us a gift."

"How so?" interjected Carlos.

"Before you contacted me, I had been trying to convince Greg, our captain, to replace the aging washer and dryer on board our vessel. The machines are on their last legs. He is in favor of doing so and asked me to look into it. A friend of mine is an insurance adjuster and often handles claims in which damaged commercial items have been salvaged and must be liquidated as best possible. I could suggest to Captain Mason that my friend, whom he knows, came across the appliances and got me a good deal on them. I can get them on board under that guise right before we leave and say we'll install them after our New York trip."

"What New York trip?"

"We have an obligation to be in New York in about three weeks to pick up a barge load of stone at the Brooklyn navy yard."

"Very good. I had wanted to move our schedule up because of the current situation, but this is better than I'd expected."

"We will leave on the morning of July 13. The trip up will take about two days."

Atef mentioned dryly, "Your captain and any other crew will have to be eliminated."

Wally reluctantly responded, "Yes, I understand. I know. I will see to that after we're at sea, on the way up." It was paradoxical. Wally was not as troubled by the fact he might be responsible for the deaths of thousands as he was with the death of one, his friend and captain. "My brother, I have to be candid with you."

"I would expect no less."

"I understand your need to compartmentalize your operations, but I sense a certain hesitancy while you're speaking with us. Considering the planning necessary to achieve our objectives, I would think it's time to be straightforward among ourselves. I would like to finalize most of the plan now, minimizing communication later."

Atef responded for both of them, "You make a very good point. Excuse our secretive nature. It is just how we're forced to conduct ourselves. I imagine you can understand the need to be so."

"Agreed."

Wally Kurri led the conversation into particulars. "I expect to arrive in New York City early on the morning of Thursday, July 15. Gentlemen, what should I do at that time? I know I'll be carrying an explosive device, but what is it and what am I doing with it?"

Atef looked at Carlos and nodded, gesturing to him to speak. "You're delivering two sea mines and depositing them in New York Harbor."

"We don't have any training in handling that type of thing."

"That's all right. We're going to bring an expert aboard for that portion of the operation. As you're coming up the coast, we're going to rendezvous with you by boat outside of Barnegat Bay, New Jersey. We will bring people out to assist you. One of those people will attend to all the technical issues relating to the mines. He will know when, where, and how to place them in the water. He may need some physical help at times. Please assist if asked."

"Understood."

"I would like you to arrive at the location we've chosen in New York between three and four in the morning, before first light."

"I can do that. Can you tell me where the location is?"

"No, you'll be told en route. That is more of a concern for the expert I'm bringing aboard. I have a particular route I want you to take. When you arrive at the lower New York Harbor, I want you to proceed in the rear side of Staten Island up the waterway known as the Arthur Kill."

"I know it well. You want me to continue on into and up the Kill Van Kull and reach your target area from the rear?"

"Precisely, Mr. Kurri. After you've done your work, proceed, pick up your legitimate cargo, and continue as normal. On your way back down to Delaware, we'll meet again off Barnegat, and I'll take my people off. You will be well paid, and I suggest you use that money to relocate. Now I have a few other instructions for you."

"Yes, sir."

Atef then related to them his standard procedure for dumping phones and other devices after their use and gave them a cell and GPS device.

"I don't expect you will be contested. The American government is currently financially gutting its Coast Guard. Units and craft that were in place six months ago have been reduced in the harbor. Still, their law enforcement agencies are formidable and will be on us if we get sloppy. That is why I say, now is our time."

Wally briefly added, "Gentlemen, I have a healthy respect for the Coast Guard and their capabilities through many personal experiences."

After brief farewells, Carlos and Atef were back on the road to New York. As they drove back toward Route I-95, Atef turned to Carlos and said, "I believe they will do well. They, Kurri especially, appear to be quite competent."

"I agree. I was quite impressed. The die is cast, my friend. There is no going back. I'll relate the timing elements to Damascus. Our expert should arrive on Thursday, July 8, which should give him enough time to properly establish himself."

CHAPTER 35

Anthony Thaci and Syed Remmalli had been at Islamaville for a month and a half, being treated to liberal doses of Shariah dogma for hours on end. At first glance, they found the imposition of Shariah law appealing. It was all very grand and noble—until one morning, after prayer, they were called to make their own martyrdom videos. They both prepared farewell letters to their families, along with their last will and testaments for whatever meager possessions they had. Ali Aziz's people did all they could to trap the boys in their commitment to *istishhad*, the act of martyrdom.

Syed Remmalli was completely brainwashed by the teachings of Sheik Ali Aziz. Anthony, youthful as he was, saw his situation more clearly. While he could appreciate the tenets of his faith, he now balanced them with a mental vision of himself as a *shaeed*, or martyred hero. Simply put, as an eighteen-year-old, he loved life more than what he increasingly began to regard as a drastic political statement. He realized the nagging hypocrisy of his older mentors and instructors while he was being asked to sacrifice himself.

Still, Anthony knew how dangerous it could be to reveal his lack of enthusiasm for his trainers' rationale, which he saw as a collection of dangerous fanatics who scared the crap out of him. He saw no way out of this godforsaken place that he'd learned to hate. Instead, he'd stay the course for now, hoping that possibly, in the end, he would not be forced into any drastic action and would be moved home. Possibly, he could get to a telephone and his father would somehow get him out of this mess.

Without any warning, on a warm Monday morning in late June, Anthony and Syed were told that they'd be leaving for an undisclosed location that afternoon. Though they both ached to ask questions about where they were going, they knew better. Too often, they spoke out of turn and felt the sharp burning sting of the cane across their backs, which their mentors seemed to relish. At 3:30 p.m., their head tormentor, Razi El Quaffi, loaded them and their baggage into a blue Dodge Caravan with tinted windows and drove them away.

*****

Manny arrived at his office shortly after nine on Monday morning, June 14. He was having his coffee when he found himself facing two rather stern-looking FBI agents.

Scott had his game face on. "Good morning, Mr. Pabon. I'm Special Agent Burton, and this is Special Agent Krieger. We're with the FBI. How was your vacation?"

Manny answered with obvious suspicion, "It was fine. What's this all about?"

"Mr. Pabon, do you know Carlos Reyes?"

"He works for me."

"In what capacity?"

"He facilitates grants to deserving artists."

"When was the last time you saw him?"

"He's been on vacation for a few weeks. Listen, what's this about? I'm not at all comfortable with your tone."

"Tone? I'm just asking a few questions. Did you vacation alone in Atlantic City?" Scott had pulled Manny's credit card records. Unwisely, Manny booked his hotel on his card.

"I did. Why?"

"Why two rooms?"

"I was with friends."

"But you just said you were alone, Mr. Pabon. Once again, sir, you were with friends? Who might they be?"

"That would not be a concern of yours."

"Interesting, a simple question engenders an automatic lie. A poor way to begin our relationship, wouldn't you say?"

"I forgot. You made me nervous."

"No, Mr. Pabon, lying made you nervous. You're sweating. How's your stomach feel, sir? It feels terrible, does it not? It's about to feel worse. Mr. Pabon, can you tell me why Mr. Reyes went to Canada recently? That's right, Manny, we know, and I'm sure you do too."

"That's it! If you have any more questions, speak to my lawyer!" He handed them his attorney's card.

Scott purposely turned it up another notch as he was about to leave. "Mr. Pabon, you are aware that it is a serious federal crime to lie to a federal officer during the course of an investigation. The federal prison system is full of such people. A nasty place our prison system is. You have drawn my complete attention, sir." Scott fixed his glare directly on Manny. "We'll speak again, sir. You can be assured of that, with or without your attorney being present, which of course would certainly be your prerogative. We will do so, however, next time, at our offices down at Federal Plaza. Until then, I would use that time to contemplate the future, your future that is. You have a good day, sir." As they left, he smiled at Manny's secretary, Abigail, in a very direct fashion. She was visibly pale; she unconsciously licked her dry lips.

After his visitors had left, Manny sat down nervously at his desk. They had gotten to him, and they knew they had. Manny ached to pick up the phone and call Carlos, but common sense told him otherwise. After two trips to the bathroom, he took a disposable cell from his desk drawer and left the office, telling Abigail he was going for a walk. He hailed a taxi on Seventh Avenue and told the driver to take him to Thirty-Fourth Street and Seventh Avenue.

Upon arriving at the corner, Manny walked to the Empire State Building. There, he became a tourist and rode to the observation deck. He took out his disposable phone and made his call, which would be lost among hundreds of other calls that were being made at the same time in that eighty-six-story building.

"Carlos, the FBI was at my office this morning. They know everything!"

"Manny, if they knew everything, you would not be making this phone call. What did they ask you about?"

Manny related the particulars of the visit. As Carlos listened to him, it was obvious just how unnerved Manny had become.

"They said they're going to take me into custody the next time!"

"Manny, calm down! If they had as much information as you believe, they would have already taken you into custody. They were trying to upset you, and apparently, they have. Let's meet at the boat Thursday morning at 10:00 a.m. We'll go out and take a peaceful ride and talk this out. Everything will be fine, I promise. Please remain calm until then, and speak to your lawyer."

"This is not good, Carlos. I'm telling you, this is not good."

"Try to calm yourself. We'll talk on Thursday." Carlos hung up. He told Atef of the conversation with Manny. It was apparent to both of them that Manny was becoming dangerously unhinged.

*****

Razi arrived with his two trainees at the apartment on Bay Street shortly after 11:00 a.m. on Tuesday, June 15. Even though they'd laid up at a Days Inn for the night, they were all beat from the trip. Both boys noticed that Razi's attitude didn't mellow until he was greeted by Atef and Carlos. His deference toward them was apparent immediately.

"As Sala'amu alaikum, my sheikh," Razi first addressed Atef then Carlos. As they embraced and kissed and greeted traditionally, Atef responded, "Walaikum as sala'am wa rahmatollahi, my brother." Much to Syed and Anthony's delight, they were similarly greeted as equals, as men.

After a few more brief expressions of welcome, Razi excused himself, announcing that he was going to return to North Carolina and left.

There were a few awkward moments before Atef spoke to the boys. "My brothers, you will be with us for a few weeks. Please excuse the spartan nature of your accommodations, but they are born of necessity. Take mattresses from the pile against the wall and set up in the front bedroom. At least for the time being, I would ask—no, I would insist—that you not leave the apartment without at least one of us to escort you. It is for your sake, so you don't get lost."

Carlos continued, "My brothers, we are on the brink of changing history, and you two will play an integral role. We must be discreet. Atef and I have cell phones for emergencies only. Now I notice that you have few belongings with you. This evening we shall take a trip to the local mall, get you some new clothes, and get a bite to eat."

That lifted the spirits of both of the boys. Things were looking better. Carlos continued to remake the point: "Gentlemen, you are the hope of Islam. We would like to treat you as such, but please, adhere to our few simple rules."

They both responded in chorus, "Yes, sir."

Carlos softly suggested, "Why don't you fellows set up inside and rest for a while. We'll wake you later."

They took the suggestion gratefully and dragged two mattresses into the front room overlooking the street and were asleep in short order.

*****

Wassim Bin Nouri had been well served by his years in the Syrian Navy. Now retired, the former chief petty officer had served on a number of different vessels and had been seriously wounded in 1973 while serving on a missile boat. As a result of that incident, he became recognized within the Syrian Navy as somewhat of a hero. At the completion of his lengthy recuperation, he was rewarded for his heroism by being chosen to attend an advanced Russian course in mine warfare in Leningrad, now St. Petersburg. Upon completion of the course, he educated personnel of Syrian and other Middle Eastern navies in the intricacies of mine warfare. While in Leningrad, he also learned the techniques of minesweeping and mine laying, along with the operation and technology of many non-Soviet bloc variations of mines. His national intelligence agency, the Air Force Intelligence Directorate, or Idarat al-Mukhabarat al-Jawiyya, gave him additional tasking. He also trained in the EOD aspects of land mines. His training resulted in participation with the United Nations antimine missions and symposiums. Much to his own and his intelligence director's satisfaction, he was granted a diplomatic passport that afforded him incredible ease of travel.

A meticulous individual, Wassim became a man in demand since his retirement and soon found that his consulting work paid handsomely. A loyal Baathist Party member, his talents opened doors to places he couldn't have previously imagined. He taught, surveyed, consulted, and when asked, performed certain special assignments that were sometimes high-risk.

Wassim didn't have to take every special assignment that was offered, but he did. He'd gotten used to the money, or more correctly, his wife and his son Ali had gotten used to their cultural upgrade. He used his newfound financial freedom in a number of ways. The family home in Latakia was renovated, and his wife received a generous stipend to maintain a luxurious lifestyle.

Recently, he was informed that he would be sent on a special assignment to New York in early July. While he was not given particular details, he discovered that the assignment would last a little more than a week. The consulate in New York arranged a series of meetings and appointments with the United Nations Demining Commission that would cover his presence. The fact that the meetings were a ruse was known to very few people, none of them in New York.

Wassim was provided with tickets, cash, and a disposable cell with one number in its memory. He was instructed to call that number upon his arrival at Kennedy International Airport. Wassim Bin Nouri could not possibly have imagined the magnitude of what he was about to be asked to do.

*****

Brian, Louie, Scott, Al, and Jack sat around the conference table in Jack's quarters on the *Intrepid*. They had been racking their brains for weeks and were no further along in understanding exactly what Carlos and Atef were up to.

"Jack, when you took your boat rides with these humps, did they ever indicate they wanted to go anyplace other than Staten Island?" Brian asked.

"Nope."

"So we've got no dispute that Staten Island or at least the waters around Staten Island are their possible target, right?"

There was a collective positive head nod.

Brian continued, "Carlos bailed after he figured that Jack here had given us the information he did. He obviously doesn't want to have his operation clipped before it gets off the ground. What's most important to these guys…"

"Is their operation." Scott continued, "I don't think either one is concerned about themselves other than because their participation is integral to the completion of their mission."

Brian continued, "Let's try to think in their heads. Where is their highest risk of apprehension?"

Al Krieger answered, "At locations where they might have to interact with authorities, like terminals, subways, toll booths, yada, yada, yada."

"Right, Al, so you know what that leaves us," Brian answered this time.

"They have to be someplace where that possibility is minimized and still allows them the ability to work. No subways to ride, bridges to cross, or anything similar. What's bothering me right now is I think these guys have quite possibly relocated out to Staten Island. Scott, when your guys interviewed the clerk in New Jersey at that sporting goods place, he ID'd Carlos, didn't he?"

"Yeah, he said he bought six kayaks and a used trailer."

"Where in Manhattan is anyone going to hide or discreetly move that stuff?"

"Don't know," answered Scott.

"Nowhere but, man, we've got all kinds of garages out on the island that you could lose that stuff in. Guys, I haven't seen Carlos and can't tell you where he might be, but if he's out there, he has some fifty-odd square miles to hide in. Think about it, it just makes sense. I know that the inspector doesn't want to panic the public, but

I think we need eyes and ears in the field who at least know what they're looking for."

Louie, not surprisingly, bolstered Brian's point, "Maybe the job can find a way to allow some sector cars out on the island to be on the lookout for odd things, like people moving kayaks on trailers?"

Scott jumped in, "I think this whole conversation should get kicked up to our bosses. They need to hear this, Brian. If you want, I'll take care of that."

Brian gestured in agreement, and Scott continued, "Brian, Lou, you both make very good points. Even beyond that though, we have to get proactive. We don't know how much time we have left before these guys act."

"Pardon me, Counselor. I stand corrected." Just the fact that they were beginning to get proactive lightened the mood.

Brian spoke again to the group in general, but more to Scott in particular. "In that last meeting, I suggested that we get Orlando and his boat involved. How about we get Orlando hooked up with Lieutenant Robles and at least get Orlando into the Coast Guard Auxiliary so we can use his boat legitimately?" Again, there was approval around the table. "One other thing comes to mind. Jack, you've met Orlando, haven't you?"

"Yeah, sure. I rode with him. He seems like a decent guy."

"Could you work with him?"

"Sure."

"Jack and Orlando could make a helluva team on the water. I mean, who knows the nooks and crannies of these waters better than Jack? I think it's time to get Jack out where he can be most useful. You know, maybe we should have the bosses out for another meeting. What do you guys think?"

There was unanimous agreement. Scott would act as the de facto spokesman for the group and make the meeting come to pass. Jack, although he had developed a place in his heart for the *Intrepid*, was ready to get sprung. As the meeting broke, everyone parted company with a newfound sense of purpose.

CHAPTER 36

Carlos was up and out by 7:00 a.m. on June 17 for his trip to meet Manny in New Jersey. Both he and Atef were in complete agreement on how to mollify or at least manage Manny's jangled nerves, so Atef remained behind to babysit Syed and Anthony.

The drive down the Garden State Parkway with the sun on his face and the warm breeze made the act of getting out of bed a pleasure. By the time he pulled into the yacht club parking lot in Barnegat, it was already eighty degrees and absolutely clear. Carlos grabbed the light lunch he'd packed, walked across the lot, and let himself through the cipher locked gate leading to the boat slips. Carlos saw Manny and called out cheerfully, "Good morning! How are you on this fine day?"

Manny, standing on the aft deck, saw him and waved back but much less exuberantly. Carlos disregarded Manny's dismal mood and climbed aboard, ever mindful that other part-time mariners were present and watching. He then addressed Manny. "Well, Captain, how about showing off your newly acquired skills? Let's get going!"

Manny started the engines with a faint smile. "Absolutely. Give me a hand, will you? Cast off my lines."

Carlos obliged and got back on the slip, first casting off the stern line and then the bow line just before he hopped back aboard. Manny put his rudder over slightly and applied a little power. *Mariel* moved smartly off from the slip and into the channel.

"You've been practicing. I'm very impressed. Nicely done." They stood side by side at the helm as Manny maneuvered slowly through the bay waters.

"We must talk about what's happened." Manny's tone was low and gravely.

"In a little while, but let's enjoy this beautiful day a bit first. Have you gone beyond the bay into the open sea yet?"

"No."

"Let's try it. We'll hone our skills."

Carlos, appreciating Manny's value as an asset, really wanted him to calm down. After an hour of sailing, they had exited the channel and were feeling the swells of the open sea.

"Manny, why don't we practice with the navigation equipment? Let's use the GPS to sail to a predetermined point. Try and pick a point away from the rest of traffic, and then we'll use the equipment to find our way back in."

Manny responded with only a nod while proceeding.

They continued to a point to the southeast with no other vessels in the vicinity.

"Now we can drift for a while and talk. What has you so disturbed, my dear friend?" Carlos broke out the lunches and drinks he'd brought with him and sat on the transom.

"These federal police seem to know so much. They've got me scared to death. I don't think I can handle being sent to prison."

"As I've said to you before, if they knew as much as you think they know, you'd be in custody right now. They're purposely doing what they are in order to produce just this reaction. Manny, you've allowed them into your head! They will continue to harass you in order to extract whatever information they can. That's why we've made sure that you have legal representation. Use it, let her guide you, and she'll handle your concerns. It is obvious that before Jack died, he told them some or all of the information he was privy to. You can't add to that, can you? Can you even confirm any of it? No, you don't have that knowledge, do you?" He was speaking to Manny much like an older brother might, even though Manny was ten years his senior.

"No, but what if they find out about the boat?"

"What if they do? Don't you own the boat?"

Carlos tried to reassure him for over an hour, but to no avail. Manny seemed worse than ever afterward. Now he was crying in deep sobs. "I can't sleep, I can't eat. I just can't get any rest." Manny dissolved into tears.

Carlos put his arm around him, trying to console him. "I know, I know. We'll get you your rest, I promise." Carlos excused himself for a trip to the head, leaving Manny sobbing at the transom. On the way back, Carlos removed the fire extinguisher from its mount on the bulkhead and walked back toward Manny. He came from behind Manny and, without warning, struck Manny a solid blow across the back of his head with the heavy metal extinguisher. Manny never knew what hit him. He went down hard, knocked unconscious, lying spread across the transom, with the back of his head split wide open and his skull fractured. The head wound was a mess and bled heavily. Carlos cautiously avoided getting blood on himself while he lifted Manny's lifeless legs over the transom and dropped his body into the rolling sea. He'd clean the mess up shortly, but he had one more thing to do.

Just then, Carlos looked aft, and there was Manny, bobbing in the sea behind the boat. *The contact with the water must have revived him,* Carlos thought. He was waving and screaming in the water.

Carlos took the controls, opening the distance between the two of them, and then turned the boat back toward the struggling Manny. When he was pointed directly at Manny, he buried the throttle at full ahead. As Carlos closed the distance rapidly, Manny's terrified expression showed above the waves as he realized what was about to happen. Manny stopped flailing and accepted his fate. As the boat ran over his body, there was a slight thump underfoot. Passing the spot, Carlos looked aft over the stern to his wake. There was nothing, not even a telltale pink blur. Carlos thought it unfortunate that it had to come to this, but Manny had become an unacceptable risk. Now he would have his rest.

Carlos took the boat a few hundred yards more, cut the engines again, and attended to the cleanup. Luckily, the blood splatter was restricted to the transom and other composite surfaces, easily washing away. He then plotted a course with the GPS and made his way back to the slip. When night fell, Carlos left the boat and took Manny's car keys, which he'd left in the cockpit near the helm on the boat.

He moved the car away from the yacht club into the parking lot of a nearby bar. He then walked back to his car, quietly left the area, and drove back to New York. It would take a few days before the bar owner would report the apparently abandoned car to the police. They would run the plates, and they'd come back with no wants or warrants. It would eventually be towed to a private impound area where it would accumulate a hefty storage fee.

*****

Bringing Orlando into the fold had not been all that easy. True to his word, Scott had organized another meeting on the *Intrepid* with the powers that be, including Inspector Halvorsen and Agent in Charge George Denby. The concerns about Carlos and Atef had expanded well beyond 1 Police Plaza and 26 Federal Plaza, however, reaching all the way up to the national level. The FBI's counterterrorism unit in Washington had properly identified Carlos and his associates. There was no doubt that some type of terrorist act was coming down the pike. Now it was their case and up to them to figure the when, where, and how.

Denby and Halvorsen listened to Brian's theory about Carlos possibly being on Staten Island and found his logic compelling. They also agreed that it would be beneficial to have Orlando and his boat brought into the fold. It was an unusual practice to bring a civilian witness into a case, but considering their present shortness of afloat assets and given Orlando's personal knowledge of Carlos, they decided to take the unorthodox approach.

Denby asked Todd Robles to make sure the appropriate applications were made with the Coast Guard Auxiliary. He further instructed Scott and Brian not to mention anything about Jack being alive and being Orlando's potential partner until after Orlando had completely agreed to participate.

They had to enact other protective measures. The Coast Guard raised the warning levels to MARSEC level II. Throughout the harbor, maritime company tugs, barges, ferries—everyone—increased their security postures. The public was only told that the elevated level was a precautionary measure due to an increased level of terrorism-related chatter.

Finally, Inspector Halvorsen spoke to his chain of command and arranged for more intelligence street presence on Staten Island through increased patrols known as Hercules Units. They would be acquainted with terrorist threats and would be alert for any movement of recreational boating craft, such as kayaks, through the streets. For the first time, Staten Island would see the spectacle of a critical vehicle response, or CVR, of seventy-six police cars descending simultaneously and unexpectedly on one location, a bold display and statement of deterrence.

On a late June night, Brian called Orlando at his apartment and asked if he could stop by to discuss something. Brian brought Scott with him and made the pitch for Orlando's participation. Orlando was enthusiastic about becoming involved and jumped into the operation headfirst. Aside from it being a chance to see justice done, it also allowed him, at some level, to regain his self-dignity. He thought he'd been relegated to the background. But now with him on board, the ever-growing task force had the *Sofia* at its disposal; this could come in handy, especially considering some of its advanced electronic systems, including its forward-looking infrared equipment that he had installed at his own expense to address night patrols in the areas around the Narrows, Kill Van Kull, and Arthur Kill.

As requested, Todd Robles fast-tracked Orlando's application into the Coast Guard Auxiliary. The Coast Guard was trying to compensate for the reduction in MSST units in the harbor, and now the *Sofia* would be one of the most capable vessels involved in the operation.

A few days later, there was another meeting when Brian and Scott returned to Orlando's apartment on East Third Street. Orlando was pleasantly surprised to see Brian and Scott at his door, even if it was 10:30 p.m. "Gentlemen, how very nice to see you!"

"Orlando, we have something to show you. Can you come with us for an hour or so?"

"Sure, but can you tell me what this is about first?"

"No, we're going to a secure location. Just indulge us?"

"Okay, let's go."

They got into Scott's Chevy and headed across town.

Fifteen minutes later, they stood on the pier under the mass of the USS *Intrepid*. Brian explained, "We have a facility aboard the ship we use as a command center. It is completely secure." Orlando was understandably impressed. "Orlando, how would you have liked to work with Jack O'Connor?"

"You know, I would have liked it. He was a nice enough guy and a great sailor. I gave him a ride on *Sofia* back to his place in Brooklyn one day. He knew the ins and outs of this harbor better than some of the rats who live here. Poor guy really didn't deserve the end he got. I felt very bad when I heard about his passing."

Brian couldn't help himself, shooting Scott a quick sly grin that Orlando couldn't see as they passed through the inner passageways of the ship. For his part, Scott maintained his stoic demeanor.

Orlando was clearly impressed. "Wow, this is something else!"

Brian showed Orlando into the meeting room, and they sat down at the table. He set up what they were there for. "Orlando, we have a partner for you and the work we asked you to do using *Sofia*." After bit of small talk, he had planned to tell him Jack's story before actually introducing them, but then the small talk just kept going. In the meantime, Scott brought Jack into the room, assuming Brian had already brought Orlando up to speed about Jack. Orlando turned to see Jack standing in the door. The color completely left Orlando's face.

"Whoa! Whoa, Madre Dios! What the fuck!" Orlando stood, with his back plastered to the rear bulkhead of the room. For his part, Jack stood speechless amid the chaos of his reunion gone awry.

"Orlando, easy, easy! I'm sorry, we didn't mean to scare you!" Brain said, trying to calm Orlando.

The best Orlando could do was to stammer in return, "What... what the fuck?"

Scott sat them all down at the table and explained Jack's entire story in detail. After settling down, Orlando swore an oath to keep secret everything he had just been told. The plan was for Jack to remain living aboard the *Intrepid*, and they would both be paid as government contractors. Each night, Orlando would pick Jack up from the pier in *Sofia* and patrol the harbor until daybreak. Two victims of Carlos's mayhem were now working for the same thing: justice, a return of their dignity, and yes, some small measure of revenge.

*****

Wassim Bin Nouri entered the country on a Thursday morning in June aboard an Air France flight. He was met by Abu Hagali, aide to the Syrian Mission to the United Nations. Mr. Hagali was not there as a friend; instead, his orders from the mission were to ensure Wassim's admission with the least amount of physical restrictions. It was Wassim's responsibility to patiently appear diplomatic, professional, and nonthreatening. His blue suit fit his wiry five-foot six-inch frame impeccably, and his demeanor matched his appearance. It was time for Hagali to do what he did best.

Wassim and Hagali were politely ushered into a small room to the side where a male customs officer asked Wassim the reason for his visit, where he'd reside while here, and how long he planned to stay. He answered slowly in a soft, measured tone, attempting to put the TSA officer at ease. His diplomatic status spared him the indignity of a personal search. Their questions answered, Wassim was then told he would be required to report to the Department of Homeland Security at 26 Federal Plaza on a daily basis for the duration of his visit. Hagali went on the offensive.

"Excuse me, Officer. Do you not understand that Mr. Bin Nouri has diplomatic status?"

"I do, sir, but still, he must report daily," answered TSA supervisor Ken Richmond. He was polite but quite matter of fact.

"Mr. Bin Nouri is an esteemed member of our mission, and what you are doing here is nothing short of profiling. Mr. Richmond, because of Mr. Bin Nouri's good works in his field, there are innumerable children in what you Americans refer to as the Third World who have not lost their lives and limbs to the plague of land mines. There are places where he is held in higher regard than your Mother Teresa. I demand to speak with someone in authority. This cannot stand!" Hagali's outrage was measured and calculated. TSA Supervisor Richmond made a short phone call, and ten minutes later, TSA terminal manager Ursala Johnson entered the room. She calmly addressed Hagali.

"I'm Terminal Manager Johnson. How can I be of assistance?"

"You may be of assistance by rescinding this insulting order that will require my esteemed colleague Mr. Bin Nouri to report daily as if he were a common thug! This is profiling and a direct insult to not only me and Mr. Nouri but to the Syrian people. Do you know why Mr. Bin Nouri is here, Ms. Johnson?"

"I assume, as he has said, that he is here for meetings with the UN Commission on Land Mines."

"That is correct. I then fail to understand why this personalized attack on Mr. Bin Nouri's integrity continues. What is it that you fear from him? Do you have some other information about his intentions that I should be aware of?"

Johnson flatly responded, "I cannot respond in that regard."

"Cannot or will not, madame?" Johnson did not reply. Hagali continued passionately pleading Wassim's case.

"Ms. Johnson, Mr. Richmond, I must tell you that this situation is rapidly descending into an unfortunate diplomatic incident. I will be filing a report with your state department. I cannot allow the seriousness of Mr. Bin Nouri's mission to be diverted or distracted by this vindictive assault on Syrian honor! If correcting this slight is beyond either of your capabilities, I would suggest you put me in contact with someone who can, or I visualize my ambassador having a personal conversation with your secretary of state this very day!"

Terminal Manager Johnson excused herself and went back to her office, where she called her supervisor, Federal Security Director Henry Plecher. "Mr. Director, this is Terminal Manager Johnson. I'm having an incident at the entry point." Johnson filled her boss in on what had happened to that point.

"Johnson, does this fellow show up on our lists?"

"Yes, sir, he does."

"Why?"

"He is an armaments expert, mines."

"That's what he's here for at the UN, isn't it?"

"Yes, sir."

"Johnson, I'm awfully busy today. I'll tell you what. Back off on the daily reporting. Apparently, he's here to do positive work at the UN. Check his hotel reservations and have him followed for at least today and maybe tomorrow. If he turns out to be lying, pull him in, but if not, well, does this look like it would be worth an all-out incident?"

Johnson caught the drift. "Not really, sir."

"Johnson, by the time we get spun up for a full surveillance, this guy is going to be long gone back to Syria. Do I have to come down, or can you handle this?"

"I've got it, sir." She walked back down to the entry point office where Wassim, Hassan, and Richmond waited. She relished the opportunity of shining for her boss when given an additional responsibility. All she had to do was cut this one insignificant pain in the ass loose.

"Mr. Bin Nouri, Mr. Hagali, I've consulted with my superior and apprised him of our situation here. He is acquainted with Mr. Bin Nouri's good works and has agreed to rescind the requirement to report daily."

This time Wassim answered, "On my behalf and on behalf of Mr. Hagali, thank you ever so much, Ms. Johnson. I regret my presence has caused so much extra work and aggravation. I appreciate your diligent efforts in finding a positive solution to the problem."

"Mr. Wassim, you're staying at the St. Raymond?"

"Yes, I am."

"We will verify that."

"Please do."

Johnson turned to Richmond and said, "Ken, see Mr. Bin Nouri on his way. Good day, sir."

Wassim fetched his baggage and laptop and was on his way. In the taxi into Manhattan, Wassim turned to Hagali with a smile. "My brother, you are an extremely able individual. I must inform the ambassador of the level of talent he has in his employ." Hagali smiled coyly. They made pleasant small talk for the remainder of the trip.

A little more than an hour later, he found himself checking into his favorite Manhattan hotel, the small, discreet Hotel St. Raymond on East Fifty-Third Street. An older establishment from a bygone time, it offered him a level of service not available at other midtown tourist traps. Wassim saw the St. Raymond as a fitting symbol of his stature.

Prior to leaving Syria, he'd been told he would be serving the needs of jihadists. He had already decided that he would not allow these madmen to dictate terms to him. Wassim was the keeper of his own fate and would speak with them at his convenience. He was a professional and was well aware of how to maintain his security posture. Wassim would settle in and then call from his room.

Wassim unpacked, and after fastidiously assuring himself his clothes were neatly arranged in the closet and dresser, he took out the cell phone he'd been given and dialed up the only number in its memory. Atef answered.

"I've arrived. What are your instructions?"

"Tomorrow afternoon at three o'clock, walk out and away from your hotel at least to the next avenue and hail a random taxi. Ask to be taken to Staten Island, to the corner of Bay Street and Hylan Boulevard. We will meet you there. I have a green Volkswagen Passat. The taxi driver may very well be reluctant to go to Staten Island; it is an expensive trip. If that is the case, show him some currency. Do you have American money yet?"

"I do. That will not be a problem."

"Good. Allow at least an hour for the trip. I will be there at the appropriate time."

"I will see you then."

CHAPTER 37

The following morning, Wassim arrived at the UN office for a meeting about the neutralization of land mines in Cambodia. The meeting lasted until slightly before noon. After returning to the hotel and changing, he departed to catch a cab per Atef's instructions. He gave the driver a fifty-dollar bill and said, "Drive south immediately, no questions please." The cab driver, already fifty bucks ahead of the game, had no complaints when told he was going to Staten Island. Wassim sat back and enjoyed a pleasant ride.

The drive, slightly hindered by the onset of rush hour, took a little more than an hour. Wassim got out of the cab at the corner of Bay Street and Hylan Boulevard. The corner was an unremarkable mix of tired commercial retail businesses housed in two-story buildings. Wassim immediately saw the green Passat parked on Hylan Boulevard just off the northeast corner of Bay Street. Wassim walked purposefully to the car and got into the rear driver's side door. They exchanged greetings as Carlos pulled from the curb.

"Welcome, Wassim, I'll try to make this brief." Carlos looked into the rearview mirror and smiled at him as they drove.

"You must be the gentlemen my briefer referred to as Carlos, and you are Atep."

"Atef."

"Yes, pardon me, Atef. You gentlemen have two Italian MN-103 Manta mines in your possession?"

"We do, at a secure location."

"Are their batteries with them?"

"I have been assured that the devices are complete in all respects," said Atef confidently.

"These mines are powered by lithium batteries. The batteries are generally kept separate and in cool storage to prolong their lives. They are only placed in the devices just before they are deployed."

"They are stored as we received them. They came prepackaged and sealed."

"I believe I know who your supplier is. They are usually reliable. Where are the mines now?"

"In a storage facility in Maryland."

"Is that facility climate controlled?"

"I don't know."

"Please pull the car over, right here."

Carlos did so without question. He found that Wassim projected a certain degree of authority in his persona.

While passing through the waterfront area on Front Street, Wassim had noticed a nautical chart shop snuggled in next to a garage to his left. "Do you know the area where the devices are to be planted?"

"Yes, of course."

"Go in there and purchase a chart of that area for me."

Carlos did as he was asked and was back out in ten minutes. They continued on another quarter of a mile when Wassim asked Carlos to stop again. "Stop next to that seawall over there. Let's talk."

"My brother, I live a short distance away, and we can speak there in somewhat more comfortable surroundings."

"Not necessary. Here will serve the purpose adequately. What is your plan?"

Carlos laid out what he had planned in detail, including when he expected the mines to arrive. Wassim seemed appeased.

"It is all reasonable, but I need you to do a few things for me. First, find out if the facility where the devices are stored is climate controlled or, better yet, air-conditioned. How long have these devices been in storage?"

"About two and a half months."

"That's not bad. Do I have any way to examine the packages they're in, to see if the batteries are there?"

"Not really. They should be moving up to us within the week."

"Well, if the batteries aren't there, this will all be pointless. So I need to know. Secondly, take that chart and mark, lightly in pencil, where these devices are to be placed. Other than that, I'll meet you at the same corner where you picked me up at 7:30 a.m. on Tuesday morning. Everything else we have to discuss can be spoken about after that. Now take me to the ferry please. I have a dinner appointment this evening."

Atef smiled to himself; he appreciated this old sailor's style. Carlos, on the other hand, was experiencing the same sense of ill at ease and subservience he'd felt when Atef first came to New York. He didn't know whether or not he trusted Wassim, but he was sure he disliked him.

*****

Levant's shipyard was located just outside of Wilmington near the Delaware Memorial Bridge and was home to LePlane's Towing. The facility was a bare-bones wooden affair in appearance, a throwback to the days of World War II when it had been built to supplement the need for dockage. Bill LePlane had a long-time arrangement with Greg Mason's father that transferred over to his son and the *Triton*.

On June 13, Wally pulled down to the pier in a delivery truck with his neighbor, Cal Winstrum, who owned a small parcel delivery business. Cal thought he was just doing a favor for his neighbor down the block who coached his kid's soccer team. The transfer of the "washer and dryer" went quickly. Cal's truck had a pneumatic lift gate that made rolling the devices on and off fairly easy. The truck was met by a mobile crane at the head of what was known as Echo pier, the last of five in the yard. The crane trundled the two devices the last hundred or so feet down the pier and placed them aboard as Greg Mason watched.

"I didn't think you'd it make on time. As soon as you get them lashed down, we'll be on our way. Thanks again for helping find them so cheaply."

"I'll take care of it, Cap, and we'll be out of here in fifteen minutes." He held true to his promise, and the devices were lashed down and lines were cast off at 8:35 a.m. Wally then joined Mason down in the pilothouse.

"How'd you make out with the price?" asked a curious Mason as he slowly backed out into the channel with a prolonged blast of the horn.

"How about $900 for both units?" He was really overplaying his hand.

"Really? That's great! We'll install them after we get back down. Will they fit through the hatch?"

"Just barely, but we'll have to heft them around a little bit."

"Don't worry, just make sure they're secure."

"I'll give it another look before we get outside."

By 11:00 a.m., they had cleared Lewes and were ten miles off of Wildwood, New Jersey, when Wally decided it was time to dispose of the crew. He called both able-bodied seamen out on the aft deck and made sure they were out of Mason's view from the pilothouse. He pulled a Smith & Wesson 9 mm from his rear waistband and shot them both in the chest before they could react. One fell over the starboard side immediately. Wally pushed the other overboard with some weights around his midsection. Wally trusted that the deep, loud throbbing of *Triton*'s diesels masked the sound of the shots. A moment later the phone on the aft bulkhead rang.

"Wally, what was that popping sound?"

"Cap, we've got a problem. Could you come down to the fantail?" There was no emotional tone in Wally's voice. He had given himself over to what he perceived as his holy mission.

"I'll be right down."

Wally had been truly apprehensive about this moment for a very long time. This was not something he wanted to do, but he understood it had to be done. As soon as Greg Mason cleared the hatch, he was confronted by a purposeful Wally with a blued automatic pistol in his hand.

An incredulous Mason could only say, "Wally, what the fuck?"

He didn't prolong the moment, but raised the 9 mm, saying only, "I'm sorry, Greg. I really am." He put one round into the middle of Greg Mason's forehead. Mason fell backward with both eyes open.

Wally wrapped some chains and other weights around his midsection and gently shoved Mason's body into the blue water of the Atlantic Ocean to join his mates.

Wally called Charlie in the engine room, "Charlie, it's done. They're all gone."

"Allahu Akbar!"

Wally answered flatly, unemotionally, "Yeah right, I'll be up in the pilothouse."

Wally went up in to the pilothouse, took out the GPS he'd been given, and adjusted his charts to reflect the pickup point that was indicated. He adjusted the throttle. Then he took out the cell phone he'd been given and made his call. After it rang twice, he disconnected. *Triton* proceeded forward slowly in the swells of the gray overcast morning.

*****

George Denby called Scott Burton and Al Krieger into his office.

"Guys, please have a seat. You'll need to be sitting for this one. This Carlos Reyes case just got a little stranger, or I should say a lot stranger." Denby had their rapt attention. "A guy on a party fishing boat hauled in an eight-foot bull shark off the New Jersey shore the other day. When they got back to the pier, he cut the shark open and found this in his stomach." Denby reached inside a manila envelope, took out an eight-by-ten glossy photo, and slid it across the desk to his agents. It was a photo of a severed left hand with an onyx ring on one finger. Even the stoic agents recoiled slightly.

Denby continued, "They printed the hand for missing persons, and are you ready for this? It belonged to Manny Pabon!"

"Wow," was all that Scott could muster. "I didn't even know he was missing."

"Neither did I. These guys are aggressively covering their tracks. I want you to take this picture out and re-interview Manny's secretary."

"Okay. For what it's worth, I think you're right. We're running out of time." They took the photo and left the office as Al turned to Scott. "You want to go now?"

"Oh yeah, right now." Scott's eyes flashed with anger.

They returned to their office, briefly reviewed their notes, and headed for the parking garage. Pabon's office was just a few minutes away.

Abigail Prince stiffened when she saw the agents enter and braced herself for the discomfort she knew was about to come her way.

Scott led. "I hope we haven't come at a poor time. We have a few questions."

"Your arrival is always at a poor time." Her hackles were all the way up.

"I'm sorry you feel that way, Ms. Prince. Is Mr. Pabon in?"

"No, he is not."

"Where is he?"

"I do not know. He is out of town. I don't know where."

"You really don't, do you?"

"No, I do not."

"There's a note of fierceness in your tone. You resent not knowing where he is, don't you? He's more than your boss, isn't he?"

After a prolonged silence, she replied, "We've been together for a very long time. Why are you here?"

"When did you last see him?"

"More than a week ago. Why?"

"Ms. Prince, you know Manny's associates, and I'm sure you understand that a number of them are dangerous people."

"I know no such thing. Listen, make your point."

Scott softened his tone. "Ms. Prince, Abigail, if I may, when you associate with such people, eventually, when and if it suits their needs, they will turn on you. Ms. Prince, regrettably, I have to inform you, Manny is dead."

Abigail's eyes widened in panic, and she shouted, "You're lying!" Her hands gripped the front of her desk, her nails digging in until Scott could hear them scrape.

It was then that Scott played his card and placed the photo of the severed hand in front of her. She turned stark white and vomited on her desk, then she recoiled back in her chair.

"Ms. Prince, is that Manny's ring?"

She could only give them a positive nod. She struggled but failed to regain her composure. Scott and Al helped her clean up after herself.

Finally, after about fifteen minutes, she was able to ask, "How?" She glared at the agents, her eyes dark with accusation.

"I don't know how it happened, but the hand was found in the stomach of a dead shark." Scott tried to be as consoling as possible, but considering the subject matter, it was nearly impossible.

"Jesus Christ! Where, ah, where ah, is the rest of him?"

"I don't know. Abigail. Why was he down in New Jersey?"

"I really don't know. At times he went out of town on business trips. He purposely wouldn't tell me when, where, or why he was going. He used to tell me it was for my own good. Maybe it was after all."

"How so?"

"Look, why am I talking to you? I really don't know if I should be."

"Look, Abigail, we're just talking. You're not suspected of anything, and you're not the focus of our investigation. We came over only to speak with you about Manny. Manny's associates are of interest to us, especially Carlos and a fellow named Atef. Do you know those men?"

"Carlos, yes. The other fellow you mentioned, no."

"It's Special Agent Burton. This is Special Agent Krieger, but please, I'm Scott, he's Al. Abigail, you don't seem to be an evil person, but Manny was in the company of people who we've come to recognize as just that."

"Manny was not evil! He treated me very well."

"I'm not going to disagree with you, and I'm sure you've seen a different side of him. Mr. Reyes and Atef seem to be leaving a path of death and destruction though, and we think, although we cannot prove it as of yet, that Manny got in their way."

"Why? I don't understand."

"Abigail, what is Carlos's nationality?"

"He's Cuban, why?"

"You see there, no he's not."

"What do you mean?"

"Carlos and Atef are Middle Eastern, and both, as far as we can tell, are terrorists with a plan to kill hundreds of Americans. Nothing you know about them is as it seems. We're not here to judge Manny. That's beyond us. Frankly, we're here to try to save some lives. We'd like some help."

Abigail sat perfectly still, her face completely unresponsive. She had seemingly withdrawn into a place where neither Scott nor Al was welcome.

"Abigail?"

She said nothing and began to bend in her chair into a semifetal position. Scott had gambled, and now he'd apparently blown it. He'd pushed too hard at the wrong time. Her loyalty to Manny, even in death, was beyond what he could touch. She had completely tuned them out. Scott let out a prolonged sigh of defeat and rose to leave. She kept looking away as she began to speak. Her voice was now composed, resolute.

"Whatever Manny's sins, he has always been good to me. He is, or was, a conduit between certain foreign agents and governments and people here. He has earned a great deal of money fostering those relationships. I'm not going to pass judgment, as you've said. I never felt comfortable around Reyes. He made my skin crawl. He always seemed to have an agenda. Now you tell me he's evil beyond even what I know, and I can't say it surprises me."

"Abigail, when you last spoke to Manny, was it by phone?"

"I called his cell last week and gave him his messages. He was supposed to be back the other day."

"Can I have that phone number?"

"Yes, but why? He's dead."

"But his phone may or may not be. If it's not, we can possibly reconstruct a picture of what happened to him."

Abigail reached into her desk drawer, withdrew a cell phone, and scrolled through its memory. She stopped and turned it to Scott, displaying a phone number that he copied into his notes.

"Manny's agenda was his own. Mine doesn't include harming anyone," she said as she crossed her arms defensively over her chest.

Scott nodded and then went fishing with his next question in the spirit of "nothing ventured, nothing gained." "Abigail, we do appreciate your cooperation, especially considering what you've just been through. If you think of anything or anyone else who may also have been associated with Carlos and Atef, please give me a call." As he said that, he handed her his card. He expected no response to this shot in the dark.

Abigail took the card, looking straight ahead, maintaining her poker face. Burton and Krieger were rising to leave when Abigail said without expression, "Well, there was Faisal."

Scott arched his eyebrows. Then, looking straight at Abigail, he incredulously repeated, "Faisal?"

"Yes, he was Reyes's brother."

That truly shocked Scott and Al.

"I thought you said you thought he was Cuban? *Faisal* doesn't sound Cuban. Didn't it strike you as odd that he had a brother with a Muslim name?"

"It did at first. Manny and Carlos spoke Spanish together all the time. He spoke about Havana like a native. The only thing that crossed my mind was that Faisal must have been a half brother or something. As I said before, I didn't second-guess a lot of things that came through here. Maybe I should have, but if I had, I may have ended up like Manny."

"What did they speak about?"

"I don't know. They never spoke openly in front of me, but I remember Faisal arriving one day and Manny surprising Carlos with his arrival. He and Carlos met and then left together."

"Do you have an address or phone number for Faisal?"

"No, no, I don't. I did have the impression that he didn't live locally. He had something like an English accent."

"Abigail, thank you. Thank you very much. I'd ask that you keep our conversation to yourself. Try to do your business as if Manny were still out on one of his trips, okay?"

She agreed.

Scott continued, "We'll speak again. Once more, our condolences."

CHAPTER 38

Scott and Al drove directly back to their office and immediately called George Denby to inform him about the interview. Scott and Al were now more convinced than ever that they were all sitting on the edge of a disaster. Denby reluctantly agreed. He decided it was time to call Phil Halvorsen at the Joint Task Force.

"Phil, George Denby here. We've got a real problem. Have you heard about Manny Pabon?"

"Nope, what's up, George?" Halvorsen twanged his native Vermont accent, thicker for some reason this morning.

"I'm sorry. Maybe I should have told you. Some fishermen down on the Jersey shore found his left hand in the belly of a bull shark."

"Just the hand?"

"Yup, just the hand. On the positive side, his girlfriend is now cooperative."

"George, these fellows seem to be tidying up their loose ends. They're coming toward their end game."

"Agreed."

"Scott and Al came across what may be a break. Manny's girlfriend provided them with his cell phone number. I'm going to see if my tech people can track it. If we're lucky, maybe he didn't have it with him when he went in the water and the battery hasn't died. She also told us that Carlos has a brother, Faisal. We're seeing what we can find out about him."

"That's interesting, George. I wonder what the significance of New Jersey is?"

"I don't know, Phil, and that frankly worries me. I wish I did. As far as we knew, this was all centered around Staten Island. Now this issue seems to be spreading. I'm going to contact a marine biologist who's familiar with shark feeding patterns around the Jersey shore and see what he can add to our knowledge. I know that Manny and two guys who fit our boys' descriptions were down in Atlantic City a couple of weeks ago, but by the time we got people down there to check it out, they were gone."

"Phil, I'm going to ask Robles to speak to the captain of the port and see if he'll raise the MARSEC level to three and ramp the harbor all the way up. I think we're about to get hit."

"I agree, George. I'm going to have my people speak to the morals squad down in Atlantic City. If these guys were players down in AC, maybe they were fucking around with the girls."

"Good idea. I'd like to bring my people up to speed."

"By all means, I'll have Scott and Al get together with them."

"Thanks, let me know how you make out with the Coasties?"

"Absolutely."

*****

The Passat was uncomfortably overcrowded even before Wassim got in. Atef sat in the rear with Anthony and Syed. Each had packed clothes for three days that now sat in the trunk. Wassim eyed the boys a bit warily as he climbed into his seat.

The ride to Barnegat took two and a half hours during which Carlos explained the itinerary of the next few days to the boys. They would fill in as crew aboard the *Titan* and follow the directions of the crew to the letter. The kids were pumped. This was heady stuff for a couple of teenagers. Wassim then requested one more pair of hands aboard *Titan*, and since Carlos was needed to man the *Mariel*, Atef volunteered his services. Carlos would have to restructure his plans.

"We'll both go."

That confused Atef. "Who'll take the boat back?"

"We'll no longer need the boat. After the devices are planted, we'll ride the *Titan* back down to Wilmington. We'll rent a car down there for the trip back to New York. After we board the *Titan*, the *Mariel* is left where it is."

Wassim was quick to interject. "Excuse me, but I have reservations to leave New York for London on Saturday the seventeenth."

"Wassim, I understand we are testing your patience, but I will pay you well for your time and airfare, and we will upgrade your passage to first class."

"I'm already booked in first class, but I appreciate the offer. When may I expect to leave?"

"I'll have to ask the crewmen from the ship. I don't know, but I expect it will only be a few more days."

"I would ask that you let me know as soon as possible, so I can reschedule."

"Absolutely."

*****

They got underway at noon and spent the rest of the day and most of the night on *Mariel*, awaiting their rendezvous in the waters twenty miles off Barnegat Bay. The Atlantic swells had everyone aboard puking their guts out with the exception of Wassim. He said he was sure they would acclimate, or at least he hoped they would.

*****

Denby called Scott at 10:00 a.m. on July 13 and gave him the good news. "Scott, tech called me back. They were able to trace Manny's phone, and it's still active."

"Really, where is it?"

"A place where you and Krieger are going. An auto impoundment yard, Bo-Bo's Auto Salvage in Barnegat, New Jersey. Leave immediately. Call Brian Devine and take him with you."

"Boss, do we know what type of car we're looking for?"

"Yeah, it's a 2006 Buick sedan, maroon, New York registration ABS-6755. Oh, and there is one other interesting thing we've come up with. When we ran his name and history, we came up with another vehicle, a gray Jeep Cherokee."

"Carlos's?"

"That's why we couldn't put an ID to his car. He registered it through Manny."

"I should have made that connection!"

"Don't beat yourself up too much, so should have I. And there's more."

"I can't wait, what?"

"Manny owns a thirty-eight-foot boat." There was no sound. "Scott, are you still there?"

"Yeah, boss, this is really starting to freak me out."

"He bought the boat last month, that's all I know now. Get down there and get to that car. Take it and we'll go over it. We'll have somebody up here look into the boat, Robles or one of his people. But just get on the road."

"Done."

Burton and Krieger picked up Brian at the Ninth Precinct and brought him up to speed on the way.

Scott, Al, and Brian arrived at Barnegat at the auto impound around two thirty. The office was a double-wide at the front of the lot that was fenced and topped by razor wire. In the office, they found Bob Stiver, known in the area as Bo-Bo Stiver, a large friendly man in greasy jeans, an equally soiled T-shirt, and a Phillies ball cap resting backward on his head.

"Can I help you, gentlemen?" Bo-Bo greeted them with a smile.

"Hi, sir, I'm Special Agent Burton. He's Agent Krieger, FBI, and that's Detective Devine, NYPD."

"How can I help you, guys?"

It didn't take more than a minute for Bo-Bo to locate Manny's car in the yard. They walked out to it immediately. There it sat in the front row.

"Mr. Stiver, we'll have to take this vehicle off your hands. It's evidence in a federal investigation."

"Am I going to get paid?" Bo-Bo got right down to business.

"Pal, I wish I could tell you we could give you a check right now, but I can't. Give me an invoice for your fee, and I'll see what I can do. Where did you take it from?"

"It was parked in the lot of a local bar for a couple of days, and the owner asked that it be towed out. What's the story with the car?"

"It was used in the commission of a crime. Sorry, that's all I can say right now. Where is this place?"

"Not far. Lenny's Sand Bar over by the bay. It's a local hangout. A lot of folks who live here and work over in AC hang out there after work. Sometimes, a guy or girl will hook up and a car gets left in the lot. Lenny is willing to overlook that, but this car was there for three days. We towed it away for him."

"Were the local cops involved?"

"No, it was a private thing, no crime. Lenny just wanted it out of his lot. I get seventy-five dollars a day for storage."

"We're going to have to know all the people who have touched it so they can be printed for elimination purposes. I'm going to ask the local police to sit on it until it can be removed to our facility. Is it open?"

"It is now. It was locked, but we slim-jimmied it open."

"Anything in it?"

"Not that we found."

"Did you know the owner?"

"No."

"Did anyone try to contact you about it?"

"No."

Scott put on latex gloves and opened the door. Stiver was right; there was nothing apparent. Scott did a more thorough search and found the phone under the rear seat. It would go back to New York with them but provide no useful information. The car was secured, and authorization was obtained to transport it to a New York facility for processing. Scott asked and obtained permission from Denby authorizing Bo-Bo to do the tow to offset his loss, making Bo-Bo a much happy camper.

"Bo-Bo, could you direct us to Lenny's Sand Bar?"

Bo-Bo smiled and said, "I'll do better than that. I'll take you there." He walked back to the office, told his secretary he'd be back, and got into his truck. "Follow me."

At 4:15 p.m. they arrived at Lenny's and pulled into the lot.

"Bo-Bo, thanks a lot. Give me your card, will you?" He did so obligingly. "As soon as we're done here, I'll give you a call and let you know where the car has to be delivered. Make sure you get me that list of people whom we have to print. Tell people not to touch the car unless they want to be printed."

"Got it!" Stiver was more enthusiastic, feeling he was now an integral part of what was going on.

Scott quickly found that neither Lenny nor anyone else at his bar had ever heard of Manny or could recognize him through his description. They were about to leave when Scott's cell rang.

"Scott, this is Denby."

"What's up, boss?"

"Scott, we got something back on Manny's boat. I've got its serial number, but I don't know its name. He bought it at a place called Garden State Boat Sales right there in Barnegat." Denby gave him an address on East Bay Avenue, and he plugged it into the GPS.

It took him about twenty minutes to reach the location, which was a two-story white wooden building set back about twenty feet from the road with a boat yard to the rear. He pulled the car into the sandy pebble parking lot, and the three of them got out of the car. Brian happened to be the first in the door and spoke to the receptionist.

"Good afternoon, miss. My name is Detective Brian Devine, NYPD. These are Special Agents Burton and Krieger of the FBI. Is the manager available?"

The receptionist immediately acknowledged them and excused herself as she dialed an extension. "Paul, I need you up front. I have the FBI here."

A short, rotund man wearing khakis and a turquoise company polo shirt came up to the front and extended his hand. He was visibly concerned. "Gentlemen, I'm Paul Lofton. I'm the owner. How can I help you?"

"Is there someplace we can talk?"

"Certainly." He guided them back to his office and commandeered some additional chairs.

Scott explained that they were looking for information on the sale to Manny Pabon. Lofton excused himself and looked up the sale.

"Yeah, we sold him a used Lehr thirty-eight-foot boat. The sale was handled by Brett Blasingame."

"Is he here, sir?"

It was now close to 5:00 p.m. Blasingame had left at 4:00.

"Mr. Lofton, can you find him? It's important we speak with him immediately."

Lofton was able to reach him on his cell. Blasingame turned around and was back at the office in thirty minutes. Blasingame was a dignified white-haired man in his sixties, a head taller than Lofton, with a pencil mustache. He remembered Manny vividly.

"Yeah, Mr. Pabon bought a used thirty-eight-foot Lehr. He was with his brother-in-law, a fellow by the name of Santiago. They were new to boating and said they wanted to go fishing. What did they do?"

"Well, among the things I can't talk about, murder."

"I'll be damned. They didn't seem that way."

"Mr. Blasingame, do you know where that boat is?"

"Oh sure, if it's in, should be right behind here in the marina."

"Could you show us, please?"

"Sure, come with me."

Blasingame led them through the maze of slips until he came to an empty one. Scott, Al, and Brian almost simultaneously unclipped their sidearms.

"This is their slip. They must be out."

Blasingame led them to the yard master's office, where they met crusty old Bill Tillotson, the facility manager.

"Bill, the boat at slip 22, Pabon's thirty-eight-foot Lehr, when did they go out?"

"Oh, the *Mariel*. Early this afternoon, twelve or one. There were four or five of them on board, but I only knew that one fellow, Santiago. Ya know, his brother-in-law? There were three older guys and a couple of teenagers."

Scott and Brian looked at each other quizzically when Tillotson mentioned "teenagers."

Scott asked, "Did they say when they were coming back, sir?"

"They didn't say anything beyond hello and goodbye. They just fueled up and left. They might come back at any time. I just can't say."

Scott, Al, and Brian were understandably annoyed that they had missed them. Scott called Denby and informed him of what had transpired. Denby in turn notified the Coast Guard, who immediately commenced a search for the *Mariel*. Unfortunately, they all knew that the search would be greatly inhibited by the waning daylight. While they waited, Scott, Al, and George set up a surveillance on Manny's slip.

*****

Carlos did his utmost to hold the vicinity of his rendezvous coordinates. His queasiness had subsided, and his head was considerably clearer. Atef was also much more stable now, but the boys were completely useless. Carlos hoped that they would recover in time to make the transfer.

At 11:00 p.m., Carlos pointed out a set of running lights growing larger to the south. It occurred to him that planning to make the transfer at night had not been his best idea. Carlos did his best to hold his position.

Charlie joined Wally in the pilothouse of the *Triton*, providing an additional set of eyes for the next half hour. *Triton* had a direct drive to the engines, which allowed Charlie a degree of freedom. The engines could be controlled directly from the bridge without Charlie being present below. Wally glanced at the radar and nodded. "Charlie, I think I have them at about four miles off the port bow. Can you see anything?"

"No, not yet." The elevated pilothouse would be a great help as they strained their eyes to see the *Mariel*, but it was just as black as a witch's heart out there. Wally corrected his course to intercept the target off his port bow. Forty-five minutes later, Charlie called out, "I see him, and I think he's your radar contact."

"Yeah, I think so." With only the two of them aboard, the vessel was ghostly quiet aside from the constant engine sounds.

Carlos was sure that this oncoming vessel was the *Triton*. He asked Atef to rouse the boys.

When the vessels were side by side, Wally hove to. It was much easier for them to remain stationary and have *Mariel* maneuver than vice versa. At its lowest point, the sides of the *Triton* were more or less even with those of the *Mariel*.

Carlos tried to come alongside the larger vessel and lost a piece of his main deck coaming and a cleat for his trouble. The wave action had him pitching erratically from four to six feet up and down and rolling just as sickeningly. They were riding like a cork in the swells. He decided to move from his bow to the larger vessel's port quarter, but the wave action made the task much more difficult. The *Mariel*'s bow was taking a terrible beating. Carlos maintained contact with the *Triton* using forward power to push his bow between the large tires along *Triton*'s side that were used as fenders. The transfer was done as fast as possible without anyone going overboard. First, Wassim and his gear were transferred, and then Atef, and then the boys, whose agility remained apparent even through their nausea. Then it was Carlos's turn. He used a bit more forward power to snug the mangled bow of the *Mariel* in between the tug's fenders. He abandoned his post and jumped from the bow. He had allowed for the pitch but not the simultaneous roll; his right foot caught the debris of a cleat, and he landed heavily but safely on the aft deck of the *Triton*. Charlie grabbed him as he landed and led him up to Wally in the pilothouse.

"Good evening," Wally bid. "Your seamanship was a bit rough around the edges, but it proved adequate. Welcome aboard."

"It is done. Can you come down and meet my people?"

"Shortly, let me finish my work here."

Wally began to bring the *Triton* back up to speed. As he was doing that, he turned widely to port, in toward the *Mariel*, causing the larger vessel to shed the smaller *Mariel*. With forward power applied still, the *Mariel* moved off to the northeast and the *Triton* moved northward, undamaged. Wally left the wheel to Charlie and accompanied Carlos to the aft deck to meet the new arrivals.

After Carlos made introductions all around, Wally stated what he thought to be the obvious: "Gentlemen, why don't you come into the mess deck and allow me to offer you something to eat." The adults took him up on the offer, but the boys had not yet fully recovered.

Wassim wanted to immediately inspect the mines, but Wally suggested they rest until morning. They had another complete day at sea to make all the preparations, and it was far too dark on deck at the moment. Common sense won out, and after soup and some hot tea, all retired.

CHAPTER 39

Sofia slowly motored along as Orlando and Jack patrolled the dark waters of Staten Island's Kill Van Kull. As members of the Coast Guard Auxiliary, they were assigned to a patrol sector on the northern side of Staten Island two nights a week. This week, they were assigned Wednesday and Thursday. Orlando and Jack were accompanied by an armed coast guardsman, twenty-one-year-old Petty Officer Tre Oliver, a native of Austin, Texas.

Tonight the three were patrolling from the ferry terminal in St. George down past the Bayonne and Goethals Bridges and the remainder of the west shore of Staten Island. The snaking waterway would take them past the Howland Hook Container Port, the Linden oil refineries, and at the end of their route, the ship graveyard at Witte Marine. First, however, they'd pass the Bayonne Bridge and confront Shooters Island. Jack repeated what Orlando already knew.

"Carlos sure was interested with this area."

"Yeah, I know. Everything comes past here, which is why we're going to give it special attention." As they came up on Shooters Island, Orlando called out to Tre Oliver in the bow cockpit, "Petty Officer Oliver, I'm going to light up that island. Give it a good look." Oliver just gave him a thumbs-up. Orlando slowed the *Sofia* even more and snapped on his powerful searchlight, but it barely penetrated the dense foliage of the deserted bird sanctuary. There were only a few breaks in the trees and bushes where the beam reached in, and they were able to see the crumbled foundations of a once-thriving shipyard. They circled the small island, returned to where they had started, and applied power again. "See anything, Tre?" Oliver shook his head no.

Jack verbalized the experience: "This place is as dead as Kelsey's Nuts."

"Amen to that," answered Orlando.

They hit a few more spots on the shoreline among the wreckage and skeletons of barges from ages gone by with the same result: nothing.

They continued on, using their light in every desolate nook and cranny where a kayak could be launched. Jack seemed to know where every last one of them was, and the ship graveyard at Witte Marine was of particular interest to them. It was the end point of their patrol sector and a fascinating display of harbor history. Orlando had to be extremely careful picking his way through here, especially in the dark. He could easily punch a hole in his hull. The shoreline around the facility was dotted with dozens of surfaced, semisubmerged, and skeletal remains of tugs, ships, ferries, and barges of a bygone era that were now awaiting their fates at the hands of cutting torch. It was an excellent place for kayakers to lurk. But again, they found nothing.

Finally they reversed their course and inspected the same shoreline once more in the same thorough manner as they had on their first inspection. They would soon be relieved at the other end of their patrol area, near the Staten Island Ferry Terminal, by a boat from the New York State Naval Militia. Orlando would take Jack back to the *Intrepid* just before first light, and tomorrow night they'd be back to do it all over again.

After they were relieved and heading through the upper bay, Jack turned to Orlando with a wry smile and said, "I guess the way you and me and Scott, Al, Brian, and Louie work together makes us sort of like that TV show *Band of Brothers*."

"I guess it does, doesn't it?"

*****

The morning broke off the central Jersey coast with a sunny haze. The sea was calm, much to the relief of Syed and Anthony, who were up and already about. Wassim had been up for hours, as was his daily custom. He'd performed static tests on both weapons and found them in perfect working order. Wassim and Wally then gave the boys a cram course on basic seamanship and line handling. The boys would need to develop these skills quickly to assist in order to make this thing work. All Wally could do was thank his lucky stars that Wassim was aboard; one more competent man on deck was a huge plus. Because of him, Wally was able to stay in the pilothouse, for the most part.

Wally adjusted his speed so they would arrive in Raritan Bay after midnight on Thursday and stay on schedule to make Arthur Kill and Kill Van Kull. For the most part, the day would be a slow and relaxed event, almost recreational. Wassim decided that he'd leave the devices crated until after dark, remaining secured to the deck under a tarp, strapped to their wheeled dollies. He planned to wait to set and arm the mines until the last minute.

*****

Scott, Al, and Brian had spent an uncomfortable night, contorted like pretzels all night in their medium-size government car at the marina just observing Manny's boat slip. While they waited, Brian and Al walked through the Marina parking lot and took down the plates of the nine cars that were in the lot. One of those cars was a green Volkswagen Passat. They ran the registrations of each car through the *Malibu*'s onboard computer. When it came to the Passat, they just looked at each other in amazement. Brian said what they were all thinking, "No wonder we couldn't hook the car up to Carlos."

Shortly after seven the next morning, they were wakened by Scott's cell phone.

"Yeah, Burton here!"

"Scott, it's Jack Robles. Our people found the boat this morning."

"Where?"

"It was about forty-five miles northeast of where you are. There doesn't appear to be anyone on it."

"Appear?"

"Yeah, a helicopter spotted it. It's drifting. We've got a surface unit going to it who should be there shortly. The helicopter said it appears to be seriously down by the bow and may be sinking."

"Jack, I really hope they can keep it afloat. We'd like to look it over."

"I'm sure they'll do the best they can, and I'll call you as soon as I know more."

"Listen, we found Carlos's car. It was registered to Manny."

Scott relayed what had been said to Al and Brian, and then they continued to hurry up and wait.

Luckily, they didn't have to wait very long for Roble's next call. A 110-foot cutter had reached the *Mariel* at 9:15 a.m. and immediately got pumps working on board. Unfortunately, their efforts were in vain; minutes later the *Mariel* slid under the waves, bow first.

Robles called Scott as promised, and his disappointment was apparent. The next obvious question was, What had become of the occupants? Robles volunteered, "I spoke with the CO of the cutter. He said the damage didn't seem to be catastrophic. It looked more like they'd hit something and not the reverse. He wasn't able to fully examine the boat, but he told me that the radio seemed to be intact and the boat was out of fuel. It doesn't seem as if they hit anything hard enough to throw everyone over the side simultaneously. We also know there were no reports of accidents last night or maydays."

"Does it look like they abandoned the boat?"

"It would appear so, but for what reason?"

"Is there any way of checking what's gone past this area since last night?"

"Well, yes and no. There isn't any requirement for most of the recreational vessels that come out of this area and pass through to make any type of notification. Commercially, vessels over one hundred tons must identify themselves. They could have transferred to God knows how many different vessels. Why, though?"

Scott thanked Robles for his efforts and conveyed what he'd said to Al and Brian, adding, "No reason for us to stay here. Let's head back to New York."

Brian couldn't help but state the obvious. "Questions that lead to questions that lead to questions. I could really learn to dislike this guy."

*****

All aboard the *Triton* welcomed the sunset and its blanket of anonymity. They continued to move up the Jersey shore, passing Sandy Hook at 9:30 p.m. After midnight, they turned into Raritan Bay and moved toward the Arthur Kill on schedule. The trip up the kills would be an exacting piece of navigation. They would need to change course frequently going up the narrow waterway—at least five times in the first two miles. The multitude of wrecks that had been abandoned along the shoreline over a lifetime jutted out into the channel in more than a few places. This passage would have taken Wally's full attention in broad daylight; in the dead of night, even though the channel was well-marked and the charts precise, he could not be disturbed.

Wassim had placed the uncrated devices under their own tarps. The boys held the tarps up to form small tent-like structures under which he could work. Wassim popped a glow stick; he hooked up the connections from his laptop to the control panel on the mine. He set the time delay to activate the devices early on the twenty-seventh. The sensitivity was set for a midsize vessel and the proper depth. All in all, in less than ten minutes per device, the mines were armed. All that remained was pushing the mines up to the deck edge. Wassim's last act would be to cut the fabric straps separating the mines from the packing that had castors installed to their bottoms. When they were rolled over the side, the packing would separate from the truncated mines, and they would fall in place to the harbor floor. For now, the mines were rolled to the deck edge, still under their individual tarps and chained to the deck. Wassim sent the boys back to the galley, and then he joined Carlos, Atef, and Wally in the pilothouse. There wasn't much to be said.

Carlos asked, "Done?"

Wassim answered with only a nod. He looked forward to the end of this mission; he had a feeling of foreboding he could not shake.

*****

On Thursday, Orlando and Jack began their third tour patrolling the kills shortly after midnight. They were manning the forward cockpit of the *Sofia* with Tre Oliver again. The finger of their searchlight slowly probed the odds and ends of the shoreline. Orlando noticed that everything was quiet, even traffic on the Kill. On their first pass of Shooters Island, they repeated their actions of their last two patrols with the same result: nothing. As they passed the tugboat yards at Kirby Marine-Sea and McAllister, they gave way to a departing tug, exchanging waves with the deckhand. They finished their circuit of Shooters Island and continued on their way. Then they turned around and did it all again.

After returning to St. George near the ferry terminal, they took a break and threw a line to a bollard at the ferry fueling pier. They idled for a half hour, enjoying some coffee. Then they moved out again. Neither of them vocalized what they both felt. Boredom was setting in.

On their next pass, Orlando varied the routine by giving extra attention to the oil terminals on the New Jersey side and the scrubby wooded area near the landing at Sailor's Snug Harbor. The extra security at the oil terminals was apparent even from their view, but the area under Sailor's Snug Harbor was a different story.

Sailor's Snug Harbor had been a residence for retired merchant seamen from 1833 until its remaining residents were relocated to North Carolina. The eighty-three-acre site was—and still is—a cultural center, which was successful in many ways. The society that operated the property had always hoped that making the facility more accessible might bolster attendance.

The next thought was that building a pier on the perimeter of the property would attract excursion boats. They built a state-of-the-art pier that rose and fell with the tide. It was built where the dilapidated remains of the previous railroad now lay in decay. The excursion boats were hopefully yet to come.

What did remain was an overgrown three-hundred-foot wooded area and refuse dump. Barely inaccessible from the street, it was occasionally frequented by sports fishermen and was rarely patrolled by the local police. You could hide almost anything or anyone down there; it was only one of dozens of such hides that existed along the shoreline.

As Orlando passed, they lit it up but only rousted some homeless folks who were peacefully asleep. As they continued up the Kill, Orlando and Jack encountered more traffic. A large APL containership passed them starboard to starboard just east of the Bayonne Bridge. When they came up on Shooters Island, they gave the shoreline a good look from a respectable distance. Orlando had seen this area at low tide. There were enough ribs protruding from long sunken barges that festooned the bottom near the shore that going any closer was a very dangerous proposition. He moved back out into the channel, allowing a large tug to pass in the opposite direction. Again, they passed starboard to starboard. A deckhand waved amiably as they passed, and Jack returned the greeting. Jack looked aft and caught a quick glance at her name on the stern, the *Triton* out of Wilmington, Delaware. Orlando continued on. He wanted to take a closer look at the oil terminal in Linden this time. He still had another round trip after this one, and the night was dragging.

*****

Wally Kurri was in the zone. While he gave a lot of credit to his GPS navigating system, there was a lot of skill involved on his part as well. He'd previously plotted all his points and now had everything under control. Wassim went back aft and double-checked the chains holding the mines down. There was really nothing more to be done until they reached the drop area. Wassim sat on a mooring bit and took out a cigar. In Syria he had access to Cuban cigars, but he had never been a big fan of them. Instead, he took out one of his favorites, a Padron Maduro, which was in the Cuban style but made in

Florida by what he considered cigar artisans. The cigar was just what he needed to alleviate his tension. He sat and watched the marsh lands on the starboard give way to what appeared to be a salvage yard. The *Triton* moved past large earthen mounds to starboard and oil refineries to port. Wassim looked up the channel and could see a searchlight probing the shoreline from the channel. Wally saw it up in the pilothouse too and made a mental note of it.

The *Triton* passed under the Goethals Bridge and the Howland Hook Container Port, where two huge containerships were loading simultaneously, but no one paid them any heed, and they continued to glide through the night unnoticed.

The Bayonne Bridge was now coming up ahead. Wally found the source of the searchlight coming from what appeared to be a recreational boat searching the shoreline. Wally judged it for what it was, some type of auxiliary patrol boat, and then he saw the Coast Guard colors flying, confirming his belief. They passed each other, acknowledged one another with a wave, and then continued in opposite directions.

After he passed the Bayonne Bridge, Wally realized he was in the home stretch to the target area. He called Carlos, Atef, and Wassim to the wheelhouse and told them to ready themselves. Carlos, in turn, alerted the boys.

Wassim would have preferred to drop the mines in the vicinity of the Bayonne Bridge to maximize the effect, but this wasn't his operation. These guys were jihadists, and they were in it for the body count first and the tonnage second. Every time he looked at Anthony and Syed, he thought of his own son and he had to force himself to remember, again, that this wasn't his operation.

It was just after 3:00 a.m. when the ferry terminal came into view. The three o'clock boat was leaving the slip for its trip to Manhattan. Luck was on their side; there was no other traffic in the vicinity.

The water in the harbor was flat, without a single ripple. Atef, Carlos, Anthony, Syed, and Ahmed gathered on the fantail with Wassim to receive instructions. Wassim had Wally enter the drop points on his electronic chart. When the *Triton* was about five hundred yards from the drop point, Wassim unchained the mines and took the tarps off. Wally would queue the release with a buzzer signal from the pilothouse. At about two hundred yards from release point, Wassim cut the fabric tie on the starboard mine. Wassim gave the assembled group their last instruction.

"When I say push, push! These things are heavy, but they'll roll off. Be careful not to go over with them. After the first one goes over, we're heading over to where the other one goes in. There's no time to dally, gentlemen." The buzzer signaled 150 yards in front of the ferry terminal.

"Now! Push!" They did and the squat device went over the fantail. As the mines splashed in, their religious fervor bubbled over in a chorus of mutual yet restrained cries of "Allahu Akbar!" Wassim only hoped no one had seen the splash. "The other side now, please!"

They quickly moved to the port side, and Wassim cut the strap on the mine. The *Triton* moved forward in a slow turn to the left, and after 150 yards, the buzzer sounded again.

"Push, now!" The second mine splashed in, and it was done. Wally never altered his speed but continued his turn and began traveling northward toward Manhattan. In less than an hour, he'd be tying up at the Brooklyn navy yard awaiting daylight to pick up his cargo. He couldn't help but wonder which ship would be the eventual victim of his other load.

CHAPTER 40

The trip back up to New York was made under a pall of disappointment. The three large-framed men were cramped, tired and in need of showers. Scott's interview with Abigail Pence had provided them with their first substantial lead, but now that had sunk, literally, to the bottom of the Atlantic Ocean.

Brian was especially affected. Carlos had stayed one step ahead of him in what Brian considered his own ballpark. Brian's frustration was approaching a level he'd never experienced. "It's almost as if they're playing with us," he grunted.

Scott contributed, "Playing with us, no. I don't think they have any idea of how close we are, but they were always aware that we could take them out. Are they professionals? Oh yeah. The fact that we can't wrap them up bothers me too. What eats at me even more, though, is a nagging feeling that we're not seeing the bigger picture here. If their intention is to attack a ferry boat or any boat by ramming it with an explosive-laden kayak, then what's with all this other stuff?"

"What do you mean?"

"As nasty as the thought is of somebody in a kayak planning to attack a ferry, the operation seems to be a whole lot more intricate than that. The intel people have already told us about Manny Pabon. He is, or was, up to his ass in subversives and radicals. He's actively hooked up to Cuba and facilitates radical relationships. Now for some reason, this scumbag buys a boat, and then Carlos and a few others decide to mourn his recent passing by taking some kind of Manny memorial cruise. They hit something, but they don't hit that something hard enough to sink the boat outright. In fact, it doesn't sink until the next day. Since Robles tells us no one reported either an accident or picking anyone up, these guys are still alive. Where and why, I don't know, but obviously our cast of characters has just increased."

Brian chimed in, "I was introduced to a guy, retired from my job. He works in maritime security and has some great insights and connections. Al Calcaterra. He knows an awful lot about the Port of New York. How about we run our situation past him?"

Scott shrugged his assent. "I haven't got a problem with that, but haven't we got someone in the Coast Guard with that level of knowledge?"

"I'm sure we do, Scott, but I've been told that this guy is really sharp. He's written articles on maritime terrorism, works as a consultant on the subject, and what he doesn't know, his people can find for him. I'm liking this guy because he doesn't have any official line he has to follow. Maybe we should start to think outside of the box."

"Don't you think Robles can help us?"

"Sure, to whatever extent Todd can, he will. But think about it. He's privileged to all the same information we are, but he doesn't seem to know any more than we do."

Scott very seriously considered what was being said and then added, "Okay, I get you, but I think I'm going to run your thoughts past Robles and his people. I don't want to insult them or have them feel like we're cutting him or the Coast Guard out of the loop."

"Sure, Scott. Call him."

Scott did so immediately; Todd answered on the third ring. Scott began explaining the conversation that had just taken place in the car and waited for Todd's response. There was an uncomfortable period of silence until Scott started to think the call had been dropped. "Todd? Todd, are you still there?"

"I'm here, Scott. Listen, I wish we had some magical answer I could give you. I hear everything you're saying. I share your frustrations and fears. We're physically doing everything we can to prepare for what's coming at us. I've met this Calcaterra fellow. He's legit, and he does know his stuff. Sure, let's run it past him. Maybe he can give us another perspective. He's got both police and retired naval intelligence credential with the associated clearance background. Go for it, Scott. Let me know what he says. And, Scott, thanks for the heads-up, brother."

Scott ended the call with Robles and just looked at Brian and simply said, "Call him. Set it up."

Brian wasted no time and did it right then. "Hello, Al, this is Brian Devine. Do you remember me?"

"Sure I do, kid. How ya doing?"

"I wish I could say better. Listen, Al, my friends and I have a problem that we'd like to pick your brain about. Are you available for a meet?"

"Yeah, don't say any more. When can you get together with me?" Calcaterra could feel the concern in his tone. He invited Brian to his home in the Westerleigh section of Staten Island. "How about tomorrow morning at my place?"

"How about 10:00 a.m.?"

"Good."

"Do you know where I live?"

"Waters Avenue, right?"

"Yeah," Calcaterra gave him his address.

"Al, I'm bringing a couple of friends."

"I'll have the coffee on. See ya then."

*****

For Wally and his associates, the trip back down to Wilmington was slow considering the weight of the tow that was following them. After delivering their cargo, they returned to their mooring at the shipyard early that afternoon. They got off after securing the boat and went over to Wally's car. The others in the yard said hello; they didn't give any thought to the fact that Greg Morris wasn't walking off the boat since he lived aboard. They also didn't pay attention to the crewmen since new deckhands came and went with regularity, though technically most of these guys were markedly older than most.

Wally took Carlos and his party to a car rental agency where they could rent a new set of wheels to get them back to New York

City. Carlos looked at Wally's pickup and its tow connection and realized he'd come upon another opportunity. He still needed a vehicle to move his kayak trailer in New York, and the Passat was not rigged for towing. He took Wally aside.

"Wally, I have need of your truck. Take me to the rental agency, pick any vehicle that will suit your needs, but I'm taking the truck."

Wally hadn't known Carlos or Atef for long, but he had seen enough to understand they weren't people to be trifled with. While Carlos and his cohorts may have been hardcore and into martyrdom, Wally and Charlie were mainly thinking about survival and putting distance between themselves and a murder indictment that they felt for sure was on its way.

"Certainly, my brother, go with Allah. The truck is yours. The papers are in the glove box."

Gonsalves left in his truck while Wally and Carlos's party went directly to the rental agency. Carlos and his people were on the road to New York in less than two hours in the Tacoma after thanking Wally profusely. Wally got on the road in his new SUV with an escape plan that involved passing south through the Mexican border toward his eventual destination, Venezuela.

*****

Brian, Louie, Scott, and Al were standing in front of Al Calcaterra's small colonial home on a peaceful tree-lined street at ten the next morning, feeling antsy. Calcaterra answered the door and introduced them to his wife of thirty-four years, Helen, before they sat at the dining room table. Laid out before them was a gracious spread of coffee, buns, fruits, jams, and juices. Helen excused herself as the men sat down, but not before she reminded them, "I didn't put this food out here just to look good. Please enjoy."

While portly, sixty-year-old Al was Sicilian by heritage, and the décor clearly reflected his wife's Irish heritage. Their home was a gentle and welcoming place.

Ships had always been a passion with Al, and living so close to the harbor had only increased his fervor. Even before 9/11, Al had been an advocate for paying greater attention to maritime security in the harbor. Still 9/11 had been a transformational experience for him, as it had been for so many others. He saw right away the need to increase harbor security. Toward that end, Al became an active advocate of what would come to be commonly referred to as Maritime Domain Awareness.

As time went on, the 9/11 attacks became his passion. Al educated himself about radical Islamic extremism to a remarkable extent. If anyone wanted to see this gentleman's demeanor change, just bring up the subject of violent jihadists. He was often heard to say, "I know I can't go back in time and return to the Navy, but if I could, I would. Now I'll do whatever I can, whenever I can." So in his retirement years, he had done consultancy work, taught, lectured, educated, and developed an unclassified data bank that was the envy of many.

After they sat down, Al looked directly at Brian and opened the conversation as all internally police-based interrogatories do by flatly asking, "What ya got?"

Brian laid the story out to Calcaterra in detail, omitting only that Jack was still alive.

After they'd fully briefed him, Calcaterra sat back in his chair. His snow-white hair, glasses, and stout build gave him a paternal persona. Al thought deeply about what he had been told, and after a prolonged silence, he began to offer his diagnosis.

"First, your scenario involving the kayaks is perfectly feasible. It sounds like a play on a contemporary pirate tactic. They've been known to lash two small boats together on a long tether, usually in narrow waterways. The boats separate to the length of the tether in the path of the oncoming target vessel. The ship is allowed to snag the cable, and when it does, the boats are drawn into the sides of the larger ship. Pirates do this as a boarding technique. It could just as easily be employed with explosive-carrying kayaks. Then again, it's just as feasible for the kayaks to paddle up alongside a ship and detonate their explosives, sort of like manned limpet mines."

Al had their complete attention.

"Their technique is fairly simple, I have to agree with you. However, there seems to be an awful lot of effort being expended on their part for such a straightforward tactic. It's important to remember that these jihadis plan in great detail and way in advance. The kayaks may only be a portion of their overall plan. They could have additional targets in mind and additional weapons in their possession."

"What else could they use?"

"Jeez, the options are practically limitless. They could use all types of underwater improvised explosive devices, like mines and explosive-filled pleasure boats. Unfortunately, their only limitation is their imagination. Guys, you have to understand that the people we have come to know as Islamic terrorists come in all shapes, sizes, and degrees of competence. They can span the spectrum from homegrown wannabes to a frighteningly inventive cadre of people who are dedicated to our demise. It would be a terrible mistake on our part as a society to dismiss all of them as amateurs. From everything you guys have explained to me, unfortunately, you are dealing with the higher-end people. I really believe you're dealing with al-Qaeda or one of their franchises. Their flexibility and training may account for your difficulty in catching up with them. They also have the finances to obtain the most sophisticated weapons."

Al continued, "Back when John Kerry was running for president, he was about to campaign in New Orleans. He was scheduled to take a ride on Lake Pontchartrain. A local boater was out on the lake before he was scheduled to appear. The fisherman looked down in the water and saw what looked like a floating bag, but it ended up being a rubber bladder filled with ammonium nitrate floating just below the surface. It was eventually disabled with fire hoses, but it would have really put a crimp in Kerry's day had it not been found. Now that's home-grown stuff, but in today's world, there's a whole lot of stuff out there on the black market, including some pretty sophisticated mines. People will tell you that's far-fetched, but before 9/11, so were flying airliners into buildings."

Brian asked, "So these explosives are like mines from World War II with the horns sticking out, floating in the harbor?"

"Sort of, Brian, but things have really progressed a lot since then, although those old mines can still be procured. Those particular mines, the ones with the horns, are M-1908 Soviet contact mines.

The target ship actually has to make physical contact with the mine. The ship breaks one or more of those horns. They contain acid that, when broken, finishes an electrical circuit that causes the mine to detonate. They were first introduced in 1908 and last employed in the Gulf War. Guys, I could go into a long tutorial on mines, but I don't think that's necessary. Cutting to the chase, these things are getting more and more sophisticated. One of the areas of concern here in the harbor is the use of suicide boats to carry explosives, like those that were used against the USS *Cole*. You have to understand that there are countless civilian pleasure and work craft that have access to this harbor, and they have no reporting requirements placed on them. They can be used to launch an attack and pull it off before ever being detected. Coast Guard and police boats often escort high-value targets, like ferries and ocean liners, like the *Queen Mary*. Facilities, like bridges, often have police boats assigned to protect them. Still, there are an awful lot of opportunities for small craft or divers to plant explosives or ram targets."

"What about mines?" Brian asked.

"That's a bit of a different story. You could set a bottom mine on the harbor floor, arm it, and set it to react to a certain set of parameters, such as the size of a target. These things react to changes in water pressure as the vessels pass over or even react to their magnetic signature. What really makes them a nightmare is that they can be left, preset, not to activate for weeks or months. When these things detonate, they're devastating. They send a pressure wave up that can rip a vessel into pieces. They can also be laid by any number of vessels."

"Gee, that's reassuring. Can't the Coast Guard find these things?" asked Louie.

"Ah, now you've come to another interesting problem. The Coast Guard will tell you, and rightfully so, that only the Navy is physically responsible and equipped to hunt and sweep mines. The Navy will tell you, again rightfully, that it's the Coast Guard's job to provide harbor security. They're both right, but neither will cross over into the area of responsibility of the other. If a mine is somehow found in the harbor, the Coast Guard calls in the Navy to sweep them. That process could take weeks, stopping shipping and thereby crippling the economy."

"Can't the police bomb squad handle the job?"

"No, only particularly trained people can handle these things. It would be incredibly dangerous practice to deal with them otherwise."

Brian asked the obvious question, "How do you find these things?"

"They detonate under ships and kill people, and then you know where they are or were. I don't mean to scare you, but the contemporary school of mine detection involves either the early employment of superior intelligence which nips plots in the bud before the mines are planted, or it is about how to react after the fact. The system, as it is now structured, is geared toward the latter. That in itself is an additional problem. It's difficult for the powers that be to wrap themselves around this threat and really work to prevent it. You talk to them about this stuff, and their eyes start to glaze over. Of course, another big part of it is that they don't want to spend the money, though it's a miniscule amount when compared to the potential threat. In reality, any money spent in this area is an insurance policy. If the worst happens, believe me, heads will roll. And that will be of little consolation to the families of the dead."

"Damn, that is scary," Brian chimed in.

Al grimaced and continued, "You seem to be busting your ass closing in on your prey. They've obviously got a stock of alternative identities and until recently were hiding behind this Pabon fellow. It's fairly common to find them dealing in fake ID's and credit card fraud. Now that Pabon is dead, your man is going to have to reach into his stash of phony ID's. It shouldn't be a problem for them though. Credit card skimming is one of their more lucrative funding sources. They can get those cards from the strangest places."

"I can attest to that," Brian retorted.

"If I could advise you personally, I'd say these guys aren't going to set up far from a Muslim neighborhood or far from the water."

"Thanks. Could you put something together to educate us on mines?"

"Sure, I'll shoot you an email."

"Ya know, Al, if I'd walked in here with four drinks in, you would have scared me sober. Thanks for your insights." Brian had spoken for the group.

Scott added, "Al, we'd like to stay in touch."

"By all means, I'll help you in any way I can."

Brian and the group ended the meeting and retired to their respective cars. Brian and Louie were riding together, and Scott and Al had their company car. Brian gave Scott and Al clear instructions about how to get back to the highway. They'd see each other during the week, but Brian and Louie were finally taking a couple of days off. Brian suggested that it wasn't too early for a beer at Duffy's Tavern down in their neighborhood. Brian twisted Louie's arm ever so slightly, and he surrendered. They both agreed that there was nothing better to knock down a buttered sesame bagel, fresh fruit, and coffee than a couple of Amstel Lights. As Brian drove through the residential back streets toward Duffy's, Louie looked over and saw that same old look on Brian's face.

"Brian? Brian?" Nothing. Louie had seen this look too many times before behind those blues eyes nestled inside that big melon head of his. The wheels were whirling like crazy. "What's up, man? What's bothering you?"

"Before we went to Al's house, I was confused and felt like I was missing something. Now I'm not confused anymore, but I know I'm still missing something, and, man, I'm telling you. Whatever it is, it's right there. I'm just not seeing it. This is really driving me crazy, and frankly, that meeting scared the hell out of me!"

Louie saw the writing on the wall as he privately lamented, *This is going to be a long weekend.* He knew Brian wouldn't let go of this until he figured out what was bothering him.

They got to Duffy's and took two seats toward the middle of the half-empty bar. The attached restaurant to the rear was beginning to fill with the lunch crowd; the bar would fill very shortly. Their privacy would be short-lived. Through the first two beers, not a hell of a lot was said.

Brian turned to Louie with a quizzical look on his face. "Louie, ya know what keeps sticking in my head? That stuff he said about Carlos using native identities and stolen credit cards."

"Well, yeah, the fuck is a parasite. He used Manny, he used Jack, and he used Orlando."

"Yup."

Louie lamented, "Carlos must have taken Orlando to the cleaners after Fausto put him in the hospital."

"What are you talking about?"

"When Orlando was admitted to the hospital, Carlos safeguarded his wallet. If that hump was forging ID's, he had all of Orlando's stuff to use."

"How do you know Carlos had his stuff?"

"He told me."

Brian fixed Louie in a protracted stare modified with a wry smile. After a short while, it started to make Louie feel uncomfortable. "What? Why are you looking at me like that?"

"Because you're a genius!"

"Obviously, but why?"

"Carlos left his car, this green Passat, down in Barnegat. Wherever he is, he hasn't got a car. He hasn't got Manny to buy his cars for him anymore. If he's got copies of Orlando's ID, the complete package, maybe, just maybe, he'll screw up and use it instead of any other ID he's got. If he wants to rent a car, they're going to demand a credit card and a matching driver's license. I've got to call Orlando." Brian got up and walked toward the restaurant portion of the place and ducked out the back door into the rear parking lot.

The phone rang five or six times before Orlando picked up. It was apparent from his raspy tone that Brian had awoken him. "Orlando, Brian. Did you work last night?"

He came back in a low, sleepy voice, "Yeah, what's up?"

"Sorry, I woke you up, man. Orlando, after Fausto worked you over and you went to Bellevue, did Carlos safeguard your wallet when you were there?"

"Yeah, and I got it back while I was in my hospital room a day or so later."

"Did you have your credit cards and driver's license in your wallet?"

"Yeah, one or two cards. I just use my American Express card. And yeah, my license was in it."

"Have you noticed any odd charges on the cards?"

"Not that I've heard of. My secretary takes care of paying that stuff. She hasn't said anything to me."

"Was everything in your wallet when you got it back?"

"Yup, as far as I could tell. Where are we going with this?"

"I think Carlos may have made copies of your cards and ID. Could you have Rosemarie pull copies of your billing?"

"Sure, but that only takes care of up until last month. I'll cancel the card immediately."

"No, no, don't do that, let him use it. If he's using it, we can track him. Do you mind if I ask the Feds to pull the current usages on the card?"

"No, of course not."

"Good. I'll reach out to Scott Burton right after we hang up. I'll speak to you during the week. What nights are you working this week?"

"Tonight and tomorrow night."

"Sorry to wake you. We'll talk."

"Don't worry about it. Talk to you later."

As soon as he hung up with Orlando, he called Scott Burton, who was still in his car; he quickly briefed him. The wheels were set in motion. Brian walked back into the bar and sat down next to Louie. Brian's feeling of dread had begun to subside. He clapped Louie on the shoulder.

"Am I still a genius?"

"Oh yeah!"

"Good, I could get used to this recognition thing."

They both had a laugh and ordered another beer.

CHAPTER 41

Carlos, Atef, Anthony, and Syed returned to Staten Island late Monday afternoon to make their final preparations. Tuesday morning, Carlos drove out to the storage facility in the marshlands on the west shore of Staten Island. Once there, he examined the contents of his two large storage boxes. He'd rented two units, and one unit was stockpiled with enough surplus MREs, water, clothing, and camping supplies to last six days. Nestled behind everything else, in the rear of the unit, was a canvass-covered wood cargo pallet. It contained a breathtaking quantity of shrink-wrapped US currency. They would not eat or live luxuriously, but they could successfully subsist for at least a week. When he rented the boxes, the contract listed a number of items that were strictly prohibited from being brought into the facility. But the caretaker at the facility, a bookish retired postal worker, rarely interacted with the clients unless they specifically asked for assistance. He could not have cared less.

The contents of the second box violated every prohibition in the rental agreement. There was a trailer, eight kayaks, four AKM submachine guns, four hundred rounds of 7.62 × 39 ammunition, and enough Semtex to blow that portion of the facility sky high.

The plan was about to enter its most dangerous phase. The items in the storage facility had to be transported out to Shooters Island and stockpiled before the operation could begin. It was a difficult task made even more daunting by the fact that they had to make the transfer in the dead of night by towing the kayaks in one of the busiest shipping channels in the northeast. And before that could be done, Carlos had to locate a secure point where they could enter the water with minimal chance of being noticed. He chose a spot on North Shore, Staten Island, in a mixed industrial/residential area just to the east of Shooters Island. It was near Staten Island's former Bethlehem Steel Shipyard and the Great Lakes Dredge Company facility. While the dredge company was a functional operation, the shipyard was defunct and had been divided into half a dozen maritime-related companies. The sad surrounding neighborhood had been struggling to resurrect itself after the shipyard's loss for years but could never quite recover. Its desolation worked in Carlos's favor.

The two-lane Richmond Terrace wound its way along the entire length of Staten Island's northern shore and the Kill Van Kull, along with a portion of the Arthur Kill. Carlos had reconnoitered the area of the Terrace and found a spot suited for his needs. The roadway there was lightly traveled and even less so in the early morning hours.

The shoreline at that point was less than thirty feet from the road, ensconced behind a metal guardrail and through an overgrown grove of maple and blackberry trees. There were also nondescript weeds and mounds of trash, some of it discarded from the street and some washed up onto the shore. Beyond the guard rail, the terrain dropped eight to ten feet into the black oozing muck that was the shoreline of the Kill.

The city bus passed only once every half hour after midnight and rarely stopped at the corner in those hours. There was no pedestrian traffic at all in the early morning hours. A dozen men could easily hide in that scruffy grove and remain unnoticed.

Carlos was a little worried about irregular police patrols that could show up any time, but he was more concerned about Coast Guard patrols in the waters around Shooters Island. He had a plan for the police, but timing the Coast Guard patrols would entail a couple of nights sitting and conducting surveillance in the filthy grove. The patrols had increased considerably recently, which Carlos deduced was due to the authorities picking up on his scent.

The waterfront adjoining the grove had been formed into a shallow cove created by an unintended breakwater composed of sunken and half-sunken barges, along with the overflow vessel storage of the adjoining dredge company. A small gap existed between the dredges and barges that led to an access point to the open kill itself. It would provide good cover along with the dense foliage of the grove. Once out in the main channel, they'd have to paddle approximately two hundred yards out to Shooters Island. Carlos was absolutely certain that this could be done, but it had to be soon. He knew their time was running out.

*****

Scott was in his office Wednesday morning when he got the results of his inquiry into Orlando's Amex card. "Well, I'll be a son of a bitch! Al, look at this," he said and handed the fax he'd just gotten to Al Krieger. As Al read it and smiled, Scott dialed Brian's number. "Brian, Scott. We got a return on the inquiry we made on Orlando's Amex card. Carlos is still alive."

"No shit, where?"

"Unless Orlando rented a car in Delaware on Monday, he's somewhere down there. Monday afternoon a GMC SUV was rented by an Orlando Rodriguez. I'm assuming Orlando didn't do that."

"No, of course not."

Scott continued, "Well, just like you said, it looks like he cloned Orlando's personal information. We'll put an alarm out on the vehicle. We got all the particulars from the rental agency. He even used a forged New York state driver's license in Orlando's name to do it. He probably isn't sure where our investigation stands, so it shouldn't be long before somebody grabs him. I just have to speak to Orlando so I can do an affidavit confirming he didn't rent the car."

"Scott, I'm over in that area. I can speak with him and do a five. Would you want me to do that? It's not a problem, really."

"Would you mind?"

"No, not at all. Keep me informed if anything changes."

"Absolutely. And, Brian, nice catch, man. Nice catch!"

Brian called Orlando next.

"Orlando, Brian here. Can we get together for lunch today? We've got to talk."

"Yeah, but this is going to cost you, pal. You're buying lunch."

"Let me guess, pastrami, rye, and a Manhattan special from Katz's."

"There you go! My apartment, twelve thirty. Okay?"

"You're on."

Brian got the sandwiches at the deli on Houston Street and was at Orlando's apartment right on time. They sat in his kitchen and ate heartily while Brian told Orlando the results of the Amex card check. He half-laughed as he asked, "I mean, Orlando, you didn't rent a car in Delaware on Monday, did you?"

"No, of course not. You called me, and I was home sleeping, remember?"

"Yeah, I do, but I had to ask the question." He smirked at Orlando, but Orlando was too frazzled to grin back.

Orlando frowned and put his hands on the table as he said, "I got the report back from Amex. This guy was playing me even worse than I thought. He didn't use my stuff often, but he did use it. He rented two storage boxes someplace out in Staten Island in my name. Rosemarie hadn't thought about it because around the same time, we'd spoken about how my storage bin in the building was getting cluttered with boating stuff. She figured I'd rented the boxes out there to keep that stuff near the boat, but I didn't."

"He's got a box out in Staten Island in your name?"

"Two boxes in my name." Both men looked at each other as the weight of that sunk in.

"My immediate thought is to go out to Staten Island and take you with me. Since the boxes are rented in your name, they should open them for you. Ya know, though, why don't we just be smart and run this past a judge and get a legitimate search warrant so we won't have any problems in court?"

"If you say so. Sure, why not? I guess better safe than sorry. Shouldn't you keep an eye on it or something in the meantime?"

"Yeah, normally I would, but I don't want him to know that we're watching them. I'd rather stay away for now, until we have the warrant. I want this fuck in a nice neat package. Ya know, tell ya what, let's do this. I'll call TARU and have them put a camera on the place from, say, a block or two away so we can keep an eye on the area without being obvious. We can watch from a remote location."

"Sounds good, but who is TARU, and how long will it take to set up?"

"TARU are our technical guys, and they're damned good. They'll be up and running in a day or so."

"Okay, if you say so. You're the expert."

"I'll get Scott to run it past a federal judge. We should be ready to go tomorrow. We're going to get this guy, brother." Cold pragmatism was giving way to optimism.

*****

Carlos sat on the ground with his back against an old maple tree halfway down the embankment, watching the waterfront in front of him. So far, he'd witnessed a parade of tugs, barges, containerships, and tankers.

Other than crickets, there was only the sound of an occasional car or bus passing on the road up behind him. There wouldn't be any pedestrian traffic, and even if there were, they would have to go out of their way to see him. On the down side, it was oppressively humid out, and a bluish haze hung over the streetlights. He thought to himself, *My god, it's hot at home, but this weather is beyond miserable.*

A patrol boat passed by every hour or so, and the crew made a point of illuminating the shoreline with their piercing searchlight. They were very thorough, but Carlos was quite sure that if he didn't move, they would not see him, and he was right. They took their light off the shoreline and then lit up Shooters Island just as thoroughly. When the boat crew fixed their light on one side of the island, the beam was unable to penetrate the dense foliage to the other side of the island.

Carlos was becoming increasingly concerned as the authorities seemed to know something more than he thought they might. He nervously ran his hand through his thick brown hair, thinking, *How much had Jack told them before he died?*

Carlos waited for the boat again. Like clockwork, at four thirty in the morning, the same boat passed by and performed the same search. It was clear to him that the walls were beginning to close in on his operation and his secret was unraveling. He had intended to move onto Shooters Island in the early hours of Saturday morning, but that would have to be changed. Carlos moved the date up to Thursday morning as paranoia began to consume him. He waited for the patrol boat to leave the area and then abandoned his post and returned to the truck. He'd lay the new plan out to Atef and the boys tomorrow.

*****

Brian's cell rang shortly after he returned to his office in the precinct. It was Scott.

"Hey, Scott, what's up?"

"You're going to love this."

"What are you talking about?"

"We found the car that Carlos rented. Texas police grabbed it near Austin." There was a long pause on Scott's end after that.

Brian could only respond with a demanding, "And?"

"Carlos wasn't in the car."

"What! Then who the hell was?"

"Wally Kurri."

"Who the fuck is Wally Kurri?"

"Some guy from Newport, Delaware, who lawyered up. We're holding him on a variety of federal charges involving fraud and conspiracy to commit the same. I'm going to fly down tomorrow and interview this guy as soon as I can."

"Where?"

"A place called Wide Creek, Texas, an affluent suburb of Austin."

Brian told Scott about his need for a search warrant.

"Brian, I'll ask Al to put the wheels in motion on that, but do me a favor and sit on the warrant until I've had a chance to talk to this guy Kurri. I just want to see how all this fits together before we move. Are you okay with that?"

"Sure, no problem. Listen, I've called TARU. They're going to put a camera on the place from a discreet distance until we're ready to pop the warrant. They should be up in a day or so."

"Good, perfect. I'll call you from Texas."

*****

George Denby had been brought up to speed and fully realized the significance of Wally Kurri's arrest. He made a call to a friend at McGuire Air Force Base Operations and called in an old favor, a very big favor. Denby and Bill Haggerty were both graduates of the US Air Force Academy; they had been and still were the best of friends. Denby had left the Air Force after his first hitch, but Bill had stayed and found his career there. He was now in charge of base operations at McGuire, and as luck would have it, Haggerty had a Beechcraft T-1 Jayhawk scheduled for a flight to Lackland Air Force Base in San Antonio the next morning. It wasn't uncommon for the Air Force to accommodate an FBI request for transport on a space-available basis. After an explanation of the importance of the situation, Haggerty ensured a priority and secured a return flight.

*****

Carlos got back to the apartment at a little after five in the morning. He sat at the kitchen table, lost in a thousand thoughts. There was no air-conditioning, and the only meager breeze that offered some respite from the oppressive humidity was the cross ventilation from the front and rear windows. Even with that, the air was fetid in the apartment. There were no curtains on the windows, just stained secondhand shades. At 6:15 a.m., Atef woke and came into the kitchen where Carlos was having a cup of tea. Atef heated some water for his own tea and sat opposite Carlos and asked, "How was your night?"

"It was dank and worrisome." He explained the persistent patrols and the curious and exacting probing of the searchlights. "The authorities have gained knowledge about us, and I fear for our plans. Our window of opportunity may be closing. I was going to move out to the island early Saturday morning, but I have reconsidered and I want to move tomorrow tonight."

Atef nodded in agreement and turned his hands, palms up, toward Carlos, as if to comply with a request. "As you wish. After the boys awaken, we will explain what must be done."

As he said that, Syed passed through the room, heading for the bathroom. Carlos looked surprised, stating, "Good, you're awake. Take care of what you were going to do and then wake Anthony and come out here."

Five minutes later, Atef and Carlos were joined by the two drowsy teens. Carlos took the meeting in hand. It was his intention to draw the boys in by addressing them as full partners in a noble mission. Carlos spread a local map on the table in front of them.

"I've had to revise the plans for our mission. Our danger factor has increased considerably. I believe the Americans have our scent, but we are a wilier fox, and we will prevail. We are moving out to the island tonight." As he spoke, he pointed to the applicable points on the map. "We must stay ahead of the Americans. We will have to move a large quantity of equipment to the island and need to do it very secretly. Anthony, Syed, I look to both of you to continue your dedication to jihad. We'll move our equipment from the shore in kayaks. We must load most of our supplies out of the storage facility tonight. Starting at midnight, we'll pack our gear in the truck and tow a trailer with our kayaks. I had wanted to do this over a period of time, but that delay, unfortunately, will not be possible. I will not lie to you, the next few days will be difficult and rather unpleasant, but our reward will be at hand. We must work quickly but carefully. The area that I have chosen to enter the water is the most secluded area I could find. It is off of a main road that is not heavily trafficked, but we will still need a lookout as three of us transport the supplies. Our entrance point is located in a depression just off the road, in a very quiet area. At that point, whoever stays back on security will be able to see vehicles approaching for at least a quarter of a mile in each direction. We will all have small hand radios, but please use them sparingly and in muted tones if contact must be made. It is of the utmost importance that we do not compromise security at this point. Is that completely understood?"

All acknowledged with nods. Atef was his stoic self, while Syed was hardly able to control his enthusiasm. Anthony, on the other hand, remained quiet as the reality of his situation set in.

CHAPTER 42

Scott was momentarily stunned by the Texas July heat when he disembarked the Beechcraft Jayhawk at Randolph Air Force Base in San Antonio. He'd forgotten how oppressively hot summer could be in the Deep South. He was more than grateful to step into the air-conditioned SUV that the Houston FBI office had provided. During the ride to Wide Creek, his Houston counterpart, Special Agent Tony Perez, briefed him on the background information they'd been able to accumulate on Wally Kurri. A check of federal records revealed Kurri's status as a merchant seaman and that he had a permanent position on the *Triton*. At that moment, agents from the Philadelphia office were heading down to the Delaware waterfront to investigate the *Triton* and her possible connection to the blossoming plot.

The Wide River Police Department building and its surrounding grounds were an attractive complex. A one-story red brick structure gave it the appearance of being set in a park. A small department by most standards, it enjoyed the enthusiastic support of an affluent community that endowed its officers with technical and logistical facilities equal to most departments many times its size.

Upon their arrival, they were cordially greeted by the local chief of police, who placed an office at their disposal. It was there that they experienced the first oddity of the day; they would have to wait in line to interview their suspect. New York attorney Daniel Fitzroy of the law firm of Monahan, Stolz, and Cordero was interviewing Wally at the moment. An attorney interviewing a client is not unusual, but one who had flown in from New York to do so and had arrived before Scott and Al was noteworthy.

Carlos had left clear instructions for each of his underlings of what was expected of them should they be captured. Wally, for his part, understood he was to say nothing and call for the lawyer whose name was on the business card Carlos had given him. He was to say nothing to the authorities while waiting for his attorneys to arrive. This tactic had held up well, and he could only hope it would continue to do so.

The law firm also received specific instructions from Carlos. There was to be absolutely no cooperation in regard to interviews or interrogations by authorities beyond providing individual identifying information. This minimal cooperation would be necessary before any one of them could possibly qualify for bail. Beyond that, the attorneys would not be told more than what they needed to know.

Scott and Al both realized that the presence of this high-octane attorney underscored Carlos's level of preparation and attention to detail.

When Scott and Al were led into the interview room, Wally was already seated next to Fitzroy. The room was ample in size with light-blue walls and a plain metal table set in the middle with four seats surrounding it. Scott and Al took chairs opposite Wally and his lawyer and introduced themselves. Fitzroy was a thin-looking forty-year-old associate who was rather pale and appeared uncomfortable. He presented both agents with his business card.

Scott asked matter-of-factly, "I'm assuming that your client has been given his Miranda rights?"

"He has, Agent Burton, and I have to inform you that he will be invoking his Fifth Amendments rights. I expect we will make bail in this minor traffic case."

"Counselor, this 'minor case,' as you refer to it, is a charge of forgery, conspiracy, and interstate flight to avoid prosecution. We do intend to add to that list very shortly. I would not expect Mr. Kurri to be walking as a free man anytime soon. Unless, that is, he'd like to help himself and cooperate in our investigation."

"Agents, I have conferred with my client. He wishes to stand on his Fifth Amendment rights. He has nothing to say to you."

"Is that true, Mr. Kurri?"

Wally was obviously nervous and conflicted when Al posed the question. "Is that how you feel, Mr. Kurri?" Al repeated, softer this time.

Fitzroy's bony left hand tightened his grip on Wally's leg. "Mr. Kurri, say nothing!"

Wally looked at them and then back to his lawyer and cast his view away and downward and quietly said, "Yes."

"Okay, Mr. Kurri. Then we'll speak, and you just listen, okay?"

Fitzroy barked back, "We're not interested in listening, Agent Burton. We're out of here."

Scott tightened up his attitude. "Sit down, Mr. Kurri! I'll tell you when we're finished!" Scott was pushing it, but Fitzroy and Kurri sat down.

Scott began again in a calmer tone, "You took possession of a 2007 GMC SUV from a Hertz rental agency in Wilmington, Delaware, that had been rented by one Carlos Reyes, aka Khalil Wafi, who represented himself to be one Orlando Rodriguez at the rental agency. You then left the area prescribed in the rental agreement, which again had been obtained with a fraudulent credit card, and fled to Texas. That, my friend, is an unauthorized use of a vehicle, conspiracy, and interstate flight to avoid prosecution, the last of which is a federal crime. But I'm sure your attorney has told you that." With that, Scott slammed down a photocopy of the rental agreement on the desk in front of Kurri and his lawyer.

A near-panic-stricken Wally blurted out, "No, no, he didn't."

Fitzroy put his hand on Kurri's shoulder and flatly said, "Shut up, Wally. Say nothing."

Scott continued, "We have photographs, Mr. Kurri, photographs!" He slammed down the rental agency's security camera record of the transaction showing Wally standing next to Carlos as he signed the rental agreement.

"Mr. Kurri, your name is not on that agreement. That constitutes unauthorized use of that vehicle. The evidence, Wally, is placing you deeper in shit, but your attorney has told you that, hasn't he? No? Gee, I wonder why not. Could it be that he's not here to protect and serve you but to represent the interests of Mr. Reyes, aka Wafi? Could it be that he doesn't give a rat's ass what becomes of you as long as Reyes is protected?"

Fitzroy squeezed tighter. "Don't listen to him, Wally. He's got nothing."

With that, Scott stood up and pointed his finger directly at Kurri's face and loudly stated, "Wrong, Mr. Kurri. I've got you, sir! I've got you, and I'm not letting go!"

Fitzroy moved to stand up and remove his client from the interview, but Scott was in full control and, in a raised voice, commanded, "Sit down! Prisoners do not move without permission, sir! I'm not finished speaking to your client, counselor. Mr. Kurri, your opportunities to help yourself are rapidly dwindling. You're not here in Texas to visit relatives or vacation, and it is our personal opinion that you're here passing through on your way to Mexico and God knows where else, but then again, I'm just a cynic, right? Listen, you're running because you know exactly what Carlos Reyes is planning and just how serious that plan is. He's going to kill many Americans, and you know how, when, and where. Time to step up and help yourself, but the window's closing, and soon you're going to be standing on the outside. Wally, if you don't cooperate and Reyes's plan comes to fruition, I will be there, smiling on the other side of the window when they slide that needle into your arm. So help me God, I will."

Scott stood up at the table and walked around to spin Wally's chair out toward him. Burton got right in Kurri's face and told him, "When Reyes does commit the terrible sin he's planning to commit, you will be charged equally with him. Wally, I'm sure you've heard that tired old saying, 'The wages of sin are death.' In your case, that adage is particularly applicable."

On board the boat, Wally was a leader, but apart from it, he fell victim to the persuasion of the strongest influence. Now he was torn between two strong influences. Scott watched Kurri's eyes dart back and forth as he desperately tried to find a way out of his situation, but he had no options. He was trapped, and it was beginning to take a toll. His fingers tapped methodically on the tabletop as he hungrily stared at the shape of the cigarette pack in Scott's shirt pocket. He desperately craved a cigarette. There was dead silence in the room when Burton was finished. Then there was the sound of water running on the floor of the room that featured no apparent plumbing fixtures. Wally's bladder had failed him.

Scott quickly realized what had happened and added, "I see that the point wasn't wasted on you. Counselor, take him back and clean him up. We can continue this later. And, Mr. Kurri, I hope you understand that you can fire your lawyer if you're dissatisfied with his performance. The clock is running, sir, and it's not in your favor."

Scott and Al rose from the desk and moved toward the door as Fitzroy snipped, "I'll be reporting your conduct here today!" Scott turned toward him as he opened the door to leave and said rather dismissively, "Right, whatever, you do that, counselor." They left without another word.

As Scott and Al walked down the hall toward their office, Al remarked without looking back, "Impressive, very impressive."

Scott smirked and shook his head. They needed to take a few minutes and find out what further background New York had come up with. Kurri might have the answers they were looking for.

*****

Carlos, Atef, Syed, and Anthony arrived back at the storage facility at 12:30 a.m. The four of them emptied the storage boxes in about an hour. Standing inside the metal box, Carlos called his band together. Holding a block of Semtex in one hand and a detonator in the other, he instructed them about the explosives they were about to be handling. Having riveted their attention, Carlos quietly, precisely, and calmly explained the use and the result of the misuse of their explosives, especially the sensitive detonators. It had a sobering effect on them all. After the briefing, the boxes containing the Semtex were gingerly placed on the bottom of the truck bed, well apart from the detonators. Carlos enigmatically smiled, noticing the boys exhibit a newfound sense of seriousness about their duties as they loaded the truck.

The metallic clank of the of kayak trailer being hitched to the truck reverberated in the quiet of the night in their deserted surroundings; they were ready to move. Carlos knew this would be the time they were most vulnerable to observation, in this initial move from the storage facility through the back roads near the vicinity of the shoreline. Rather than drive through the local streets from this point, they would travel the local West Shore Expressway toward the Goethals Bridge on the north shore of the island. Even though they'd be exposed on the open highway, it would be for a shorter period of time. Leaving the storage facility, Carlos pulled over on the highway on-ramp and stopped. Carlos picked up his cell phone.

"Police operator 217, where is the emergency?"

"I'm at the Kansas Diner at Forest Avenue and Richmond Avenue. There's been a robbery, and an off-duty policeman has been shot. Hurry!" He hung up before the 911 operator could question, and waited. Twenty seconds later, two police cars passed him heading eastward toward the diner at speeds in excess of eighty miles per hour. Carlos smiled. *That should occupy the local cops.*

Carlos moved the heavily burdened truck slowly onto the highway and proceeded out into traffic. He had bought himself at least twenty minutes of police-free travel as units from all over the area would converge at the site of his bogus call. He traveled north on the arterial highway without hitting any traffic and got off at the last westbound exit. They passed quietly into the local streets bridging marshland and a mix of maritime industrial sites of a bygone era.

The truck pulling the trailer drove eastbound on Richmond Terrace, the rattling metal frame of the boat trailer echoing through the sleepy streets. The Terrace, as it was referred to locally, was the main roadway that passed through the quiet Mariner's Harbor at the shoreline. Carlos followed Richmond Terrace eastward, now nearing his ultimate destination, the scrubby T-shaped intersection of Richmond Terrace and Van Name Avenue. He pulled the truck into the quiet residential Van Name Avenue next to the vacant remains of the boarded-up American Legion Hall.

Carlos posted Atef as a lookout at the corner as they got the kayaks off the trailer and down into the trees. Once free of the small craft, Carlos had the boys hide themselves on the water side of the street with the kayaks. They stood behind the guardrail, below street level and out of sight. Carlos then drove the truck a few blocks away and quietly stopped. Just as silently, he detached the trailer and left it parked anonymously on a back street, while the truck was left on Van Name where it could easily blend in with the surrounding cars. Now that the trailer was gone, it was time to get down to business.

It was 1:30 a.m., and they were transferring the food, water, and other provisions to the grove when Atef noticed the searchlight of a Coast Guard patrol boat darting through the clutter of the shoreline. He signaled Carlos with one of the hand radios. Carlos immediately began covering everything with black tarps. "Syed, Anthony, get behind those larger trees and do not move!"

The boat appeared beyond the old dredge just outside of the artificial breakwater; its engines had the deep grumble of a craft operating almost at an idle. The bulk of one of the dredges obstructed the path of the searchlight on the shore, keeping Carlos's team safe as the boat proceeded on. They would now have almost a half an hour before the Coast Guard would make its return trip. It was Carlos's intention to use that time to move the remaining cargo from the truck to the shoreline. The move out to Shooters Island would proceed only after the patrol boat had returned and completed its eastward passage toward the St. George Ferry Terminal.

The police ashore continued to act according to Carlos's plans. After responding to the bogus report of an officer being shot, half of the officers took a coffee break. Among those attending that coffee cloche were the officers assigned to patrol the sector that covered the intersection of Richmond Terrace and Van Name Avenue. A serious accident on the highway kept the rest preoccupied. Carlos and company could expect to work in peace for the remainder of the night.

*****

Scott's cell phone rang as he and Al sat in the loaner office at the Wide Creek Police Department. Scott picked it up on the second ring and simply answered, "Burton."

"Special Agent Burton, this is Major Fiske over at the air base. You hitched a ride with us from McGuire."

"Yes, what can I do for you?"

"Colonel Haggerty asked me to give you a call to see if you'd be riding back to McGuire with us. We're leaving tomorrow morning at 0930 hours."

"Yes, that would be great. But I'm not sure that I can conclude my business here by then. Could I transport a prisoner on your aircraft?"

"Would he or she be restrained?"

"Absolutely."

"Then, sure."

"Listen, Captain, can I reach you at this number?"

"Yes, sir."

"Let me see if I can wrap up my business, and I'll call you back in a couple of hours."

"Sure, but I have to leave on time tomorrow, sir. I have a flight plan already filed."

"Understood. I'll call you back either way. Thank you very much for the heads-up."

"Yes, sir."

They hung up, and Scott turned to Al. "Scott, let's speak with the local prosecutor and see if he'll defer the case to us."

The call was made immediately to Travis County prosecutor Steve Bell, who, after hearing the saga surrounding Wally Kurri, could not have been more cooperative. The appropriate paperwork was completed, and the Wide Creek Police ceded the prosecution to the government. Mr. Kurri would most certainly be leaving on the Beechcraft the following morning. Counselor Fitzroy was not happy that his client was going to be out his control for the three-and-a-half-hour trip back to McGuire Air Force Base. He admonished Scott and Al that Mr. Kurri was not to be interviewed out of his presence. Al and Scott readily agreed. Nothing was said about plain old conversation. They told Wally what was going to happen the next day and made sure the jailers would have him ready to move early the next morning. With all that done, they took Steve Bell up on his offer of some Texas steaks and Lone Star long necks.

*****

Once the patrol had passed from view, Carlos had the boys place the kayaks in the water. First, the explosives needed to be loaded and separated between three boats. To be on the safe side, the three towed boats would go out to the island in two separate moves. Loading the boats was beyond laborious as they stood in the shallow sucking muck at the shoreline. Carlos, Syed, and Anthony each towed a kayak. The seventeen-year-old boys made it out to the northeast corner of the island in a reasonable fifteen minutes. Carlos arrived eight minutes later, gasping for breath.

The solid shore of Shooters Island was an obstacle course of debris that could easily injure someone not paying attention. As Carlos approached his landing point, he was horrified to see the boys just standing in open view next to their kayaks. Part of him wanted to call out and scream, "You stupid bastards, get under cover!" Instead, he waited until he landed to instruct his young charges.

"Boys, for God's sake, use your heads! Get the hell out of sight!"

Syed and Anthony followed him into the island's interior as he pulled the boats far back into the trees. The ground underfoot was matted with a soft, springy bed of wet leaves and had a strong musky odor mixed with rotting animal carcasses. They stopped and stood still for a few moments to allow their eyes to adjust. Once their night vision kicked in, Anthony noticed a corner remnant of a collapsed building. They carefully walked toward it, avoiding the exposed roots of trees around them. Carlos took a few minutes to regain his breath. After he composed himself, he quietly explained what he wanted them to do.

"Boys, place the explosives behind that wall. Later, when we come back out here, we'll dig a pit and put the explosives and the remainder of our supplies further out of the line of sight. We must remember to remain conscious of not being seen. Use the wall as cover. Never stand out in the open. Don't let me have to remind you again."

Both young men sheepishly nodded. They then got back into the boats and started their return trip, which was much faster with the lightened load.

The second trip went smoothly. Then they had to wait in place on the island for the patrol boat to pass once more. They set the boats well back in the brush and fetid soil until the patrol moved on. Other than the low growl of the outboards moving past, there was little or no sound in the thicket. All Carlos heard were the crickets and the occasional movement of animals. It was a bit disconcerting lying motionless in the dirt as rats scurried across their legs, but if that was what was necessary to maintain operational security, then so be it.

Carlos allowed everyone to sit up and rest while the patrol boat passed on toward the western end of its sector, but they would have to go back to the ground when the boat returned on its eastward passage.

While transporting these materials in kayaks sounded like a good idea on paper, in reality, it turned out to be somewhat more difficult. The small craft were designed to transport people in a confined cockpit and were limited in their ability to accommodate bulky cargo. Regardless, they finished before sunrise and brought Atef across on the final trip.

As the sun came up, the group had a better view of their surroundings. What had once been a thriving shipyard was now reduced by time and nature to a series of crumbled walls and foundations. The quiet bird sanctuary in the busy harbor had been peacefully composting itself for the past ninety-some-odd years.

The animal population had claimed it as their sanctuary, although the deer and egrets were timid and moved off to other portions of the island. The group dug holes for cover and settled in with their MREs and bottled water while beating rats away with their shovels. It was going to be a long few days.

Their supplies were covered with the black tarp. Garbage would have to be buried in pits some distance from their encampment. One member of the group was on watch at all times with a Kalashnikov AKM. If they were discovered prematurely, they'd only achieve martyrdom earlier than planned, but they were to take as many Americans with them as possible.

CHAPTER 43

The Beechcraft T-1A Jayhawk Executive Transport went wheels up on schedule the next morning with Scott, Al, and Wally securely aboard. While Scott and Al were grateful to the Texas authorities, both could not wait to get out of the oppressive Texas heat. Wally was shackled hand and foot, as the pilot, Captain Fiske, had requested. Free of having Fitzroy in his ear and now being in a secure environment, Wally seemed a little less on edge now.

As soon as they were comfortably at altitude, air-conditioning provided a soothing atmosphere in their small cabin, and the seat belts came off as Scott began skillfully working his prisoner. Neither Scott nor Al gave a damn about what the lawyer had said as long as they could gain some inside knowledge into Carlos's plans. Scott took a seat next to Wally.

"Hey, man, how you doing?"

Wally had been resting his head peacefully against the small window next to him. He broke a slight smile and only replied, "Okay."

"Do you need anything?"

"Nothing you could give me."

"Did you think about what we said the other day?"

"Look, my lawyer said we shouldn't talk."

Scott backed off a little and kept it nonthreatening. "That's fine. I'm just asking." He'd just let him be for now. He hoped Wally would like to make a little idle conversation in a while. Wally actually did want to speak with them, but he still had Fitzroy's admonitions in his ear. He hadn't much cared for Fitzroy or his advice up to this point. He couldn't help but worry that Fitzroy was more there to protect Carlos's interests, not his. It had also occurred to him that he was a liability to Carlos now, and his people might seek to eliminate him regardless of whether he cooperated with the Feds or not. Still, he was trying to keep his mouth shut so he wouldn't be in a deeper hole. About a half an hour later, Al casually stepped back to Wally's seat and tried a different tack.

"Hey, pal, would you like a cup of coffee?"

"Yeah, yeah, I would, thanks. Black please."

"You got it."

Al came back with the coffee and sat down next to Wally. Al remarked casually, "Not bad transport, huh?"

Wally took a sip as he looked out the window, taking in the panorama of plowed fields and small communities where everyone seemed to have a swimming pool in their backyard. "I'd like it more if it was going in the other direction."

"I imagine you would," Al quipped with a smile. "Wally, you seem to have worked your way into quite a shitstorm of events."

"You have no idea."

"The fact is, I actually do have an idea. I wouldn't want to be in your shoes right now. You're in it up to your neck with us, and you're on shaky ground with your own people."

"Look. Agent Krieger, I believe your name is?"

"Yeah, call me Al, Wally." Al's demeanor was quieter than Scott's and seemed to be putting Wally more at ease.

"Right, Al. Look, I hear everything you guys are trying to say to me, but I've got it coming at me from all directions, and to tell you the truth, it's driving me nuts. I didn't sleep at all last night with all this shit on my mind, not to mention that cell was hardly a five-star hotel, and I've got a splitting headache from the tension. I'm not saying you guys are wrong in what you're saying, but I feel like my head is going to explode with everything I'm trying to deal with. I need some time to process all this shit and maybe get some rest. Can you understand what I'm saying?"

"Oh, absolutely, Wally. Listen, would you like us to set you up in protective custody in the detention center when we get to New York?"

"That would be great. You can do that?"

"Sure, no problem."

Al realized that even though he'd extracted no concessions in return, he'd made a breakthrough. "Look, Wally, take whatever time you need. Lord only knows time is something you and I both have plenty of. I'm going back up to my seat, so why don't you get some rest. We'll be back at McGuire in a little more than three hours. We can talk again before that or whenever you feel up to it. No pressure, man. Okay?"

"Yeah, thanks." Wally sipped his coffee and re-rested his head on the window. He really wanted to ask for an aspirin for his headache, but he didn't want to be a pain in the ass.

Al returned to his seat next to Scott, and the two looked at each other. Al shot Scott a thumbs-up and a smile. Scott said nothing but smiled as they exchanged a fist bump. They were sure Wally was going to come their way. Al asked Scott, "Do we know if this guy has family?"

"Yeah, New York shot me a profile yesterday. He's got a family, his mother, and a couple of others somewhere in northern New Jersey."

"We should interview them."

"We will, right after we get him settled in New York."

*****

Among Wally's life priorities, his personal health was not high on his list. Aside from a trip to the local emergency room when he was in his twenties to get some stitches, he had never seen a doctor—ever. Had he done so, especially recently, his doctor would have made note of the fact that his blood pressure and cholesterol were through the roof. Wally was a ticking medical time bomb.

Wally had consumed black coffee by the quart on a daily basis for years and smoked two packs a day. At 10:00 a.m. on an air force plane twenty thousand feet over America's heartland, fate and Wally's blood pressure caught up with him. The combination of his physical condition—or more correctly, the lack thereof—stress, and sitting stationary caused a clot to be thrown from his leg to the left side of his brain.

It began with him quietly thrashing about in his seat. Wally found himself suddenly semi-awakened by his own sense of distress, confusion, and disorientation. Everything seemed to be happening somewhere in the foggy distance. He wanted to call out but couldn't. Wally was suffering a grand ischemic attack, more commonly known as a massive stroke. That resulted in the loss of his ability to speak and awareness of the entire right side of his body. He slumped over in his seat against the window in a semiconscious state, unable to comprehend what was happening.

Scott and Al were completely unaware of what had just happened behind them. They briefly looked back at Wally, who appeared to be asleep with his head resting against the plastic window to his left. As the flight winged back toward McGuire, they occupied themselves by catching up with their reports. An hour later, Scott accepted the invitation of the pilot to come forward. He was absolutely fascinated by the grand view of the state of Tennessee from the flight deck.

A while later, Captain Fiske informed Scot and Al, "We're going to start to make our descent into McGuire soon. You might want to make sure your prisoner is ready and belted in."

Al signaled that he would take care of that, allowing Scott to keep gawking like an eleven-year-old. He walked back to Wally's seat and tried to wake him up.

"Wally. It's time to belt up, man. We're getting ready to land." There was no response. Al tried again, but still there was no response. Al shook Wally's shoulder, and Kurri's body pitched forward with his face falling against the seat ahead of him with a meaty slapping sound. Al could now see Wally's face, and what he saw shocked him. His olive complexion had taken on an ashen quality. The right side of his face was drooping, and drool soaked his shirt. His deep-set eyes were fixed and staring off to the left. Al immediately called out loudly, "Wally! Wally, can you hear me?" Again there was no response, with the exception of a guttural sound. The volume of Al's voice and the sense of urgency in it drew Scott back to them fast.

"Al, what the hell's going on?"

"You tell me, man. Look at him. This is not good."

"Did this guy try to overdose or something?"

"Impossible. I searched him myself when we picked him up this morning. He may have had a stroke." They placed him back in his seat. Scott went forward and informed the pilot immediately.

"What's his status? Is he conscious?"

"I'm not sure. He's nonresponsive, his eyes are open, but he seems really out of it. My partner thinks it may be a stroke." Fiske turned the controls over to his copilot and went back to assess the situation for himself. Having seen all he needed to, he turned to go back up forward. Before he did, however, he deployed the oxygen mask out of the space above Wally's head and placed it on his face, instructing Scott, "Keep an eye on him. Make sure he doesn't puke into the mask."

Fiske wasted no time after returning to his seat and got right on the radio. "Washington Center, Hawk 644, declaring an emergency. Have a passenger on board with a medical emergency. Request immediate vectors to McGuire Air Force Base."

Washington responded, "Hawk 664, roger, turn left to 030, descend 2,000, accelerate to maximum airspeed and contact McGuire. Approach on 363.8."

Fiske acknowledged his instructions, and the controllers at McGuire Air Force Base took control and fast-tracked the Jay Hawk's approach.

A female controller with a crisp but pleasant voice responded from McGuire approach. "Emergency Hawk 644, winds are at 070 at 16, altimeter 3001, McGuire landing runway 06, turn heading 035, descend and maintain 2,000, emergency vectors to McGuire AFB. Paramedics will be standing by. Hawk 644, can you advise the nature of the medical emergency?"

Fiske briefly explained Wally's condition.

"Emergency Hawk 644, thank you, sir. I will advise the medics of that."

Approximately one minute later, McGuire replied and further cleared their descent.

"McGuire Tower, Hawk 644 crossing final approach, gear in transit, for emergency full stop RWY 06."

Throughout the approach, Al and Scott stood by Wally, who exhibited no change for the better or worse. "Wally, stay with us." Al pleaded. There was no reaction on Kurri's part.

"Hawk 644, cleared to land RWY 06, report the gear, paramedics standing by at the ramp."

"Cleared to land RWY 06, three down and locked, 644."

The aircraft touched down at 12:45 p.m., rolled out on runway 06, and responded to directions that would lead Wally to the paramedics who were awaiting him at base operations. As Fiske taxied, he could see the ambulance's lights straight ahead.

Once he came to a stop, the medics got immediately on board and worked on Wally. He was removed to the base hospital, quickly evaluated, and then evacuated by air to Virtua Memorial Hospital in Mount Holly, New Jersey. Unfortunately, he received treatment outside of the critical first three-hour period, which excluded his being treated with a touted clot-busting drug. His chances for full recovery would have been remarkably good had he received the treatment. Regardless, Wally was now barely conscious. He appeared unable to coherently coordinate his thoughts when awake.

Scott called George Denby and carefully briefed him on the day's chaotic turn of events. Denby sat and merely stared at his phone. He was speechless, and Scott actually thought the phone connection had been broken. Denby could only shake his head and remark quite loudly, "Is this case fucking cursed? Goddamn it all!" He picked up a souvenir paperweight and threw it against the far wall where it shattered. All work in the office stopped as employees' heads either swiveled toward the source of the disturbance, speechlessly frozen in place, or looked away, seemingly not knowing how to respond. This was a serious departure for the very controlled, buttoned-down, and meticulous George Denby. When he regained his composure, he asked Scott to set up federal marshal protection on Kurri at the local hospital. Once that was taken care of, they were to report back to New York. Wally Kurri, another promising lead, was now out of the picture for God knows how long, if not for good. A now very embarrassed Denby stood in his office door and said out loud for all in the office bay in front of him to hear, "Ladies and gentlemen, please excuse my inappropriate conduct."

*****

Shortly after 11:00 a.m. on Saturday, Brian and Louie were sitting at the office of the You Rent It center on a back road of the Travis section of Staten Island with a search warrant in hand.

Brian and Louie brought Orlando with them to the facility. The Police Tactical Assistance Response Unit had held the site covertly under observation from a camera located on a telephone pole a quarter of a mile away. They observed no activity and had no way of knowing that Carlos had removed most of the contents of the boxes two nights before. The group entered the modular office at the front gate of the facility and were met by the day man, Leonard Scatozzi, a forty-year-old man with thinning gray hair combed straight back, whose voice had a distinctive nasal twang. He stood next to a counter with a number of television monitors behind it, all showing various sections of the facility.

"Good morning, guys. How ya doin'?"

"Good morning. NYPD. We have a search warrant for the premises. I'm Detective Devine, this is Detective Lugo, and this is Mr. Rodriguez."

"Yo!" A man of few words, the befuddled Scatozzi didn't know how to react and carefully checked their shields and ID cards as if he actually knew what he was doing. He also gave the search warrant itself a superficial examination. Then, satisfied that they were who they said they were, he ceded to their authority and the situation. "What are youse guys looking for?"

"What's your name, sir?" asked a very official Brian Devine.

"Lenny, Lenny Scatozzi. I'm the day manager."

"Mr. Scatozzi, the warrant is for containers rented by Orlando Rodriguez."

"What'd he do?"

"I can't discuss that, Mr. Scatozzi."

"Please, guys, my friends call me Squeaky."

Brian looked at Scatozzi and evaluated the kind of guy who stood before him. He had on jeans, a light-blue short-sleeved button-down shirt completely open with an athletic T-shirt underneath, and black leather shoes with elevator heels. Brian processed this vision before him and thought to himself, *Yup, definitely a Squeaky*.

Scatozzi keyed the computer at the station in front of him. "Rodriguez, yeah, here ya go. Orlando Rodriguez, units nineteen and twenty. Ya want I should open them for youse?"

"We would appreciate that, Mr. Scatozzi."

"Err, okay, but would you mind if I just call my boss and tell him what's happening? If I don't, he'll probably get pissed off, and I need this job, if ya know what I mean."

"Mr. Scatozzi, take us to the units, open them, and then after we're done, call whomever you want. Until then, please, no calls." They didn't need him tipping anybody off before they were able to examine the boxes.

"Okay, sounds good. Come with me." He took them out into a courtyard and down an asphalt-paved path, past a sequentially numbered series of storage units on both sides, all behind the same type of corrugated steel gate. "Here you go, fellas, unit nineteen." Scatozzi unlocked the cipher and rolled up the gate. It was a pretty straightforward affair: metal walls and floor sitting on a concrete base. Lenny snapped on the light, but that really wasn't necessary. They didn't need the interior illuminated to see that there wasn't a blessed thing in the box other than three empty wood freight pallets.

"Lenny, do me a favor, close it up and don't go back in there. We may want the interior dusted for fingerprints."

"Whatever you say, Detective. Should I open number twenty?"

"Yeah, please, sir." Brian couldn't believe how humid it was back here, especially within the boxes.

Box number twenty was opened in the same fashion as nineteen, but this time, the limited light revealed an object at the rear of the box. Lenny flipped on the lights. There was nothing in the box with the exception of an object approximately four feet by four feet by four feet covered by black plastic sheeting and sitting on a wooden pallet. Louie looked at Brian. "Whatya think?"

"I think we ought to open it and take a look," Brian said to Louie.

"What do you think it is?"

"If I knew that, I wouldn't have to open it and look, would I?"

"Got a point there, ace."

Brian took a folding buck knife out of his right pants pocket and flicked it open. He carefully cut the packing tape that secured the package to the pallet and to itself. He lifted the black packing and was now looking at clear plastic shrink wrap. What was under that shrink wrap stopped them all dead in their tracks. Brian was speechless. Louie said for all of them, "Whoa, holy shit!" Lenny added a low-brow "Holy fuck" as an addendum. Stacked before them was a solid block of US currency—twenties, fifties, and hundreds. Brian regained his composure and said, "Everyone, touch nothing and move outside. Louie, do we have crime scene tape in the trunk of the car?"

"I don't know, I'll check."

Brian asked Lenny, "Sir, do you know the last time someone was in numbers nineteen and twenty?"

"I'd have to look that up in the office, but I'm sure I can help youse."

"Can you describe what the renters of this box looked like?"

"I can do better than that, Detective. We videotape everyone coming and going. See them for yourself."

"Squeaky, I think I love you!"

Lenny smiled, relieved to be able to help.

Brian had Lenny secure the boxes and number twenty's contents once more.

Brian grabbed his portable radio and asked for the crime scene unit. He then called for the local command duty officer to set up security on the boxes. Following that, he placed calls to his boss, Chief Halvorsen, and then Federal Supervisor George Denby and informed them of what they'd found. Finally he dialed Scott and Robles in order to keep them in the loop. He wasn't immediately able to contact Robles but did speak with Scott, who was absolutely flabbergasted.

As they walked back to Lenny's office, Brian put his arm around Lenny and asked, "Squeaky pal, could you get me a copy of the tape from the last time somebody went into those storage units?"

"Sure, let me bring it up."

Within minutes, Lenny had located the critical tape from early Thursday morning. There was Carlos, Atef, and what appeared to be two other young men. They were loading a silver pickup truck. The truck, unfortunately, was parked at an angle that made it impossible to view the license plate, but there was also the trailer with the kayaks. Louie's eyes widened.

"Squeaky, could you burn us a copy of that tape?"

"I'll burn a copy, you take the original."

They would spend hours examining that tape back at the office. Brian thought out loud, "I wonder if that prick can feel me breathing down his neck."

CHAPTER 44

By Sunday, life on Shooters Island had deteriorated beyond anything they had anticipated. Carlos had failed to account for several factors when he planned for the group's stay on the island. Amidst the heat and humidity of July in New York City, they were running out of water and had to ration the water that was left. On top of their hydration concerns, they had also run out of bug repellent and had resorted to covering their bodies in mud to ward off the swarms of mosquitoes that circled them. Heavy rain on both Saturday and Sunday had reduced the island to a quagmire that was beyond bleak. They might as well have been trying to survive in the jungles of the South Pacific. The conditions and their inability to move about freely were beginning to take a physical and psychological toll on all of them.

Syed and Anthony occupied holes side by side, and in the late evening, Anthony carefully probed Syed, hoping that he might have an ally in his desperation.

"Syed, is this filthy hole what you expected jihad to be?"

"My brother, this place is disgusting, but our misery is only temporary. Soon we will be seated at the feet of the Prophet Mohammad in paradise. Hear me when I tell you that hundreds of infidels will burn in hell because of our work. Our mothers will cry over us at our funerals, but they will be tears of joy, my brother!"

Anthony smiled benignly and said nothing but thought to himself, *They're all out of their minds. It hasn't even occurred to this lunatic that after the hundred pounds or so of explosives detonate under him, there won't be enough left of him to bury in a thermos! I'm not ready to die for Allah, or anyone for that matter, especially like this!* Anthony desperately fought off the waves of panic that were flooding his mind.

He had previously been fully submissive and obedient to his over-bearing father's wishes and the dogmatic harangues of his overzealous teachers, but for the first time in his life, Anthony was thinking for himself. He would have to fight to maintain his composure unless he wanted one of these lunatics to slit his throat. But he also knew how unbelievably wrong this mission and jihad was.

*****

It was early Monday morning, July 26, and Jack had company. Supervising Special Agent George Denby had called an early morning meeting of the task force principals to discuss a situation that was becoming more and more ominous. Denby and Phil Halvorsen sat at the meeting table in Jack's quarters with his team. Denby's mood was more dour than Scott and Al had ever seen.

"Gentlemen, I know I can speak for Inspector Halvorsen when I say you've all done an incredible job to this point, but we continue to have a real problem on our hands. I'm sure, based upon our investigation to this point, we're about to hurt really badly, and I'm afraid very soon. We need to know the when and where of this story. I have to believe there is more to this plan of theirs than a kayak attack on a ferry. Kurri's tug is capable of moving much larger cargoes, so what is its role?"

The Coast Guard's representative, Al Robles, suggested, "UIEDs?"

An expressionless Denby agreed, "Possibly, why not?"

Jack O'Connor hesitantly chimed in, "Excuse me sir, UIEDs?"

"That's okay, Jack. Those are underwater explosives. They could have a fifty-five-gallon drum filled with some type of explosives, or rubber fuel bladders filled with explosives, or even actual sea mines."

"Al, can't the Coast Guard look for them?" Brian asked.

"You mean sweep for mines?"

"Yeah?"

"I wish it were that easy. The Coast Guard does not have the expertise or equipment to do that. That's the Navy's job."

"Can't we have them check the harbor?"

"We could, once we get them here. The closest detachment is in Virginia, though. Then, where should we have them search? Jack, the thing of it is, unless we can give them some substantial proof that some sort of mines is actually present, I doubt that they're going to respond. The problem is, they usually expect to be contacted after the fact. I'm still going to try, though. Oddly enough, there was a time during the Cold War when we had a mechanism to address this type of situation. But not anymore."

Robles had the floor and an attentive audience. "Agent Denby, Inspector Halvorsen, do you mind if I continue?"

Denby gestured approvingly with his right hand, stating, "No, please go ahead. You've got my attention."

"Thank you, sir. During the Cold War, as late as 1991, the government performed underwater sound surveys in major US ports. You do an intricate survey and catalogue every mine-like object on the bottom of the harbor, which is a virtual junkyard. There might be hundreds and hundreds of mine-like objects down there. Some of the stuff are fairly obvious, but some aren't. If they found a suspicious object, they would send somebody down for a look. In the end, there would be an archive routinely assembled of the contents of the harbor bottom. If a device was suspected or one actually did detonate, the Navy could refer back to the archive to facilitate reopening the harbor, already knowing what did and did not belong."

This time it was Denby asking the question, "We no longer do that?"

"When the Cold War ended, the practice ended too, and it hasn't really been done here properly since 1991."

"So we have no idea what's on the harbor floor?"

"Nope."

"Has anybody tried to resurrect the practice?"

"Yeah, but it falls on the deaf ears of politicians. Brian, do you remember that guy who retired from your job, Al Calcaterra?"

"Sure, he's a very knowledgeable guy on this type of stuff."

"You bet he is. Outside the intelligence community, there are few people who are as on top of this stuff as he is. He has been trying to sell the powers that be on sonar archiving of the harbor floor for years, but no one's biting."

A curious Louie asked, "How many millions of dollars does it cost to do?"

"Millions? Try a paltry half a million for the entire harbor, including Newark Bay. Let me try to put that in some sort of perspective. In the early 1980s, there was a longshoreman's strike on the West Coast that lasted about ten days. The ships and trains that serviced them backed up, and the economy suffered. The cost of this completely predictable event was $1.9 billion a day! Can you imagine what an unexpected attack on a harbor like ours would do to the economy? It would be economic devastation."

After Robles finished, there was a more than awkward silence hanging over the group. Denby finally broke it. "Thanks, Al, that's really a sobering evaluation. Can we elevate the MARSEC level?"

"We're at level II now. The Coast Guard captain of the port has the authority to do that, but without some type of tangible evidence, I don't think it's going to happen. I don't think the government is going to want to panic the public without something to hang their hats on." Now even Denby fell silent after a deep exhale.

Robles quietly added, "There may be one way to step around that. There is a stakeholder's group in each harbor. It's called the Area Maritime Committee, which is composed of the principal players in the harbor. We could speak to them individually and have them subtly raise security levels on their own with no fanfare."

Al asked, "Would the captain of the port go along with that?"

"He's on our side, guys."

"Wonderful! In the meantime, we need to tighten up security around the ferries." Denby turned to Halvorsen, who didn't need to be prompted. "George, starting tomorrow, police divers will be checking out each of the undersides of the boats before they go into service for the day."

Robles added, "And each boat will be escorted back and forth by at least one of our twenty-five-foot transportable port security boats. They'll be carrying their full armament of .50-caliber and two M240B 7.62 mm machine guns. Nobody will get near those ferries."

The color began to return to Denby's face. "Very good. They're here, gentlemen. They didn't vanish into thin air. Let's get them."

Brian raised his hand with a frown. "Mr. Denby, if I might add something, sir?"

"Absolutely, Brian."

"Sir, Kurri was found in Texas driving an SUV that Reyes rented for him, but why? He owns a four-by-four pickup, so he didn't need the GMC that was recovered in Texas. It's my feeling that Reyes took Kurri's vehicle for his own use. Scott, hear me out. I don't think Kurri's vehicle was found in Delaware, was it?"

"No, Brian, it hasn't been."

Halvorsen nodded. "Great thought, Brian, put an alarm out on Kurri's truck. Do we have a make and model on it?"

Scott answered, "A 2008 Toyota Tacoma. I'll give Brian the particulars as soon as we break."

Denby took the reins again. He stood and solemnly said, "Gentlemen, let's get home and get a few hours' rest. Tomorrow's going to be an ass kicker of a day. This thing may still happen, but let's not make it so because we glossed over something right under our noses." The meeting broke with a huge sense of urgency hanging in the air.

*****

A bright and seasonable July Monday afternoon found a bleary-eyed Scott and Al Krieger in Ridgewood, New Jersey, at the home of Maurice and Albert Malouf, Wally Kurri's next of kin. Their house was a pristine example of a main hall colonial that harkened back to the 1940s or 1950s. Set back from the road about a hundred feet, it was hard for Scott and Al not to notice and admire the meticulous condition of the grounds, a tribute to Albert, an avid gardener.

It was Maurice, a stocky man of medium height in his late sixties with a thick mustache and an even thicker shock of white hair, who met them at the door. After warmly inviting them in, he led them through a foyer area that Scott thought could have easily been larger than the living room in his Brooklyn apartment. Scott and Al followed through a formal dining room, rich in oak furnishings and wainscot walls, turning through the kitchen toward the door to the rear yard. "If you gentlemen don't mind, I thought we might be more comfortable out here." He led them out into a portion of a large rear yard under a canopy of grape arbors. Under the middle of the arbor, Maurice had set a large table covered with a blue-and-white-checkered tablecloth and a bowl of summer fruit.

Al spoke as he admiringly surveyed the intricate rose garden farther out in the rear of the yard. "Yes, sir, much more than comfortable. You have a beautiful home. Thank for your hospitality."

Maurice smiled and graciously acknowledged the compliment with a slight nod.

Albert Malouf was already seated, but he rose and offered his hand in welcome when Al and Scott approached. Albert was a bit younger than his brother and had a smaller yet well-toned physique. Both brothers had a dignified presence about them.

As they sat at the table, Rania, Wally's mother, came out carrying a tray with a pitcher of ice tea and glasses. "I hope you like ice tea." Albert introduced his sister.

Seated at the table, Scott opened the conversation. It was an obligatory interview, and neither Scott nor Al expected any massive revelation, but then again, you could never know.

The background information that had been accumulated on Wally led the agents to Maurice and Albert. When they called Maurice and told him who they were and that they wanted to speak with them about Wally, they expressed concern but no hesitation. Now the family hung on to Scott's every word. They had not been in Wally's life for a very long time, but it was quite obvious that he had remained in their thoughts. Scott led Wally's family through the events surrounding his current predicament as gently as possible, including his medical situation.

The Maloufs immediately became distressed at the news of Wally's stroke. A now-ashen Rania could only hold her hands to her head and repeat, "Ya albi! Ya albi!" Maurice placed his head in both as he let out a deep sigh.

"I knew one day that it would come to this."

"What do you mean by that, sir?" asked a restrained Scott.

Rania interjected, "Maurice, not now! Mr. Burton, I need to be with my son!"

"Madam, I will try my best to arrange that. However, you must understand that in addition to being a patient at that hospital, he is also a federal prisoner. He does not enjoy normal visitation rights, and the reason for that, partially, is for his own protection. Mrs. Kurri, let's get through our conversation here, and I promise you before we leave today, I will call the hospital and try to have you speak with your son's doctor."

"Why can't I speak with Wally?"

"I don't mean to upset you further, but as a result of the type of stroke Wally has suffered, his ability to speak has been impaired. Right now, he probably can't speak with anyone."

"Oh my dear God!"

Scott felt a twinge of guilt for the pain he was bringing to these people whom he found to be sincere and loving. "Mrs. Kurri, he's getting the best possible care."

"Mr. Malouf, what did you mean by what you just said before?" Scott asked, gently probing.

"After Rania and Wallid immigrated to the States, he had a very good life. He enjoyed a typical life for any American kid and teenager. For a while, he seemed to adapt very well, or so we thought. We had apparently underestimated the demons that had immigrated with him. Now, sir, you do understand his past, the how and the why he came to America?"

"Briefly, sir, please tell me his and your stories."

Maurice sat back in his chair and ran his hands slowly back through his thick white hair and paused for a moment. His English was perfect with just the slightest vestige of an accent. He very slowly and with great emotion explained Rania and Wally's history in Beirut and America.

Once finished, Scott replied, "I'm very sorry, sir. That's a very sad story."

"Yes, it is, Mr. Burton. Yes, it is, and it is also strange."

"Strange, sir?"

"When Rania and Wally were forced to flee Lebanon and come over to the States, my business was not as prosperous as it has since become. Businesses have ups and downs, and mine was in a down cycle then. The money to bring Wally and my sister here was a loan from a business associate, Abe Scheinbloom, a Jew."

"Did you ever tell Wally that?"

"Sure, but it made no difference."

"Wow, how ironic is that?"

"Yes, it is. Mr. Burton, these dangerous people are among us and mean us harm."

"Well, Mr. Malouf, I can say that our last conversations with Wally led me to believe that he may have been having a change of heart. He might have spoken with us if he had the ability, but now, I'm not certain that he is capable of doing that. Maurice, Albert, Mrs. Kurri, did Wally ever mention or identify his radical friends?"

"Occasionally."

"If I mentioned some names, could you tell me if you've ever heard of them?"

"Certainly."

"Carlos Reyes?"

"No."

"Atef?"

"No."

"Charles or Charlie Gonsalves?"

"Yes, he was the arrogant one of Wally's friends. I nearly ejected him from my home when he accused Rania of being immodest."

"Interesting. Have you ever seen him again?"

"No, but I believe that when Wally moved out, he lived with him."

"Why do you think that?"

"That's where Wally's mail was being forwarded."

"Do you still have that address?"

"I'd have to look. If I find it, I will call you. Do you have a card?"

Scott gave him a card from his jacket pocket.

Rania injected herself into the conversation, "Sir, may I speak with the doctor now?" She had been differential to her brothers to this point, but she was also clearly distraught.

Scott turned directly to Rania. "Yes, Mrs. Kurri. I'll call now."

Scott dialed the hospital and was connected with the US marshals guarding Wally. After being vetted through to Wally's doctor, he was handed to a neurologist, Dr. Stanley Endicott. "Doctor, this is Special Agent Scott Burton of the FBI. Mr. Kurri is my prisoner. How is he?"

"He's in guarded condition, agent. In his condition, he could go either way. If he doesn't have another stroke—which is a possibility—I think he'll survive."

"Can he talk? Or communicate in any way?"

"No, not in any meaningful way. The type of stroke that he's experienced has severely affected his speech center. It's called expressive aphasia. Movement on his right side is compromised as well. Additionally, he also lapses in and out of coherency. The good news is that if he doesn't have any further problems, he should be able to return some degree of function over time through intensive physical therapy."

"Including speech?"

"Possibly."

"Is he conscious?"

"Yes, for the most part, but incoherent most of the time, like I said."

"No speech, though?"

"Not that anyone could understand. He seems at times to be trying to say something with an *M* type of sound repeatedly. He can't say what he really wants to though, and it frustrates him terribly."

"Could he be calling for his mother?"

"Could be anything or nothing at all. His ability to communicate as you and I do has been seriously compromised."

"Dr. Endicott, I'm with his mother right now, Mrs. Rania Kurri. Could you brief her as you've done for me? It would be tremendously comforting to her."

"Certainly, Agent Scott, put her on the phone."

"Thanks so much, Doctor. On my end, I'm going to do what I have to in order to secure his family visitation privileges."

"That type of stimulation might be therapeutic for him but only in limited doses."

"Dr. Endicott, I'm going to pass the phone to Wally's mom now."

Scott passed the phone to Rania. Dr. Endicott very patiently explained her son's condition to her. She knitted her fingers together, hanging on his every word.

As Scott watched Rania talk to the doctor, he felt an odd relief. In an occupation where guile, deception, and outright lying got you to the end you're looking for, this bit of simple honesty felt good. But what neither he nor the doctor could not have known was that the *M* word that Wally had been trying to mouth so desperately and frustratingly wasn't *mother*; it was *mine*.

CHAPTER 45

Captain Tom Reagan parked his car at the Department of Transportation's ferry maintenance facility where the ferryboat *Andrew J. Barberi* lay quietly at her mooring. It was 5:15 a.m. on Tuesday, July 27, and even this early in the day, it felt unseasonably warm in the St. George section of Staten Island. A few weeks prior, Tom had been assigned as the captain on board the *Barberi*, a promotion he less than enthusiastically accepted. As much as he tried to explain her away and rationalize his unease, *Barberi*'s record spoke for itself. She was a hard luck boat.

The *Barberi*, named after a local football coaching legend, was commissioned in May of 1981. On her inaugural trip from Staten Island to Manhattan's Whitehall Street Terminal in August of 1981, the 310-foot vessel's engines and steering failed, resulting in her grounding near Governors Island.

Diesel powered, *Barberi* was driven by an innovative propulsion system that gave her the ability to change its direction almost instantaneously. The system had malfunctioned repeatedly over the years, causing passenger injury and extensive damage. Nothing, however, could exceed the events of October 15, 2003, for sheer mayhem.

On that day, an assistant captain was at the helm on a late afternoon passage to Staten Island. Sleep deprived and under the influence of painkillers, he drove the 3,335-ton ship into the cement maintenance pier next to the St. George Ferry Terminal at full speed. The boat's side was split as if by a giant can opener. The final count was eleven dead and seventy injured, including several decapitations and the loss of limbs. The assistant captain was arrested after a failed suicide attempt and eventually sentenced to prison. Hundreds of lawsuits followed, and recriminations abound to this day.

*****

The captain, assistant captain, and engineers of the *Barberi* routinely boarded earlier than the remainder of the day crew to get the boat up and operating for the day's work. Reagan had a large coffee from Dunkin Donuts in one hand, his uniform on hangers from the dry cleaners in the other, and the daily paper tucked under his arm. Out of uniform, he could have easily been mistaken for one of his Wall Street–bound passengers. In fact, Reagan was considered one of the more talented captains within the ferry system. Reagan juggled his possessions as he crossed the gangway to the *Barberi* and became dimly aware of a presence ahead of him already aboard his boat. A police officer was standing before him.

"Good morning, sir. Are you the captain?"

"I am. Is there a problem?"

"No, no, sir, there is not. I'm Sergeant Petraglia from the harbor unit. We have divers down examining your hull for foreign objects. We'd just ask you not to start your engines until we're clear, Captain."

"Sure, are you going to be long?"

"No, sir, not at all, we're almost finished. We're not going to be more than another fifteen minutes."

"Okay, if that's all it is, but I have to get started soon. We have to be ready for the first run at seven thirty."

"Don't worry, sir, you'll make it." Petraglia excused himself and reboarded the police launch, which was tied to the port side of the large orange ferry.

Reagan boarded the boat. As he got to the main deck, he stopped to rearrange his gear. He looked back and saw his chief engineer, Ted Stavakos, walking through the parking lot toward the boat. Reagan stepped out onto the rear deck and waved, calling out, "Ted, could you join me up here for a second?"

Stavakos acknowledged the request with a smile, a nod, and a thumbs-up. While Reagan waited, his phone rang.

"Tom, this is Tony at the operations office." Tony was Tony Sicilia, the ferry's port captain. "Tom, there are a couple of things I have to brief you on."

"Like the police diver I just met?"

"That would be one, yes."

"What would the other be, Tony?"

"Actually, I wanted to tell you that the Coast Guard will be escorting you today during your crossings."

"Is something going on that I should know about?"

"They didn't tell me any more than I'm telling you."

"Tony, if you find out anything, would you update me, please?"

"Absolutely, Tom."

The call left him uneasy. Security drills weren't uncommon, but this was not a routine change. Tom Reagan had never considered himself to be a superstitious sort, but he would have been all the happier had he never been assigned to the *Barberi* for these last few weeks. As he sipped his coffee and pondered his situation, Stavakos joined him. Reagan filled him in and then made his way up to the pilothouse.

*****

Captain Rolle Peterson slowly turned his articulated tug and barge into the midstream of the Kill Van Kull off the fuel depot he'd just left in Bayonne. He moved forward, slowly gaining headway as he pushed the 100,000 barrels of aviation gasoline that filled his 399-foot barge to capacity, bound for Kennedy Airport. The *Mary Margaret* was one of a fleet of a dozen such tugs owned and operated by McMullen Transportation. She and her sister tugs were married to fuel barges by large stainless-steel pins built into their bows. Rolle regularly made this run with his seasoned crew, one of whom was his son, Ronnie. The barge itself was actually four times the size of the tug, but the *Mary Margaret* had more than enough horsepower to compensate. The immense load, which converted to some 4.2 million gallons of highly flammable gasoline, ensured that they'd have a slow but steady trip at approximately five knots. Because of the barge's size, the tug had an upper pilothouse raised some fifty-five feet above the waterline, where Rolle sat, allowing him to look over his barge and navigate safely.

At sixty-one years of age, Rolle Peterson had happily been at the job for the last thirty years. Looking out over the barge, he took in the sun rising ahead of him and reveled in what promised to be a beautiful day as the pungent aroma of diesel wafted into the pilothouse. With a smile on his face, he once again reassured himself that given the chance to reset his life's priorities, he wouldn't change one damned thing. He was even more pleased by the fact that his second-eldest son, Ronnie, had chosen the same life and was working with him as the second assistant engineer. A self-satisfied Rolle sat back in his chair on his elevated perch at the helm with a cup of coffee and prepared to enjoy the day the Lord had given him.

*****

Shortly before 7:30 a.m., a subdued throng of commuters slowly shuffled toward the large modernist glass doors that led to the ferries. As they did so, a few glanced over and admired the large tropical fish tanks in the middle of the entry hall.

The large glass doors would soon roll open as they did every fifteen minutes at this time of the morning, and 2,500 sleepy-eyed individuals, coffee and/or bagel and newspapers in hand, would shuffle down the interior of the terminal to the boat. Tom Reagan had brought the *Andrew J. Barberi* over from the maintenance pier. It now sat in the three slip, held in place by two large cables and a slight forward engine thrust, awaiting her passengers. Commuters barely paid attention to the layers of increased security in and around the terminal.

Boarding this giant orange boat toward the rear of the pack was an ambling Louie Lugo, who hated being stuck in the middle of any crowd. Louie would normally be traveling with Brian, but today he was on his own since Brian had taken the day off. The week before, Maureen had asked him if he would accompany her to a doctor's appointment. When a sincerely concerned Brian asked what the problem was, she very calmly told him that she was pregnant. The news sat him down in a kitchen chair and left him speechless. Louie laughed again now as he recalled the first time Brian had told him the story.

Louie was the last to board the boat. He took his regular seat toward the rear on the main deck as the accordion metal gates were secured, and the passenger ramps were raised as the cables unhooked and retracted to the pier. With one long blast of the diesel horn, they were on their way. Louie settled in with his *New York Post*. It was amazing how subdued over two thousand people could be.

In the pilothouse, Tom Reagan stood at the controls with Pat McTigue, a deckhand who would provide an extra set of eyes. As the ferry slowly powered out of the slip, McTigue made a note of the *Mary Margaret* and her barge, which was about to plod across their bow.

"Cap, ya got a tug and barge coming out of the Kill."

"I've got her, thanks, Pat." Reagan adjusted his thrust so he was barely moving as he picked up the UHF radio on channel 16. "Tug *Mary Margaret* off my bow, this is the ferry *Barberi* coming out of the St. George terminal. I'll lie to while you cross my bow, over."

Rolle came right back, "Thanks, *Barberi*, I'll be out of your way in just a minute, *Mary Margaret* out."

Rolle would have gone faster but couldn't and chugged along just inside the KV buoy a couple of hundred yards short of the *Barberi*. Reagan also made note of the Coast Guard escort idling to their port side, also waiting for the tug and barge to pass.

The first indication that something was awry occurred loudly and dramatically. All on the *Barberi* were startled by a deep, sharp boom from somewhere below the vessel. At the same time, those looking forward witnessed the *Mary Margaret*'s rise on a huge geyser of muddy water, dragging the tug upward with her, twisting both the tug and its barge at their connection, and separating them with a distinct metallic pop.

The *Barberi* began to vibrate violently. Windows shattered, and unsecured objects took flight. At the point of detonation, the depth of the water was a mere forty-five feet. The barge, fully loaded, was just twenty-nine feet above the Manta mine that had just been detonated by the tug and barge's magnetic signatures as they passed over. The explosion not only caused the barge to absorb the effects of the high-pressure water column, but it also felt the full force of the explosion.

On the *Barberi*, trashcans and other unanchored objects ricocheted off seats, walls, overheads, and passengers as if a giant hand had randomly flung them. Even worse, passengers were thrown violently in all directions. A sudden deadly wave of nondescript shrapnel and broken glass mangled passengers and crew, causing an array of broken arms and legs and deep lacerations.

In the pilothouse, an incredulous Tom Reagan witnessed the event occurring before him that his mind could not adequately process or react to. It became only too real when the bridge windows disintegrated before him and the *Barberi* seemed to twist and vibrate simultaneously. Both he and McTigue were barely able to cover their faces with their arms as the flying glass tore into them.

As Reagan watched, the barge separated from the tug and settled back down in a jack-knife position, its back broken. Moments later, the unthinkable happened. Whether due to a spark from a severed electrical line or a spark caused by rending steel, 4.2 million gallons of gasoline detonated 150 yards from the *Barberi* with a blinding flash and deafening explosion. At the moment of the detonation, Reagan happened to be bent over forward, still reacting to the original blast, which had driven him down to the deck. The blast was immediately followed by the effects of the blast over pressure, pushing thousands of steel shards and other debris with and before it.

The negative pressure wave followed a millisecond later, sucking most of the debris back through the vessel. The searing fireball was being fed by a seemingly endless supply of fuel. Hell on earth had been unleashed. Passengers who had set themselves up at the rail on the port side and on the forward deck to enjoy the morning were the first victims of the effects of the blast and were roasted by the expanding fireball. Reagan, who had been bent over by the pain of his injuries, survived with lacerations and second-degree burns. Tom raised his head to look out to where the barge had been, but all that remained was a fiercely flaming and expanding pool of gasoline on the surface of the water, constantly being fed by the now sunken barge. The form of the *Mary Margaret* was listing heavily to starboard; its extended pilothouse was gone, and the entire vessel was on fire end to end.

The harbor surface in front of Reagan was ablaze for a hundred yards in either direction and was quickly expanding toward the *Barberi*. The choking smoke had blocked out the morning sun. Reagan momentarily considered returning to the slip he'd just left, but as he turned, he could see multiple fires had broken out in the terminal and in the streets of the municipal area outside of the terminal. He also saw Pat McTigue seated dead on the couch at the rear of the pilothouse, his skull cleaved in half by a jagged piece of steel that was embedded in the bloody bulkhead behind him.

Reagan noticed that a small channel was open between the surface fires and the maintenance piers a short distance away. He turned his boat and accelerated toward the opening. His intention was to take his passengers past the danger and moor at the defunct naval station a short distance beyond. Even though seriously injured himself, he felt sure he could navigate into the clear. He was aware of the anguished cries for help from the passengers below him but tried desperately to blot that out and concentrate on the task at hand.

Louie, like many other passengers on the main deck of the *Barberi*, was thrown head over heels from his seat as a result of the initial blast. Somewhat bruised, he immediately got back on his feet and began to assist the more seriously injured. It was then that the world around him disintegrated in a deafening crack and a blinding flash. Once again, Louie was on his back, now bleeding from a deep facial wound. He forced himself up and looked out of a hole that had previously been a window. He was astounded; the entire surface of the harbor within his field of vision was on fire. Pockmarked by debris, sides singed black, the *Barberi* was still on an even keel. Louie again attempted to help those around him.

The *Barberi* had not advanced one hundred yards before the magnetic signature of her mass triggered the second mine. In milliseconds, a bubble jet created by the explosion rose toward the surface at a velocity in excess of 22,000 fps. The bubble collapsed from the bottom due to differences in pressure as it rose. Because the hull was so close to the detonation, the bubble's pressure jet penetrated right through the thin bottom of the *Barberi*, opening a jagged hole roughly ten feet wide and twenty feet long from the keel along the port side of the boat. It punched right through to the salon deck. The blast effect and the ensuing shaking and vibrations were *Barberi's* final death knell. Equipment separated from mounts and took flight. People were flicked about like insignificant specks joining the piles of wreckage and jetsam. The laws of physics exhibited neither animus nor mercy. Ted Stavakos and his entire crew were dead, and all fire-fighting systems and pumps were destroyed or rendered inoperable.

The *Barberi's* back had been broken. The superstructure forward of the stack had been visibly pushed upward by the force of the blast. The hull was open at its bottom, her time limited.

Injuries were what one could expect in such cases. Broken bones, multiple traumas, and lacerations were the order of the day. All those injuries occurred, but in no special order. In reality, the end result were random piles of passengers with broken bones and penetrated multiple organs, in many cases ruptured by the force of the explosion. Of the approximately 2,500 commuters aboard that morning, almost no one remained uninjured. The dead and injured lay among each other and jagged pieces of equipment. There were pitiful cries for help that, for the most part, went unanswered.

One person who would have answered those cries if he could have was lying on his back among the debris of a fallen cable run. Louie Lugo's back was broken. He had been thrown into a vertical beam like a rag doll. The blast had taken his hearing. As he lay there, he fully realized what was going on around him. He felt strangely at peace, understanding that he would be unable to affect anything that was happening. As the boat began to list to its port side, the hull plating groaned as the *Barberi* began to start a stuttering downward slide that steadily picked up momentum. Louie found the water unrepentantly warm as it swept over him, almost soothing.

In total, over two thousand people went down in the boat, which sank out of sight in a little more than eight minutes. But even after the *Barberi* went down, those cast into the warm July waters had yet another test to endure. Less than ten minutes after the initial blast and after only a few minutes in the water, the remaining survivors in vests were engulfed by the moving tide of fiercely burning gasoline. That fuel had now been reconstituted into a sticky gel by diesel oil escaping from *Barberi*'s bunkers.

The twenty-five-foot Coast Guard defender-class patrol boats that had been waiting to escort the *Barberi* on her scheduled run were now making courageous efforts to rescue those in the water. They repeatedly braved the burning fuel to answer the screams and plucked survivors from the water with complete disregard for their own safety. Unfortunately, even after additional rescue vessels joined the effort, only thirty-seven people were taken from the water alive.

The area that surrounded the ferry terminal also fell victim to the blasts and its effects. The positive and negative pressure waves of the blast blew out windows throughout the area. Flying glass and other debris injured hundreds. Large steel shards of *Mary Margaret's* barge landed heavily ashore. One portion of the deckhouse flew like a skipping stone into the ferry terminal's waiting room, causing additional deaths and injuries. The ability of local hospitals to handle the huge surge of injured caused them to be rapidly overwhelmed, and they soon had to send the injured to Brooklyn and Manhattan hospitals.

The Coast Guard captain of the port immediately raised the MARSEC level to three, the highest level, which put the harbor on virtual lockdown. The Coast Guard, police, and other city and state agencies reverted to preplanned emergency management procedures to bring the situation under control. The first and immediate concern, naturally, was rescue, but in no time, it became painfully apparent that rescue would be on the shorter end of a list of needs and necessities.

The media was involved in reporting the story almost immediately, which resulted in both government and the public wanting to know who and what had struck them. The harbor had to be protected from further attack and be still reopened for shipping as soon as possible. The task before the government and the maritime industry was daunting.

*****

The destruction of the *Barberi* was a rude awakening for the American public, especially New Yorkers. On the same day of the New York attacks, a tanker struck an underwater explosive device in Chesapeake Bay, and only after extraordinary damage control efforts did it remain afloat. Later that same day, a small containership struck an as yet unidentified underwater explosive device on the Savannah River and had to be grounded, partially blocking the channel.

Beyond the immediate concern of securing the harbor from further attacks was the realization that the port of New York and New Jersey had to be closed down—a very costly proposition in excess of $2 billion a day. The owners of ships currently moored in the harbor ordered that their valuable assets remain where they were. Still, there was no guarantee that they were not in danger from other underwater devices lurking on the harbor floor. Arriving shipping stopped short of entering the harbor and anchored out until the government could ensure their safety.

How fast the afflicted harbors and waterways could reopen to business depended on a number of factors. How fast could the Navy bring their minesweeping assets to bear? The general rule of thumb had always been that they could be on the scene within three days. Could they maintain that schedule now that three main harbors had been affected?

Recovery would have been greatly enhanced and accelerated in those harbors if proactive policies, such as the archival bottom sonar searches Al Calcaterra had preached for years, had been in place. The harbors that had performed archival comparisons and could provide that information to the Navy upon their arrival dramatically shortened the Navy's sweeping task and considerably accelerated their reopening of the harbor. Oddly, almost all ports that were home to naval facilities had active archival survey programs in place. This should have spoken volumes about their validity.

*****

The sharp crack of the explosion detonating under the hull of the *Mary Margaret*'s barge was heard for miles. On Shooters Island, Carlos and Atef immediately jumped to their feet and embraced while chanting "Allahu Akbar! Allahu Akbar!"

Atef sat down in his hole with a self-satisfied smile. He had succeeded beyond his wildest dreams. Looking at his randomly patched together band of compatriots, he thanked Allah more sincerely than he ever had.

Carlos retrieved a small portable radio from his equipment bag and tuned it to a local news station. What he heard just further buoyed his spirits. Shortly, there were heavy clouds of smoke hanging over the vicinity of the ferry terminal four miles away. As he listened to a shaken and solemn news analyst, a very self-satisfied Carlos continued to stare at the columns of smoke rising from the ferry area.

A highly emotional Carlos gushed, "Allah be praised. My brothers, we have done it! Victory is ours! We should rest ourselves today, because tomorrow we will wake with Allah in paradise. Tonight, glory will be ours!"

Again the cry went up, "Allahu Akbar! Allahu Akbar!"

Anthony's stomach went into immediate spasms. He knew what he had to do. He settled back down into his squalid hole as they all listened to the radio reports of the chaos near the ferry terminal. No matter how many spiritual lectures he'd endured, he knew what was being done in the name of Allah was wrong. He was beyond guilt ridden; he was panicked by what he now perceived as an insanity he had become a part of.

CHAPTER 46

Brian sat with Maureen in the second-floor waiting room of her obstetrician at Staten Island University Hospital. He couldn't help but stare at her; in his eyes, she was the most beautiful woman in the room. She was dressed simply in brightly colored summer shorts and a top, but she stood out. As happy as he was to be with her on this occasion, he was equally uncomfortable sitting among all the women who were considerably pregnant. Maureen could sense his uneasiness and suppressed a smile.

"What's the matter, stud?" She toyed with him, holding the emphasis on the *d*.

He slid over closer to her ear and half whispered, "They're all so, ya know?"

"Pregnant?"

"Yeah."

"I guess it's your towering powers of observation that earned you that promotion to detective?" She grabbed his hand tightly and smiled.

Brian couldn't help but notice that the incoming ambulance traffic at the rear bay of the nearby emergency room seemed endless. "Damn, I wonder what the hell is going on. You hear all those sirens?"

"I do, but I don't know or care, and you shouldn't either right now, if you know what's good for you. You haven't forgotten why we're here, have you? No police, not today."

Brian did an exaggerated visual scan of the room. "Nope, hard to forget why we're here."

"Good!"

It was then that his cell phone range. It was Scott. "Brian, you've got to come in. It's all gone bad."

"Bad, how? I'm over at the doctor's at the hospital with Maureen, and there's like a parade of ambulances here. It's like endless."

"Brian, they blew up a Staten Island Ferry and a gasoline barge. Man, it's very, very bad. Tons of DOAs."

"Oh shit, I'll be right in. Where should I go?"

"Come into my office. We'll work out of here today. We'll be here for a while. Where's Louie?"

"He's on his own today. He came in by himself. He should be there by now." His stomach tightened, and he felt flush as he added, "He came in by ferry today." As soon as he hung up with Scott, he rang Louie's phone, to no avail. He began to panic.

He rapidly filled in Maureen. In a minute they were both on their feet and heading for the door. As they passed the receptionist's desk, Maureen curtly said, "We'll reschedule."

*****

Orlando and Jack were slowly pulling the *Sofia* into the marina with their coast guardsman, about to end their midnight-to-eight tour when their attention was drawn behind them by a low-rumbling explosion. At first their vision was blocked by other boats and the piers, but a moment later, visibility ceased being a problem. A brilliant flash to the north of their position was followed by a deafening crack and explosion. Black billowing clouds of smoke merged with towering orange flames and large pieces of debris, all of which seemed to be falling in the area of the St. George Ferry Terminal. The two men stood transfixed by the enormity of what was unfolding before them.

Paralysis only lasted a few moments though, and then Orlando throttled up, spinning the *Sofia* around and back out of the marina. He turned north, back toward the source of the explosions. Once he had a full and unobstructed view of the carnage, it was almost too much to mentally process. Almost the entire surface of the harbor outside of the ferry terminal was ablaze. There was a gap between the fire and the pier head of only a few hundred yards. Coming directly at him through that gap was a bright-orange Staten Island Ferry; its entire left side was singed black with most of its windows blown out. Then, before their eyes, the harbor seemed to explode under the ferry. The front of the ferry was lifted off the surface of the harbor on a column of water. When the boat fully landed, it was obvious that her back was broken. She immediately began to settle on her port side with the fire closing in on her. All Orlando could say was, "Sweet mother of Jesus!" He buried the throttle and headed toward the ferry.

What Orlando found when he arrived beside the *Barberi* was truly horrifying. In the short time it had taken him to arrive on the scene, it was already apparent that the large ferry was a goner. It was slowly but steadily going down by the bow with the superstructure already underwater up to the pilothouse. Clusters of passengers were jumping off the rear of the boat while those alive in the water struggled and screamed for help amid the dead and dying, many of whom were on fire. Orlando immediately began working with two Coast Guard boats and a police launch already on the scene, all of them struggling to get screaming victims out of the water before those survivors were sucked into the advancing flames. All present were making heroic efforts, but the advancing burning gasoline was moving and threatening both victims and rescuers alike. Orlando spun the *Sofia* around and placed his three large outboards at the edge of the fire. He buried the throttles and used the wash from the outboards to temporarily push back the advancing flames. As he exposed himself to the flames again and again, backwashing the fire away from the survivors, the other boats came in and plucked swimmers from the water. More than once there was a sickening thump as his props struck a floating body. The rescuers continued until no more swimmers were found and they were about to be trapped by the flames themselves. The ferry boat had slipped below the surface. The small flotilla took all those that had been rescued to the nearby former navy base where ambulances awaited.

One fireboat had arrived on the scene and began to spread foam on the flames, as more fireboats made their way to the site. News helicopters examined not only the chaos in the harbor but also the devastation ashore where Staten Island's downtown business community had been peppered with flaming debris.

Orlando was getting low on fuel, so he took the *Sofia* into his home marina. As he was refueling, he noticed that the stern and rear sides of his boat were singed and the fiberglass was bubbled up in places. He filled his tanks and went back out into the rescue effort that now was a recovery effort. The whole thing was being neatly framed by the media in a photographic image of the harbor that showed the harbor surface aflame with the Statue of Liberty framed dead center. As Jack looked on, the word *apocalyptic* kept coming to the forefront of his mind. The harbor was rapidly responding with additional police, fire, and Coast Guard vessels, as well as many commercial and private vessels. All had a grim task in front of them.

*****

On Shooters Island, the focus of the day was conserving energy as much as possible as they prepared for the evening's operations. Carlos had determined that they would leave on their final martyrdom mission that evening at slack tide, shortly after 1:00 a.m. He had determined they would then launch an attack on an oil tanker moored about a mile away in Linden, New Jersey. He hoped that an initial explosion aboard the ship would instigate secondary explosions within the refinery where it was moored. If that one-hundred-thousand-ton vessel was loaded or half loaded, it stood an excellent chance of detonating with catastrophic effects.

Anthony couldn't help but notice that Carlos was more animated than usual, as was Syed. He'd never seen Carlos so chatty. Atef, on the other hand, was his impassive self, maybe even a little more introspective than usual. Anthony's assessment was that each of his companions was a little more demented than the other. Anthony had come to the full realization that he was not cut from the same cloth as the other three. He found himself sickened by the unrestricted joy that they had exhibited upon learning how many thousands had been killed in the earlier explosions.

As night fell, Carlos took Syed and Atef with him to prepare and load the kayaks. Carlos ordered Anthony to take a position near the eastern edge of the island to keep watch for approaching patrol boats. Anthony stifled his excitement, realizing that Carlos had just handed him a gift-wrapped opportunity.

Anthony set himself up just inside the tree line, about twenty yards from the water, staying low. Looking through the trees, he could see the others moving about. At about 10:30 p.m., when he could see that everyone had settled in on the other side of the island, he decided that it was now or never. Observing that there was no traffic on the water, he crawled down to the rocky debris-strewn beach below the wooded area and out of the line of sight of anyone behind him. Trying not to panic, he crouched and ran along the island's southern inside shore to the midpoint where it faced Staten Island. From there, it was approximately one hundred yards to the Staten Island shoreline.

Anthony entered the water fully dressed. As he began to swim, he had only one thought: escape. The water was initially colder than he thought it would be, but he soon got used to it. He took great care not to splash excessively or otherwise cause him to be noticed. He landed at a spot about one hundred yards west of where they'd originally launched the kayaks. He got his footing but immediately noticed he was standing in an oozing muck. Each step was difficult, and when he finally climbed out of the water, he found that he was still slogging through thick, sucking black mud. Stepping clear of the water, he felt his left boot get sucked off by the slop he'd just walked through, but it didn't matter. He was alive and free of his maniac companions; he'd figure the rest out on the fly.

He found himself in a small private ship repair yard that was closed and unoccupied. Anthony scaled the eight-foot corrugated metal wall standing on Richmond Terrace, which was all but deserted. He found a dark break in a fence and ducked out of sight. A muddy mess, dressed in black with one boot, he clearly would stand out and risk being apprehended. At this point he was driven by one overpowering thought: *Please let this nightmare end*. He had to get back to Carlos's apartment in order to clean up and change. He wasn't sure where the apartment was, but he knew it was somewhere along this shoreline.

After taking five or ten minutes to acclimate himself, he left his shelter and began to move northward. He walked close to the building line under the pale glow of the streetlights. When he saw headlights, he ducked back toward the building line, behind a hedge or fence. He it made it past the Bayonne Bridge, a quarter mile east from his starting point and about another two hundred feet before his plan fell apart.

Anthony hugged the fence line of a used-car lot that occupied the south sidewalk as it approached the intersection of John Street and Richmond Terrace. The vehicles in the car lot obstructed his view, creating a blind corner, and just as he was about to reach the corner, a police car suddenly appeared from behind a line of parked vehicles in the lot. There was no time to react. They were only twenty feet away.

Police Officers Harry Lindale and Barry Green were in their 120th Precinct RMP 1225 operating in Sector Y on this evening. Both Lindale and Green were normally easygoing sorts, but tonight they were quiet and tight-lipped. They had just witnessed the carnage of the day, both on TV and up close; their precinct was in sight of the ferry terminal. As they came out of John Street, where they had been investigating one of many reports of suspicious persons, they were presented with a young male dressed in black, caked in mud, with only one shoe on. Green said it first.

"Harry, what the fuck is this?" They stopped the car and attempted to confront the bedraggled male. Anthony broke and ran past the two down John Street. Barry was the faster of the two and took off running right on the kid's heels, yelling, "Police, don't move!" Anthony was moving like a gazelle and began to open the gap between them. Meanwhile, harry turned the car around and moved to cut Anthony off.

Barry's eyes narrowed on the back of the suspect and thought his eyes were deceiving him. Throughout his panicked escape, Anthony had not even felt the AKM assault rifle strapped to his back.

Harry went to the top of the street, knowing that John Street was a dead end with nowhere to go, and screeched to a stop. Jumping to come to Barry's aid, he looked to Barry for direction. Barry locked his eyes on the AKM, drew his 9 mm, and screamed one word to his partner, "Gun!"

Lindale and Green both called out the same order, "Police, don't move!" It was then that Anthony Thaci made the most intelligent decision of his young life: he stopped in his tracks and threw up his hands in surrender. They had to order him to drop the weapon multiple times before he realized he had it on; he then took it off and set it down. As the policemen grabbed him and placed him in handcuffs, he felt relieved; he was finally safe.

*****

Denby offered his offices at 25 Federal Plaza as a command center in order to maintain continuity and prevent duplication of the efforts between his and Phil Halvorsen's people. Halvorsen gratefully took the invitation. They maintained a direct link with their command, as they had an enormous amount of information from the day's events to sift through.

Denby sadly looked at Brian, who had been thoroughly immersed in his thoughts about Louie. Brian had called every hospital that was receiving victims. He'd visited the temporary morgues and checked every list of survivors and dead that was available. Louie was not among them. He knew Louie was scheduled to work and had not arrived. It was apparent to everyone that Louie was gone, but that had not deterred Brian in the least bit; he just kept checking and rechecking the lists.

Denby was seated next to Halverson and tapped him on the shoulder while he was watching Brian. "Phil, why don't we cut Brian loose? He's of no use here, poor bastard. I wish there was something we could do for him."

"Unfortunately, there's not."

"Brian!" Denby called.

"Yeah, boss!"

"Come over here, please."

Brian crossed the large office in long steps. "Yeah, boss, what'd ya need?"

"I need you to go home or go to Marie. We can get by here."

"If it's just the same to you, boss, I'll stay. My Maureen's with Marie, and anyway, I told Marie I'd keep looking."

Just then, Scott called out to Brian, "I've got your operations desk on the line. You want to take this."

Brian asked, "What line?"

"Four."

Brian clicked the extension button. "Detective Devine."

"Brian, this is Gayle Kranick. I just got a call from the 1-2-0 over in your neck of the woods. You might want to check this one out." Kranick had been a tried and true friend and top-notch investigator. If she thought something was worthwhile, then it was.

"What have they got?"

"A sector car over on patrol in the 1-2-0 brought in a guy in something like a black camouflage outfit, covered in mud, carrying—are ya ready for this?—an AK-47!"

"Really? Wow! Are they still holding him at the precinct?"

"Yup! They called and asked if we'd want to come out and talk to him."

"You bet your ass we do! Thanks, Gayle."

"Anytime, Brian. And, Brian, I'm sorry about Louie."

"Thanks, Gayle. Could you call the 1-2-0 back, and tell them we're on the way?"

"You got it."

Brian hung up and briefed Halvorsen and Denby. Denby reacted by calling out, "Scott! Scott Burton! Come here."

Scott came over, and Denby briefed him about the new information and said, "Go out there with Brian, check it out. I guess I don't have to tell you to step on it. You drive."

Normally, the trip to the 1-2-0 would have taken at least forty-five minutes. Using lights and sirens, they arrived in twenty-five minutes.

The 120th Precinct was an old-school police building. It was an imposing stone structure made even more impressive by the fact it had been constructed within a hillside and stood above sidewalk level. Brian wore his shield on a chain; Scott's creds were clipped to his pocket. They stopped at the antique wooden desk, and Brian presented themselves to the sergeant.

"Hi, boss, I'm Detective Devine, and this is Special Agent Burton from the Joint Terrorist Task Force. We got a call you're holding a guy for us to speak to?"

"Oh yeah, Rambo, he's up in the squad. Do you know where that is?"

"Yeah, yeah, I do." They climbed the creaking stairs to the detective squad on the second floor.

The "squad" was housed in a bare-bones suite of offices that had been minimally upgraded over the years. The furniture was utilitarian, the result of someone's lowest bid. The only outward sign of the times was the desktop computers. Off to the rear side of the main portion of the office was a sorry-looking detention cell with walls stained by years of fingerprint ink stains. One simple wood bench rested against its rear wall, and on it sat a forlorn, skinny kid in some type of pseudomilitary garb. As Brian and Scott stepped in, they were met by Detective Mike Squires and Officers Lindale and Green. After the appropriate introductions, Devine asked the two uniformed cops, "What'd ya got?"

Green did most of the talking and laid the story out for Brian and Scott, adding, "He's a scared kid. He's Mirandized, and we actually got him to sign that he got his rights."

"What's his name?"

"Anthony, Anthony Thaci. He says he's from Virginia. We didn't speak with him too much. He's into something beyond what we know about, and we didn't want to keep talking and fuck anything up."

Scott reassured both of them. "No, you guys did just the right thing. You've done a great job. He had a submachine gun, we were told."

"Yeah, it's over here."

Green handed the AKM over to Scott. Brian asked, "Can I see that, Scott?" Brian had seen his share of Kalashnikovs while he was a marine in Kuwait. He picked up the weapon and closely examined it, checking it to make sure it had been safety-latched. "This isn't a commercial knockoff. This is the real thing. This AK is still capable of firing fully automatic. Did he have rounds for it?"

"Yeah, a full thirty-round clip and one in the chamber," Lindale replied.

"You guys were lucky. Is that him in the holding cell?"

"Yeah."

"Can you take him out and seat him at that desk?" he asked, pointing to a plain gray metal desk in the far corner of the room.

"Sure." Lindale took Anthony out and sat him down. He was filthy. His Nomex clothing reeked of the decay of the fetid shoreline. It was more than obvious to both Brian and Scott that Anthony was the link they had been searching for. The fact that Wally Kurri and Manny Pabon had slipped through their hands was still a fresh and painful wound. Anthony was not going to be allowed to follow a similar course. Brian led off with his part of their duel effort.

"Son, I'm Detective Devine, and this is Special Agent Burton of the Federal Bureau of Investigation. What's your name?"

Anthony, looking dejectedly at the floor, mumbled under his breath, "Anthony Thaci."

Brian firmly grasped Anthony's chin and raised his head so their eyes fully met. With two fingers of his right hand, he pointed to his own eyes. "Here, sonny boy, right here!" he said demanding the kid's full and direct participation. "Am I going to have to drag every fucking word out of you, laddie buck, hmmm?" Brian raised his voice slightly. "Look at me when I speak to you, you little shit!" Anthony raised his head; there was no sense of arrogance about him, only fear.

"Where are you from?" Brian asked brusquely, taken aback by his surprise at the boy's sad eyes.

"Virginia."

"Big state. Where in Virginia?"

"McLean."

"How old are you?"

"Seventeen."

Seeing Brian's agitation mounting, Scott joined the conversation, "Seventeen, very good. You're an adult in the eyes of the law. You realize that, don't you?"

"Huh?" Anthony peered at Scott in confusion.

Brian went back at him again. "Would you care to explain what a young man your age, from McLean Virginia, is doing walking on our streets, carrying a loaded Russian assault weapon?"

There was an uncomfortably long pause in the conversation as Anthony looked down at the floor again.

Scott took a shot in the dark. "Well, Anthony Thaci, do you travel much?"

"No, not really."

"You're about to start. You see, we know about you and your friends. We're the FBI. We know that you are responsible for killing all those people on the ferry this morning. I also know that you're about to make one of two trips. One trip is after your trial to a federal prison; the other is much worse. Detective Devine here is even more anxious than me to get you there." The color faded from Anthony's face as he settled more deeply into his seat. "The other option, if you're lucky, is a trip to Guantanamo Bay. And you to be coming back until you're a very old man, if at all."

The tears began to well up in the boy's eyes as he shook uncontrollably. "Please, mister, all I want to do is go home, sir. I didn't want to be like the others. I left the island. They're out of their minds. I'm not like them. That's why I left the island. Please, sir, I just want to go home."

Brian and Scott both internally said to themselves, *Island.* Their pulses began to race. The key had been turned, the door opened, and they were about to carefully step in.

Scott fought the urge to jump all over the revelation and instead calmly engaged the boy. "Son, you are in an almost impossible situation. You will most definitely face the death penalty unless you do something to help yourself."

"Death penalty! What do you mean help myself?"

"In conspiratorial situations, such as you find yourself in, it's usually the first person who cooperates with the authorities that tends to save his or her ass. Right now you're in that unique position. Help us and maybe, and only maybe, we can help you."

"I just want to go home! I was running away!"

"Kid, you're a little dense, aren't you? You may have been running away from them, but you also ran away from us when you had the opportunity to surrender. A jury is going to believe that the only thing you're remorseful about is getting caught. We are the only future you have that may not ultimately involve you taking a long dirt nap. Am I being a little bit clearer?"

"Yes, sir." Anthony's eyes darted back and forth between Scott and Brian in an attempt to find some softness or a glimmer of compassion.

Brian stepped back to the newly glazed window as Scott continued. He gazed out on the nearby ferry terminal and the disaster scene in and around the harbor beyond it. The fire department had extinguished the fires with a blanket of foam, but the scene buzzed with the flickering blue lights of police and Coast Guard boats now engaged in the grim duty of body recovery on the periphery of the scene. Brian could only imagine Louie trapped somewhere in that scene. It took a lot to maintain his composure. He turned and looked at Anthony, thinking to himself, *This son of a bitch is really clueless about what he did.*

"Are we talking about the same island?" Brian threw it out to see if it would stick.

"The one near the bridge I got caught by."

"Shooters Island?"

"Yes, sir, I think that's the name."

"Your friends are still there?"

"I'm not sure. They may have already gone." In the next few minutes, Anthony gave them both the thumbnail sketch of what he knew of Carlos's plan.

CHAPTER 47

Carlos, Atef, and Syed loaded the kayaks and prepared the fusing system attached to the Semtex explosives by eleven thirty. Carlos then instructed Syed to retrieve Anthony and meet them at the mid-island encampment.

Syed first searched the shoreline where he expected Anthony to be but did not find him. Syed hoped against hope that Anthony might have returned to the camp on his own, because the thought of bringing bad news to Carlos scared the crap out of him. His worst fears were realized when he returned to the encampment and found Carlos talking with Atef, very much alone.

Carlos immediately became agitated, and his dark, sunken eyes flashed. "What do you mean you can't find him? You incompetent fool, he must be here somewhere. We'll all spread out and search again." Atef, Carlos, and Syed split up and divided the island into roughly equal segments. They stumbled through every ruin of a building, trash dump, and beach area on the island; they found no one. Carlos was floored by how badly he had misjudged Anthony.

"If I had him here right now, I'd take his eyes before taking his head," Carlos ranted wildly. On the other hand, Atef was troubled by the transgression but was even more concerned with whether or not their mission had been compromised.

Calmly and in an even tone, Atef gently held Carlos by the back of his neck and said, "My brother, there is nothing to be done to or with him now. He certainly will be made to suffer at the hands of Allah for his actions. We must now concentrate on the task at hand." Atef's pragmatic leadership skills were on display as he calmly, even softly, refocused Carlos. "Do you think we should consider moving our timeline forward?"

With Atef's hand massaging his shoulder, Carlos took a few deep breaths of the foul night air. "What time is it now, my brother?"

Syed softly volunteered, "Twelve twenty-five, sir."

"Thank you. No, the timing shall remain the same. Our optimal movement is dependent upon the tides. If we go before slack tide, we'll make little or no progress. We'll go at 1:30 a.m. Brothers, let us take the time that remains to recheck all the fusing and our other equipment." He fairly hissed, "We'll not let this unfortunate turn of events deter us." Syed could only shake his head.

Atef handed Carlos one of the last bottles of water and flatly said, "Drink." Carlos took a deep draw on the bottle as he looked out solemnly on the dark waters. He found the scene odd since there was little or no traffic on the bridge and surrounding shoreline. The lights on the adjoining shorelines and the Bayonne Bridge were blazing, but practically no one was out.

Atef drew close to him, "Are you all right?"

"Yes, yes, I am. Thank you, and please pardon my temporary loss of control. It's comforting to know you're here to maintain the equilibrium of the operation."

"My brother, if we are not here for each other, Allah be praised, we are here for nothing."

*****

Brian called Detective Squires over to put things in order. The squad room had been closed to routine comings and goings. "Squires, I have to ask a favor of you. Could you sit on this guy until our people can get over here to take him off your hands? Don't let anyone talk to him or even get near him. Please, it's extremely important. We're going to get real busy with other things right now. This guy is more important than I can even begin to explain to you right now."

"Sure, don't give it another thought."

"Great. Can I use the phone?"

"Right there, bro. Help yourself."

Brian reached out to Denby. "Boss, we've got a critical situation out here on, or maybe I should say near, Staten Island."

"I'm listening."

"The guy that the 1-2-0 bagged is the real deal, and he's talking some very significant stuff. The thing of it, though, is he just told us there's another attack planned within the hour on the water out here. Can you get somebody out here to take this guy to a secure location? We can't debrief him at length right now. Boss, he knows the whole story. Now I know why Carlos was so concerned with Shooters Island."

"Why's that, Brian?"

"Well, the short story is that they staged from there."

"Okay, I'll come out with Krieger right now. What else do you need?"

"Is Robles around? We have to address these people on the water right now. This kid, Anthony Thaci, confirmed all that stuff we'd heard about using kayaks."

"Yeah, he's right over here. Todd! Todd Robles, come over here, please!"

The young Coast Guard lieutenant took the phone from Denby, who briefly gave him the gist of what was transpiring. "Brian, what do you need from us? What can we do?"

"Todd, this kid has told us that Carlos and two others are planning to attack ship traffic on the water in the vicinity of the Staten Island and New Jersey shoreline with kayaks loaded with explosives."

"Do you know when or where?"

"The when, unfortunately, is like almost right now, according to this kid. He says he doesn't know where, but they will move out of Shooters Island over into the Kill Van Kull."

"Shit! I'll call the captain of the port and see what's moored over in that vicinity. He has to dispatch his boats over in that direction. They should get any air units, city, or Coast Guard over there."

"Jack, these guys are armed with AK-47s, so make sure our people know that."

"Gotcha, Brian. I'll take care of the water side right now and see about having the police put people on that island to secure it."

It occurred to Brian that the area they were talking about had been Orlando and Jack's patrol area. Brian picked up his cell and called Orlando.

*****

It had been the most horrific day of Orlando, Jack, and Tre's lives. After the first half hour, there was not a survivor to be found. They lost track of the number of charred and broken bodies they pulled from the water and deposited ashore.

After a short break and meal over at the Coast Guard Sector New York in Fort Wadsworth, the crew started back to the *Sofia* when Orlando got a call.

"Orlando, it's Brian. Where are you?"

"Staten Island, heading back to my boat. Why?"

Brian explained what had transpired while they had been off duty.

"Brian, do you mean to tell me I've been passing that godforsaken island night after night and they were there all along!"

"Orlando, I haven't got a definite answer to that, but that may be the case."

"Son of a bitch! We looked all over that miserable island every time we passed it and saw nothing."

"Spilled milk, Orlando. Listen, Sector New York is being notified as we speak, and I expect they'll be sending a force in that direction."

"Thanks, Brian. We're just pulling up to the boat, and I'll be on my way."

"Listen, Orlando, if you get to them before the cavalry, do the right thing."

"Yeah, right." They hopped aboard and headed out to St. George.

The radio came alive on Senior Chief Boatswains Mate Ken Kitchner's forty-five-foot Coast Guard medium response boat idling off the ferry terminal in Staten Island. "Coast Guard *45/602*, Coast Guard *45/602*, Coast Guard *45/602*, Pat Com." Kitchner was a nineteen-year veteran, with as much of an emotional overload as anyone else, but he was still managing to perform his job.

"Pat Com, this is *602*."

"Six-oh-two, we have a report of three individuals underway in the vicinity of the area between Shooters Island and Bergen Point on the Kill Van Kull. The subjects are in three kayaks towing three other kayaks. All the boats are reportedly carrying explosives. The occupants are armed with automatic weapons."

"Pat Com, this is *602*. Do you know their ultimate destination?"

"That's negative, *602*. Take *25/112*, *25/457*, and auxiliary vessel *Sofia* with you, and assume the duties of on-scene leader. Search the area from the Bayonne Bridge westward on the Arthur Kill past Howland Hook. I will have the New Jersey State Trooper's boat and the New York State Naval Militia 440 search Newark Bay toward Port Elizabeth. And, *602*, use caution and respond at all possible speed."

"Understood, Pat Com; *112*, *457*, and *Sofia*, did you all copy that last traffic?"

All his subordinates answered in the affirmative, one after another. They fell into a line-ahead formation, *602* leading and *Sofia* picking up the rear. They lost some time as they were forced to make a wide detour around the area of the sinking. Once clear, Kitchner took a last check and made sure their wakes would not disturb the sight. Once sure, he merely said "Okay, let's go" over the tactical channel.

Kitchner was seated at the control console of the latest piece of Coast Guard technology, joystick in hand, and throttled all the way up, setting everyone aboard back as the water jet propulsion on board ate up the distance toward the Bayonne Bridge. The trip took barely five minutes at speeds in excess of fifty knots over the flat, calm gray-green waters of the Kill. As they came up to the bridge itself, they throttled way back. The *602* lit off their FLIR and led the way as the other fell into a rough line abreast, slowly searching ahead and to the sides, like a pack of hungry dogs.

*****

Just before they got into their kayaks, Carlos held a final brief for his depleted force. His optimum target was the oil refinery in Linden, New Jersey, which was another two and a half miles farther west in the adjoining Arthur Kill. Hopefully, they'd find an oil tanker moored there. If for some reason that was not to be, the secondary target would be a containership that was moored at the container port in Howland Hook on the opposite Staten Island side of the Arthur Kill. Carlos knew both vessels had passed his island inbound, and neither had left. He preferred the 99,000-ton tanker *Utica Star* as a target. He instructed the others to follow him and hug the New Jersey side once they had passed the entrance to Newark Bay near Bergen Point.

Once in the water, their varying levels of skill became quickly apparent. Of the three, Syed showed himself to be the most adept. Carlos managed, but Atef floundered about as Carlos explained the techniques of operating the small boat. His impromptu schooling cost them a precious fifteen minutes. They set up in a rough echelon formation with Atef to the left and nearest Staten Island as they paddled out. Carlos soon realized that he'd underestimated the effort needed to tow the explosive-laden kayaks. They had only gotten to the area known as Arlington when Syed first heard engine noises.

FLIR picked them out of the darkness first, a few hundred yards forward of *602*'s position. They were very low in the water and slim, barely apparent on the surface search radar, when the FLIR was compared to the radar picture. Kitchner quietly shared their find with the accompanying vessels and asked them not to use their searchlights, at least not just yet. They would track in on the FLIR image and place themselves in favorable tactical positions while hopefully denying their targets the same ability.

Kitchner placed *112* and *457* to the west beyond the kayaks and had the *Sofia* stay behind them on the Staten Island shore side. The *602* assumed a midposition and moved in to block and challenge. They were inside of one hundred yards; Kitchner could see them now, six small targets ahead and to his left. He was sure that just as he could see them, they could see him. As they approached, a gunner on each boat jacked a round into their M240B 7.62 mm machine guns.

When they were all in place, Kitchner ordered, "Lights!" All their searchlights came on as if triggered by the same hand.

"This is the United States Coast Guard. Stop and put your hands up!"

Carlos and his two compatriots heard the boats approaching but chose to remain silent, hoping they would be missed in the darkness. A youthful and excessively wired Syed turned with his AKM raised and cried out, "Allahu Akbar!" as he emptied the clip at *602*, amazingly taking out its searchlight. All Coast Guard vessels open fired simultaneously, obliterating Syed's kayak. Red and green tracer rounds zigzagged, bouncing off the dark waters between them as Atef and Carlos wildly opened fire in the general direction of *602*. Syed was dead before he knew it, but he added a final spasm to the day's destruction. His last act was to depress the electrical trigger in his right hand. The kayak exploded in a blinding flash. The pressure wave took out every piece of glass on *602*, and shrapnel lacerated everyone aboard; the reflective wave only added to the effect. Kitchner regained his composure, buried the throttles full forward, and aimed *602* directly at Carlos. The Coast Guard vessel closed at an amazing rate as Carlos sat frozen, unable to react. Within twenty feet of each other, Kitchner threw his joystick over hard right at full speed. The forty-five-footer turned on her beam's end on command. The ensuing wave rose five feet, slamming into both Carlos and Atef's kayaks, rolling both on their backs and dumping them into the murky Arthur Kill.

The coast guardsmen closed and came to a stop, standing over the capsized kayaks, all with M-16s and Remington 870 shotguns that they were only too willing to use. When they righted the kayaks with boat hooks, they were empty.

Orlando played his searchlight over the now quiet water as he circled but saw nothing. He brought *Sofia* to an idle as Jack and Tre used handheld lights to search the surface around them. They seemed to be drifting on a surreal seascape where searchlights played crazily across the dark water. They could hear helicopters in the rear as the FBI assaulted Shooters Island.

It was Jack that saw him first. "Orlando, over there!" He pointed to a spot off their starboard bow. "Over there, do you see him?" There was a man afloat on the water between them and the shoreline. Orlando slowly brought *Sofia* alongside the figure of a bloodied body. Tre hooked the body with the boat hook and brought him to the transom at the aft deck to retrieve him. Oliver rested his M-16 against the transom as he and Jack retrieved the body. It was Carlos. Between them, they hoisted Carlos aboard and laid him on the transom deck. Before they could catch their breath, Carlos ended his ruse and grabbed Tre's M-16 in his hands. He stood on the transom deck, weapon in hand, pointed right at Tre and Jack. He looked up at Orlando and smiled, "Mr. Rodriguez, you have indeed been a formidable adversary. Unfortunately, I will have to once again impose upon you for the use of your boat." Pointing his weapon at Jack's, he calmly said, "Move off to the east, please, slowly."

Jack replied, "Whatever you say," as he slammed his throttles forward and three 300 horsepower engines roared to life and surged the *Sofia* forward at full power, which sent Carlos somersaulting backward off the transom and into the wake of the rapidly accelerating boat. This time, Carlos Reyes would not have to feign death, courtesy of the Donzi's razor-sharp props.

They would find Carlos's body, or what was left of it, the next morning in the reeds on the Staten Island side of the Arthur Kill. Syed's remains at the epicenter of the Semtex explosion would simply not be retrievable. Atef still had not been found.

CHAPTER 48

The United States Navy mine-sweeping assets arrived within the promised three days, but their presence was abbreviated. Assets had to be split between New York, the Tidewater area of Virginia, and the port of Savannah, Georgia. Three of their giant MH-53E Sea Dragon helicopters began sweeping in New York on the fifth day with their AQS-14 Mine-Hunting Sonar and MK-105 Minesweeping sleds. One concentrated its efforts in the vicinity of lower New York Bay; another in Newark Bay, the Arthur Kill, and Kill Van Kull; and the last focused its efforts on the northern reaches of the harbor and East River. All in all, the area they were asked to sweep was huge.

Their task was labor-intensive, to say the least, since the bottom of New York Harbor was a virtual junkyard. The search became painstakingly slow as hundreds and hundreds of mine-like objects were discovered. Some objects were dismissible by virtue of how they lay on the bottom, but many were not. These items had to be individually examined by navy EOD divers, a time-consuming effort. An additional impediment was brought about by the necessity of having to sweep close to and in between piers.

Beyond the heartbreaking human toll, there was the mounting economic consequence. Two weeks after the event, the majority of the harbor was still not open. Locally, and as far as the Midwest, gasoline passed eight dollars a gallon, and many of the consumer goods were becoming increasingly hard to find. A public who had, to this point, been ignorant to the fact that they lived in a maritime nation, suddenly got a crash course in where their standard of living came from. The overall economic loss exceeded $2 billion a day, driving the national economy precariously close to collapse. Predictably, deprivation gave way to anger and calls for an accounting of how this could have been allowed to happen. Initially, politicians and administration types tried to tap dance around responsibility, but then along came Al Calcaterra and people like him.

Al had been speaking publicly for years about the maritime threat posed to this country from mines and the possible threat to New York, along with suggesting preventative measures. He had cultivated relationships with the media during that time, and now they sought him and other experts for their commentary. Al had methodically documented those who had neglected to provide protection from the devastation the country had just endured. Now a more educated public took up the time-honored American practice of placing blame, and they went at it with blood in their eyes. Al had gone from an obscure security maven to a media personality almost overnight.

*****

The high funeral mass at Sacred Heart Church on a clean, crisp August day was a spectacle as much as it was a heartfelt tribute to Louie Lugo. Louie was receiving his rightful police department inspector's funeral.

The tides had eventually brought his body ashore on the eastern side of Staten Island, just past the Verrazano Bridge at a place known as South Beach. He was found by a dog walker, and police identified him by his police shield and ID card, still in his pocket. Brian took the news to Marie after he'd found out. She had not been living under the illusion that he had somehow survived, but that did not make the reality of the situation any easier. The police fraternity came together and wrapped themselves around Marie and the children. She would want for nothing, now or ever.

A conservative estimate placed the number of local and other police who attended the funeral at five thousand. They came from as far as Virginia to pay their respects. Ranks were swelled with representatives from state and federal police agencies, a contingent from the Navy, to honor their veteran brother, and Louie's friends and neighbors. There was a very small representation of elected officials as the events had engendered a spirit of near hatred for some politicians.

Marie was visibly moved when she first saw the massive presence waiting at the church. The ranks were six deep and ran for blocks and blocks, all silent, all at attention, and many openly weeping. The cortege had moved from the funeral home a few blocks away on Forest Avenue to the church in solemn procession. The hearse was preceded by an honor guard from the police motorcycle unit and a department bagpipe unit, silent but for a drum mournfully marking cadence. As the procession passed intersections where traffic was being held, motorists stood outside their vehicles with their hands respectfully over their hearts.

At the church, Brian waited with Scott, Marie, and the children for the coffin to arrive. Brian was in his dress uniform and Scott in a dark suit. Both walked into the church on either side of Marie and the children. They were greeted by their local bishop, their local pastor, and the police department chaplain.

The Mass was long but dignified. The mayor made a few appropriate remarks, but the keynote was Brian's heartfelt eulogy of his partner and best friend. When it was over, Louie was laid to rest at the local Saint Peter's Cemetery. As he said goodbye at the gravesite, Brian couldn't help but think that this grand fuss would have embarrassed Louie. Looking at Marie and Maureen consoling her, Brian realized that the threat that had taken Louie and so many others was not gone but had retreated into the hearts and minds of others. At the funeral reception, held at a local catering hall, Brian sat in a corner with a Sam Adams and reflected over what had occurred. He called Orlando, Jack, Al Calcaterra, Scott Burton, and Al Krieger together and simply said, "When this is over, we've got to get together and sit down to talk. This isn't finished." Brian raised his bottle along with the others and simply toasted, "To Louie." They all nodded; nothing more needed to be said.

*****

Atef had struggled mightily to get out of the capsized kayak. He was bloodied from the blast that Syed had ignited and sore throughout his body. As he surfaced, he sputtered a bit until he saw the

Coast Guard vessels all moving away from him. He then began a very subdued breaststroke and came to rest in the cover of the rushes on the Staten Island shoreline. One of the smaller Coast Guard vessels lit up the shore where he lay but did not uncover his presence. He lay still for at least another hour and then decided he had better get out of the warm water before the authorities organized a more careful search or daylight broke.

Climbing out of the water, he found himself in a marsh area. To his left, he could see a lit area, a twenty-four-hour deli. The owner and a few others stood across the street near the water's edge, watching the ongoing search. An unoccupied gypsy cab stood at the curb with its engine running. Atef guessed correctly that one of the onlookers was the cab driver. Atef quietly opened the rear door of taxi and lay down on the floor. In about ten minutes, the driver, a black man, said a friendly goodbye to the others, climbed back into the driver's seat, and slowly drove off. Atef waited until he felt the vehicle make a turn. Feeling safe from prying eyes, he took his knife from its sheath on his belt and slowly came up from behind the driver and placed the knife to the driver's throat.

"Do exactly as you are told and you may survive," he said in a low menacing tone. To demonstrate his intentions, he nicked his throat.

"Aw, Jesus, man. Please don't kill me." The driver was completely terrified.

"Listen to me, friend. What's your name?"

"William."

"William, drive me to a wooded area where we won't be seen."

"What are you going to do?"

"Just do as I tell you."

"Mister, maybe I could find you a secluded wooded area twenty years ago, but that ain't easy to do anymore."

"William, find me a secluded area." He pressed the knife.

"Yes, sir, I'll try. Please don't kill me."

William drove for about fifteen minutes along the western shore of Staten Island through marshlands and back area industrial zones. There was no traffic during nonbusiness hours, nor were there residences. As they pulled past an auto salvage yard, Atef spoke and pointed to the right.

"There, down that alley next to the salvage yard." William drove another hundred feet, and Atef said, "Here, stop here and turn off the engine."

Atef loosened his grip around William's throat and stepped out of the car, ordering William ahead of him. He reintroduced the knife to the driver's throat, this time frontally. "William, get undressed."

"Yes, sir." He took off his shirt and slacks and stood there.

"William, I mean completely undressed."

"Everything?"

"Everything and throw it all in the car."

William did as he was told.

"William, kneel down and face away from me down the alley."

As he did, the naked man begged for his life, "Please, don't kill me. I have a family. I'm just out here trying to make a few bucks."

"Shut up and close your eyes."

He did what he was asked. Atef could hear him praying as he stepped back into the still-running gypsy cab. He backed out on the deserted street and drove off in the direction they'd come from.

Atef calculated that it would take the driver at least a half an hour to figure out how he was going to walk out onto the nearest road naked and get assistance. Even when he did begin walking, it would take him at least an hour to reach any road where he'd find anyone. Atef only wanted an hour to himself.

About a half a mile away, on a still deserted road, he pulled over and changed into William's clothing. He threw his still-wet and muddy Nomex clothing into the weeds. He had William's wallet containing a MasterCard and twenty-five dollars in mixed denominations and a few more dollars in mixed loose change. He also had approximately sixty dollars from the taxi's cash box, but more importantly, he had William's cell phone.

Atef drove back to the highway and followed the signs for the Verrazano Bridge and Brooklyn. On the way, he listened to the news broadcasts and updated himself. His only close call was at the bridge itself where a road block had been set up. He patiently waited in line; police stopped him and looked in.

"What's the problem, officer?"

The young officer shone his flashlight into his eyes and said, "Just a routine check. Where are you going?"

"Brooklyn, to pick up a fare. All this shit has got him stuck over there."

The officer blandly said, "Yeah, know what you mean, have a good night." The kid was looking for terrorists, not cab drivers.

Atef parked the taxi, leaving it near the Ninety-Second Street Station of the R Train on Fourth Avenue. He used William's cell to make a connection to a safe house. Ten minutes later, he was aboard a Manhattan bound R Train enveloped in total anonymity. Two hours later, he would be securely lodged in a two-family home in Queens. Two weeks later, he'd be in Arizona, and a week after that, he'd be in Mexico on his way toward Venezuela.

*****

Slightly more than $4.5 million sat in the police property clerks custody, awaiting its disposition. The City of New York claimed the cache was the proceeds of a crime, which was frankly thought by many to be a legitimate claim.

Orlando asked his attorney, Bill Faroe, to make a claim for the cash on his behalf, which he did. Orlando's argument was simple: The storage facility where the funds were found had been leased in his name with his credit card and a copy of his driver's license. Faroe's assertion was that nothing other than the pallet of cash was found in the storage bin. There had been no physical connection made between Carlos and his operation and the cash. It was an intellectually tantalizing argument that not many gave a snowball's chance in hell of succeeding, even Orlando. He had proceeded with the case in the spirit of nothing ventured, nothing gained. Fatefully, the only person who didn't see Orlando's claim as outrageous was Supreme Court Judge Charles Bleiman, who astoundingly found in Orlando's favor. After the judge's pronouncement, Faroe was leaving the court in the company of the city's corporation counsel attorney and good friend Leonard Bitman. Faroe barely made it out the doors before dissolving in uncontrollable laughter. Not even Bitman could suppress a wry smile as he shot his friend the middle finger of his right hand. The city immediately appealed the ruling and, just after some minor twists and turns, lost. No one was more shocked than Orlando Rodriguez, who became $2.25 million wealthier after taxes. The first thing he did was call Brian to tell him they now had the money needed to start the joint security venture they talked about. It was time to avenge Louie.

*****

Thilak Yatthavan followed the events of July 27 on the radio and television as thoroughly as any native-borne American. On the twenty-ninth, the identity and death of Carlos was released to the media. Very little of the remains of Syed had been found. Only a faceless portion of his head with the lower jaw attached were recovered at the water's edge. The medical examiner had them in his possession, hoping to make an eventual identification via dental records. Anthony Thaci provided the police with Syed's pedigree information, and his parents would eventually be notified by their local police departments.

Thilak's interest, however, was narrowly focused on Carlos Reyes, or as he was now being identified in the media, as Khalil Ebrahim Wafi. Thilak, a devout Muslim, had suggested to the imam at his local mosque that he would be interested in financing an appropriate Muslim funeral ceremony for Carlos. A very soft-spoken man, he respectfully requested the imam's assistance and intervention with authorities in order that Carlos's body be released to him, Thilak.

The imam enlisted the aid of a local funeral director who specialized in Muslim funerals. Together they were able to contact a city councilman and convince the city medical examiner to release the body just before it would be assigned to the city's potter's field.

A Thursday morning in mid-August found Thilak Yatthavan and his two elder sons, Lavindra and Ruwan, at a nonsectarian cemetery facing an open grave. To that point, the services had been completely in line with a traditional Muslim funeral. The remains of Carlos's body had been cleansed as per the appropriate ritual and placed in a plain white linen shroud.

The imam became suspicious, however, when Thilak's youngest son Ravith, who had been charged with driving him to the cemetery to say the Salat al-Janazah, the funeral prayer, took him back to the mosque. Ravith dryly explained that a family imam would do the graveside service and he would not be needed. The imam protested strenuously as he was just about shoved out of the car at the mosque.

At the gravesite, Lavindra and Ruwan removed the shrouded body from the hearse at their father's direction and brought it to the edge of the grave. Sensing the ceremony was taking an abnormal turn, the funeral director began to protest.

Thilak stepped close to the funeral director's ear and said in a very purposeful manner, "My friend, if you feel the need to report what you see here today, you will join him in that hole. Is that clear?" The man had no choice but to agree.

"Lavindra, Ruwan, push him into the grave."

Lavindra asked, "Father, shall we place him in the appropriate position?" Ritual dictates that Muslim deceased be placed in their grave either on their right side, preferably facing Mecca.

"Son, just push him in, let Allah and gravity decide in what position he spends eternity in."

Lavindra shoved the body, which fell in a jumbled heap into the grave. He looked to his father for a sign of approval, and Thilak nodded.

"Ruwan, you and your brother bring the package here from the car." They removed a large paper-wrapped package from the trunk of the car and brought it to the grave. "Put it in."

They unwrapped the package and dumped the freshly slaughtered hog into the grave atop Carlos's body in front of a thoroughly horrified funeral director.

Thilak said softly and unemotionally, "It is done. Now, fill it in." The boys obediently followed instruction. Thilak turned to the funeral director and quietly said, "Remember what I said." The man sheepishly nodded.

Thilak had appropriately avenged the murder of his eldest son, Aruran Yatthavan.

*****

Jack no longer needed to be sequestered on board the *Intrepid*. He went back aboard in late August to gather his belongings with mixed emotions. He'd gotten the secure feeling of coming home while living aboard the old girl. He'd made friends in his time aboard, but it was now time to move back to his place on the Brooklyn Waterfront to prepare for whatever the future held for him.

He was now a creature of the night, and 2:00 a.m. felt as if it were midday, so he'd have to reorient himself. He packed his belongings in one bag and stopped at the quarterdeck to ask the guard a question.

"Excuse me pal, is Dom Langianella working tonight? I just wanted to say goodbye. I'm leaving."

The guard smiled. "You met Dom, huh?"

"Yeah, he's a nice old guy."

"Yes, yes, he is, son. Come with me for a second. Leave your bag here. It'll be okay." The guard led Jack back through the hangar bay to the midship memorial area. He pointed to the tablet dedicated to *Intrepid*'s heroes. Jack read through the alphabetic list, and there under *L* was Lieutenant Commander Dominick Langianella, who had died on October 25, 1944.

ABOUT THE AUTHOR

I've had dual careers that have led me to write this book. I served twenty years in the US Navy, Reserve and Active, as an intelligence specialist, retiring in 1995 as a chief intelligence specialist (E-7). In August 2007 I had an article published in the US Naval Institute's *Proceedings* magazine entitled "Mines in Ports: A Serious Threat." The story outlined in great detail our vulnerabilities to sea mines in our harbors and how that threat might be mitigated. I have also used my accumulated knowledge to educate people within the maritime industry on the subject of maritime terrorism. Simultaneous to my naval reserve service, I served twenty-six years in the New York City Police Department, serving many of those years in the precincts described in the book. I retired from the NYPD in 1996 as a sergeant/investigator.